AMAZON/Library VERSION ONLY

Original Ebook/Print Cover: Carol Marques Design
Editing, Proofing, backgrounds, & Formatting: Dirty Sexy Words/ Storm shield
Editing/Little Tailfeather Publishing
Cassandra's logos: Pretty in Ink Creations/Artlogo
Goosebusters Alpha team: Kat Silver, Becky Ross, Erica Taryn
Duckhunters Proofing: Jackie H, Jaemi Serrano
Sensitivity Readers: Brit Mason, Gail Jericho
Translation Consultant: Mo Jacobs
Promotional Team: Literary Inspired
Legal Services: Joshua Farley, esq.
Images/Fonts/Maps: Depositphotos, Shutterstock, Canva, Inkarnate, & Photoshop

No GenAI was used within this book. All errors and greatness are by an ADHD muppet.

F.E.A.R. ACADEMY

FAILED STATE

CASSANDRA FEATHERSTONE

CONTENT INFORMATION

This is a *paranormal whychoose romance with poly elements*—our FMC, Sydney, will not have to choose between love interests.

I *purposefully* include **all** pertinent information in this section from tropes to triggers to included content to silly things. It's an attempt to cover my bases which is probably futile since some will be upset with *and* without it.

However, it's my book, and I'll do what I want, so here we go.

There are many situations included that are intended for mature audiences (18+).

In this book/series, there may be instances/references (be they small or lengthy) that could trigger some individuals such as:

- dystopian themes (which means political and rebellious leanings within the text)
- demons, shifters, magic users, vampires, and more
- attacks on the FMC (physical)
- discussion of bodily autonomy
- inexperienced FMC
- within series: MM, MF, MMMMFM, and more
- bullying (light from MMC)
- forced proximity
- consistent discussions of consent
- imprisonment
- alphahole/possessive MCs
- cinnamon roll MC

- power imbalance
- outspoken, sassy FMC
- big tough guy MC
- unhealthy coping mechanisms
- spoiled, rich MCs
- extremely aggressive boundaries
- age gap (unknown)
- discussion of oppressive power structures
- allegorical content
- BDSM in future
- horns, tails, forked tongues, and unusual equipment
- traumatic childhood
- alcohol use and abuse
- threats of bodily harm
- death
- body modifications (both consensual and dubious consent)
- physical assault by non-MCs
- treacherous authority figures
- bullying (in person)
- discussion of sex work
- blood
- emotional abuse
- body dysmorphia
- adult language
- pop culture references
- literary references
- emotional manipulation
- power play
- adorable nicknames
- physical intimidation
- manipulative authority figures
- markings/tattoos
- discussion of birth control and menstruation
- family dysfunction
- absolute disrespect for shitty parents
- scary re-imagining of history and parallels to present
- official corruption
- discussion of groups being rounded up/killed during species purges and imprisonment
- rituals
- inappropriate professors
- name calling

- occasional misogyny
- shitty parents
- discussion of physical abuse
- elitism
- bribery
- corpses
- drama
- physical threats to FMC and others
- species-ism

No practices in this book should be taken as safe or appropriate for real life application.

Content information is important to me and I do my best to include things people might enjoy and not enjoy.

READER'S NOTE

A FEW THINGS YOU SHOULD KNOW...

Failed State is book **one** of the *F.E.A.R. Academy* series.

There are five books planned and they will start on Ream, then come to print/KU after they are re-edited and formatted. The books don't *change* from one medium to the other so much as get refined, etc.

This book belongs to its own universe, called *Fury of the Forsaken*. It is not related to the *Legends of the Ouroboros*, *Heirs of Prophecy*, or *Apex Society* universes. All universe information is available on my website.

This is a **multi-book series**, so *everything will not be revealed at once*. Some plot lines will continue through series in a larger arc and *not get resolved in the first or even the third book.*

I write lengthy books with intricate world building, strong character development, and *lots* of tiny threads that stretch throughout a series that may not always seem important at first glance. However, I promise nothing I put to paper and leave in the book is unimportant; it may simply become *more* important later on. There is no 'throwaway' detail in my worlds, so every scene will mean something eventually.

I promise it will all get tied up and have a HEA; don't worry!

Failed State is a why choose/poly romance, which means our FMC will not have to choose.

I would consider it a **SLOW** burn because of the plot details regarding the FMC. It will get spicier—slowly—in the following books as Sydney's situation changes. If you're looking for porn with little to no plot, no judgment, but this isn't the series for you. I realize spice scales are subjective and everyone has different opinions on it, so forgive me if mine and yours aren't totally aligned.

Note: In the South (where I'm from), it is fairly common to call people by their full names when you're being condescending or dressing someone down. It's not just family, and if they don't know your middle name, sometimes they even make one up! It's an authority flex to do so. This happens in my books a lot—even if they are not set in the South—so I'm just giving you a heads up that it's stylistic and purposeful.

There are some characters and creatures that speak in other languages. I made the *translations clickable end of chapter notes* to help.

There are some words that are slang, jargon, or foreign that may seem to be spelled wrong—*please email the author or find her on social media rather than report to Amazon* if you find a typo. This has been proofed and edited *several* times, so the error could be a stylistic or dialect choice. Every effort is made to find these pre-publication and since the publishing industry standard is below two percent of word count (and my books are almost always over 100K), I promise what you find is not out of the accepted range for the editors and teams who have reviewed it.

Please do not email critical feedback that is not a simple typo or formatting issue—this book is written and released. It will not be changed after publication to suit personal preferences.

If you see this book *anywhere besides Kindle Unlimited in ebook format,* please reach out to me via social media or email. Pirating kills my ability to write full time and I am so grateful for your help.

Contact my team for typos or to report piracy: teamcassandrafeatherstone@cassandrafeatherstone.com

AUTHOR RAMBLINGS

Readers,

I need to start this book by making it ***very*** clear that Sydney's story lives in a ***dystopian alternate reality***. That means that like most dystopian books (*1984, Handmaid's Tale, Hunger Games, etc)*, it is *inherently* political by the nature of the genre.

Anyone who reads my books/series can easily figure out what I stand for and what I won't abide, but this series is definitely one that reflects that. I started writing it in June of 2024 for a Vella contest, and while I thought it would be a chilling 'what-if' in the style of *Man in the High Castle*, it has become eerily prophetic and sometimes scared *me* as I wrote it.

Like, am I clairvoyant? Ahhhhhh!

However, before I am beset with angry feedback, I want to make certain you are aware that it has some scary parallels, not-so-well hidden social commentary, and plot points that might be a little disturbing to some.

If you are bothered by that, it's probably not a good series for you, and that's okay. This isn't a dark romance, but I feel like it is gritty at times, and explores themes that might be upsetting to some, despite being paranormal rather than contemporary.

Sydney and her guys have some ugly experiences as a result of this dystopia and are put into places where they make decisions or act in ways that damaged people might… but they're going to learn and grow. They're going to figure out how to heal from it together…***just slowly***.

As usual, I've done a lot of research and added quite bit of mythology, depth, and information to my rich world. But if I get something wrong, know I did the best I could to make certain I had the right information.

*Plus, you know… magic. Magic explains everything. *wink**

While I definitely cannot ever make every reader happy—and that's *okay*—I'm so grateful for all of the people who enjoy my books in my group, REAM, and other venues. You guys are the sunshine in my day when I happen upon less than kind opinions on the internet by mistake.

For that, I can never repay you.

However, I never give up, so I'm going to be here with silly puns and smart FMCs who aren't afraid to show how big their hearts, libidos, *and* brains are.

Enjoy the beginning of this new universe, and rally behind Sydney as she and the misfits they pair her with strategize and plot their way to victory.

Blood and guts,

Cassandra Featherstone

A NOTE TO MY LOVING FAMILY MEMBERS AND THEIR FRIENDS...

THANK YOU FOR SUPPORTING ME BY BUYING THIS BOOK!

THIS SERIES IS SLOW BURN, BUT IT'S GOT SOME INTERESTING THINGS THAT WILL EVENTUALLY SQUICK YOU OUT.

I DON'T RECOMMEND STARTING IT, EVEN IF THE WHOLE 'DYSTOPIAN REBEL' THING SOUNDS REALLY GOOD TO YOU IN THIS ATMOSPHERE.

I JUST DON'T WANT TO ANSWER QUESTIONS ABOUT SOME OF THE... EQUIPMENT YOU MIGHT DISCOVER.

SERIOUSLY, DON'T.

CAVEAT: IF YOU CHOOSE TO KEEP READING, KNOW THAT AT NO TIME WILL I EXPLAIN TERMS, POSITIONS, THEMES, TROPES, OR ANY OTHER PART OF THIS NOVEL AT FAMILY EVENTS, IN GROUP CHATS, OR ON SOCIAL MEDIA.

DON'T ASK.

FAILED STATE PLAYLIST

BOOK VIBES SONGS

Book Vibe Playlist

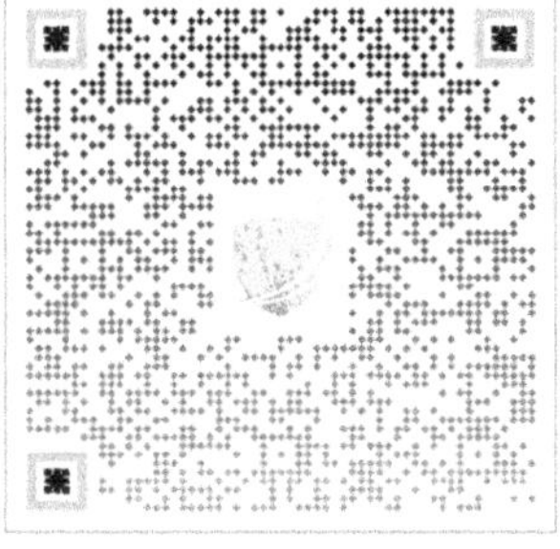

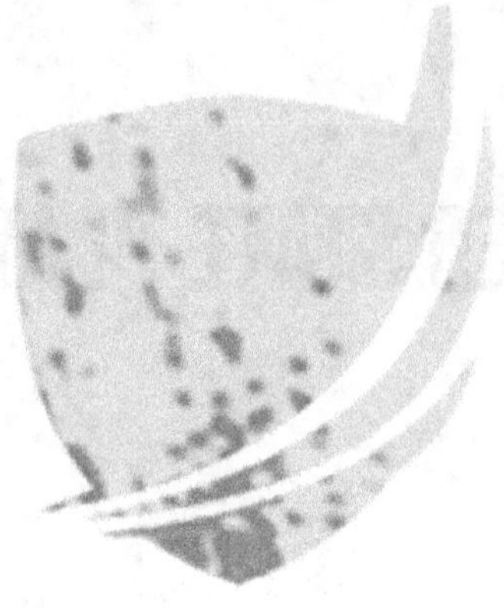

To all the people who are getting up every day and
    fighting,
who refuse to let this nightmare become reality,
For those who are bringing light to the world
    through their gifts
being beacons in the darkness that's falling...
This is our fight song.
Illegitimi non carborundum.

In a time of universal deceit, telling the truth is a revolutionary act.

~George Orwell

TEMPEST SEVEN
SUPERNATURAL
RESIDENTAL CAMP
SYDNEY'S
APARTMENT
THAD'S
SLEUTH
HUC
HOM

F.E.A.R.
ACADEMY
CONFESSION
ENFORCEMENT
ZONE
SHRIEKING
SUCCUBUS
LOCKDOWN
LOSERS
GAMES
COMPLEX

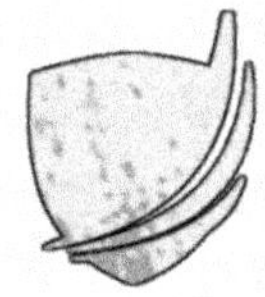

TEAM BITE CLUB

SYDNEY JOLIE, THADDEUS CALVIN, RORY STORMBRINGER, HUCKLEBERRY MONROE, SEBASTIAN WHITMORE. ELIAS DANTE

TRAINING SCHEDULE

time	monday	tuesday	wednesday	thursday	friday
8:00 AM	Social Media Savvy	Cultivating A Cult	Social Media Savvy	Cultivating A Cult	Social Media Savvy
9:00 AM	KRISTA	Chantelle	KRISTA	Chantelle	KRISTA
10:00 AM	Style & Flair Shoshana	Strategy & Planning Westlake	Style & Flair Shoshana	Strategy & Planning Westlake	Style & Flair Shoshana
11:00 AM	Larson	Lunch	Larson	Lunch	Larson
12:00 PM	Lunch	Weapons, Magic, & Armed Battle Brick & Lancaster	Lunch	Weapons, Magic, & Armed Battle Brick & Lancaster	Lunch
1:00 PM	Fighting Hand-to Hand Brick & Lancaster		Fighting Hand-to Hand Brick & Lancaster		Fighting Hand-to Hand Brick & Lancaster
2:00 PM		Coaching Catch-Up Krista		Coaching Catch-Up Krista	
3:00 PM	Intrigue & Socialization All Teams		Intrigue & Socialization All Teams		Intrigue & Socialization All Teams
4:00 PM		Beauty Maintenance Bolero		Beauty Maintenance Bolero	
5:00 PM					
6:00 PM					
7:00 PM	Dinner & Free Time	Dinner & Free Time	Dinner & Free Time	Dinner & Free Time	Dinner & Free Time

FEDERATED HUMAN STATES OF AMERICA

EVERY DAY IS MONDAY

SYDNEY

"JESUS FUCKING CHRIST," I mutter as I slog through the streets of Tempest Seven. "Just because they locked us up like animals doesn't mean we have to live like them."

Pausing in my walk to the education center, I look around myself in abject disgust. The inhabitants of this end of Tempest Seven aren't the bottom of the proverbial barrel, but outside of the 'lockdown losers', people stuck here never seem to get out of the cycle of poverty and despair. I don't think it means we have to throw garbage everywhere and give the drones nice shots to prove to the humans that we're as unworthy as the leaders of this stupid country say we are.

What would it hurt to tidy up, even if we don't have much?

Honestly, I believe it's only a third rooted in laziness. I think the other parts are exhaustion and hopelessness. Since the First Infected Being Sweep of 2020, supernaturals all over this country were tracked, catalogued, reassigned, and declared property of the government. By the time they ran the second through fourth sweeps, the population of some supernatural species dropped by fifty percent. The rules on how to track us down and receive your bounty were infuriatingly vague, which gave the most violent psychopaths in the world a free license to kill, maim, rape, and disappear anyone caught on the 'Non-Human Watchlist'.

I was a baby when my mother left, but my father taught me everything I needed to know about being a shifter. Unfortunately, he was one of the people who ended up on that list and was killed in the Second Infected Being Sweep of 2020. That sweep was brutal, and since I was a 'half-breed' orphan, I was placed in the orphanage in Tempest Seven. From the moment every child and teen arrived, they were forced to attend the Federal Enrichment Assimilation & Re-Education Center.

Our human professors taught us that being born this way is a punishment from their God, especially if you were a mixed type. At first, we tried to tell them about our various species, but it became clear very quickly what would happen if we didn't fall in line. You either learned to smile and nod, providing the rote answers and scripts they gave you when tested or interrogated, or you died.

Now, in 2024, there are no rebellions against the Federated Human States of America, nor are there any aid workers from other countries left to help or try to get us out. The world has given up on the former United States—it's been ruled a failed state by the United Nations and cordoned off at every border on land and sea.

We're on our own in the former land of the free and home of the brave.

"As if anyone would want to come here anyway. Shit went downhill fast after that baboon was elected," I mutter to myself. I realize I've spoken louder than I thought and I look around carefully, making certain I'm not near a Confession Enforcement zone or any other beings. My breath releases slowly when I confirm that I'm totally alone and not in a hot zone.

No one watches out for others now; the temptation to gain things your family or group needs is too high. A random person would dime me out for a week's supply of crackers and I can't blame them. Food and drink are rationed, our clothes are drab and provided, and the world is dimmer since the Sweeps. They force us to stay small so they're in control, and we have to live with it because of the fucking Markers.

My hand flies to the back of my neck, grunting in irritation as I scratch at the tattoo that covers the skin where the implant is located. These were the second step on the path to the current tyranny of our 'benevolent' government. That spray tanned fuck won the election because the humans here were that goddamn stupid, and then the virus hit. COVID brought America to its knees and like all good con artists, President Taterman used the distraction to funnel money into secret programs under DARPA.

Men who stare at goats my skinny ass.

They released a widely contested study that blamed the virus on the 'infected'. Unfortunately, they defined that as beings living in our country that had paranormal capabilities. The rest of the world laughed at the senile old fuck until the media hype was so huge that the various species around the world convened a leadership meeting. With so many cameras and videos everywhere, it was only a matter of time until a random human caught one of us doing something and bam! A viral TikTok would expose all of us whether we were ready or not. The vote was close, but the supernatural community decided to come out of hiding to protest their innocence.

'The Unveiling' was the most watched TV event in decades, and the consensus was our leaders had done the right thing. At least, until the next study was released. This one made Taterman damn near salivate as he screamed into the TV cameras about the 'unclean' liars and thieves who have been hiding in plain sight, taking our jobs, and stealing the lives humans should have. It quickly devolved into a mass panic and our kind were left scrambling.

We'd told them who and where we were, like a bunch of fools.

Thus, the evil assholes at the top started their mission to protect the humans from us and reclaim their country. Supernaturals in other nations were fine, but the atmosphere here became dangerous within the blink of an eye. Taterman stacked his own deck in the courts and the legislature by fear-mongering, especially since the world was still reeling from a pandemic. Eventually, he was able to get the support he needed for the first Sweep.

Secret Supernatural Enforcement Agents used databases, social media, DNA websites, immigration records, and everything they could to gather the biggest dragnet of personal information ever assembled. Civil rights advocates and other world leaders were vocally opposed to such violations, but nothing could stop the juggernaut of hatred. Once they identified every supe in the nation—to the best of their ability—that's when they stripped our citizenship, robbed us blind, and re-assigned every single one to the sectors they'd been building in secret.

Let's be honest—they're supe prison camps.

But the humans felt safe once more because while we were all being shuffled all over like cattle, the rest of the scientific community worldwide started to get COVID under control. Taterman crowed about the United States' involvement, taking credit for slowing the spread by locking up the infected beings. No one but his nutty followers believed him, but at that point, it didn't matter.

So when they came to implant the Markers, no one spoke up.

We all have them, and depending on what you are and how powerful you are, they are different. But resting above the spot where they cut us open to shove in the controller, there's a matching tattoo of the logo that is now on the flag of the Federated Human States of America… but that came much, much later.

Democracy dies in the dark, the old slogan said… and here lies her rotted corpse.

"Hey, Syd. It's a beautiful day in the neighborhood, huh?"

My brooding gets interrupted by the arrival of Thad, my friend since we got placed here four years ago. He's a bear shifter and the size of a small SUV, but it doesn't bother me. I survived the sector version of high school partially because we stuck together. My brains and his bulk were a good match and it kept us from getting cornered by the gangs and cliques.

Okay, fine, it kept me from getting cornered. Obviously, Thad held his own with-out me.

"That sentiment hasn't been applicable for half a decade, man." I toss my braid over my shoulder and wait for him to catch up. It's our second week at the F.E.A.R. Academy's college level program and being late is more than frowned upon. I have to give us extra time every morning because Thad lumbers out of bed like his animal—slow and grumpy. "We gotta get moving."

The dark haired shifter looks at me, scratching the piratical scruff he's usually sporting. "You're ridiculously concerned about rules for someone with such a rebel spirit."

"Rebels die, Thad. I'm very aware of that." Turning on my heel, I head toward the huge building at the end of the main drag with a heavy heart. Losing Dad was hard and I'll never forgive him for assuming humans are anything but ignorant beasts that barely rise above their simian relatives.

We continue walking in silence until we reach the steps. The line is stretched down them as the guards run the wand over each student to check for weapons. After that, we put our bags on the conveyor belt for the magical detection while the security mages in government issued loyalty collars scan us for anything the wands wouldn't catch. It's not quick, but it keeps fights in the schools non-lethal most of the time.

That's the official reason, but the real purpose is to allow the staff to abuse students if they step out of line. The Markers not only brand and track us, but they siphon energy and power in small bits to keep us all weak enough to be controlled. Weapons would even the score and the humans who run these stupid ass brainwashing cults would be at risk.

"Look who's last at the trough again." The wry voice of the only demon in Tempest Seven gets my attention. Huck Monroe saunters up, tilting his worn black cowboy hat back as he smirks at me. "Y'all are just cruisin' for a bruisin'. I swear, you don't have the sense that the Devil gave a goose."

My eyes narrow at him briefly, then I turn forward and shuffle along as the line moves. "You don't have to hang out with us, Huck. In fact, it'd be great if you fucked off and stayed there."

Thad laughs, bumping his shoulder against the annoying fear demon's and I sigh. Huck was sent here during the First Sweep, like us, and he's been a Southern bramble in my side ever since. It's my bad luck that Thad enjoys his folksy charm and it means he sticks to us like glue during school hours.

"Sometimes you're meaner than a wet panther shifter, Sydney Jolie. I should take you at your word and mosey off, but I like your boy."

Huck's pitch black eyes are hidden by his Ray-Bans, but I know they're sparkling with amusement. He finds my dislike funny, and I don't get why. But then, I don't get a fucking thing about men, especially supes, nor do I want to. Life in our sector is hard enough without having to consider birth control or babies or even finding privacy. I'll save that for the day when I get the fuck out of here.

"I heard they're bringing in a new group of students today." Thad changes the subject quickly, knowing I'll continue to needle Huck and vice versa until one of us loses their temper. "The rumors say the shipment has vamps, losers, and traitors. I'm worried this sector is turning into a dumping ground for psychos."

It wouldn't surprise me if the humans started segregating the camps by species, value, or even criminality. Even after they corralled us into the sectors, the leaders have continued to exert their influence and power over us. The Markers were first, then the lockdowns for the ones they deemed dangerous, and now they're shuffling people weekly at random. I've often wondered if all of this is covering up something like what went on in the 1940s among the humans, but I haven't seen any proof.

Our media is monitored and curated, so unless you know someone with a highly illegal device, you have no idea what's happening outside of the FHSA.

"Next! Keep it moving, you little shits," the yell from the front of the line brings me back to reality again.

"Wicker is the fucking worst," Thad mumbles as we ascend the steps to stand behind the person being inspected. "Watch his hands, Syd."

"I'm aware." Despite thinking we're the scum of the earth, some of the human staff and enforcement in the sectors are fucking creeps. Some supes are willing to trade sex for perks, but that doesn't stop the predators from being creeps to those who don't. "I'll let you go first so Bishop gets me."

"Got it," he says as he muscles in front of me. "Huck, stay behind her."

"Why, I'd be delighted, Thaddeus."

I guess he's useful sometimes, but he'd better not let it go to his head.

LIFE IS NEVER FAIR
THADDEUS

"NEXT!"

I step up to the open spot in front of Guard Wicker, noting his frown when he realizes Syd won't be in his line. The dude is a fucking sleaze and I'd like to punch him right in the mouth, but I don't want to end up in the 'Self-Awareness' room. Misbehaving students from elementary to college level get thrown in these isolation cells and basically renditioned until their spirit breaks. Usually, people last about a week before they at least *pretend* to be reprogrammed. If you end up there often enough, they pull you from F.E.A.R. to be fitted for the lockdown version of a Marker.

Who knows what that is because those people never speak of it, nor do they mix with the general populace afterward.

"Hold your arms out, Calvin," Wicker grunts in irritation. "I don't have all day."

He actually does, but I'm not going to let him rush me through in an attempt to get to Sydney. I put my bag down, lifting my arms slowly as I give him a fake apologetic look. "Sorry, boss. Spaced out for a second there."

"Don't let it happen again."

Biting the inside of my cheek, I harness the anger of my grizzly at being treated like I'm lesser by a guy who couldn't punch his way out of a paper bag. The damn Markers are the only thing keeping these fuckers alive, especially with the way they treat beings who could tear them apart bare-handed. Our world is topsy-turvy at the moment and nothing is fair—I don't know if it ever will be again.

Wicker is human, so he doesn't sense my fury, but I know the chained magic user scanning my bag does. The small witch raises dead eyes to me, and we share a long look as she casts. Her voice is low, almost too low to hear, but I think she's ignoring the plastic blade I have zipped into the lining of the satchel. My lips quirk for a brief moment, then I go back to frowning at the moron who points me to the body scanner.

It's dangerous to smuggle weapons into the academy, but I have someone besides myself to keep safe.

"Move it, Calvin." The guard rolls his eyes as I lumber forward and he groans. "Fucking Monroe. Of course I'd get you."

I can almost hear Huck's shit-eating grin behind me. He shuffles up as I enter the body scanner, whistling under his breath. I know he's in place when he coos, "Oh, Wicker, I didn't know you cared. Are you offering to be my hombre?"

"Shut it, demon. No one wants anything from a crazy ass fear fucker who thinks he's Doc Holliday."

Huck is very aware that our nemesis is a total homophobe, so he's happily pushing his buttons. It distracts the entire contingent from Sydney's scans, and that's his plan. She always sneaks things in—more than me—and neither of us want her to get sent to the Bad Place for a week. Females come back a lot more haunted than most males. It's fucking disgusting, and I refuse to allow her to be subjected to it.

"You wound me, Wicker. I thought we were becoming *friends.*"

I swear to Odin, that demon is absolutely insane. Since he feeds on fear, he doesn't feel it himself, and that leads to interesting behavior. Most people would call it unhinged and maybe it is. But he's loyal as fuck, even if Syd pretends to hate him.

She definitely doesn't; my shifter senses can tell.

"Huck, for fuck's sake," Syd growls as she crosses to the entrance. Her scans are done and we can stop screwing around. "Stop being an idiot and get inside."

Pausing to pick up my bag, I give a very subtle chin jerk to the poor witch locked up by Wicker's line and join my friends to head inside for another day of being told we're the cause of the entire world's ills.

None of us use the old rusty lockers that line the wall. Some kids do, but it's foolish. The guards can search us at any time, but the admin can rifle your locker without you even knowing. It's the perfect way to frame someone you don't like. Syd, Huck, and I simply carry our shit everywhere, then head home. We're more suspicious than the younger supes or the ones who weren't caught in the earliest sweeps.

Watching people die in the early court system had a chilling effect on our ability to trust anything we can't see with our own eyes.

"I will never understand why they make us attend a college level program. None of us will *ever* be allowed out of the sectors, so a higher education is a waste of time," Sydney says as we walk down the hall.

"Maybe it's for appearances?" I offer. Truthfully, I don't know why, either, except it means they have all the younger supes under their thumbs for four more years. Rebellion is the watchword of the young, and perhaps they believe they'll keep future generations under control by continued indoctrination.

Huck snorts. "Nada, little buddy. Since the blockades went up, the rest of the world could give a fuck less about the supes on this land mass. Taterman doesn't need to pander to their wishes."

Sydney whirls around giving us both a dirty look. "Did you fucking check for a Confession Enforcement indicator before you said his *name*?"

The demon has the grace to look chagrined as he shakes his head. "Sorry, filly. It's hard to remember, though I know it shouldn't be. We're four years out and this shit still gets me."

"We didn't grow up in a world like this one," I murmur softly. "By the time this came along, we'd formed normal habits. It's not weird that you're still adjusting, Huck. Hell, we all are. Look how hard the lockdown supes fight against their situation."

Syd frowns as she shrugs. "I don't know why they do it. No one is coming to save us; that much is clear. And we're unable to save ourselves now, so the Unveiling sentenced us to this life until we die. There's no point in getting murdered."

Her father's death still haunts her and I wish I could help… but no one can.

Death gives no quarter, even to those who deserve it.

Our first class was *History of Supernatural Interference 100* and how the asshole giving the lecture kept a straight face, I don't know. Most supe groups—be it packs or covens or clashes or whatever—still used oral history to keep our existence secret while preserving our history before the Unveiling. Humans rely on governments and the internet and schools to teach doctored versions of theirs. The disconnect is why they're failing to convince the young supes in sectors of the evils that supernaturals have done over the centuries.

Leaders in the supe sectors make sure we are not vilified before everyone who knows how it was before dies.

"How in the fuck can they stand up there and straight-up lie to people old enough to remember shit?" Sydney grumbles. "I know for a goddamn fact that supernaturals didn't cause the fucking Gulf War fighting with djinn."

"Djinn are a funny lot. They'll go to war, but not unless they have to." Huck chomps on the toothpick he's been chewing since the beginning of class. "If it were true, that shitgibbon would never have been able to win. They'd owe all the American supes wishes. Dangerous game, but amazing spoils."

"You've never met a djinn," I scoff as we walk up the stairs to our *Human Literary Masterpieces* class. "Demons lie like they breathe."

Huck rolls his eyes as we get to the door, holding it open for us. "I sure as hell have. She was as beautiful as can be, like a fever dream of spices and dark nights in the desert. But she had her Marker and wishes were not an option."

Ah, he met her in the holding area before he was shipped here.

"I've never met a supe that exotic," Syd says wistfully. "My dad kept us pretty under the radar so we wouldn't get found out. We lived in a small town and there weren't many supes at all, aside from witches and a few common shifters."

"You're not missing anything." Shrugging, I follow her into the lecture hall and plop down in the seat on her left side. "We lived in Kansas, so lots of open space and that means bigger shifters and mythicals sometimes made their homes nearby. Most of them were dicks because they were powerful and rich—especially the vampires."

"Fanged fuckers aren't big," Huck says with a sneer. "And they're not uncommon. They're just traitors to us all."

Here we go…

"Huck, they were smarter than the rest of us," Sydney mutters. "If I had a Wayback Machine and could tell the other species to mimic the fangers, I would."

"Good afternoon, students!"

The loud bellow from Professor Ashley makes me wince. He doesn't have magic or supe powers, so the dumbass uses this outdated bullhorn to teach the huge section of people. The squeal always hurts my sensitive bear ears, and I can't do a damn thing to protect myself from it.

"Today, we will continue discussing *Frankenstein*. Shelley captured the need for eliminating the monsters within her world perfectly, I must say. We would all do well to respect the lesson this book teaches about what happens to those who rampage against their betters."

Sydney tenses next to me and her hand is gripping her pen like she's going to crack it. Obviously, she doesn't agree with the interpretation being presented. I've never been much of a reader, but what I read doesn't jive with the text, so she's probably right. But then, the professors here don't want us to learn; they want to control us. Of course they'd twist a narrative to suit their agendas.

Leaning down, I whisper in her ear. "You gotta calm down, Syd."

"That's *not* the lesson of this book, *Thad*."

Huck shakes his head, slouching in his chair so no one notices him leaning into her other side. "Doesn't matter, sweet pea. It's what we're forced to vomit up for their tests, so you need to have a come to Jesus moment and get good with it."

Her eyes narrow as she looks at the demon. "You know that's a fairy tale, Huckleberry Monroe."

Ouch, the full name; she's pissed.

"I do indeed, but I'm not fixin' to get sent to the hole today. And I'd appreciate it if you could avoid it as well so I don't have to lose my temper."

We have to distract her and I hate to do it this way but… "Didn't you just say it's useless to fight? What good did fighting and trusting them do for your dad, Syd?"

It's like a wave of ice hits our section of the room and I wince as she goes silent, staring ahead silently. She won't make trouble while that dill hole up there continues, but our friend is also going to be a zombie for the rest of the day. I hate having to do that to her, but since Sydney is a mixed breed with a question mark where her mom should be…

I have to help her until she figures out what she has beyond magic.

"You're a dick, Thad."

"I'll take that over silence any day," I whisper as she scribbles notes in her notebook.

She's very good at functioning in the low tech world sectors brought us back to, while I miss the hell out of phones and computers. We have an agreement that she'll take the notes and we all study together so Huck and I can help her memorize. Since they put in her Marker, Sydney has trouble with memory gaps, blackouts, and sometimes, gaps in time. It's like they short-circuited something important in her and it caused a magical dementia.

"I'm only talking to you because I need you. Otherwise, I'd freeze you for the day," she says, her voice full of irritation. "Unfortunately, the damage done by my Marker will put me in the shit. Even Huck knows that by now."

Our demon friend pushes his knee against hers, surreptitiously trying to siphon the fear off of her. It's a win-win for him because he feeds, but it also helps our friend stay on an even keel. "Sweet pea, I don't know why you act as though I'm a gnat buzzing around your pretty head. You know I'm your second favorite person in the entire world."

"I only associate with two people, Huck. That's not as special as you make it sound."

No, we're the lucky ones and she doesn't have a clue.

MAY THE ODDS
SYDNEY

THE REST of the morning was filled with the jabbering of the guys and ducking the mean girls that—no matter how bad life is for everyone—form groups to poke at those they consider beneath them. There's a hierarchy at F.E.A.R. despite our dire circumstances, I keep under their radar as much as I can. All I want is to stay in our asshole overlords' good graces and *not* have to be in conflict with other supes or the humans. If I keep a low enough profile, I might qualify for a menial job outside of the sectors at some rich vampire or human house.

Getting out of this place is the ultimate goal and nothing will stop me from achieving it.

It's lunchtime now, and I'm in line for my daily serving of slop with Thad and Huck trailing behind me. Today's garbage smells awful and will likely taste worse, but the sectors don't get anything fresh. Leftovers, factory seconds, low grade meats—supes are sent all the shit their FDA deems unfit for human consumption. Places like F.E.A.R. slap it all together in random goulash and tell us to eat or starve—you learn to hold your nose and eat it pretty quickly.

"It doesn't look like it's movin' today. That's a plus," Huck says as he takes my tray from me. I give him a dirty look, reaching for it, but he shakes his head. "Just let me be polite, sweet pea. I don't get to flex my chivalry muscles often here."

Sighing in annoyance, I nod, following him and Thad to our table in the corner of the room. We stay away from the cliques, gangs, and psychos, but strength in numbers helps. When we're settled, I reach into my bag and pull out my copy of *Frankenstein* intending to ignore them so I can do my reading in a place with reliable electricity. Plus, Thad's on my shit list even if he wasn't wrong.

"Syd, come on," Thad whines as I hold my book up and eat while I read. "I don't deserve the freeze out. I was being honest, not mean."

I know that, but I'll never heal from seeing my dad executed in front of me.

"She's smarting, partner," Huck says as he elbows our friend. "Give her time to lick her wounds. Our girl's a strong one."

"Not your girl," I mutter around a bite of the semi-solid crap from my tray. "Not a girl at all. I'm a woman and I belong to no one."

Thad chuckles and I hear the sound of him opening the nutrient shake shit they give us. I feel like it's also part of why supes have stayed so weak—poor diet and the unidentifiable supplements we're forced to take or go without food and drink. "You're practically a nun, Syd."

Lowering my book, I press my lips together then respond. "Thad, nuns are human shit, and choosing celibacy doesn't make me a religious zealot. It means I'm exercising what little right to my own body I have left because I'm focused on getting the fuck out of this hellhole."

"But if you didn't, you might be in a better mood occasionally," Huck says with a grin. "A little meaningless release is good for the soul—or lack thereof."

Dudes are the same no matter what species and it's almost comical.

"No thanks. The FSHA gives us enough drugs I don't trust; why add their form of birth control that's probably secretly sterilization to the list? It's not like I *want* kids, but I sure as fuck refuse to let them take that choice, too," I mutter quietly.

They both frown and I cut my gaze to a blinking light just outside of our table area. There's a Confession Enforcement Drone flittering about and I don't want to be caught explaining further. Huck growls and mumbles something about six shooters and Thad leans back in his chair with a dark look on his face. Their bad boy looks paired with our loner status means girls actively look for them for a good time, while my bristly exterior brands me a 'challenge' for assholes to conquer.

"I refuse to be someone's high score," I say a bit louder so if the drone is close enough it will hear. "Guys can keep their fucking conquest lists to themselves in my opinion."

"Aw, sweet pea, that will disappoint nearly everyone I know." Huck tsks, then looks around the room for someone to feed off of. His eyes turn to slits when he locates a suitable target and I go back to reading and ignoring Thad.

After all, he earned this.

The period's nearly over when the huge speakers on the walls crackle and I put my book down, lacing my fingers on the table as the screen comes down from the ceiling. Everyone knows that sound means we're going to be forced to watch a video either from the administration here or from the government officials at some level. We're taught to sit straight, look up and have our hands where they can be seen every time and punishment for fucking around during their indoctrination bullshit is severe.

"Good afternoon, students of the Federated Human States of America's Supernatural Sector Academies."

I have to strain not to roll my eyes at Taterman's sheer laziness. He does absolutely fucking nothing in that gilded mansion in the capital, but he couldn't be arsed to record a few different takes for the academy names so it was almost like he gave a shit. Nope, that Spraygolf Pissler wanna-be has recorded one of these announcements for the entire nation and we're probably all watching it.

"Since the glorious victory over the virus is now fully in effect, and we have gathered those responsible for its spread in your new homes, your government has been working hard to find more ways for you to show your gratitude to your nation."

"Oh, yeah, we're so excited to be in prison camps where you try to brainwash us," Thad mumbles and I give him a *look*. That damn drone is here for a reason, and I might be mad now but if they kill him, I'll be inconsolable.

"I am so pleased to announce that classes in the university-level academies will be altered for the next three months as we prepare our amazing students for the opportunity of a lifetime. "

The jackass pauses and if you look closely, you can see the evil in his piggish eyes. I shiver, but I don't avert my gaze. I'm not afraid of *him*, only the power he wields like a goddamn guillotine.

"In three months, students from ages nineteen to twenty-three will have the honor of competing in the first annual Supernatural United Challenge of Endurance!"

No one speaks; hell, I don't know if anyone is even breathing in the cafeteria. Taterman is still smirking at the camera, the lights in his office glinting off his veneers coated in Vaseline. Finally, he shuffles what are likely blank papers on his desk and winks.

The motherfucker who killed ten million supes in two years just winked at their survivors.

My hand tightens around the spoon I was eating with as if I could stab someone with it, and if I could I sure as hell would. The souls of the lost relatives and friends in our world are screaming for justice, but this asshole is pretending to be a fucking character from the goddamn *Hunger Games*. I just… I can't, but I can't move or they'll put me in the isolation area.

"The Challenge will be fraught with danger, but never fear my loyal citizens, for the entire world will be able to subscribe to the live video feed from every academy as your

competitors level up through their sectors towards the main event. The final challenge will include one team of six that are the champions of their home school battling it out for the prize."

"That son of a bitch thinks the sun comes up just for him to crow," Huck grits out. "He's picturin' himself as a fuckin' Roman emperor, guaranteed."

I don't respond. The amount of shock and resignation flowing through me is making it hard for me to formulate an answer.

"You're likely wondering what the winners of this globally watched battle of ferocity will receive? My personal Cabinet and the very auspicious members of your governing bodies have worked long and hard on that answer. There will be a small, modest town constructed in the Southern part of what was previously California where the winners will live in comfort with non-menial jobs. They will be allowed to bring their immediate families and will not be required to stay in the sectors or supernatural only areas."

My eyes widen and I almost stop staring at the screen. The gasps around the room tell me Taterman achieved what he set out to: instant obsession. No one will fight the entry to these stupid games or challenges now that they've heard what the prize is.

Of course, they're forgetting these are the same people who swore *they would never use supe status to deny us anything.*

That went away the moment they realized they could put the blame on supes for the man-made bullshit they lost track of and started killing off half the planet. Supes were a perfect scapegoat because human media has been predicting the takeover of their feeble race by 'others' in every format for centuries. The dumbasses Taterman courted simply stopped evolving in the 1950s, and they liked having someone who agreed with their bigotry.

"Syd, say something," Thad whispers. "You look ready to keel over."

I shrug, unable to force sound from my mouth. There's simply no way they will allow anyone who is able bodied to refuse to participate and I have a feeling you're only out when you're maimed or dead. This is the new version of the Infected Being Sweeps, and people all over the world are going to pay those wrinkled old dickbags for the privilege of watching us kill one another.

Huck kicks my foot with his booted one, his dark eyes glittering with concern. "Syd, you're makin' us worry, darlin'."

"I…" Licking my lips, I shake my head. "I don't even know what to say. My ears are ringing."

The video finally ends and Taterman's face leaves the screen only to be replaced by the ugly mug of our Dean. Patrice Wallace-Brickman looks like she's just sucked on a lemon—as usual—as she stares at the camera.

"F.E.A.R. Academy students, I am certain you are as honored as I am that President Taterman chose you all to represent the Federated Human

States of America on the global stage!" She grins toothily, looking terrify-ingly like a human jack 'o lantern in her orange power suit. "Tomorrow morning, we will be augmenting the student body here with new recruits to flesh out the teams of six for the challenges. You will be expected to accept the teammates assigned to you as you would new pack mates as your lives will depend on working together."

"Shit," Thad says softly. "They're really doing this. The humans are going to pit us against one another to the death for paid TV."

I wish I could find it as surprising as he does, but I don't.

Wallace-Brickman claps her hands, her eyes sparkling with excitement as she continues. "You will be sent home early to rest up. When you arrive tomorrow, you will head straight for the auditorium to sign up in teams from your current classmates. Any team short of six will be assigned the balance from the new students."

"Great," I mumble. "We're going to have three more people for me to want to stab myself in the eye over."

Huck snorts. "They can't be worse than me, right, sweet pea?"

Unfortunately for me, he was dead wrong about that.

PITCHING A HISSY FIT

HUCKLEBERRY

THE MOOD WAS DARKER than a hog pen on butchering day as everyone filed out of the cafeteria to go home.

There were plenty of students talking in groups—the time for those who aren't affiliated with a group to get attached is now. No one wants to bet on whatever supes are brought in to flesh out the teams. If I were in charge, I'd schmooze some of these known entities before allowing them to put unknown people with us. But Sydney hates most of the supes in our school and I'm not going to piss her off further by mentioning it.

"Wonder where they're getting the overstock from?" Thad says as we walk down the front steps of the F.E.A.R. building.

Syd sighs, her shoulders hunched as we trudge down the street. "Probably re-balancing the larger settlements amongst the small ones. We're medium size, I think, so they won't have to send too many new folks. It will make the boarding house crowded, though."

I frown. Our girl lives in the adult version of the orphanage she was dumped in as a kid because she has no relatives and no supe group to associate with. Thad's tried to convince her to move in with him at the bear compound and I've even offered to let her bunk in my hidey-hole, but she refuses to move. New blood we know nothing about makes my ass twitch.

"You could always—"

"Thad, I'm not moving in with your mini-sleuth. Your uncle has enough on his plate between you, your siblings, and the other orphaned bear shifters."

Damnit. She's so stubborn.

Grinning, I tip my hat back and look at her. "You know I'd let you bed down with me in a New York minute, sweet pea."

This time she actually scoffs, shaking her head. "Huck, I can barely stand you all day at school, much less living together. Plus, the demon places are too close to the lockdown losers. I don't like the vibes."

"You realize those supes aren't there because they're all criminals, right?" I tsk softly as we continue down the path together. "The government locked down anyone from species powerful enough to challenge them. Some of my kin are locked down in other sectors, Sydney."

My quiet rebuke stops her in her tracks, and she looks at me apologetically. "I'm sorry. I didn't mean… I mean… Okay, I meant it, but I think it's because they keep shoving that down our throats. I shouldn't judge the supes in lockdown because it could be any of us if we lost control of our shit."

"Aw, come on, guys. We have bigger fish to fry now. What the fuck are we going to do about this damn challenge thing?"

Our burly bear friend has an annoyed expression on his face, but I can *feel* his fear. It's delicious, so I use my power to siphon some of it off so he won't go home radiating it like a beacon. He'll have to tell his uncle the news, and the kids will smell it as easily as I did. It gives me a boost and helps him, so I don't mind invading his privacy a bit.

Sydney shifts her bag on her shoulder, shrugging again. "Nothing. I mean, we obviously don't have a choice about entering. We're going to get three other supes to fill out the team and if we're lucky, they won't be total fucknuts. Then we all get to dance to the government's tune and hope we don't die. That's it—the only option we have."

I hate that she's right; her aura feels like she's given up.

"We're not going to die, Syd," Thad says. "Everyone has the Markers, so power levels are evened out. All the supes have the same chance."

"Um."

They both look at me and I roll my eyes upward, not believing that I'm going to share one of the things that got me shipped off from my last sector. The information I have is super top secret, and I never shared it because I didn't want to put them in danger.

"What, Huck?" Syd growls as she steps toward me. She's got the scent now and I'm not going to be able to deny her.

Besides, I don't want to—it makes a difference in terms of her safety in these damn games.

"Vamps don't have the same…limitations… as other supes. That was part of the deal when Taterman did all this shit." I hold my hand up before they can ask, shaking my head. "We can't talk about how I found out or who told me."

When I wave my hand around, to indicate why, their eyes fill with understanding. Anyone who overhears that story would sell me out in ten seconds flat. It's highly guarded info and if it got around the sectors, the knowledge would foment dissent. Supes wouldn't win, but a lot of people would die on both sides. Humans wouldn't hesitate to use the vamps and force the locked down prisoners to fight for them.

Their Markers are different, too.

"Huck, you've been holding out on us," our girl says in a tight, dark voice. "Why?"

"I'd prefer you stay alive, sweet pea. People who know this shit tend to die." I duck my chin, unable to meet her eyes when I think about my sister. She was tortured until she spilled the truth, and then they killed her. I refuse to let that happen to anyone else I care about.

Thad crosses his big arms over his chest, frowning. "You think they'll mix them in with the new supes in the sectors. It will make their telecast more entertaining."

"Yes."

Syd makes a strangled sound, stomping away from us down the street with her braid flying out behind her. Thad looks at me in confusion, but I know why she's upset. Her father died trying to work with the humans, but because vamps are sneaky, rich assholes they were given special treatment. It's triggered her grief, and she won't allow us to see it consume her.

"Let's head home, Thad. She needs space and time."

At least, I hope so because tomorrow is coming whether Sydney is ready or not.

After I drop Thad off, I take a detour from the route to my tiny home. I want to see what's crawling along the thorny vines of the underworld in Tempest Seven. Every sector has a darker side, and ours is no exception. The black market traders and less than scrupulous species live south of the demon horde, but before the lockdown bunkers. That's where I'm going first because some of these supes, like the Fae, look humanoid enough for the humans to allow them to work in their offices.

I need someone who works in the logistics department or maybe in the Supe Relations division.

"Wonder if Angus is home yet?" I mumble as I slink along the shadows of the side streets. "Nah, he'll be at the Shrieking Succubus and so will all his cronies."

Angus McSherry is an angry little leprechaun who resents the fact that he wasn't able to outwit the humans and escape the US when the sweeps started. His cohorts are all Fae, pixies, fairies, and other supes who should have flung themselves back into the Veil when the madness started. He runs his own little gang of informants and while he's about as pleasant as sitting on a hedgehog, his crew is wired into the humans' bullshit.

A low buzzing noise distracts me and I look over to see two enforcement drones zipping along the street. One is the audio confession type and the other looks like it's a thermal video transmitter. They're looking for someone, I bet, and whoever it is runs either very cold or very hot. Since vamps aren't on the humans' bad side, it must be an elemental magic user of some kind.

"Careful, demon. The drones are out in force tonight. No one knows why." An old crone jerks her chin at the robots I already saw, her gnarled hand waving in the air. "The whole area is blanketed and no one can suss out what the skin bags are planning."

I snicker when I realize she's not an old witch—no, she's a onibaba and she's skulking around hoping to find a random human worker in the wrong place at the right time. "Understood, ma' am. I'll keep my peepers peeled."

"Good. Far too many of them have gotten away with abusing our kind for too long."

The old bat is a million years old, so if she gets caught whispering treason, they won't execute her. However a young spry demon like me would get locked down so fast my head would spin—if I was lucky. Death is a much more likely outcome and since I enjoy living, I'm not going to take the chance.

Thaddeus is too soft to keep Sydney safe; I can't leave them alone.

When I finally get to the Shrieking Succubus, I've clocked at least ten different types of spy bots flying around. The leaders of Tempest Seven are either hunting the shit out of someone or they're *really* worried the announcement today is going to cause unrest. Either way, this is a hot zone of human squealers and everyone who lives here needs to be cautious.

"Huck! What brings ye here, boyo?"

My lips curve up as I stalk across the floor to the back corner where the shout came from. Angus is a pissy little shit, but he likes me because I help siphon his crew for a small stipend. After all, unlike Huck and Syd, I have to pay for my residence. A demon has to do something to earn money while they're in school.

"Where's me Lucky Charms, you old coot?" I shoot back, earning a dark glare from the short, red-haired man playing poker with a table full of ne'er-do-wells. "They're magically delicious, you know."

"If you don't shut yer yap, I'm going to make lucky charms out of yer bollocks, boy."

Chuckling as I drop onto the chair that appears out of nowhere, I lean in to study the players. Angus is sitting on the lap of a very curvy Seelie Fae girl half his age. She might be one of my classmates, but I don't pay attention to girls who aren't Syd. Next to him, a half-shifted wolf is holding his cards in his claws. The way everyone gives him space tells me he's high in the pack hierarchy and I don't need to piss him off. The third player is a gorgeous mage with aquiline features and a poker face that doesn't even seem to move when he breathes.

Then there's the last motherfucker—Saleos Ignia, the ugliest pit demon I've ever had the displeasure of knowing. He grins at me, his sharp teeth sparkling in his maw as he clutches his cards.

I'd like to stab Ignia so many times he turns into a cube steak, but I can't.

"What brings ye to my lair?" Angus asks as he knocks on the table to call.

"The challenges."

There's a variety of grunts and scoffing noises from his fellow players, but Mc Sherry scratches his beard as he studies me. "Worried about the new meat coming in, are ye?"

"Not worried, but I'd like to be prepared."

"I bet you would, Monroe. You've always been weak," Saleos hisses.

My fists clench at my side and I have to count in my head to keep from wringing his traitorous neck. "A complacent demon is a dead demon, Ignia."

"You would know, wouldn't you, Huckleberry?" He laughs evilly and I have to hold myself back again. "Your kin weren't prepared when the humans came for them, were they?"

"*Saleos,*" Angus snarls as he slams his small hand on the table. "You know I don't allow fights in my bar."

If I weren't aware, I might have jumped over the table to strangle this asshole the minute I laid eyes on him. This demon owes me blood and I will eventually collect on that debt.

Saleos Ignia is living on borrowed time and I'm going to be the one to kill him.

PLEASE, SIR, MAY I HAVE ANOTHER

SYDNEY

LEAVING them behind wasn't my intent, but I had to get away. I've made peace with the fact that my dad's naiveté and faith in other beings got him killed, but that doesn't mean the trauma of losing him is gone. It wasn't fair and it shouldn't have happened, but then my mom shouldn't have left when I was a baby, either.

Enough feeling sorry for yourself, Syd. This place is full of people who had raw deals.

I look around my small, dingy room, sighing as I acknowledge my inner voice is right. My sponsored flop house is packed with former orphans created by the Sweeps. There are twenty singles on this floor alone, and each one of them has a supe with a sob story of varying levels of tragedy. Mine is pretty low-level in comparison to most, though no one's grief is the same.

"This place is depressing as hell, but I cannot take the boys up on their offers." I lay back on my bed, hugging my stuffed Bulbasaur. My dad bought it for me as a kid because I was obsessed with Pokemon because it felt like if humans could accept them, they could accept shifters and such. "And they still can if they fucking enslave them."

Stop being such a lemon-sucking asshole.

"I need to get out of this room. Otherwise, I'm going to brood all night and by tomorrow, I'll be an even meaner bitch," I mutter to myself. "I should go down and see what's left from communal dinner, if anything."

Sitting Bulba aside, I slip on my flip-flops—no one should ever go barefoot in a shared living space—and make my way down the quiet, dark hallway to the stairs. Two floors later, I'm entering the main living area. It's abuzz with people talking about today's announcement, something I wish I could ignore. A group of six magic users are huddled together in a corner with a bunch of materials I assume have to do with a pact. Several shifter groups are also chatting, and I have to bite my tongue not to sigh.

Trusting someone who you live with but haven't formed a friends group with is… well, it's something.

"That something isn't smart, but whatever," I mumble as I step around and over people lounging with books.

No one pays me any mind because I don't hang out with anyone who lives in my tenement. I'm not fond of giving supes who know what room I sleep in access to parts of me. The other residents think I'm anti-social, which is fine with me, but our life in Tempest Seven is precarious. Random supes go missing every day, and who the fuck knows where they go? There's never an explanation offered unless they've joined a group of their own species.

The missing could be dead, trafficked, or even shipped off to other sectors, but we don't know. I'm not going to die because I was gullible like Dad. With a glance over my shoulder, I head into the large kitchen area to raid the fridge. Nothing here will be very good, even if it's mostly fresh. These homes are funded by the increasingly stingy government and they think we're lesser beings. What gets sent to places like this is no better than what the schools serve.

I open the industrial-sized door, squinting at the various containers suspiciously. There's one with meat and when I crack it, it smells like it's still good. Searching quickly, I grab some okay-looking tomatoes and lettuce, then the watery condiments we have to scrape to extend. As long as the bread isn't moldy, I'll have a decent sandwich.

"What are you doing, weirdo?"

My spine stiffens as I hear the high-pitched voice of a hybrid wolf shifter girl from the floor below mine. I have no idea what her name is, but she arrived about three weeks ago. Word was they'd caught her living amongst the humans with some exotic collector pervert. The pack here hasn't taken her in yet, so she was shoved into our home.

Remember, I said I don't talk to people, not that I don't listen.

"Making a sandwich. I got home late." I turn away, heading for the counter to find the bread. That was more than I owed a stranger anyway, so I consider the conversation over.

She huffs, making a sound that makes my fists clench at my sides as I peek into the cabinets. "Why were you late? We got out early. Sounds like you were up to no good."

I close my eyes, winging an irritated prayer into the aether that she leaves me alone soon. "You aren't my keeper. Walk away."

"There are rules here. Everyone has to follow them," she presses as I open the bread bag and sigh in relief when it's edible.

Gritting my teeth as she moves closer, I concentrate on getting a portion of meat on the bread, then dressing it up with the condiments and veggies. I'm not used to someone bugging me and if she behaves like this with others, she'll be the pariah of this place quickly. "I didn't break any of the rules and if I had, you wouldn't be in charge of enforcing them. Get your nose out of my business."

"You aren't very friendly. The other girls told me about you, loner girl. You snub everyone but those boys. You're probably fucking them, right?"

For fuck's sake. I am running out of patience.

"Look, whoever you are. What and who I do are also none of your goddamn beeswax. I just want to eat and study. It wasn't a great day, which I guess is why you're pestering me." Putting my sandwich on my paper towel, I walk to the fridge and get the water, pouring myself a glass. "Find another punching bag to take your fears out on. Today is not the day and I am *never* going to be the one for you to screw with."

Her mouth drops open and I smirk at her as I walk away.

Dogs aren't the only ones who bite when cornered.

I lock myself in my room with my food, not wanting any surprise visitors. This announcement is drawing all the dickfaces out of the woodwork and though my stay here has been pretty drama-free, the addition of new faces to round out the teams may change that. Dropping onto the bed, I wiggle until I get comfortable and finally take a bite of my dinner. It's not great, but it's been four years since I've had anything actually tasty.

Even your taste buds adapt eventually.

Eating quietly, I close my eyes and let the stress of the day flitter away. This bullshit would be easier if I had a damn clue what the hell my mom was, but Dad insisted it wasn't important. We'd deal with it if I ever manifested anything from her, he always said. But I only gained magic, like him, and none of it was very powerful. The collar isn't keeping me from doing much, though its presence irks the fuck out of me.

Once I'm done, I clean up the trash, making sure it goes down the chute in the hall fully. People who don't keep their rooms tidy get rats or bugs pretty quickly and no one from the management gives a shit. You're on your own getting rid of them, and no one has the extra money unless they're doing something I want no part of. Having spare cash is reserved for the orphans who do illegal or questionable things to get it, and again... no, thanks.

My luck would be that I'd get caught and sold in some stupid human market.

The door shuts behind me and I turn the lock again, then walk over to grab my textbooks. I have a few hours before they shut the lights off in my building and I need to get this damn studying in. I know they said they were going to change up our schedules, but I don't believe a thing the people in charge say anymore. They lie, they steal, and they have zero regard for our lives—this challenge proves that.

They're not going to catch me unprepared—not ever.

The loud klaxon announcing it's time to wake startles me out of a dream. I can't remember what it was when my eyes are open and I frown. I hate that; it happens all the time and every time, I try harder to figure out what my mind was doing while I slept. It's always just out of reach, though, and it drives me batty.

Rolling out of bed, I freshen up in the communal shower, avoiding all the other females hanging about using banned products to highlight their features and hair. Everyone shares whatever they can get their hands on, and I bet they'd let me in on it, but I don't need that shit. My ticket out of here isn't being someone's mistress or lover. I'm getting the hell out of here based on something besides my ass.

No shade—out is out and we all use what we have to work with.

After I dry off, I pull the dark pants, dark shirt, and socks that comprise my uniform for F.E.A.R. Academy. There's a logo on the left breast of the short sleeved shirt and the pants have pockets like the cargos people used to wear. I chose to take the male uniform because I didn't want the attention or inconvenience of the skirt and skimpy blouse they give the females. The guards bitched, but when I insisted I could tailor them myself so it wasn't baggy and ill-fitting, they gave up.

One of the things our old next door neighbor, an Arachne shifter, taught me pre-Unveiling was how to sew. I've been good at it since I was young, and I did exactly what I said I would, so no one complained. The other girls seem perfectly fine with me being dressed down, and I'm *definitely* fine with it. The big bonus is the steel-toed combat boots they get rather than Mary Jane flats. My feet don't ever get trampled because I'm protected.

They're gonna regret their choices when these damn challenges get handed out or whatever.

I run a brush through my long hair carefully, then braid it tightly as I do every single day. Keeping it out of my face and out of other's reach is practical, plus it doesn't get dirty as often as the chicks putting crap on theirs in the bathroom right now. I check myself to make certain everything is exactly how the guards expect it to be, then I pick up my bag and sling it over my shoulder.

Today is the day we're supposed to meet new supes to fill out our teams. I don't know how they planned to get them here so quickly or where they've been keeping the new residents of Tempest Seven. Huck might have info once I meet the two of them on the street; he always has his ears to the ground.

At least he's useful for something besides pissing me off.

Trudging down the stairs, I breeze through the front room and into the kitchen to grab a few small snack items to put in my bag. If I'm up quickly enough, I make it in here before others take the individually wrapped shit, so I always move quickly in the morning. I'm able to get one weak ass cup of coffee out of the pot, tossing it down as fast as I can before I sneak out the back door. The less contact I have with the buzzing supes in my tenement, the better my day will be.

I walk fast, unlike yesterday, and I'm at the crossroads where Thad and Huck find me within minutes. As predicted, the huge bear shifter is yawning and ambling along, while the demon is nowhere to be seen. I frown, trying to figure out if I'm upset that he's not here or relieved. Before I can decide, a finger taps me on the shoulder and I whirl around, my fist making contact with a face hard.

"Jesus jumping Jehoshaphat, sweet pea." Huck groans as he rubs his jaw ruefully. "Your left hook gets better and better. Thad, our girl is a powerhouse."

"Quit freaking her out before school, man." Thad yawns again, then reaches out to give my shoulder a squeeze. "Morning, Syd."

For once, the soft-hearted bear has it right—it's morning, but it's definitely not good.

THIS IS GOING TO SUCK

THADDEUS

TODAY IS GOING to be pretty fucking interesting. Not only do we have an influx of new 'students' being shipped in, but they're going to pair up those who don't have a full six person team. That's purely to screw with anyone stuck here solo or from an unusual species—no getting around it. Magic users and wolves are plentiful enough to have multiple pre-filled teams; it's obvious the 'wise' overlords think those more common groups will advance quickly because they have packs or magical bonds to help their teams successfully work together.

Unfortunately for them, shifter strengths don't work the way their human shit portrays us, especially with the Markers.

"Do you think they'll do it randomly or…?" Sydney asks as we ascend the front steps of F.E.A.R. Academy. "I don't know which way is better, honestly."

Huck snorts as he pulls the door open for her. "Mixing us up with folks who aren't well-matched and don't get along makes for good TV, I'd reckon. Making scratch off our performance is their aim—that way, that Dorito-colored tub o' lard can have another solid platinum outhouse."

My lips quirk. He's not wrong in the slightest. Taterman is damn near an avatar of greed and sloth, filling the former stately mansions of human government with tacky overpriced shit that only the newly rich would even look at. He declared many cultural masterpieces as traitorous filth done by secret supernaturals leeching off America's unknowing generosity of spirit. That meant every priceless artwork and historically valuable item he could get his grubby hands on went into 'top secret storage' so it wouldn't influence younger generations of 'true Americans'.

I'm pretty sure if this country ever digs out of this hole, history will find he stole it all to enrich himself.

"Taterman's a con man, pure and simple, and people here fall for it every time. Remember the human who enslaved all those shifters with the help of mages? He called supes freaks and abused all the shifter performers, but he got a catchy musical and movie made about him. They're so damn gullible; it's frightening."

Syd sighs as we head down the hallway, following the signs that point toward the gymnasium. "Yeah, I figured as much. We should expect our additions to be dead weight or assholes. They want to make sure people the world over are tuning into our demise, thanking their stars they don't live in this hellhole."

With that grim truth, we get in the line at the entrance to the athletic center. It's full of nervous looking supes from nineteen to twenty-three either chatting in formed groups or burning off their anxiety about not having one. Nothing about this process bodes well for the rest of the day and I watch as Sydney rubs her palm over the hidden blade in the seam of her pants. It's carbon fiber, so it passes the wanding and magical inspection— nothing like human ingenuity to thwart their own systems. Huck and I have matching ones stowed in our spots that the eldest bear female in my sleuth crafted for me.

Feels like it wasn't so paranoid now.

"You," Wicker spits, pointing at Sydney as we get near the front. "You're next."

I'm about to fire back a retort when Huck steps in front of us both, the energy in his frame dark. "Oh, no, sugar. You've got that backwards. I'm next… that is, after you account for the ten people standing in front of our little club."

The female guard across from Wicker—Baxter, I think—narrows her eyes as she looks between us, then barks, "You know the rules, Travis. No cutting the line. Take that group of six wand lickers."

My relieved breath comes out in a whoosh as I jerk my chin at the woman gratefully. I think she understood what was happening and for whatever reason, decided it wasn't going on while she was present. Humans don't often give a fuck about supes being abused; Taterman's convinced them we're lower than household pets in terms of worth. But this one was okay, and I'll keep that in mind for later. I owe her a small debt and I'm sure I'll find a way to repay it.

"That motherfucker is begging to be castrated with a rusty spork,"

Sydney grumbles as we move towards the female. "One of these days, I'm going to be the one to show him the error of his ways."

"I'd pay the Devil his due to watch that, sweet pea," Huck chuckles as he gives her a little push toward Baxter to make certain she doesn't get yanked to another guard. Sydney rolls her eyes at him and I make a face.

I wish she'd stop pretending she hates him. Huck is more our friend than any other supe in the sector.

"Maybe you'll get lucky and I'll extend my special treatment to your soft bits," she says. Her wink is saucy as she holds her arms up and lets the lady run the wand over her slowly from head to toe. You'd never know the girl's packing a secret weapon or that she's nervous as hell about this shit if you were human. Huck and I can smell and sense it, but these unevolved dipshits can't see a damn thing even when it's right in front of their noses.

The fear demon just tips his cowboy hat back a bit and hooks his fingers into his belt loops as he watches her get checked and waved to the doorway. I step up next, running through the process, and then Huck goes, flirting with Baxter the entire time. I consider that maybe he's banging the human and that's why she intervened, but that thought flies away before it fully forms.

Huck hasn't bragged about a conquest once since I introduced him to Sydney.

She doesn't know it, but I think he's almost as besotted with the mystery supe girl as I am. He's no better at getting her to pay attention to his advances than I am, though he is more obvious about it. Syd's just so fucking damaged by all the shit that happened since the The Unveiling that she's locked herself down to keep from getting hurt again.

Yeah, I signed on for that even though I sensed it the first time I met her; I'm a fool.

Baxter finishes scanning me and moves onto Huck, then we join Sydney where she's standing in the doorway looking around the gym shrewdly. I know the wheels in her head are clicking in rapid succession; the girl can break down a situation faster than anyone I've ever known. She's studying the gathered students as if she's assessing a battlefield. I nudge her elbow, tilting my head towards the bleachers.

"Time to go in," I murmur. She nods, then strides across the floor without a word. Huck and I follow, but no one thinks we're in charge of this little cadre—they can't. The dirty blond ahead of us has the air of confidence I know she doesn't feel, practically emanating from her pores. It's an act meant to fool any established groups into thinking we're a threat, but it's a good one. She drops onto a bench at the far edge of the room, wrinkling her nose when it's in the first row.

"I hate being this close to their bullshit," she mutters as Huck takes the aisle and I sit on her other side. "It feels dirty."

"That's because these assholes are meaner than polecats, sweet pea.

They just put on pretty faces when the right moment comes." Huck cuts his gaze to the cameras mounted on the ceiling then to the huge projection screen they lowered from the ceiling. "And this is part of their highlight reel, I'd wager."

I look around, noting the teachers and staff are dressed better than normal and there are decorations placed around the gym to make the atmosphere seem festive. Two slick looking humans that must be in charge of… fuck, something important by the look of them… are walking around pointing to things the maintenance crew are fiddling with. I don't see the Dean, but anyone special is here, she's likely sucking their asses in private.

Supes are always a stepping stone to something bigger for these people; nothing is done out of the goodness of their hearts.

"Who are the fancy fuckers?" Syd says as she leans into me.

I close my eyes for a moment, inhaling her scent. She'd tell you that she stinks of poverty and cheap supplies, but she doesn't. There's an underlying scent of jasmine and rose that always clings to her, no matter how gross we get. Calm washes over me and I finally answer her. "No idea. Maybe they're people in charge of this damn project? But they look too soft to be running death matches."

"Media, I think," Huck drawls as he leans back. "They got that slicker'n greased owl shit look about them. Taterman must be paying some idiots a small fortune to brand and package us like fucking action figures."

Sydney scoffs, tucking her legs up so she's sitting criss-cross on the bench. "I knew this was going to be a damn circus. We're all the trained seals and shit."

Suddenly, the lights in the gym go out and the doors audibly close. Syd sucks in a sharp breath, and I switch to my animal's vision so I can see what's going on. I don't like the sudden pitch blackness, either, but at least she's safely between Huck and me. "Stay calm."

"Easy for you to say, big guy," she mutters.

A spotlight turns on, illuminating the two strangers and Dean Brickman as they stand proudly in the center of the floor. Brickman is dressed in some ridiculous get-up like humans wear to horse races with a giant hat. It makes her look even dumber next to the city-slick visitors, but I've never gotten the feeling this woman has a clue about anything, the least of which is fashion.

"Good afternoon, lucky students of F.E.A.R. Academy! Tempest Seven is *honored* to be hosting one of six trials our competitors will be challenged to complete. Each trial will test strength, intelligence, skill, and teamwork in ways you have never imagined. Only winners will progress to the next challenge—those who are unable to complete their trials will be handled in their home sectors."

Syd takes my hand, drawing a skull on it with her finger, and I shrug. It would be a lot of supes to kill off at once, but maybe the spectacle of this stupid farce is to hide the humans' newest genocide. It wouldn't be the first time in the history of this world, nor will it be the last.

Not thrilled to be part of this many world altering events in my formative years, but what can I do?

Brickman claps her hands, beaming brightly, and I realize the single spotlight in the dark isn't just for effect. The government is probably streaming these performances to the surrounding human territories and cities—they can't risk catching the expressions of fear, horror, and anger on the faces of the supernatural youth in the schools. It might go viral and re-start the rest of the world's concern about our treatment.

"Without further ado, I want to introduce the *esteemed* Tempest Seven *Supernatural United Challenge of Endurance*'s Head Coordinators, Melinda Turner-Grant and Pat Bates. They will assist us with matching the unpaired teams, getting our contestants in fighting trim, as well as make certain we give everything we have to offer to our country and our President."

The fake tanned man and woman wearing expensive enough clothing to feed a family in the sector for two years step into the middle of the stage. Bright white veneers reflect the light and for a second, I almost have to block my view. It's clear these two humans have never done a single day's work in their entire lives and likely won't ever have to. They look like wax figures that have been animated for a theme park; that's how plastic and unreal their appearances are.

I mean, if that's what you want, whatever—but it's not going to convince the crowd in this gym that they're on our side for a millisecond.

TROUBLE IN RIVER CITY

SYDNEY

THE FAKE ASS people Brickman just introduced remind me of animals that look cute and friendly, but are actually plotting how to kill you from the moment they lay eyes on you. I suppose that's accurate—no one here believes these games are about giving anyone freedom. No, this is about making money off of the base instincts of humans worldwide wanting to watch us kill each other for sport. Anyone who takes a job 'coordinating' that shit has the moral compass of a great white—existing to do nothing but consume everything in their path.

I'm far too poetic for this early in the morning; what the fuck is with me?

"I reckon these city folk are going to shovel a whole lot of bullshit, then try to make us eat it with a smile," Huck murmurs. "Listen closely, friends. I smell magic in the air and I don't fucking cotton to it."

My brow furrows as I lean closer to him, whispering near his ear. "You think they're forcing witches or other supes to infuse their tech with compulsion magic? Like, to get us all to agree to their madness on camera?"

Huck shrugs and I roll my eyes to the ceiling. Even dampened, he's better at ducking that kind of shit than Thad and me. He's a shifter and I'm… mostly unknown… so we don't have the ability to block mind tricks as well as him. "Just fucking great. The witches are so easily bought. Being so close to humans makes them believe they'll be accepted some day."

"Not you, sweet pea. You know that a bull without horns is still smart. The rest of 'em are useless as chicken shit on a pump handle."

Thad groans and looks over at us. "Are you just going to get *more* annoying with these people here? 'Cause that was almost unintelligible, man."

I duck my head, smiling a little. "I knew what he meant. I'm smart enough to realize that the Markers don't take away all the things that make me powerful while the other witches are dumb. Right, cowboy?"

The demon reaches up and tips his hat a little as he winks at me. "Beautiful and brilliant as always Sydney."

My elbow finds his ribs and he has to cover his yelp so we don't draw attention. "Translating your shit doesn't mean I'm going to let you flirt with me, idiot."

"You wound me, sweet pea, both physically and emotionally," he says dramatically. "But I'll never give up, so be prepared."

Ugh. Men are so fucking incapable of comprehending reality.

"Thad, what did your uncle say last night?"

The bear shakes his head, pointing at the stage. "Not now. They're finally going to talk finally."

My gaze moves to the plastic people in their designer outfits and expensive shoes. The woman Brickman called Melinda is built sturdily for a human with dark, glittering eyes that lack emotion. She smiles broadly before she speaks, but there's not an ounce of emotion in it. "Good morning, F.E.A.R. Academy!"

Silence descends on the room and the smile falters for a brief second before Brickman gestures behind the two coordinator's backs. It takes a moment, but a low rumble that repeats the greeting echoes in the gym. Melinda's lip twitches on the projection screen behind them, but she goes on. "Pat and I are here to get you all ready for the biggest event of your young lives. We each have detailed plans for both the boys and the girls that will guide you through the preparations your teams must make for the competition. But first, we must balance the scales, as they say."

I snort, leaning into Thad. "Biggest event of our lives? Bigger than being put in prison camps?"

"Justice is what balances scales, Syd. Obviously, this woman is drinking her own Kool-Aid if she thinks supes will believe either of them have the power to do more than put lipstick on a pig," Huck mutters. "We'll be okay."

"That's right, Melinda," Pat says with a big, game show host looking smile. "We can't groom these students for success until we have their teams settled and formed. So with the guards' assistance, we'd like any full, six member team to stand, then make their way quietly to the back left corner of the gym so our staff can fill out your necessary paperwork."

Looking around, I estimate the stands have about three hundred students. That would give them fifty teams of six, but some of the students won't be qualified to play. There are a few that are injured or medically unable to do much—whether it's an injury from birth, a pregnancy, or one from the sweeps and camps. If my estimate is right, it'll cut that down to forty-one full teams, so they'd need at least fifty outsiders to make this work.

That's not terrible.

But the number of people who stand in groups is much smaller than that, and I watch as about twenty-five groups make their way to the area we were instructed to go. I guess I thought more of the shifter groups would band together, but it seems like a lot of people aren't ready to put their lives in the hands of the supes they live with. They can't be bringing in *that* many new mouths to feed, right?

"Excellent, kids. We love your enthusiasm!" Melinda beams as she claps. "Now, the remaining half of you are in for a real treat. We're going to have you shuffle down to the front right corner there to fill out your forms so we can match you with our newest Tempest Seven residents. These players have been brought from sectors all over the country and our very own seers have volunteered to read the energy on your forms to match you with the remainder of your teams."

Is she mental? That's not how seers work.

Thaddeus shifts, his voice low as he looks at Huck and me. "This woman doesn't know her ass from her elbow. Seers went to ground long before the first sweeps. Any race that had a live line made sure they were hidden before The Unveiling. It was the only smart thing our leaders did."

"And they were rare as hen's teeth anyway," Huck says. "Fae probably had some, wand wavers might, maybe demons—can't rightly think of anyone else who would have. And *none* of those groups would ever share someone who knows the damn future."

I squint at the two blindingly vapid people on the stage with Brickman. "Then what the fuck are they talking about?"

Huck sucks in a breath, then lets it out slowly. "My guess is they have a group of supes who are skilled at cons. They likely read auras, have empathy, and the like, but are well versed in micro expressions, cold reading, and the like."

"Shit," I say when it dawns on me. "They finally tagged all the supe circus folk."

Thad groans and stretches his legs out as he puts his hands on his face. "Man, those assholes were like folk heroes. Everyone pointed them out when the young ones get discouraged. If they got the circus—the entire circus— and broke them up to use for this shit, how long have they been planning to do this?"

I blink. "From the beginning, Thad. From the beginning."

~

Our realization makes everything feel drastically worse, and we're quiet as Melinda and Pat call down rows of the unmatched supes one by one. They started at the top, so it will be a bit before they get to our section, but a stone is sitting in my gut as I watch students in twos, threes, and fours make their way to the table where they each take a clip board and fill something out. After that, a guard leads their group out of the gym to fuck knows where, and they start with another waiting group. It's smooth, but only because the Markers keep everyone from using their powers in a panic.

You can tell by the look on most of the students' faces that they've figured out a pay-per-view death match was in the cards from the start.

I flex my fists in my lap, wishing I had something more to contribute than some shitty basic magic. At least Huck and Thad have strength, speed, and power despite their Markers. I'm as useless as the witches Huck described earlier unless someone wants heated coffee or plants to grow. Very basic earth and water magic is all the Marker left me. The new team members are going to want to abandon me, I just know it.

"Stop fretting, sweet pea. Your brain is worth ten strong bears or wolves," Huck says with a smirk.

My eyes narrow. "Don't read me, asshole. You know I hate that. Are you sure you aren't part carnie like these seers they claim to have?"

He winks at me, but doesn't answer. I frown as he goes back to watching the descending groups with eagle eyes. It's always bugged me that we don't have Huck's whole backstory, but Thad has good judgment. I know he wouldn't put me in danger, so I have to trust that he knows what he's doing keeping the shady Southern demon in our orbit.

But he's got a lot of skills I wouldn't expect from anyone who hasn't dabbled in the darker crevices of life.

"I don't get where they got all these extra people to shuttle all over to fill the teams. Did they do more sweeps? Find people hiding?"

My ursine friend drapes his arm over my shoulders, squeezing me against his side. "I heard the camps below the Mason-Dixon are bursting at the seams. The ones out West, too. That sound right to you, Huck?"

He nods. "Even a couple years ago, parts of the country were overloaded. Lots of supes hide from humans in places like mountains, swamps, forests, and such. Large communities were scooped up that consisted of generations of supes living communally, especially those that like to be in packs or prides or covens. They used vampires to locate a lot of 'em. That's why they started processing centers after the Second Sweep, Syd. They gather us all up and ship us to different parts of the country depending on space."

"But what about families?" I say softly.

"Sorry, sweet pea. Humans don't give a flying pig's fart about that. They tore babies and kids and parents apart, shoving them into different housing then supposedly sending them to specific places. But…"

My eyes widen. "Holy fuck. You don't think they…" Thad hugs me a bit tighter as the realization dawns on me. "In the crowded areas, you think they trafficked supes to cut down on costs and shit."

"Wouldn't surprise me. Human hunters, fetishists, killers… There's a lot of money to be made if no one can track down where people go. It's intelligently designed, weaponized incompetence. Something has to pay for all those fucking platinum shitters, and Taterman thinks we're lower'n roaches."

"I'm gonna be sick," I mutter as I lean forward and put my head between my knees. "I knew these assholes were evil, but…"

"That's why I never underestimate this shit," the demon says. "I visited friends in low places last night just to see if I could get the scoop on what kind of shit they're doing to bring these people in for this."

Turning to look up at him, I groan. "Huck, spill it or let me focus on not puking. No third option."

"Dude, you never said—"

"Shhh," Huck says to the bear before continuing. "I went to see Angus. The grimy little shit had to lose half his damn take for the night before his tongue loosened, but I got a wee bit. The humans used the rail lines to cargo in over a hundred supes, some in goddamn cages, a week ago. They built them housing just outside the borders of Tempest and not a peep has come from that camp since they arrived. They've got a barrier around it."

I lift up, my body suddenly stiffening. "Cages, Huck?"

"Yep. Seems like some of the teams will be getting lockdown losers to fill their ranks."

"Are you kidding me? Isn't that dangerous?" I hiss.

The fear demon smirks. "I highly doubt they give a fuck about our well-being, sweet pea. Using the powerful, crazy, and criminal makes for good TV."

Raking my hands over my hair, my mind races with the possibilities. Using lockdown species means we could get a vast number of supe types that I've never seen, much less know how to work with. A look at Thad tells me he's more than a little worried as well. We've both been here since the beginning and grew up within a hundred miles of Tempest unlike Huck.

"So we're forcibly entered in bullshit death matches for the world to watch while the humans rake in cash and we might have teammates who want to kill us? That sum it up?"

Unfortunately, our friend doesn't get the chance to answer because our row is called down to the table and we have to face the music.

Nothing in this world has been right since that stupid virus; I don't know why I expected this to be any different.

LOSERS LIKE ME

HUCKLEBERRY

WHEN THEY GESTURE for our group to approach, I flank Sydney's left side while Thad takes the right. The drugged looking supes at the table we're sent to are older students. The female wolf looks up at me with dull eyes as she asks for our names and I wince. Based on the bruises I can see, she must be one of the fillies who trades 'favors' for perks.

I suppose I'd need to be blitzed out of my noggin, too.

"Sydney Jolie, Thaddeus Calvin, and Huckleberry Monroe," she says. Her voice is confident, despite the fear I'm practically licking off of her. "We have a bear, a fear demon, and unknown magic."

The wolf girl nods robotically, taking three clipboards from the equally zoned out eagle shifters sitting next to her. That guy has a nicer uniform, makeup, and less marks where they could be seen. His sugar human has money and wants the merchandise to look appealing from the outside. It says woman to me, but that kind of preference got much more flexible after the camps.

"Take these. Fill them out. No lies or the form will know. All deception will result in punishment."

I frown as I take mine, walking with my friends to the chairs against the wall the wolf pointed out. They're using a fuck ton of magic users for this damn sideshow. Usually, the humans stay away from supes unless they're getting something they need. As I fill out the stupid information, I wonder how many supes they've bought off or enchanted to make the games happen.

That feels like an important piece of intel and I'm going to find the people I need to get it.

"Huck, why the *fuck* do they want to know this?" Sydney points to a question on her form and panic fills me.

If she lies, the form will know—supposedly. But I'm not at all comfortable with these dickheads knowing how her fertility cycle runs. My eyes drift to Thad's and his eyes widen when he sees where she's pointing. We communicate our fears silently, and I ponder the situation for a moment.

"Put a date but set it way back. It's truthful, but if you don't say why it's that far back, it might not trigger the spell," I finally say. Picking at the wording is a Fae trick and I have no idea who created these things.

Hell, they could be normal paper and I might not know because of the fucking Markers.

"Skirt the truth because it's none of their fucking business. Got it," Syd mumbles as she continues working on the questions.

Relief floods me as I scribble a bunch of shit on my own, finishing it quickly so I can watch our girl. I know the bear is doing the same because this shit just got very real. Deathmatch games have no goddamn use for information on fertility unless they're trafficking losers or… I don't want to imagine what else they might have planned. Angus' description of the 'new student' camp didn't fill me with hope that we'll get teammates who are trustworthy.

In fact, it made me worry about Syd and Thad even more. Tempest Seven doesn't have a huge criminal element—not like the bigger camps on the coasts and borders. They're not used to the darkest parts of Taterman's takeover and I'd like to allow them to keep their innocence in regards to the depravity. These Games may prevent that, though, especially with the species they've brought in.

"Are you done?" Sydney asks as her pen hovers on the page. "I want to go back together."

Thad nods, rising to his feet and holding his hand out to her. "C'mon, Vicious. We've got music to face."

I wait until both of them are turned away before I let the frown settle on my features. Thad is incredibly worried; he used the nickname for Syd that he *never* uses in public. The last time I heard it was when she got sick with the virus for three weeks after I first arrived. He was scared to death that she was going to die. It seems like he's similarly afraid for her now.

"We're going to be okay, you know," I say casually. "Syd's smarter'n a room full of clocks and the humans' porch lights are on, but no one's home. We can outwit them, and if we're very good, we can wing this thing. We just have to stick together and make sure our new 'friends' understand the goal."

Sydney frowns as I get even with them. "You're a ray of sunshine all the sudden."

I shrug, winking at her. "I don't see the point in letting these fuckers see they've affected me."

That comment works because Thad straightens up, looking big and intimidating once more, even if it's a lie. Our girl straightens her spine and her gait changes to an annoyed stomp as she heads for the table with the high supes. When we get there, she slams her clipboard down and glares at them until their bleary eyes focus on us.

"Take us to our fucking team. I'm ready to play."

You'd think that kind of statement would jerk these idiots out of their stupor, but it doesn't. They must be so doped up they don't even know their names. I slam my board down, making the eagle jump a little, and Thad follows suit. The wolf grabs the papers and hands the empty boards to the fancy bird, who hands them off to yet another cranked out supe.

"Step over to the door numbered 3. Stand at the door until it opens. When it opens, walk inside in a single file line. At the end of the hall, a team building assistant will greet you. They will take you to an intake room and when we have your extra players selected, they will meet you in the monitored team intake space you've been assigned."

I rub my temples, hoping to hell I can keep us all calm until this ridiculously long and bureaucratic nightmare ends. "Okay, darlin'. We'll stick to your boundaries for the moment."

The shifter looks at me with an empty expression. "I don't have boundaries. But you should follow their instructions or it will not end well."

Baphomet's big hairy goat balls, that scares me more than anything I've heard today so far.

Door three opens slowly, and I jerk my head at Thad as I walk in first. I'm the least destructible of us all, so I'll play the hero demons rarely get to be. Nothing comes whizzing out to kill me and I gesture behind my back for Sydney to follow me. The bear will have her back and when I hear the sound of the latch clicking, I know we're all inside. We've only been attending the university level of F.E.A.R. for a short time, so not recognizing this area isn't surprising; it's a huge complex and I'm sure there are *lots* of places in the building we don't ever want to witness.

The self-awareness rooms are only one example, but they spring to mind first.

As instructed, we walk down the barren, sterile path quietly in a single file line. My eyes skitter around, taking in the structure of the building, looking for cameras, and generally memorizing the place for future reference. It's cool, which means well-ventilated, and other than that, unremarkable. Unmarked doors are evenly spaced along the inner walls, so this is used for something, but who the hell knows what.

The lack of detail makes my horns itch to break free. I don't like situations I can't gauge and this is definitely in that category. The junkie wolf said to walk forward and meet the person at the other end, though, and I don't see as how we have a choice to do anything but. There's nowhere to escape to and I'd wager my last spur those doors are all locked up tight.

"Fucking creepy," Syd mutters and I shake my head a tiny bit.

We don't know who's listening or watching.

When we finally reach the door at the end, a loud buzzer sounds and it opens to reveal a woman who could be Melinda's double dressed in a bright pink pantsuit. She beams at us in a clueless way, her white teeth shining as brightly as her platinum hair.

"Welcome, brave competitors! My name is Krista Philbert and I'm here to guide you on your personal journey to fame and fortune!"

Syd's eyes widen and the abject horror streaming from her fills my tank. I have to smother a chuckle when I realize this Barbie-style bimbette's enthusiasm scares her more than the thought of teaming up with imprisoned supes. Our girl is nothing if not fiercely independent and down to earth, so the idea of someone so opposite being tied to us is making her teeth grind.

"Good mornin', Miss Krista. I'm Huck, that's Sydney, and the big guy is Thaddeus. Pleased to meet you," I say. I'm laying the accent on thick because it charms most humans and if this woman holds the keys to the kingdom in any way, I want her on our side. I don't trust humans—*ever*—but I'll use them for my own needs.

She beams wider, pushing the door open and gesturing for us to walk inside. "That's the spirit, Huck! Now, we're going to an intake room. Don't you worry about that name—what we do is have doctors examine you in privacy pods, then a mage will assess your powers, and after that, we'll have a tailor measure you for the base uniform for the games. You'll get five of those, but any other clothing or decorations will have to be won through various methods during the training period."

Thad frowns. "What about weapons?"

"Same!" she chirps. "Everything you could ever want will be yours *if* you're smart and brave enough to get it. That's a win-win for everyone, you see, because it gives the hard workers advantages and the viewers a treat."

That's... not good—to put it lightly.

"After we get you suited up, you'll take your packets, clothes, and information we give you from our medical and magical assessors with you to meet your new teammates. The algorithm uses that data to pair the teams appropriately and we've been assured its artificial intelligence is state-of-the-art. I'm certain *my* team will be on top quickly!"

"Mother Morgana," Sydney mutters and I imagine she's rubbing her temples in absolute misery.

I'll admit, this much sunshine in one go is going to make me puke soon, too. Clearing my throat, I attempt to ward off the woman's sudden death and our execution by walking faster. "Miss Krista, I imagine there will be some sort of orientation. Am I right?"

Her dirty blond head bobs as she claps her hands. "Yes, indeed, Huck. We're having a *big* fancy party in five days to introduce all of our fierce competitors to the world. Your team—and all the others—will have that length of time to get what you'll need to shine for the cameras. Best to keep those ears and eyes open!"

"Things we need?" Thad echoes. "Like… clothes?"

Krista stops in front of a door marked with a three again, nodding. "That's right! The coordinators have lined up a series of starter challenges to get the blood pumping. Those who win will be dressed to the nines and those who fail will wear their uniforms. Support from fans is imminently necessary in future months and trials, so you should put your all into winning them over early!"

The amount of bubbly exclamations this woman uttered in the five minutes since we met her is egregious for anyone not wearing a cheerleader outfit.

"Fine. Win people over. We get it." Sydney growls as she glares at the human. "It's all a big dog-and-pony-show and we're the livestock. We understand."

I roll my eyes to the ceiling as she stomps into the room, leaving Thad and I behind to give Krista sheepish smiles.

We're going to have to work on her people skills for certain.

THERE'S NO PLACE LIKE HOME

SYDNEY

I HAVE zero faith that this Krista woman will do anything but truss us up like prize ponies until we become a liability. Huck, Thad, and I are determined to survive this nonsense, but who knows what the extras have planned? If they were moved here unwillingly, our new friends might be fine with taking a dive.

If they put me or the guys in danger, I'll help them along without batting an eye.

"Why do you look so adorably vicious, sweet pea?"

My eyes cut to the demon as I follow him to the fat couch against the wall. Plopping down next to him, I make a face that I hope conveys my doubt about this whole situation. "I'm not great with new people, remember?"

Thad chuckles as his big frame makes a dent in the cushions next to me. "But you're so charming and open, Syd."

Rolling my eyes as he puts his arm around my shoulder, I shrug. "This isn't a world where you can trust people anymore, Thad. If anyone knows that, it's supes like us sitting in places like this."

Krista's eyes widen and I can tell it makes her uncomfortable to hear, but I don't give a randy, red fuck. Humans fucked supes over entirely instead of figuring out how we could all work and live together. They don't get to pretend we're living it up in these fucking camps like some stupid teen summer movie. It's dirty, soul-crushing, and inhumane; that's the plain truth.

Don't want to be labeled the villain, don't do villain shit.

A soft chime, almost like a Fae call, rings and the woman looks up with a forced smile. "Ah, that would be the matchmakers. They've put your data into the system and we'll have your team complete very shortly."

I arch a brow at her. "How did they do that? You didn't leave, nor did you call anyone."

"Oh, our magical staff enchanted the forms. The input is transmitted directly to them and they feed it into our system. It's a miracle of technology!" she gushes. "Our leaders have spared no expense to ensure this challenge is remembered for centuries."

My lips press together in a thin line as I strain not to remind her that without their supe slaves, this bullshit tech wouldn't be possible. It won't help to antagonize her constantly; I imagine she's not the worst human they could have assigned us. I'd prefer not to be given someone who would use this position for more nefarious purposes than inching their way up the ladder.

"If your 'system' is so good, what exactly is it supposed to do, darlin'?" Huck is leaning back with his hands stacked behind his head as if he's relaxing, but I can feel the tension in his body.

"Thank you for asking, Huckleberry!" Krista says with a bright grin that seems real this time. She bustles over to the chair opposite of our couch, resting her hands on her lap. "The Matchmakers take the information you provided and the algorithm in the computers compares it to all of the other competitors in teams with spots. It looks within the current camp, as well as the new residents we've imported for the most balanced group of contestants possible. Once it finds the right combination, I'll get a notification. The gu… assistants in the gathering area will be summoned to bring your new best friends to this room. I'll speak to you all for a few moments, then we'll head for the medical bay."

All three of us notice her slip—the humans or supes in the 'gathering area' are guards, not assistants. That means there are beings there they don't believe they can leave without armed humans to watch them. The rumors about lockdown losers may well be on the nose. Tilting my head back and forth, I crack my neck to relieve the pressure building there. Huck lifts a hand and his fingers massage the base of my neck, and it feels so good that I let him without a snarky comment.

That should tell you how much this process is tripping my gut—I never let Huck do that shit without complaint.

"What do you mean 'balanced'?" he says with an easy smile. "Are they looking to balance species or powers or levels….?"

Krista frowns, then sighs. "Honestly, I don't know the trade secret specific details. No one besides the Camp Coordinators, the FHSA public relations team, and the government advisors have that information. It might be some of those things or all of them. They simply guarantee that your team will be balanced for the competition."

Thad snorts. "Secrets on secrets, even from their own people. Of course that's how it works."

"We don't need to worry about it! The FHSA always takes care of our people and these challenges are history in the making."

"Uh-huh," I mutter. Taterman has the entire country practically lobotomized at this point. Krista is a prime example of the cogs in the wheels everywhere who blindly follow orders and don't question it. Dissenters to his evergreen rule gained through a hostile takeover of the judicial and legislative branches of this country after the virus were dealt with more severely than us supes.

"Hopefully, you get your message soon. It sounds like we have a few more steps before we're able to strategize." Huck continues rubbing my neck, trying to keep me calm, but I know it's also to distract her from realizing his true goal. He wants to know what's coming and how we're going to avoid bad shit.

Krista nods, her hands clasping together and squeezing as she practically vibrates with excitement. "I hope so, too! And yes, you will go through the medical certification, then a mental health review, and then I will escort you and your team to the competitor headquarters to tour the facility. Your new dorms will be there for the duration of the competition, so you will have a short time to go home and get your necessary personal items."

Is this bitch fucking kidding me? We have to live with these assholes?!

Before they can stop me, I spring to my feet and start pacing the length of the room. The one thing I've been lucky enough to have since I was put in the adult home for orphans is a room to myself. It's where I'm able to let the mask I wear fade and talk to myself about the way things were before this nightmare. I can lie in the dark and try to find the ability to cry—something I haven't been able to do since my father was killed. The silence and the space are my refuge and now these motherfuckers want to take my last vestige of hope away.

They say the American Dream died a long time ago, but it's true death was the beginning of this regime.

"Sydney, it will be okay."

I whirl around, my braid flipping behind me as I glare at Thad. "It is? Oh, thank you for telling me. Now I'm totally fine."

Huck snorts, shaking his head as he tips his hat back. "I don't think he meant to discount your feelings, sweet pea."

Of course he didn't. Thaddeus is the kindest, most patient dude I've ever met, and I know he wouldn't do such a thing. But I'm so angry about everything and have been for so long, that I don't know how to parse this newest outrage. The universe has been cruel enough to our kind, yet the hits keep coming, day after day.

When does it become too much? When do we say 'no more' and give up?

"I know that." My voice is soft because I don't trust it to stay steady. Thad's eyes meet mine, and I know he sees the depths of my despair. He's been by my side for most of the injustices and despite Huck's barnacle-like fixation, the bear is the one person in the world who knows me the best.

"Sydney, I only meant that you'll have us. We'll make sure you get the space you need."

Krista frowns, studying us for a moment. "Does she have some sort of problem you didn't disclose? That's very bad. In fact, it's definitely going to—"

"No," Huck says firmly. "But you don't know what it's like to be ripped from your home and family, by distance or death, and thrust into prison camps to live because some politician wanted to become a king. So maybe back off and let us handle our own shit, Krista."

That shuts our bubbly sponsor up. She looks ruffled, as if she doesn't know how to respond, then settles into her seat with her phone. Since there's nothing she can say to change our situation, that's probably for the best. Refuting his claim will only lead to enmity, and I refuse to let a human tell us what we've experienced since their betrayal. We would have all been at odds very quickly.

"Any idea why this shit is taking so long?" Thad says after a few moments. "This algorithm must not be that advanced if it's taking this damn long."

Krista doesn't answer him, so I pace again. "Probably me, you know. Unknown magic user is pretty vague, but it's all I have to give."

"Sweet pea, come sit down. You'll wear a hole in the rug, and I'd prefer it be clear whose team you're on when they bring our rogues along."

"Rogues? Huckleberry, we would never," the human glares at him, giving into his taunt. "Your teammates will be perfectly safe to interact with. What a horrid thing to suggest."

Thad leans forward, putting his forearms on his knees. "The rumors aren't true, then?"

Her cupid bow mouth purses and Krista looks at him. "What rumors?"

"The ones that say you've imported lockdown losers to help fill the gaps in the teams and make better TV," I growl. "I've been told people witnessed caged transports."

Her smile falters again, and a panic comes over her features. She definitely knew that was a possibility and all her misdirection was to keep us calm while we waited. I believe that she doesn't know everything, like she said, but she knows more than we're being told. This entire thing is one big mind fuck, and the humans are moving us around like chess pieces.

I fucking hate them so goddamn much.

Another weird sound echoes in the room and our sponsor claps her hands excitedly. "That's the notification. Your team members will be here in seconds."

My eyes meet Thad's and he nods, so I walk over to join them on the couch. Huck is likely right about presenting a united front, especially because Krista seems uninclined to share what she knows about the supes coming this way. Huck's arm drapes along the back of the couch to extend to both Thad and me, and he whistles an old tune softly as time ticks by. Finally, something gets our bear's attention, and he tenses.

"They're coming."

The door opens, revealing heavily armed humans and I roll my eyes. "We're definitely not working with them."

Krista titters, waving her hand at me. "Don't be silly. Those are the escorts, Sydney."

The biggest dude grunts and shoves the door open far enough to allow a trail of people into the room. My eyes widen as I take in the amount of guards they sent, and I have to school my features to keep from giving away my surprise. Usually, they reserve this show of force for criminals and gang members.

A shock of white hair belonging to a tall, lithe male with bedroom eyes and equally pale skin is the first thing I see of our new team. I'm curious for a moment, but he flashes long, sharp fangs, and my breath catches in my throat.

Please tell me that a motherfucking vampire—traitors to supe kind—isn't one of ours?!

"This is Sebastian Whitmore," Krista chirps as she reads from her phone. "Sebastian is a resident of the outskirts of Tempest Seven. His coven have homes in the Blood Red sector on the west end."

Huck grins, but it's not a nice smile. No, it's evil from stem to stern. "You mean his family was complicit with the imprisonment of our kind, so your government set them up with wealth and comfort to reward them. However, they didn't have Fae to review their contract with the humans because of their treachery, so like all vampires, they still have to live in camps… just the fanciest, least objectionable parts of them."

Sebastian snarls as if he's going to come at Huck, but the guard puts a hand out to stop the undead asshole. He sucks in a breath and glares with red eyes as he spits, "The rest of you dipshits think you know so much, but you're clueless."

"We know you fuckwads got screwed, too, just not as hard as we did,"

Thad mutters. "Bring the rest of them in so we can get this show on the road, Krista. I've got nothing more to say to this waste."

I can't stop staring at the vampire and it makes my body sing with frustration. He's hot as sin, easily as good looking as Huck and Thad, but in this dark, ethereal way. His clothes are nicer than our uniforms and I note that I've never once seen any of their kind in our schools. They must have their own education system or the sires teach them everything. I'm about to speak when the bloodsucker smirks at me as if he knows what's going through my mind.

Fat chance, dickwad.

EVERYONE LOVES A BAD BOY
THADDEUS

SYDNEY IS BRISTLING SO MUCH she's making my bear restless. Ever since the bloodsucker sauntered into the room, it's like she's gone from high alert to Code Red. Her scent has changed, too, but I can't pin it down. Her odd blend of magic has always eluded my shifter senses and the Markers make it even harder to use my animal to figure out what's going on with her. My eyes cut to Huck's, but he shrugs—looks like he's as lost as I am.

Just fucking great.

Krista nods at the big guard and they call out to someone in the hallway. "Your next new friend is on their way."

"You're a wee bit delusional, aren't you?" Syd mutters and I have to cough to cover my laugh.

The chipper team mascot—or whatever her title is—looks annoyed for a second, but then she perks up when the roided out dude at the door catches her eye. "Not at *all*, Sydney. I'm so excited to work with all of you and I know we're going to achieve *great* things together."

Lights in the room flicker briefly and the guard whips his head around to bark something at the people in the hallway. Their ire makes me wonder what kind of supe they're bringing in; someone with enough juice to thwart the Markers and disrupt anything is pretty fucking powerful. Despite my musings, I'm still not ready for the guy who walks in the door.

Holy mother fucking donkey balls.

A fucking cover model looking guy with blondish-brown hair swept to the side, barely there scruff, and icy blue eyes strides in clad in tight jeans and brown leather that makes him look like a goddamn adventurer, not a prisoner. There's a static feel to his presence—like the air in the room is charged just by his mere presence. He smirks at the vampire for a moment, then looks at our small group curiously.

"Who the fuck are these randos?"

Syd shoots out of her seat, moving like a flash to stand toe-to-toe with the cocky asshole. "Who the fuck are you to ask?"

That shuts him up and Huck snorts as he kicks his booted feet up on the small table in front of us. "That's it, sweet pea. You give this stuck-up snake a piece of your mind. I've got your back."

Sparks crackle through the air around the two of them as Mr. Tall, Blond, and Douchey stares down at our girl for a moment. He finally cracks a grin as she stays in place, not giving him a centimeter of quarter. "I like this one, Krista. I don't know about the other two. The mosquito can go fuck himself."

"Well, he's right about that." I shrug as I lean back against the couch. I'm still surprised by his ability to make this much magic with the human constraints, so I'm not ready to challenge him as yet. That is, unless he upsets Sydney, and then all bets are off.

"Now, now, children. Including your last team member, you will all need to work together to get ahead in the challenges. Thaddeus, you're an ursine shifter and your fear demon is also formidable. Adding a full blooded vampire and a mage will only raise your profile."

Huck glares at the woman as if he'd like to disembowel her for fun. "Sydney is a good fighter, fast as hell, and her magic is very creative. You're discounting her like she doesn't matter."

The mage tilts his head, reaching out to put a finger on the tip of her nose. "At the moment, she's more of a hindrance than help. Everything within her is bound up."

"Of course it is, you dickface!" Syd flicks his hands away, her braid swishing as she moves. "The fucking Markers limit our abilities."

"They do and they don't," the guy says with a smirk. "My name is Rory Stormbringer, by the way. Thanks for asking."

"As if I give a fuck who you are, spell slinger," Sebastian scoffs from his seat in the far corner. "I'm not here to make friendship bracelets with you morons. I want to win, and beyond that, I don't care a whit what happens to anyone else."

This is the stupidest plan anyone ever came up with—only humans would think they could oppress an entire swath of people then depend on them to work together to entertain them.

"Gentleman, lady…" Krista clucks as she frowns. "This kind of ire is *very* counterproductive. You won't have a chance at this if you can't put aside your differences and embrace your unity!"

"Does anyone know where her off button is?"

Even the vampire snorts at Syd's question, and the tension in the room ratchets back a few notches. Mr. Sexy Storm Dude grins at her, looking delighted as he backs off. "Ah, the plucky heart. Yes, I see why the two of you moon over her so. I think this will be much more fun than expected."

"You're a douche," our girl mutters and she turns on her heel to rejoin us on the couch. "And I'd love to know whose ass you're sucking to look so fucking fancy and 'maybe it's Maybelline', asshole."

This time I burst into laughter and Huck joins soon after. His eyes dance as he drapes an arm around Sydney. "Perfect timing as always, sweet pea."

"Wouldn't you *all* like to know," Rory says with a shrug. He plops into a big armchair, looking not even a tiny bit ashamed of that admission as he sighs. "But our last teammate is a more interesting topic at the moment, I'd wager. They held someone back for a reason, methinks."

I frown, looking at my friends then the two clearly powerful supes who are now part of our group. What in the fuck would they hold back if they've got a storm mage and a damn pureblood vamp with us? "Are you implying that—"

"Freeze!" We all turn to look at the guard at the door in shock when he yells. The beefy guy looks at each one of us seriously before he speaks again, "Dante, Elias, number 83745089201983. All supes present cleared for interaction. Bring him in, boys."

What in the name of Odin's eyepatch is going on?

The guards cart in a goddamned enormous dude on some sort of trolley. His eyes are bright sea green—as striking as you could possibly imagine and full of rage. His dark black hair is mussed and curly on top, and he's got a lot more scruff than the mage, but not a beard. Tribal tattoos cover every bit of the exposed skin peeking out of the lockdown loser uniform of black tanks, black cargos, and work boots. He has an eyebrow ring, a nose ring, and more hoops than a sewing circle in his ears. He's chained to the damn dolly thing from head to toe like they're terrified of what will happen if he can move a pinky.

"How the fuck is this guy going to help with anything when you've got him shackled like a serial killer?"

Bright eyes immediately flick to Sydney as she gives everyone a look as if they're very, very stupid. I think I see the corner of his mouth quirk a tiny bit, but then his expression turns stoic again. The guards lower his conveyance to the ground, ignoring her question as they start unlocking the huge glowing locks that hold his chains in place. One by one, the chains go slack around him, and limbs shift slightly.

Huck arches a brow. "So no one's worried that our new teammate is trussed up like his last meal came with some fava beans and a nice Chianti… except Syd."

Sebastian snorts from his seat. "Just because humans fear something does not make it fearsome, demon."

"They are rather chicken shit," Rory says in amusement. "That's why we're all here, isn't it? Fear of what isn't like them? Who says our chained comrade is even worth such a dramatic entrance?"

"I do."

We all turn to look at the freed supe as he shakes out his limbs with a dark glare. He's even bigger and more intimidating when he's not bound, but his scent doesn't make my bear concerned. In fact, something about the ocean-y smell is pretty comforting despite his dangerous appearance. Huck gives me a knowing look, and I frown—what does he know that I don't?

"This is *so* exciting!" Krista says with a squeal of joy. "As Brutus said, your last teammate is Elias Dante and he's one of the few known members of the sea dragon clan."

The dragon growls, looking at our blond-brunette human with an angry stare. "There are *many* sea dragons you have not forced to diminish themselves with your disgusting technology. Even larger than us are the earth, air, and fire clans—most of which you've not managed to locate. It will be your undoing."

Oh, fuck, we've got a captured dragon rebel; this won't end well.

Sydney tilts her head, looking very curious now, and I groan internally. Neither Huck nor I can get her to look at us twice, and somehow the fucking FHSA people have stuck us with poster guys for supernatural kind who are juiced to oblivion with power and testosterone.

"Huh."

Every head in the room turns to look at Sydney as she crosses her arms over her chest. The move definitely gets the attention of the dragon and the mage, though I'm not sure if the vampire is lusting after her body or the blood pumping through her veins. It's a toss-up with those fuckers, and I haven't known any of them well enough to tell the difference.

"What's runnin' through your noggin, sweet pea?" Huck drawls. His tone is light but I can feel his ire from Syd's other side. The demon would be stoking these assholes' fears already if Krista wasn't here with the phalanx of guards. I don't even have to think about that twice; I just know.

Sydney Jolie is ours, and I know he'd tear the soul out of a priest to protect her.

"Seems like you've gathered the dumbest group of people imaginable, especially if your stupid algorithm is supposed to pick winners," Syd says as she shrugs. "None of us will ever get along, let alone help one another.

Anything requiring team effort will be a battle of wills and the result won't be what you hope it to be. You're fucked, Kristin,"

I wince, knowing she's called the enthusiastic human by the wrong name on purpose. Sydney isn't great at being subtle, nor is she one to gild the lily when she thinks shit is fucked up. No matter how interesting and good looking these dicks are, she believes they'll sell us out the first chance they get. That's a problem in more ways than one and we definitely can't discuss it here.

Krista rises to her feet, jerking her chin up haughtily. "Be that as it may, Miss Jolie, this is the team you've been assigned. There's no half-credit in this competition, so if any of you want to survive, you'd best start figuring out how to work with one another."

"Not likely," the edgy dragon mutters. "The males are soft, even the demon, and the vampire can't be trusted."

"Good to know I didn't fail your sparkling assessment," Stormbringer snarks as he stands. "I feel warm and fuzzy inside now."

Sydney rolls her neck, cracking it loudly and I know whatever comes next isn't going to be pretty. "Fine. If our lives depend on pretending we want anything to do with a traitor, a criminal, and a human sugar baby, we'll learn to adapt." Her lips curve and she gives our bubbly manager a withering look. "That's what supes do and humans can't fathom—we find ways to survive without subjugating others in pursuit of our own comfort."

Huck chuckles, slapping his thighs before he stands up as well. "Since we're done being contrary, perhaps it's time to move this little party to the next step? I'm fixin' to burst if someone doesn't give me a potty break and the toxic bullshit in this room is makin' my stomach turn."

If we were looking for a way to shut everyone up, my demonic friend just found it and I could kiss him for it.

I'M A DOCTOR, NOT A BRAND STRATEGIST

SYDNEY

THE BACK of her neck turns pink and I know I've hit the mark. The government brought in all these randos to help run this shit who have *no idea* how the camps are run and what they're walking into. These humans don't know the rules, the cheats, or the terms of the schools or camps; it's going to get someone hurt without a doubt. And if they think the actual bad guys who live here haven't figured out how to cover up their misdeeds, the less evolved species subjugating us is in for a real lesson in reality.

Not that I'm going to tell this chick a damn thing—it's not my problem.

"It's a rule where they keep this fucker," Rory says as he hitches his thumb over his shoulder to Elias. "We should all be careful how we handle the soap at the dorm."

Huck spears the mage with a dark glare. "That better not be as homophobic as it sounds, hombre. We don't cotton to that kind of talk 'round here."

Sebastian snickers, shaking his head. "Oh, the naivete of the less talented."

"What the fuck does *that* mean?" I growl at the fanged snob. "And get fucked, by the way. You have no idea how talented any of us are just from sitting in a corner."

The crackling power skating over Rory's skin leaps to mine and I yelp. His grin widens as he replies, "I apologize if it came off that way. None of the elite are concerned about trivial issues like… gender. We're far more fluid since there are less of us—as the vampire failed to point out. I was riffing off his imprisonment, though… I suppose that's not fair, either."

Elias scoffs, but doesn't correct him.

"Not all supes in prison deserve to be there," Thad says solemnly. "For some, it's about their powers and what they're capable of."

Huck clucks his tongue as we arrive at the medical bay, walking closer to the group as Krista confers with the doctors. "Look, furry friends. We don't have much time, but keep them guessing. Docs and mages—fool them, hide shit, and don't disclose. We may not like each other, but we'd all like to live and win freedom. If they find every card in our hand, we can't hedge our bets."

The dragon eyes my demon for a second and nods slowly. "Agreed. The demon speaks truth and his plan is solid—for now."

Thad groans softly. "Dude, they know I'm a bear. What the fuck can I hide?"

Sebastian tilts his head, his red eyes intense. "Any past history—injuries, familial strengths or weaknesses, skills—is good to keep to yourself. Keep the chatter about your sleuth general so no one gets kidnapped or held for some sort of ransom. Think like you're playing chess or checkers or anything that requires multi-step thinking, ursine."

I frown as I consider what I need to keep to myself. My magic is hit or miss, and that's well documented in my school records. People know I hang out with Huck and Thad, but I live at the halfway house and I don't have friends there. I'm perfect for being a blank slate with these jackholes, but my guys are not. "I'll be okay. There's not much for them to find out about me that isn't on record."

Rory tilts his head to study me. "No, there's not, is there? It's all locked up tight, twisted in ropes and chains long before you ended up in this hellhole."

What the hell does he mean by that?

"Whatever the fuck you meant by that, button it up, son," Huck says as he pushes his hat back. "We don't need some dickface mage screwing this up because he gets distracted by his own reflection."

I whistle low, winking at the demon gratefully. "Huck's right. We all need to focus. Doesn't matter if we hate each other, we have to survive. Plus, I cannot fathom giving any of these plastic bobbleheads the satisfaction of winning bets on my corpse. I'd rather pay a succubus to drain me dry and leave my husk in the wastes."

Every single one of them blinks at me and I have to bite my tongue to keep from berating them when I realize it's because I said succubus, not incubus.

Men are the same dumbass couch humpers no matter what the species.

~

The med bay Krista leads me to is cold and sterile, but at least it's devoid of men being fucking weird at the worst possible moment. I don't like removing my clothing, but it's not like I have a choice. Grabbing the well-washed gown the assistant left, I step behind the screen and tug my uniform off piece by piece. They didn't have to include a barrier in here, but I'm glad they did because it's helping me hide the weapons I'm not supposed to have.

Thank hell for small favors, I suppose.

Once I get my contraband buried in my discarded outfit, I slip the gown on and pull my braid out of the neckline. Unlike our new teammates or even Huckleberry, I don't have much on my body outside of scars, one tattoo my father gave me, and my Marker. The scars are bad enough , if you ask me, and I do my best to make certain most of my skin stays covered in public. The early days of the camps were filled with humans who took out their rage from losing loved ones to COVID out on the imprisoned supes, especially unaccompanied minors and females like me.

I got a lot of beatings and punishment, but thanks to Thad's looming presence, nothing worse happened. Sometimes, I can't sleep at night when I think about the girls and women who didn't have people like Thad or Huck around. Even with Markers, some females of various species can handle themselves. But young ones or those with muted skills like me? We became prime targets for the worst of the worst.

I didn't mean to go back there right now; I have to get my shit together.

Pushing my hands over the top of my hair, I make sure it's still pulled back. The less 'pretty' you look, the more seriously everyone takes you—I learned that early on and it's worked for me. Keeping my long hair bound and face paint light is part of my armor, and it's all I have left when I'm wrapped in this stupid cotton gown. My feet slap on the cold tile as I walk over to the raised table, hopping onto it as I wait for the doctor.

"Come on, people. Don't bring us all to these iceboxes if you don't have enough fucking quacks to service the cows," I mutter to myself. I realize how weird the phrasing of that was as I swing my legs off the edge, grumbling about Huck's stupid country bullshit rubbing off on me.

That's when the big ass centaur in a white coat clip-clops in with a short, round looking woman in scrubs. Squinting, I make out the names on their badges: Dr. Moreau and Nurse Ames.

Okay, very cute, guys.

"Sydney Jolie, aged twenty-one, classified as a magic user. Skills have been presumed weak, as no useful magic has been performed since entering Tempest Seven after the First Sweeps."

I decide Nurse Ames can bite me, so I just arch a brow and stay quiet.

The centaur moves closer, angling alongside the table to peek at me carefully. "Perhaps you're correct, Nurse Ames. Can you fetch your equipment to verify?" She nods, bustling to the door and hurrying away as it closes behind her. Before I know what's happening, the equine physician grabs my hand, holding it tightly. "Do *not* tell her, Sydney. Many, many things depend on the right supes getting the right chances and *you* cannot be identified. It's too early. You must fight the intrusions."

"Dude, what hay are you smoking?" I ask in a tense whisper. "I can't help anyone do anything, man. I'm a dud; she as much as said so. You probably want to find some of my new teammates. They seem like real ballers."

Doctor Mr. Ed tosses his head and makes an annoyed neighing sound, his hand shooting out to grip mine. "I understand why you don't believe me, but keep what I said in mind. In life, things do not always make sense when we hear them, but they do much later. Keep your mind clear, Sydney, and your hopes up."

Sure, I'll do that just for you, crazy horse man.

"Uh, okay," I say slowly, hoping he'll back off the intensity a little once the dumpy magic nurse returns. "I'll try. But uh, I can't promise much because I'm not powerful and they have this thing in my fucking neck, yeah?"

The doctor looks around, then gestures for me to move behind the curtain. When I don't get up, he huffs loudly and I sigh, hopping down to move behind the stupid fabric. I don't know what the hell he's doing, but I doubt the nurse will be gone much longer. He clops over, standing in just such a way that I know any hidden cameras will miss this exchange.

"This will hurt. I don't have time to make it easier."

I blink, about to protest when he grabs my shoulder, spinning me around. Within seconds, a sharp pain in the spot where my Marker rests almost makes me pass out. My eyes blink and I pant softly, trying to get control of myself so I don't vomit on the floor as his fingers wiggle around. Another pinch makes me grit my teeth, but a few moments later, a cooling liquid is poured over the aching wound.

"Hurry up. Come back to the table. I've cleaned and glued it shut. Put your braid over the marks and for the love of Dionysis, *control your mind and your core* when Ames returns."

Licking my lips, I follow his instructions, but stare at the centaur in absolute shock. "Why did you remove it?"

He shakes his head and I cough, still working to get my shit together.

Apparently, that's all the answer I'm getting for now.

ANARCHY IN THE FSHA

HUCKLEBERRY

THE DAMN UNICORN shifter in charge of my exam was a perv, I'm sure of it. He sent his mage nurse packing for some bullshit reason and after that, I got the most thorough exam of my entire existence. That's a long damn time, and it's definitely topping my list for the weirdest shit since the damn Unveiling.

I'm a fucking fear demon; what could they possibly be worried about in regards to my constitution?

Now that I'm done with my creepy check-up, I plop down next to Syd. She's sitting far enough away from Krista that I know it's intentional and it makes me chuckle. Our girl doesn't trust anyone, which is probably what kept her alive when her father was killed. It's saved her ass in Tempest a few times, but nothing quite as dramatic as evading death squads. She doesn't seem upset by her experience, so her doc must not have been quite so handsy.

"Ready for the next step in the shit show, sweet pea?" I ask in a low voice.

Her head jerks up and I realize I caught her in the middle of a deep thought. "Shit, Huck. I almost stabbed you."

Blinking, I look down to see her hand covering the knife she carries as it points at my ribs. I know she can take care of herself—mostly—but it's still hot when I get to witness it. "Gotta keep your noggin in the game right now. I got too close before you snapped out of it, don't you reckon?"

"Yes," she admits grumpily. "It's just… I can't talk about it here. I'm muddling something and it feels important. But I don't know what the fuck it means or what to do with it."

Arching a brow, I look at her seriously. "Your doc or nurse didn't… get too touchy-feely, did they? 'Cause mine was fucking weird."

"Weird, yes; creepy, no." Sydney frowns as she tucks the knife back into hiding. "How was your exam creepy?"

"It was pretty damn comprehensive for a demon exam. We're built different, with extreme life spans, and hard to target weaknesses. Medical personnel aren't typically so careful and meticulous with us. This unicorn dude was toes-to-nose with me and it was strange."

Her reply is cut off by Thaddeus' emergence from his room. The bear doesn't look particularly bothered, either, so I wonder if it was just me. "Thad's coming."

"Syd, everything okay?" His huge frame wrestles into the open seat on her other side and she lets out a slow breath. "You seem…contemplative."

I snort. "In other words, she's thinkin' too hard, as always."

"Hush," is all our girl says. Her eyes are fixed on the other doors and I realize she's focused on something I don't see. "They're coming out soon, I think. I don't want to be overheard."

The first door opens to the smarmy mage laughing as his nymph nurse leads him out to the waiting area. Sparks dance over his limbs as he walks towards us, finally wriggling out of her grasp when he reaches the seats. Rory frowns when he notices the chairs on either side of Sydney are taken and I smirk at him.

No way in hell I'm letting these douches anywhere near her.

"The two of you are just *adorable*, protecting our teammate from us big bads." The mage tilts his head as he looks at me with a knowing grin. "She hasn't even given her *name* yet and she was given mine. It's very rude."

Sydney's head whips up and she leans forward in her chair to glare at the arrogant magic wielder. "My name is Sydney Jolie and knowing that won't help you in the slightest. But hey, at least the cheesy mage won't think I'm rude now."

"Ouch," Thad says, his chuckle rumbling darkly. "Guess that's what you asked for, though."

Stormbringer just laughs, his eyes dancing with the same electricity his skin does. "Excellent response. Now, about your bodyguards…"

Her sigh is heavy and full of disdain, but Syd looks him in the eyes. "Thaddeus is the bear and Huck is the fear demon. They're not my body-guards, and you're not my friend. Stop acting like the three of you won't sell us out at the first chance for glory or riches."

"That would be counter-productive, as Krista has pointed out. Is there something wrong with your hearing?"

The motherfucking vampire moved so fast none of us even knew he'd exited his damn room.

"Why would that matter to a traitorous blood-sucking scumbag like you?" Our girl's eyes narrow, and I'm a little surprised at her venom. She can be rough, but this feels… personal.

Rory whistles, slapping his palms on his large thighs. "*Vicious.* I love it. That's your new name, Sydney Jolie—*Vicious.*"

Oh, he thinks he's clever referencing the human punk rocker. How quaint.

"Again, I believe your ability to process information must be flawed." Sebastian shakes his head, foregoing the chairs to lean against a wall opposite from us. "We cannot win as individuals and the prize is not meant for an individual."

Thad glares at the mage, then at the vampire before he speaks. "Why in the hell would we believe *anything* they or you tell us? Trusting that either of your species has a better nature is why all of us are *in* camps, Whitmore."

"Naivete is why everyone is in camps," the vampire says as he pushes the hair out of his face. "Believing that every member of any species is capable of learning new information without panic or able to accept change was a grave mistake made by the entirety of the supernatural community. That fact doesn't absolve humanity of it's role in genocide, nor does it excuse it; it simply explains *why* our situation exists."

Krista clears her throat, finally looking up from her phone. "I'm not certain this conversation is appropriate…"

"Then get the fuck away from us." The snarl comes from the enormous tattooed dragon shifter as he stalks out of his room. A doctor and a nurse scurry away from him as quickly as they can, faces white as ghosts. He stomps over to our group, looking at all of us with a narrowed sea green stare. "We should proceed to the next step before I decide I'm tired of all the yapping and do something about it."

Meddle not in the affairs of dragons, the human once said.

The 'mental health' review went about as expected—an outdated battery of questions geared for humans on a bank of computers. The predatory nature of most supes means it will classify us all as psychopaths or sociopaths, if only because we view the world differently than they do. With the trauma of the past four years thrown into the mix, it's a recipe for a bunch of angry, powerless beings who were used to having the universe at their fingertips, even in secret. I can't imagine what the hell any of those results will do beyond identify the competitors mostly likely to be feral.

That would make for good ratings, so maybe that's the goal.

Krista has stayed quiet as we trudge to the next big area. Her phone dinged while we were walking, so maybe she got the analysis of the absolutely insane team they gave her. Syd's answers couldn't have been encouraging, and it would only get worse from there. Thad might be the sanest egg in the carton, but he's an apex predator in animal form, so his relative sanity won't mesh with what humans expect, either. Regardless, the chick has shut her yap and it makes it a lot easier to think.

"Wait here," she snaps, and I smirk at my friends as we claim seats.

She definitely got the results.

"If they don't feed us soon, I'm going to eat her," Sydney says grouchily. "They've gotten us used to not eating much, but this is bullshit. It's been *hours* since breakfast and we're in the part of the building with zero ability to see outside. It could be nine p.m. for all we know."

The dark scoff from the vampire makes her bristle and she glares, but he shrugs. "It's afternoon. Again, your knowledge of my kind is shockingly deficient for someone judging me so ferociously."

Thad leans forward, putting his biceps on his knees. "You can tell time with your… mojo?"

"Yes… *mojo*," Sebastian snorts, shaking his head. "Vampires have a very sensitive internal clock. It's an old trait from when we had to be more mindful of the sun setting and rising. In recent centuries, we've evolved to have a higher threshold for its rays, so it's not an instant puff of smoke as you know."

Sydney gives him a knowing look, her eyes dark. "Ah, but eventually, you all go up. It's just variable based on age and power levels. And chopping your goddamn heads off still works."

"Now, children," Rory interjects. "Personal differences aside, we all have weaknesses. Vicious here is the most limited because her Marker has fritzed her development… I think."

Awfully intuitive for a sleazy magical himbo, but the sun even shines on a dog's ass some days.

"Her magic is none of your business, dickhead," Thad growls and I have to swallow a laugh. The boy is simply unable to keep his damn weaknesses to himself. If that was fishing, he just got hooked.

"Interesting." Sebastian tilts his head, his eyes glittering with pleasure. "The bear's weakness is not only his species based ones—overheating at speed and shitty turn radius—but also the girl. Good to know."

"The mage is overconfident and lacks control," I offer as I lean my chair back, balancing on the back legs. "Syd covered yours, fang face."

"Holy water." Everyone looks at the silent, hulking dragon standing a couple feet away from us in surprise. I tilt my head at him, curious why he was a lockdown loser beyond looking dangerous as fuck.

"Nada, compadre. That's old news since the Church scandals. You'd have to find very specific priests and unsullied people to produce any that would burn me now. Weird loophole our kind found, but we're crafty."

His huge teeth are bared when he gives us a creepy grin. "You think they won't find clean people if it makes this more exciting? Now who's over-confident?"

Fuck me, the damn monster is right.

"We all have weaknesses, by species and personally." Sydney pins each one of us with a stare, her expression serious. "It will take time for the second half of that to feel safe to share—if ever. But if the crap they've been spewing about 'all or none' is true, then you motherfuckers need to get your dicks in line. I want the hell out of here."

Elias studies her for a moment, then nods. "That should be our primary goal. We have little time to execute."

My brow furrows as his words trigger something in the back of my mind. "You speak like someone who's seen the back of battle, dragon."

"I have. This will likely be worse."

"Why?" Thad asks as his hand lands on our girl's knee. "I mean, I don't know what battles or why you're locked up, but…"

The dragon grunts as he shifts, looking around the space for a moment before he responds. "I'm old enough to have survived many wars these people don't even know happened. The seas, the air, the dragons, the leadership… My kind is built to swing the balance, no matter what flavor of dragon we are."

"You're super *old*!" Sydney gasps as she looks at him. Her lips quirk up and the tattooed lizard snarls softly. "Don't worry, old man. Huck's not a spring chicken, either."

For fuck's sake…

"The vampire is likely far older than he appears," Rory says as his chest puffs up. "That leaves us and your teddy bear as the youthful contingent."

"Shut. Up. Spellsucker."

I have to turn away so I don't laugh as the vampire grits his fangs and the dragon huffs. Caring about age is such a fucking *human* concept; it only proves Syd and the bouncy mage are the closest to their species in our group. Magic users always have been on that thin line between the two, and only when they have a great deal of power do they exceed their mostly weak meat suits.

Another reason I'm making nice with these fools—I'm fond of our girl's meat suit and I'd like it to stay intact—not that they need to know that.

The balancing act of living after The Unveiling just got infinitely harder.

SASHAY-SHANTAY

SYDNEY

WE GOT USHERED into the next area so fast I almost forgot it was to be stripped and measured. Krista, however, did *not forget*, as evidenced by her squeals of excitement as they positioned each one of us on pedestals. A swarm of fucking designers and tailors in funky outfits descended on us like locusts, jabbering loudly to one another in small four person teams. I guess this is why there's a lag between the rooms; they're all beholden to these wacky humans and their pet supes figuring out how they want to dress us up for their rabid audience.

I despise this kind of foppery on principle—not that I've had much chance since the camps—but I hate it even more when I know it's because we're circus acts. My arms and legs are getting tired from being spread out like the Vitruvian man, and I have no intention of allowing *anyone* to put me in something with glitter.

Prison be damned, I'm not a fucking Barbie doll.

"You'll have a competition uniform, of course. Then a selection of gear branded by your team with your name on them—school uniform, gym kit, sleepwear, casual wear, lounge wear, and the like. The only thing you'll be measured for, but not given at first, is formal wear for events we throw throughout the run of the show. Those will be earned in various ways that the hosts will make everyone aware of. It might be through performance or grades, winning a mini-challenge, or even through votes and social media."

I blink. *What the hell?* No one in the camps is allowed more than basic tech and it's heavily curated, so social media is pretty much out. Unlike humans, we're all basically fetuses when it comes to the whims of the populace living on the Internet now. "Social media?"

Thad snorts and the crew at his legs grumble about moving. He can't help smirking at me and I know if I turn my head to look at Huck, he'll be doing the same. I'm not good with actual people, much less hordes of dipshits online. This will be a disaster of epic proportions if they think I'm going to be able to schmooze donors or some shit.

"Why the derision, Thaddeus? It will be fun!"

Elias takes this one before my guys can. "Supes haven't been permitted unfettered internet, much less social media, since the First Sweep, you twit. Do none of you lick-spittles have a clue about what these camps are and how we're treated?"

"You've got hundreds of supes in every camp across the nation who don't have a damn clue how to work shit online. We know the names of things the news here allows in reports—like TikTok—but we have not one single clue how to work it, nor do we have devices capable of it." Rory looks like he's going to burst into laughter again, and the vampire next to him simply appears disgusted.

I think that's his natural state, though.

"None of you have… phones?" Our coordinator looks horrified and again, I want to bash her head into a wall. She's acting as if smartphones are the most egregious thing people in Tempest Seven lack—what a goddamn moron.

"We have phones, darlin', but nothing like we had before your demented leader went on an IRL Purge," Huck says with a sneer. "Flip phones, if you're lucky or know how to shake it with the right humans, and that's about it."

"But… but how do you know what's going on? Who tells you what's in style or what books to read?" The blond looks so confused I almost pity her, but if this cluelessness is indicative of how little education most of the humans in our country have, it explains a lot about why nothing has ever gotten better.

"For fuck's sake," Sebastian mutters. "They don't know shit."

"No duh," I shoot back as my gaze narrows on Krista. "We only wear what they give us or someone makes. The second is infrequent because, *again*, you'd have to *earn* material to do so. We read whatever is in the school libraries, and yes, that's one of our few ways to amuse ourselves. We're *prisoners*, Krista. They treat us all like this, and supes like Dante worse. Get it through your thick skull."

Her eyes widen and for a moment, I see a flicker of sorrow in them. It flitters away like confetti, though, and she pulls out her tablet to start making notes. I don't blame her; it's easier to swallow our condition if you distance yourself from it. "Okay, so we'll need lessons on interacting with the public, both in person and online. We'll need to requisition enough devices for all of you and then I'll have to assist you with setup as a group."

"How is everyone else doing this?" Thad looks at her curiously. "I'd think someone would have had to… order… that many smartphones or whatever before this sideshow got started."

"I don't know, honestly, but we've been told to fill out the forms for anything basic we need for our teams. This certainly falls under that, and I imagine the other coordinators are doing the same thing right now."

That is, if any of their supes are brave enough to speak up or haven't been booty calling for unregulated tech.

But I don't say that because hell if I'm going to rat people desperate enough to pimp themselves for shit like Instagram. It's not something I'd do, nor is it something I'd expect my friends to do, but everyone has their reasons. Sighing, I look down at the team moving around me in frustration. I don't know why this is taking so long, but I'd *really* like some time away from this mountain of crap to decompress.

"Okay, gentleman!" Krista claps with a bright smile. "Thank you for your help, but the guards will lead you into the waiting room for the dorm tour now. Our tailors have to take measurements from Miss Sydney that are not meant for your eyes."

Oh, double fuck me; I'm going to have to get naked in front of this bitch.

"Humiliating…. I just want to stab…"

My grumbles disappear into the loud chaos that is the waiting room for the supe teams who have tours next. Every other room so far has been one group at a time, but in their infinite wisdom, the organizers of this clown show have at least ten teams milling about in here under the watchful eyes of guards with those damn electrical prod sticks and their pet witches. A shiver of fear runs up my spine as I look around for Huck and Thad. The parallels to the human Holocaust are a boogeyman tale for all the children and teens gathered into the supe camps and have been since the First Sweeps.

If they'd execute millions of their own because of some charismatic psycho once, they'd do it to us in a heartbeat.

I let out a sigh of relief when I find them in a corner, grimacing as Stormbringer babbles, Elias glares at everyone, and the vampire leans against a wall with an annoyed expression. It could be worse, I suppose; my eyes dart around the room, clocking the vibe from the others parked here. While there are two or three bored looking teams that must have been fully formed before this, the rest of them all appear disjointed and restless. That bodes well for competition since not everyone is smart enough to grasp that fucking over your teammates will lead to losing or worse, death.

"Syd!" Thad waves me over when our eyes meet and I force my legs to propel me through the throng of people I don't know.

The amount of bodies brushing mine and the noise make my skin crawl. It's bringing me back to the round up where my dad died, and my chest constricts as anxiety spikes inside of me. I hate this weakness with a fierce passion and it's why I avoid emotions that aren't righteous fury. I don't *want* to accept his death, nor how he died. No, I want it to fuel me so I never end up in that situation because of some misguided delusion that life is fair.

Fine, I'm irrevocably damaged. Sue me.

When I get to their spot, I glance at the new members of our team. Sebastian ignores me—a blessing, if you ask me—and Rory continues talking about his family's downfall. From what I catch, they must have been as naive and gullible as my father. None of them were killed, but they were definitely stripped of money and titles, then imprisoned in camps across the country. Their family was some sort of mage royalty or something, so Rory is determined to restore their honor. He's being far too open with the information, and I'm certain it will get him killed during this bullshit.

Turning my head to the dragon, I note that he's staring at me as if he can hear my thoughts. I have no fucking *clue* if that's one of the 'dangerous' powers his kind hold that lead him to be double imprisoned, so I sneer at him. His lips curve up just a hair and he sniffs the air delicately, then smirks at me.

Son of a bitch, he knows I was scared.

"When are we getting out of here?" I say as I pull my gaze from his to look at my friends. "I'm surprised they're allowing us to… mingle… as it were."

Huck chuckles and leans back in his chair, his legs sprawled out and his hat tipped back casually. "But we're not, sweet pea. You'd think that would happen as we're not the animals they make us out to be. Unfortunately, the desire to get the hell out of Dodge has everyone closing ranks."

"It's a social experiment," Thad mutters. "They're probably watching the film. It shows them their plan worked—the teams won't band together to rise up against them because they're so desperate to win."

My nose wrinkles and I tilt my head at the bear. "That's awfully cynical for you, buddy. Isn't that my job?"

He snorts, shaking his head. "I try to be more positive to temper your rough edges, Syd. It doesn't mean I don't see all the bad crap going down here."

Fair enough. I'm bitter enough for all three of us.

"Aw, isn't that sweet?" Sebastian snarks from his corner. "He weawy wikes you."

Before he can utter another word, I'm in his face with the tip of my knife barely protruding from my sleeve so no one can see it. His eyes widen and I give him a slow, satisfied smile. "Shut. Up. Traitor. I've had enough of your shit for today."

"Damn, girl," Rory whistles as his eyes burn into my back. "You got moves for someone who doesn't have magic to throw around."

Whipping around, I release the irritating vamp and stalk towards the flirty mage. "You should shut your yap, too. I don't have nearly as developed hearing as most of the supes here and I heard you blabbing your shit from the doorway. Giving the enemy your pain is an amateur move."

Elias snorts, his lips quirking up briefly. "She's right, spellcaster. You're both idiots. This set-up isn't simply for the humans to watch us; it's also to allow teams to note weaknesses of their competition. The two of you have been feeding them information the entire time while the bear and the demon simply sat back."

I lean in, looking down at Rory when I'm close enough. "You need to learn when to shut the hell up, mage. Your mouth could get us killed."

His brow arches and my stomach flutters when his smile gets wicked. "Who says any of that shit is true? I wasn't dropped off the turnip truck yesterday, Vicious. If you think I'm not playing the angles at all times, you're out of your pretty skull."

Pulling back, I roll my eyes at the ceiling and rub the back of my neck. These fucking men are infuriating and I have no idea how the fuck I'm going to survive having to deal with five dudes who think they know better than me about everything. My hand slips over the tiny cut where the doc took the Marker out and I feel a spark of energy crawl over my fingers.

Oh, shit. Maybe he really did *unbind my fucking powers.*

BITTERSWEET SYMPHONY

SEBASTIAN

I DON'T WANT to be here, but it's not like I have an option. Father swore that it would only raise our standing with the human government to participate, but I doubt that's why he sent me. He's in with the leadership of El Dorado One so deeply that he might as well be living in their colons—nothing I do will affect that either way. His true intent is to get me killed because I look like *her*. I grind my teeth together as I try to remember my mother, but she's been gone since I was a youngling.

Every day Astaroth Whitmore has to look upon my face is one I'm lucky to survive.

The ironic part of this disaster is that everyone in this fucking place is ready to rip vampires apart, no matter who they are. These competitors don't even know who I am yet or why they should want to destroy me—they simply hate my kind for the horrors of our elders. That includes my father, of course, and once someone figures out my lineage, they'll all gun for me because of him. What they won't know is that he doesn't fucking *care* if I die in this bullshit experiment. He considers my sisters by other sires to be his heirs despite the fact that I'm older and smarter than all of them.

Even my own team is predisposed to hate me—a fact that I'll keep very much in mind when we finally get to the quarters they've promised. I'm sure it will be extremely luxe compared to the filth they're keeping the supes in here, but it won't meet my exacting standards. Living in ED1 has spoiled me, for better or worse, and the trauma-based OCD I developed because of Father's rigid rules will spiral if I'm not careful. I can't allow anyone to see that weakness or notice that it leaves me vulnerable when I'm having episodes.

Astaroth had beyond high expectations for the appearance and cleanliness of his home which he held me to account for even if I had nothing to do with the mess. His punishments were cruel and scarring, but my sisters have never felt the burn of their application. Only the staff and I received those 'lessons' over the years. The healers in our prior city ignored the wounds, cleaning and patching me over the years, but once the humans moved us to sectors, a kind of old witch took pity on me and told me why I kept harming myself because I never felt clean. She told me his demand for perfection was so severe that I developed my condition before I was even a century old—a mere baby for a vampire—but I could learn to manage it.

I suppose varied providers is one benefit of being caged like zoo animals even though vampires helped those roaches corral the others.

Looking around the small courtyard they've spruced up for our journey from the bowels of the university to this 'Victory Hall,' I sneer. If you ignored the view on the way into the camp, you might even think this is how supes live in them. Hell, if you videoed the parts of ED1 where vampires and pet magic users live, you might be convinced the government is treating everyone well. But that's not how it is in the rest of Tempest Seven, nor ED1, or any other camp in the country. The show plans on featuring only the hastily polished pieces they want the world to see, and then no one will ask questions about Taterman's supernatural prisons.

I shouldn't care; if I survive this, I'll likely be sent back to my Father rather than this mythical Shangri-La they're telling everyone they're moving to. The way they described it to the supes who were brought in to fill out the teams was... suspect... at best. It wouldn't surprise me if they simply ship the winners to places like my home until the world stops paying attention or they start all over again. Once no one's paying attention to the ex-competitors, they can do whatever they want with them—even make them disappear.

That's another possibility I need to make plans for.

"Listen up, everyone!"

Rolling my eyes as the bright-eyed humans in charge of the four teams who are taking this tour together stop in front of the Hall that must be our new home. It's definitely been constructed recently, and there's no way it was without magic because the original members of my team are looking at it in shock. They must have put a fucking cloaking spell over the damn thing, too. I pinch the bridge of my nose, wondering how much money and time has been spent setting up this farce. It seems like a fucking mint's worth, which begs the question: why?

"Fuck me," Sydney whispers as she stands between the bear and the cow-poke demon. "Where the shit did this place come from?"

The tall shifter shakes his head. "Hell if I know. We were outside a few hours ago. Even with non-chipped high-level mages and elves and... I mean, it's just not possible."

"Don't be so sure," the fear demon says as he leans into them. "This damn place coulda all been here for months hiding its light under a bushel. If they had the right folks doing the right chants, none of us would have seen it, and a little extra spice would make us all avoid the area so no one ran into the damn thing."

Well, he's not stupid. That's a point in his favor, even if he is demon scum.

"They could have given this entire sector better food and housing for *years* for what that kind of shit had to cost."

I chuckle to myself, as the girl at the epicenter of our team prattles on. She's far too good for this kind of thing and that's going to be a real problem. Given she has dick for magic, it makes her the concrete shoes of our team and it won't be long before the snarling dragon and flirty mage decide she's not worth getting killed over.

I'm not sure how I feel about that, but then, I'm persona non-grata, anyway.

After an annoying speech about the building, the rules, and every other bullshit thing the guides could think of, they finally herded us into the front doors. Admittedly, I wondered if we'd get inside and it'd be some cardboard-looking IKEA nightmare slapped together with wood glue. My eyes rove over the much less upsetting atmosphere of the lobby, taking in the comfortable looking public spaces in the sunlit foyer.

No one will use them, but it doesn't look like shit so far, which is good.

My point is made when Krista takes over the tour, babbling about the 'shared' spaces on every floor for competitors to engage with the others on their floor. Teams look at one another suspiciously when she finishes, gazes narrowing and shoulders hunching as they scowl. Putting all these frustrated, desperate people in a race for a better life was never going to encourage friendly mingling. If nothing else, those stupid spaces will become prime real estate for teams to plant nasty surprises for one another if they can muster them.

"And now your coordinator will take your team downstairs in the elevator to the training basement. Everyone, stay with your team and make sure to catch the car you belong to."

Rubbing my temples in overstimulation, I move as close to the others as I can without feeling unsafe or worse, germ-infested. Damn near *everything* about this day is triggering my issues and despite my amusement at the girl's indignation and naivete, my control is waning as it drags on. I need to get somewhere quiet, unbreachable, and clean pretty soon. Otherwise, I have no idea what the hell I'm going to do.

"Why the fuck does it matter how we get into an elevator?" Sydney grumbles to the bear.

He shrugs, his focus on the flirty mage. That idiot is beyond in love with the unemerged woman and he's terrified by the additions to their tiny clique. "No idea."

"A small enclosed space without monitoring would be an ideal place to take out players before the games begin."

I arch a brow, impressed by the dragon's quick and accurate response. He's moving around the group in what he probably thinks is a random pattern, but I can tell it's not. It appears the stoic looking criminal has problems staying still for long periods. I wince when I realize he's been somewhere where he's locked down much of the time and might have traveled a long distance in that ridiculous serial killer cage. It had to be absolute torture based on his size and the hyperactivity he's trying to mask.

The brash mage claps him on the shoulder, earning him an even darker scowl. "Don't be shirty, man. I'm congratulating you on an excellent observation."

"I don't need your praise, spell sucker. Unlike you, I'm comfortable with my assessment of myself."

Ouch. Talk about an arrow to the knee—Elias is brutal.

Normally, I'd find that fairly appealing. Supes who aren't cheery fools, idealistic rubes, or ass-kissing whores are few and far between in El Dorado One. Finding anyone who can keep up with my brain and my wit is a serious plus in my book. Unfortunately, I'm separated from the rest of them by more than physical distance. I'm one of the bad guys—as far as they know—and my opinions won't be appreciated.

"Team…" The perky woman frowns as she looks at us. "We definitely need a team name. That will help immensely with branding you. For now, let's get moving… shoo!"

Sydney rolls her eyes, but follows the demon into the carriage, and the bear immediately boxes her in. The mage and the dragon go next and finally, I have to enter the tight space full of people who hate me. My eyes dart between the others and the walls of the damn elevator, trying to decide which one is worse to touch. Krista doesn't notice, she keeps babbling about the center we're headed underground to visit.

I couldn't give less fucks about the subterranean gym and pool they have for the teams to get ready for the Games in.

"Are you people fucking *kidding* me with this shit?!"

My lips quirk as I look up at the ceiling. Sydney definitely cares about this luxury, and I doubt it will be the last thing we see that sets off her fiery temper. Even if she's not jaded enough to take on most of the people she'll need to in the Games, her temper and her spirit are a force of their own. It's a shame this competition is going to beat that moral compass out of her, but I'm also interested to see what happens when the crusader goes dark.

I enjoy seeing pretty things turn deadly; it's a vampire thing.

"Syd, they're modeling this after... like athletes. Remember the Olympics?"

The bear is trying to reason with her, but even I realize bringing up the past isn't the way to calm Sydney down. She gives him an angry huff before replying, "It's only been four fucking years, not a century, Thad. Of course I remember the goddamn Olympics."

"He's trying to say the Games are like that, sweet pea. They have to give us places to train up."

She elbows the demon and the other three guys snicker. "All of you shut the hell up. I understand the concept of elite games and training. I'm fucking furious they've spent all this money to do this here and fuck knows how many other sectors all for the amusement of humans around the world. There are people in this damn town barely surviving and it's a fucking travesty."

Spinning away from the group, she hunches into the corner diagonal from the one I'm plastered into. I can tell by the miniscule movements it takes vampiric eyes to see that she's struggling not to cry. Tilting my head, I watch quietly, wondering how it would feel to be *that* compassionate all the time. I don't think I could handle it, but obviously, she was raised this way before the Sweeps.

Krista clears her throat when the elevator dings, pasting on a fake smile as she pretends the whole thing didn't happen. "Okay, team. This is the gym. It has all the modern conveniences and there will be specific trainers and staff assigned to monitor each team during their time here..."

Everyone shuffles out, and I watch Sydney take a deep, shuddering breath before she turns to face the exit.

"What are you looking at, asshole?" she growls as she stomps past me into the room I know I'll dread daily.

To be truthful, I'm not exactly sure—and I don't know if I want to find out.

A LITTLE TRUTH GOES A LONG WAY

SYDNEY

THE MORE WE tour this facility, the angrier I get. Our dear dictator spared no expense in creating this incredibly film-able, state-of-the-art place within a sector that's hurting—and we're not even the worst one nor is this the only facility like it. I shudder to think of what kind of bullshit playground was built in wealthier sectors like El Dorado 1. All that dough *could* have gone to improving the lives of supes everywhere, but instead it went to creating this perfect facade for the world to watch. It makes me wonder what kind of ulterior motive Taterman has for these Games—other than being an asshole species racist—and how this is going to fuel that fire.

Money isn't the ultimate goal here; there's something bigger at play.

I suppose it's possible some idiot let him watch a copy of *The Hunger Games* and he figured spending money to make money was a good option. Forcing a vast amount of young supes to kill one another in these trials would lower the population and therefore, the cost of maintaining the sectors. I just don't think it's on a large enough scale to be the only factor. There's a hidden benefit in this charade and I'm going to find it and expose it. The FSHA needs to be taken down and the global stage is the best place to do it—not that I have a clue how at this point.

"Rein it in, Vicious. You look ready to gut the next person who speaks to you," the mage whispers as he sidles up to me. "Can't have the shiny happy people thinking you're contemplating their deaths."

I snort. "Yeah, because they'd be totally mistaken in that assumption."

He grins conspiratorially as he winks at me and bumps my shoulder with his. "Exactly. No one could accuse you of dark, dirty thoughts, huh?"

My eyes run over his tanned skin and perfect, blindingly white teeth as he bobs his brows. "The only dirty thoughts I'm having are to do with corruption and painful deaths, spell caster. Back off."

His laugh is rumbling and I can almost *feel* it as that smile stretches into something much more predatory. He moves closer, looking over my shoulder at me with a wicked smirk. "So tragic, the way you lie to yourself, my little killer. One would *almost* believe you if they were incredibly naive and gullible."

My head rears back, catching him in his irritatingly straight nose, and he grunts as he clutches it. Blood drips from it as he cups his palm in front of his face and the tour grinds to a halt. All eyes land on us and my face heats, wondering if I've just earned myself a punishment worse than participating in this farce. But Rory simply pulls a cloth from his pocket, looking rueful as he pinches his injury.

"Whoops. A little advice for you all now that I've learned my lesson… Sydney has an excellent startle response and no one should creep up on her unless they want to bleed."

Damn, he just gave me a public legend; people will be worried about what else I can do, not my magic.

Huck is in Rory's face within seconds, his expression hard. "Don't touch people you barely know, Stormbringer. You deserve a good smack for your rude behavior."

I catch Thad moving toward us and shake my head, putting my hand out to stop the scene from getting more salacious. "It's okay, guys. The dipshit just learned a hard lesson about consent. That's what happens when you sneak up on a woman when she's distracted by such opulent surroundings."

Thad frowns, but I know he caught the pleading look in my eyes when I looked at him. Our relationship is close enough that he can read me, and I want this spectacle to end before anyone hands out punishments for interrupting their gushing. "The same goes for you, too, Dante and you, Whitmore. Sydney Jolie will kick your ass if you try shit with her."

Whew. Good on him for being so damn intuitive.

"As long as Mr. Stormbringer is okay, we should move along," one of the Krista-like drones says from the front of the pack. "We need to show you all to your team suites."

My jaw drops when I realize she's just admitted that they're housing the teams in shared living space. The blood in my veins freezes and Huck has to grab my hand to tug me along as the group walks away from the scene of my bloody mistake. His palm is cool in mine, but I don't mind because the rise in blood pressure is making me hot. Once everyone is thoroughly distracted by the cheery moppets leading the tour, he squeezes my hand.

"Sweet pea, you gotta breathe. I know this makes you madder than a wet hen, and you're not wrong about it, but it's just another thing we have to endure." I scoff softly and he chuckles. "You're a stubborn one, Sydney Jolie, but you're not stupid. You know we're not in a position to do a damned thing about this... *now*. But the time will come, and when it does, I'm with you one hundred percent."

Damn, that good old country boy thing is soothing sometimes.

"Huck, they pen us up like animals for years and now they're gathering the next gen of possible leaders to cull them through a competitive reality competition. I'm not sure it will *ever* be the time. This isn't a YA novel, and reality is far from the glamorous portrayal movies show. People are going to die horrifically in front of us—*again*."

He shakes his head, swinging our arms like we're having a normal, everyday conversation. "That's true, sweet pea, but we've seen plenty of supes die since The Unveiling. My count is likely higher than your, but that's because my first sector was a lot darker than this one and I'm a demon. Are you going to be able to handle it?"

It's a good question, but I don't think he's prepared for my answer.

Licking my lips, I take a deep breath before I reply. "There are a few things you don't know about the time between my father's death and being rounded up to come here. I just... I can't tell you *here*."

He follows my gaze to the ceiling then to the crowd of supes and humans around us. "I see. Well, I enjoy a good edging from time to time, sweet pea, so you're in luck. I'll take a raincheck on that little tale... *if* you promise to have dinner with me."

I frown at him, tilting my head. "Huck, we're all going to have dinner. It's not like we can avoid it."

"For fuck's sake, you're awkward, woman. He's asking you out, and how the fuck you've been blond about those two even this long is a real mystery."

My gaze whips to the glowering vampire as he strides past us with a disgusted expression. "Well, fuck you, too, Sebastian Whitmore." His shoulders tense as he continues on, and I know he's heard me—which was exactly the point. I turn back to the demon still gripping my palm, frowning. "I don't date, Huck. You know that."

"I do, but since you've teased me mercilessly with your hidden past *and* I helped save you from the mage, I thought you might make a wee exception." He bats his lashes and my breath catches in my throat. "Please, little lady?"

Oh, for fuck's sake.... What is happening to me right now?

I want to protest or tell him to shove it where the sun doesn't shine, but his pretty face and pouty lip are making my stomach do weird things. Paired with the *goddamned hat*, I find myself both dry-mouthed and surprisingly moist elsewhere. This isn't fair; the Universe is just mocking me to my face now. I can't give a damn about people; they leave and I'm destroyed… then I destroy. That's the story he's going to eventually hear and I don't want him to be a part of my weird, potentially illegal secrets, even if he is more of an outlaw than a cowpoke.

"Huck, I…"

He pushes his hat up, hooking his other hand into his belt as he continues to pout and I'm a goner. What the fuck is in the air here? It's like the men are exponentially hotter, even the ones I've known forever, and I'm having trouble forming coherent thoughts. "Please, Syd?"

Yep. Now I'm screwed.

"Okay," I whisper as our fingers lace together. "One dinner, just with you, because I teased you. But that's it, right?"

The beaming smile he gives me causes my heart beat to skip and I almost stop in place. "For now, sweet pea. For now."

"Thank fuck that's over. I was about to heave." Elias stalks past us to get closer to the front, and I groan as I look up at the ceiling.

"Was *everyone* paying attention to us instead of the fucking tour? Huck, I'm going to *gut* you and wear your innards for garters."

His smirk is wicked. "I'm a demon, darlin'. You can do that, and wear them to our dinner. I'll respawn before the first course."

"Gross." Thad gives me a weird look, gesturing to the bank of elevators we're standing in front of. I was so distracted by Huck's bullshit that I didn't even notice we're all waiting for turns by team again. "Demons are so damned psychotic."

Huck gives him a bright, easy-going smile. "We are, partner, but that's our charm. You two are my besties and that means all my disgusting tendencies are on board with protecting you. Remember that when you're being a grump, big guy."

"I *knew* I got a whole 'menage' vibe from you three. Always room for one more, right?" Rory appears behind me again, his face clean and recovered from the blow I dealt him a few minutes ago. The benefits of being a damn magic user, I guess, but it doesn't make it less annoying. "I'm a very generous lover and you'll *adore* what I bring to the table."

"Get it under control, Stormbringer." The dragon gives him an evil look, then he tilts his head at the other groups waiting. "If we overheard their little meet-cute, people can overhear this conversation. Thinking she's important to us—even as a bed mate—will encourage the others to target the girl. She's… got other issues to deal with."

Like my erstwhile magic, perhaps?

My brows furrow as I remember the words of the centaur and what he did in our private examination. I have no idea when and where I'll be able to test his claim, especially since we're all rooming in a shared space. Cursing softly, I let go of Huck's hand and cross my arms over my chest. Everything about this fucking event is trapping me in an ever-shrinking box, and I hate it.

"Come along, team!"

Krista's voice breaks my train of thought, and I groan. "Oh, goody. It's time to find our new cage. I can't wait."

Thad chuckles as he gives me a small push towards the elevator. "You're a ray of sunshine, as always, Sydney. I can't wait for your take on the accommodations."

"Anything's better than the *actual* cages I've been living in," Elias says as he gives us judgmental looks. "So perhaps we can be slightly less snooty when our beds aren't made of bags of straw, mm?"

My jaw drops and I turn bright red as I follow him into the car. Guilt sits on my gut like a stone as I realize that for all my complaints about life in Tempest Seven, I'm not the one who arrived trussed up like a fictional cannibal. Hell, I don't even know how long they made him stay in that damn thing. I'm a fucking moron and I can't believe it didn't occur to me that someone in the lockdown definitely had it worse than me.

"I'm sorry," I murmur to the dragon as I stand next to him. "I was obnoxious and insensitive."

He looks at me for a moment, then laughs. His dark eyes are full of amusement as I frown again. "Don't be. I was testing you and my theory was right on the nose. You have *far* too much connection to humanity and we need to work on it."

Rage fills me when he admits to manipulating my emotions and I deck him without a second's warning. He reels for a second as my fist throbs, and then gives me another assessing look. His grin is full of sharp, dagger-like dragon teeth this time and his eyes glitter with a deep sapphire. "*That* is more like it, little rebel. You need to channel *that* energy more often and we'll have a much better chance at surviving."

What the fuck is with these dicks pushing my buttons today?

I CAN SEE FOR MILES AND MILES

ELIAS

IT'S BEEN a long time since I've been free to move like this and I don't intend to spoil it by getting involved with nonsense. The vampire and the mage are clearly hiding something, the bear and the demon are in love with the girl, and the girl is completely oblivious because she's harboring some deep trauma. This bullshit is a recipe for a disaster that I want no part of.

I do want to win the fucking thing so I'm not locked up like a serial killer, though.

My eyes rove over the contestants and our handler as the elevator shoots up higher than I've been in years. The dragon inside rejoices in the change in altitude, but he yearns to be free to fly. I haven't stretched my wings in the sky since I was caught in the Second Sweep while defending my people's compound in the Pacific. I saved many sea dragons from being sent to these wretched prisons, but the sacrifice cost me mightily. I'm sure they've been looking for me, but the human government moves the strongest supes around often so they can't be located and freed.

You'd think the larger populations in the sectors would notice, but they don't.

They've been told we're all dangerous criminals who will harm them and it's easier to accept it at face value when their lives are hard enough without feeling sorry for 'lockdown losers'. I don't have resentment about it; if any of them had enough power to free me or the others locked down, they'd be in chains themselves. It would be a futile effort and end in deaths that are for nothing. I see no reason to kill any more of the supernatural population than the humans already have.

"What's your problem, smokestack?"

Blinking, I look at the girl glaring at me curiously. She wasn't thrilled when I said she has too much humanity, but that irritation seemed to fade when we piled back into the tin can to head up to our rooms. "I don't have one; do you?"

"Hell no." She crosses her arms over her chest, but the air around her changes and I can taste the fear she's emanating in the form of a light sheen of perspiration on her lip. Sydney shifts from foot to foot, watching me like I'm going to do something, but she has no idea how wrong she is.

"I see."

I'd call her out on her lie, but for some reason, I don't want to. The discomfort is going unnoticed by her two guardians and she obviously wants it to continue to stay under their radar. It means this issue is one no one knows about, and I find myself feeling pleased by that. When that thought goes through my head, I frown.

Who cares what the hell she's afraid of? This is ridiculous.

"Being on the uppermost floors is a very good sign, you know," Krista says and I flick my gaze to the human. Even Sydney could kill this woman with her bare hands, so we'll have to be careful about the flaring tempers should anything bad happen. "You're on the second highest floor, so the testing must have been quite favorable."

"Surprise, surprise," Sebastian says from his corner. "No one but you was dumb enough to miss that this is an over-the-top mix."

Sydney furrows her brow, looking over her shoulder at the bloodsucker. "Speak for yourself. I've spent the past four years hearing how useless I am and you idiots haven't dispelled that notion."

"That's bullshit, sweet pea. You have untapped potential."

I snort, and everyone looks at me. "He can't be trusted; he's a demon."

I have nothing against demons, of course, but talking about a secret weapon in front of a human is stupid.

"And he has the hots for her." The mage smirks, puffing his chest up. "Not that he has a chance in Hell, even if he is from there."

"She's not interested in anyone." The bear looks indignant and I have to school my features. These two have no ability to mask anything and that's going to be an enormous problem.

The elevator car shakes when the woman in question stomps her foot hard, her expression full of fury. "*She is standing right here and you all need to shut the fuck up about her before she guts you.*"

"Syd…"

"Sweet pea…"

"Shut. It." Her voice is a hiss, even to the males she seems to be closest to. "We will discuss your participation later, dick heads."

Good on her.

"Maybe it would be best if we all stay on topic. We have much to discuss about the—" Krista's interrupted by the doors to the elevator opening into a plush hallway. There's only one door at each end and she gestures toward the one at the south end. "Let's go to your quarters."

"I confess, I'm interested to see what this place looks like," Rory mutters as we all follow the dirty blond human. "The amount of magic needed to do all of this under cover is staggering. They must have—"

Reaching out, I smack him in the back of the head. "Be quiet, spell caster. That, too, is a discussion for later."

"Jeez, you big scaly shithead. Take it easy," he mutters as he moves out of my reach. "You're stronger than you think, you know."

"No, I'm not." I grin toothily at him, making sure he knows I put just enough strength behind it to make it hurt. "You're weaker than you think."

Doesn't hurt to make him a bit worried, either.

Krista stops at the door, raising a keypad next to it. "You each need to place a thumb on this pad to key it to you. No one but your team will be able to enter this space unless they're cleared by the officials—this will include trainers, stylists, coaches, and the like. But that will only be at specific times and by specific permissions. You must keep the space photo-ready at any time, should PR or Marketing officials choose to visit. There are no cameras in your private space, but this is the only place where that is true."

I arch a brow, looking at my teammates. They grimace back at me and I know they understand we will not take that as truth until we verify it for ourselves. "I'll go first then."

Hopefully, that doesn't come back to bite me.

Our 'chaperone' finally leaves ten minutes after we enter our room. It took quite a bit of ignoring her attempts to get us to engage before she finally gave up, saying the alarms would sound for breakfast in the morning. As for tonight, we've been left with a fucking *menu* to select food from for our dinner. Apparently, all we have to do is call downstairs and place the order to get it brought up. That statement made everyone but the vampire look like a landed walleye, though Krista didn't seem shocked in the slightest.

For someone who's been in a cage more than half the time over the past few years… that's swank as fuck.

Rory is the first one to speak as we look around the ridiculously nice suite. "Am I the only one getting a hardcore 'for those who are about to die' feeling about all this… sudden kindness?"

"Duh," Sydney says as she strides over to yank open all the doors on the outer edge of the living area. When she's exposed all six bedrooms and a bathroom, she huffs and stomps back to us. "They're buttering us up for the kill."

The demon pats her shoulder, then stands in the middle of the room, lifting his hands in the air. "First, I'm gonna make sure they're not lyin' about the camera thing, folks. We shouldn't have conversations until we know for sure."

"True." The others look at me and I shrug. "If he can figure it out, it will save a lot of bullshit scurrying around later."

"His power is *fear*. What the hell is he going to do?" The vampire rolls his eyes and leans against the door frame of the first room. "Scare the cameras out of hiding?"

Huck whips his head around, his dark eyes glowing red as black tendrils of magic emanate from his body. He tilts his head, then whisper-hisses, "Seek."

Okay, it's a little intimidating and I can definitely feel the amount of power he's exuding; it's not trivial.

"Huck is more than a simple fear demon," Thaddeus says as he shrugs. "He apprenticed under a Prince of Hell before he came up here."

"Why don't I know that?" Sydney looks angry as she pokes the bear—literally—and he looks sheepish.

"I wasn't supposed to talk about it, but since we're all going to have to share and sing Kumbaya to work together…"

The demon tenses for a moment, his magic pausing as Sydney frowns at him.

Grumbling under my breath, I shake my head. The jailors in my sectors have always cautioned us that we cannot trust the other supes—if we do, they will sell us out in an instant. Seems it's possible they were right in spirit, if not in their assessment of intent. I doubt the grizzly told us for a nefarious purpose, but his loose lips could get his demon friend in a lot of trouble if the wrong person finds out. Demons with that much power and influence are usually locked up as I have been.

"Stop talking until he's done," I order them with a loud growl. "There are things not meant for the possible watchers, shifter."

The girl nods, wandering over to the demon as his magical tendrils waft through the air, extending into other rooms. "Make us safe, Huck. We'll talk later, okay?"

They've distracted me, and I have to get my shit back together. It's good to know the demon has more magic than I assumed, but what about the rest of them?

Sebastian is certainly full of himself enough to be hiding bonus talents —vampires are a dime a dozen and their powers aren't particularly versatile. The bear can't hide shit with his earnest look and eager devotion, so we'll have to work on it. My eyes move to the unusually quiet mage as he comes out of the bedroom he must be claiming. He's not babbling or flirting; something he's been doing since he walked into the room with our new team members.

"What's with you?" I ask as I tilt my head. "Run out of material so soon?"

The blond saunters across the floor, sidestepping the demon without blinking an eye. "Worried about me, Salty Seaballs? I'm touched."

"No, but I trust no one until they give me a reason, and you disappear."

His grin widens as he approaches me. "I'm an open book, baby. Ask me anything and I'll answer you true."

No one says that when they're being honest; he protests too much.

"Did you miss where he yelled at everyone for talking about shit until Huck's done? Hello!" Sydney rolls her eyes, moving away from the demon to flop on the big ass couch. Her eyes pop wide open as she sinks into it, and her entire body goes stiff.

"Syd, are you—"

She waves the bear off, the shocked expression still on her face as she relaxes one limb at a time. "I'm fine... I... " The rest of us wait for her to continue, waiting anxiously as she gathers her thoughts. Her face turns bright red and I swear, she gets even angrier when she figures it out. "It's nothing. Leave me alone."

Thaddeus looks confused, the demon snorts, and I watch her carefully. But the mage is the one who walks over, lowering himself to the cushion next to her carefully. Rory doesn't touch her, he just gives her a sad smile that I don't quite understand. They look at one another for a moment before he finally speaks.

"It's the most comfortable thing you've sat on in years, right?"

"Shut up," she mutters as she tosses her braid over her shoulder. "This sector isn't ritzy like the ones you and the overgrown mosquito probably come from. Tempest Seven is pretty chintzy."

Thad snorts. "That's being kind."

I arch a brow. "Try living in a cage and not being able to use your wings or fully shift for four years."

Sebastian scoffs, pushing off the wall to walk over to one of the chairs. "I don't think it will help anyone to have a misery pissing contest. We just need the demon to finish so we can order the damn food, swap info, eat, and fuck off to our own spaces for the night."

Her eyes narrow and Sydney whips her head over to sniff at him. "Maybe you'll have to fuck off because no one likes traitors, but some of us might actually end up hanging out for a bit."

"What?"

She caught the bear unawares with that one, so it tells me social interaction is not normal for her, either. I find myself unable to avoid jumping in to help though I have no obligation to do so. "We might, indeed, little rebel."

I might even look forward to it, even if I can never truly integrate with any of them because my only goal is getting the fuck out of this prison.

WASHING THOSE MEN OUT OF MY HAIR

SYDNEY

I HATE that the other clowns in this room realize that Huck was keeping shit from me. Revealing a weakness to people we don't trust wasn't on my bingo card, but then almost nothing that's happened today was, so I guess it's par for the course.

Fucking stupid men as far as the eye can see.

It takes longer than I expect for him to pull his weird magic tentacle things back into himself, and when he does, his handsome face splits into a satisfied grin. His voice is high-pitched and tinged with humor as he intones, "This place is clean."

"Again with the *Poltergeist* references," Thad mutters with an eye roll.

Huck gives him a squinty glare. "It's a demon's purview to relentlessly mock the humans' ridiculous attempts to showcase the supernatural pre-Unveiling."

"They're much less cutesy since they imprisoned us, demon," Elias rumbles. "But your efforts are appreciated."

I nod, noting the strain he's hiding at the corner of his eyes. "Agreed. However, I think we should get on with ordering dinner then we can take turns at cleaning up. I don't know about you fools, but I haven't had the pleasure of a *private shower* long enough to debate whether I want that or food more."

The mage and the vampire both watch me with unchanged expressions, but the surprised vibes emanating from their auras tell me they've had a *much* nicer life than the rest of us. Rory clears his throat, then walks over to pick up the menu. "Well, I don't know about you, but I think a metric fuck ton of pizza is in order. We can save the leftovers in the kitchenette out there, so we'll have snacks later."

Thad snorts. "Now I *know* you've been coddled."

"How the fuck would you know that, bear?"

"Because you think there will be leftovers of any kind," the dragon says with a scoff. "Those of us living the *real* sector life would never leave a goddamn scrap of food to waste."

He blinks, looking at the rest of us, and everyone but Sebastian shrugs. "Damn."

Now the question is: where have these two been lounging while most supes are inches from starving in relative squalor?

The mystery of the two privileged dicks followed me throughout my shower, and as I finish giving my long hair the best wash it's had in four years, I'm still frowning. I always assumed the vampires were given better accommodations than the rest of us to reward their betrayal, but how the hell did Rory manage it? Did he do the same shit the supes here do to get preferential treatment? My eyes widen as I work conditioner through my locks, imagining him sucking up to sugar daddies and mommies as vile as the ones in Tempest Seven to get what he wanted. A growl echoes off the tile and a small spark zings from my fingertips to the wall, bouncing like a pinball until it disappears.

What the everloving fuck was that?!

Swallowing hard, I suck in a deep breath to calm myself. My magic has *never* been that visible, not even before the Markers. My hands are shaking as I step closer to the wall of the stall, running my finger over the remnants of energy on the hard marble. "How the hell…"

A burning sensation on the back of my neck makes me wince, and I pull my hand away from the stone to rub it gingerly. Whatever that damn centaur did is finally manifesting and I have no fucking clue what that's going to mean. I didn't even *think* about shooting a magical firework; it just happened. What else can I do now that I've grown into powers I didn't have access to during puberty? The thought frightens me because if I don't mute the damn things, someone might figure out I've been un-Marked.

I'd prefer not to be executed for treason before the death matches, if possible.

"Get a grip, Syd," I mutter to myself as I grab the loofah hanging from the hook on the wall and drizzle body soap onto it. Not only do we get to have a private wash area, but the shit in here smells like heaven—a fresh floral scent of jasmine, vanilla, ylang-ylang, and vetiver that makes my eyes water with an odd happiness. I was never very girly—a hazard of growing up with a single dad—but this damn body wash has me by the throat.

Once I've used every single product in this haven of cleanliness, I've been scrubbed, polished, buffed, shaved, and scented within an inch of my life. Stepping out into the steamy room, I use the towel to wipe the mirror off then dry myself. The reflection I see when I'm drying my hair is like a different person. My skin is glowy, my hair shines, and except for the pronounced bones, I appear to be a healthy young woman.

No wonder people are pimping themselves for access to this kind of shit; I feel like a new person.

"I couldn't live with myself, though," I say with a sigh. Picking up the brush on the counter, I pull it through my brown-blond locks, then twist it into my signature braid quickly. "Even if this lifts some of the burden of being in these hellholes, I'm too stupidly proud to use myself as a bargaining tool."

My moment of epiphany may not change me, but my brain suddenly accepts the desperate acts of those who choose that path. I shouldn't have been judging them for doing what they had to in order to survive the depressing reality of supe life since Taterman took over. Happiness is more than fleeting here, and you can only use what you have. No one has money, so their bodies and service are all they have to barter, unlike me.

Not everyone's father had an unreliable gift that made him train them for something that didn't happen the way his brain said it would.

Pushing the guilt for judging people down until I can breathe again, I pull on the lounge clothes I found in my bedroom. It's a branded pair of F.E.A.R. Academy sweats, and the material is soft as hell on my fresh skin. It occurs to me that though this isn't extreme luxury, it would be difficult as fuck to go back to scratchy clothes and intermittent food on hard furniture after months of this shit. Maybe that's why death is such a prominent possibility for anyone who doesn't win.

I look in the mirror one more time, and shake my head as the reflection surprises me again. "You can do this, Sydney. Being all sector scummy was good armor, but you won't get to be like that here. People will notice you're a girl again instead of being afraid of getting stabbed. It will be okay."

Now if I can just get myself to believe that…

The dudes have been staring at me like I'm a zoo exhibit since I came out of the bathroom. It pisses me off to no end, especially when Thad and Huck do it, but I figure I need to get used to it now. I have no idea how many females are in this competition. However, if cleaning us up a little turns all the males into morons, it's going to give us an unfair advantage that we should use to our benefit. I'm not going to tell anyone my discovery, though. I might gravitate towards fairness, but I'm not stupid.

They can figure it out on their own, just like I did.

"When is the pizza getting here?" I finally ask. They give me blank looks and I close my eyes, praying for patience.

Thad scratches his chin, looking around for a clock, and when he doesn't find one, he shrugs. "No idea, Syd. They said within a half hour, and you were in there at least twenty minutes, so…"

"I was?" My jaw drops as they all nod and I dip my head as I feel heat travel up my neck. I've never taken a shower that long in my life. I'm surprised no one came to yank me the hell out. "Well, shit. I'm sorry. One of you go so we can all get clean before the food is here."

They look at one another and no one speaks until Sebastian grunts. "I'll go then."

I watch him stalk off to the bedroom he must have claimed, and then his path to the bathroom with his own set of sweats. "Where the hell are the clocks? How are we supposed to know when we have to be places?"

Huck shrugs as he looks around. "I wondered the same thing when you asked when the food would get here. Obviously, Thad didn't see any, either."

"What kind of idiots forget clocks?" I grumble as I lean back against the comfy couch again. "I doubt they'll be forgiving if we're late."

Rory chuckles, shaking his head. "Man, they really have the supes in this sector behind."

Glaring at him, I wait. When he doesn't elaborate, I grind my teeth and ask, "What the hell are you talking about, Stormbringer? Spit it the fuck out."

"Irina?" he says in a loud voice. "Irina, tell me what time it is."

A disembodied voice comes from invisible speakers and I jump. *"Hello, Rory Stormbringer. The time is six p.m. eastern standard time. Do you require additional information?"*

"What the fiddling fuck was that?" Huck asks as he looks at me, then Thad. "You guys have a clue, or are we all idiots?"

"Irina is a virtual assistant people have integrated into their homes since the pandemic," Rory says. "She's named after Taterman's daughter and she's connected to the internet. We can use her for a multitude of things… Whitmore probably knows about it, too."

Thad pops to his feet, looking irritable as he paces back and forth in front of the sitting area. "Motherfucker. We're all living like refugees and the wealthy supes and humans have invisible assistants in every house doing their brain work? What the hell kind of backwards bullshit—"

My ursine bestie rarely loses his temper and I know he's thinking about the stuffed to the gills house the bear sleuth lives in and how hard they work to keep themselves mildly comfortable. A luxury as simple yet helpful as this has set him off when nothing else in this ridiculous building did, and I'm not sure why, but I know I need to calm him down. A raging bear is no joke and it's the last thing we need right now.

"Hell, man. I had no idea. You gotta understand… they don't let us out of our sectors anymore than they let you guys out of yours. It was pretty fucking eye-opening to see what it looks like as we rolled into town."

Rubbing my temples, I walk over to Thad and grab his hand, squeezing it. He rumbles a discontented growl, tugging me into his arms and hugging me to his burly frame. This is more public affection than I prefer, but I can feel the whirling emotions coming from him, so I allow it. Once he calms, I set my chin on his chest, looking up at him.

"You gonna tear this place apart or…?"

He sighs. "No. But I really fucking hate those sons of bitches."

Sebastian wanders out of the bathroom and I wonder for a moment if he used vamp speed to get through that quickly. "Who, us?"

"Yes, *you* bloodsucker," the grizzly growls, then adds, "but humans more."

"Discovered Irina while I was gone, I suppose?"

I swear to hell, that asshole is begging to die.

"Yeah, thanks for the warning." Thad pulls his arms from around me and stalks toward a bedroom. "I have next shower. Fight me if you don't like it."

The guys all look at one another and Huck chuckles. "Anyone so inclined, gents? I have to warn you; he's stronger than he looks and that's saying something."

If even one person responds, I'm going to beat their ass myself—that's a foregone conclusion.

WE'RE ALL A LITTLE FUCKED UP

RORY

I END up going last for the shower and the *smells* in it are enough to make my eyes roll back. Our team is likely the hottest in the entire competition, and every single person could have *anything* they wanted in my sector, even the scary sea dragon. The mix of their scents makes my dick twitch as I scrub myself down with the same stuff they did, groaning as I have to avoid doing anything to relieve myself. The pizza is coming and I'm hungry, plus I don't want anyone picking up on the noises. I'm not sure how sharp the vampire's hearing is, but I guarantee it's damn good. The bear is probably heightened, the dragon might be, and that only leaves the demon and our slightly human girl.

At some point, I won't give a shit if they know, but I don't want to frighten anyone off until I get a good sense of where their lines are.

My excitement fades a bit when I remember that everyone knows how supes stay as well-groomed and fed as me when they aren't the stupid blood-sucking traitors. That's a strike in my column and even if they're desperate, these people will likely refuse to come anywhere near me. The things I've had to do to keep from living in squalor in Inferno One aren't something I'm proud of, but I survived. That doesn't mean my teammates won't judge me for it, and I get the feeling Sydney will be the most horrified. Anything I can do to keep her from finding out the bargains and activities I've had to be part of is fair game; I don't want *anyone's* pity.

"You're not dirty, Rory," I mutter to myself. It's a mantra I have to keep running in my head to ward off the sadness, depression, and self-loathing. My fingers find the elastic band on my wrist that looks like a decorative piece but is one of the few things helping me keep the outward appearance of jolliness. I snap it over and over as the soap runs over my raw skin, waiting for the clarity to finally come. This is something an ex-supernatural therapist living in my sector taught me before her sugar human killed her for some stupid ass reason.

Just keep snapping it until the feeling goes away.

It takes a few minutes, but the action curbs the words of criticism in my head and the almost unignorable urge to continue washing myself vigorously until my skin peels off. I let out a slow breath as the world stops looking hyper-focused and then rest my forehead against the wall. The bullshit I've endured makes me go off the deep end sometimes, especially when I'm attracted to others organically rather than looking to gain something. When it's about getting what I need, I put it all in this imaginary box and do what I have to. But the other feelings bring up all that self-hatred and despair because I know I'm forever tainted by what I had to do to survive.

"Stormbringer, what the hell is taking you so long? It's almost delivery time!"

The sound of Sydney's voice almost brings it all back but I tug the bracelet high and let it snap me so hard I visibly wince. *There we go.* "Coming, Vicious. My hair needed some TLC; it can't be perfect all the time without proper care, you know."

Whew. Hopefully, she believes that nonsense.

Hopping out of the warm water, I towel off and pull on the sweats that were tucked in the dresser of my room. I don't think Sydney realizes the rooms were enchanted to draw the right person into the right room—that's how everyone has clothes that fit—but it's a harmless spell, so I don't need to bring it up. However, noticing it means I have to scan this entire place when the others aren't watching. I have to make sure we're not tripping over planted enchantments that will hurt our chances of winning. Getting out of Inferno One so I never have to market myself to grubby assholes is my main priority with this stupid game. I won't let anything stop me from finding that peace.

I look in the mirror, ruffling my hair until it falls perfectly, then I use the products on the counter to finish getting fresh and clean. None of the other dudes moisturized I bet, but they'll regret that when they live for-frigging-ever and have wrinkly, dry skin. I'm not so silly, so I make sure I'm covered, then brush my teeth. Luckily, they had enough brushes for everyone, and the towel supply was plentiful. It seems they're treating this like the humans used to do for Olympians and I'm not sure if that's a good or bad thing.

What if treating it that way means they're going to hold these games every few years in some twisted Hunger Games fashion to cull our species?

"What are you thinking, Rory? *Of course* that's Burnt Dorito's plan. He's probably jacking off to the idea of watching us die on screen like it's porn."

Shaking my head in disgust, I turn off the lights as I leave the bathroom, heading for the main living area with a pasted-on smile. "Here I am, Mr. America…"

The demon raises an eyebrow. "They haven't done that contest since the virus. I wonder if we're the replacements."

"Get out of my head, demon," I say with a rueful look. "I was just pondering the same thing—if this is going to get repeated year after year to keep supe numbers small in the country."

Thad nods, his youthful face serious. "I think going in with the impression that they don't give a fuck who wins as long as supes die and they make money on the broadcast is a good way to stay alive."

"But they're adding some weird… popularity component?" Sydney chews her lower lip and I know she's worried about that. Her brusque nature and sarcasm won't draw in the toxic fuckers who are devoted to licking Taterman's ass.

She might be popular globally, though. The rest of the world let our kind exist without imprisoning them—that's who she needs to aim for.

"I'm sure that's to keep people watching every week like old human reality shows did. It's a participation piece that makes them feel like they're part of the action," Sebastian says. He looks less imposing now that he's dressed down, and I'm surprised to see glasses perched on his aquiline nose.

The nerd-look is kind of hot on that salty betrayer, I have to admit.

Sydney turns to glare at him. "*You* would know. How are we supposed to believe you're not a fucking plant?"

"Good question," Dante rumbles from the big chair he claimed.

"Because I didn't have an option in being here, either. Don't you think if I had a choice, I'd be on a team without criminals and non-magic having humans?"

That makes the demon sit up, and he growls as he leans in. "You don't get to insult her, you overgrown skeeter. Your kind is part of why we're all in this goddamn mess, so watch your tone or I'll test that regrowth theory."

I frown, tilting my head in confusion. "What regrowth theory?"

Sebastian rolls his eyes, waving the fear demon off as if he's a gnat. "Supes have a theory vampires and dhampirs can regrow shit like our cousins the Cubi. It's an old Cloven Hooves tale in Hell."

The dragon grins, his eyes dancing with wicked merriment. "I could help test it. My cage has been less than comfortable over the past four years. I'd be happy to consider it the first installment on repayment for my troubles."

"Guys…" I say, pressing my lips together as I try to think of something to say to mediate this mess. The whole 'alpha possessive' thing does it for me, so does the psycho, and Sydney is just oozing a confidence I can't help but find sexy. But now my natural instincts and my trauma are colliding, so I taper off as I cover my arm and do my aversion therapy.

I'm saved by the bell—literally—as a weird alarm sounds at the door. Everyone jumps up, looking ready to rumble, and I have to bite back a chuckle when the formation surrounds the spunky girl we all seem to have a pull towards. She snarls and pushes her way through the crowd, stomping to the door as she mutters about protecting herself.

She's going to be a handful when we're actually in danger.

We watch as she yanks open the door to find a fucking *robot* standing in front of it with a stack of pizza boxes on a tray. The thing looks like something out of that old *Lost in Space* show, which says a lot about how little innovation the humans have managed since they segregated us. I would have expected something more… twenty-first century, at least, if they're using automatons. I've been in a lot of human residences due to my 'bargains' and never once saw something like this. Looking at the vampire curiously, I'm relieved to note he seems puzzled, too.

"Are they scared to deliver us food or just too damn lazy?" Sydney mutters as she grabs the boxes and ignores whatever the thing is saying in its tinny voice. "Whatever."

With that, she slams the door in its face and stalks back over to the living room. Thad looks amused, rising to his feet to head toward the kitchen. "Syd, we need napkins at the least. They sure as fuck didn't include any."

"I wonder how we get that little fridge stocked," Huck drawls. "Thad's a pretty decent cook if we can actually acquire supplies."

"Who says it isn't stocked now?" the bear asks as he starts opening cabinets, drawers, and finally the refrigerator. "Oh, I guess, I do. There are housewares, and some travel stuff, but not a drop of food or drink."

We all swivel our heads to look at the vampire and he shrugs, "It was on the menu; don't be ridiculous."

"It would be a great way to fuck up teams before they even start," Sydney mutters. "Trap us with an unfed bloodsucker and see if we survive it."

This time, I shake my head. "As long as we stay nourished, one or a couple of us could feed him. They don't need to kill to eat. In fact…" I pretend to smirk, hoping to draw attention away from how I know. "…they often enjoy feeding while they get off. Necrophilia just isn't sexy."

My statement earns me a dark glare from both Sydney and the dragon, which surprises me. I can't imagine Elias being held in a spring meadow, so why would he be so judgy about a little blood play? It's fucking weird and I need to figure out what his deal is so I know how to keep on his good side.

"Don't knock it until you've tried it," Huck says as he winks. Thad looks at him and the demon wags a finger at him. "Look, vanilla bear, demons are kinky as fuck. In fact, many supe species are. Just because some of the shifter clans keep y'all sheltered doesn't mean *we're* the odd ones."

My eyes close and I pinch the bridge of my nose, completely unable to balance the war inside of me as he chides Thad. If they all get comfortable talking like this, I'm going to need *a lot* more bands to keep myself in line.

And where the hell will I get those? Hell if I know.

"We should eat and talk about the schedule taped to the outside of this box," Elias says as he looks at the pile Sydney put on the low table. "Tomorrow is going to be another grueling day, but we will have to project confidence at every turn so no one considers us weak."

The dragon might not be so bad after all… at least he doesn't get caught up in all the emotions constantly.

THE EARLY BIRD GETS EATEN BY THE SNAKE

SYDNEY

THE DISCUSSION of the schedule went later than anyone expected, but when you throw a bunch of people used to taking charge into one room, it leads to constant fights for dominance. Even Thad and Huck—who normally let me have the reins—threw their hats in the ring a few times. It took forever to agree on how we were going to handle the events, and who would take control in what situation. I'm not sure anyone will even honor it; I know I won't if I think they're fucking everything up.

And men always, without fail, fuck shit up when left to their own devices.

My eyes scan the tight crown of braids I have my hair tucked into, then the black shirt and pants with the F.E.A.R. Academy logo on it. They told us to wear our normal uniforms today for the first orientation, physical consultation, equipment distribution, and lunch meeting. Afterward, we're supposed to change into the athletic gear for an afternoon of physical evaluations. It didn't say whether any of these 'intro sessions' are just our team or groups of them, so I tuck my contraband weapons in their hidden spots carefully.

"Get moving, Vicious. The rest of these idiots are getting restless," the annoying mage yells from outside my door.

I could give a fuck less, but this time, they're probably right. We want to be early to the first session to get the lay of the land. "I'm coming."

"Oh, not at the moment, dangerous lady, but I could help with that later."

My eyes widen and I open my mouth to shoot back a retort, but the sound of his footsteps moving away from my door stops me. I frown at my reflection, my skin feeling tight and uncomfortable suddenly. "Stupid flirty asshole. Why do men never understand timing?"

Not that there's ever a right time for a guy to flirt with me, but it's definitely not now.

After a final check, I press my hands to my hot cheeks and head out the door to meet them in the living area. Thad smiles, rising from his seat immediately to hand me a to-go mug of coffee. Huck winks at me and tosses one of the nutrition supplement bars sector supes survive on. Catching it with my free hand, I look at the others warily. They all look well-rested and ready to go—even to the point of being clean-shaven. I guess I should be thankful they're taking this seriously, but fuck me if it doesn't increase their hotness factor by a thousand.

Huck walks over, offering his arm, and I roll my eyes at him. "Don't be a pill, sweet pea. I just wanted to make it clear to whatever scoundrels we meet down there that you're not interested in what they have for sale."

Rory's eyes narrow as he looks at me. "You're dating the fear demon?"

"She definitely is not," Elias says smugly. "Her scent mingles with theirs, but not in that way."

My head turns to look at him slowly, like I'm auditioning for Linda Blair's role in *The Exorcist*. "Don't fucking scent me for information like that, Dante. You won't like what I do to people who invade my privacy without consent."

My demon friend snickers as he gives the dragon a knowing look. "Having been on the receiving end of her wrath, I'd advise you to listen, gents. She's not only brilliant and hot, but vengeful as hell and crafty like a fox with her plots."

"Not crafty enough to see what's in front of her face," the vampire mutters and I whirl on my toes, flinging the knife I grabbed from its hidden spot directly at his head. He smirks, catching it before it strikes with that damn vampiric speed. Flipping it over, he stalks over to hand it back to me. "Well, I suppose we should be thankful you're not slow as well as magicless."

The urge to continue fighting with him is strong, but Thad walks over and growls at the traitor. "Back off. This is a stressful day for all of us. Let her fucking breathe before you start in on her, Whitmore."

"I don't need a savior," I mutter to my friend. "I can handle shit without being rescued."

Thad grins knowingly. "I'm rescuing *him*, Syd, not you."

Oh. I guess I can deal with that.

"Fine," I say, tucking my weapon away with a regretful sigh. "Let's get this shit over with. I'm looking forward to this afternoon, but I have a feeling this morning is going to make me want to stab *myself* in the eye."

Huck and Thad chuckle, waiting for me to move to the door, then they follow behind as usual. I don't look over my shoulder to ensure the others are with us; they can get on board or not. My goal for this stupid contest is to win so Huck, Thad, and I can live the rest of our lives away from the desperation of Tempest Seven. If they're as motivated as me, then we'll be able to work together.

The mood is somber as we head down the hall to the elevator, and this time when we squeeze into the metal box I despise, no one speaks. I don't mind that in the slightest; I'd prefer to get my game face on before we exit. Sipping the coffee that's stronger than anything we've been able to brew ourselves in years, I feel the divine pulse of caffeine thrum in my veins. A corresponding ache in the spot where my Marker used to be makes me furrow my brows as I stare at the floor.

What will happen if I try to use magic?

I barely had any of my abilities before the Sweep that earned me the damn tag that used to rest in the back of my neck. I'm not sure what the hell I can do or even what I'm supposed to get. I need to figure it out before the actual competition starts, obviously, but I can't do it in front of anyone but Huck or Thad.

How am I going to ditch the other assholes to find out?

My question from earlier is answered when we arrive at the atrium downstairs. Krista and some of her irrepressibly gleeful cronies are waiting with six other groups. They aren't the same as the ones we toured with yesterday, so I study them to see who I recognize. Two of the teams are gathered around Bitsy Carlyle. It's her actual name as far as I know, and she's supposedly a Chimera shifter. I've never seen hide nor hair of her powers, but that doesn't mean they aren't formidable. Her attitude and appearance certainly are—she's been using her curves to get whatever she wants the entire time we've been in Tempest.

Bitsy is to our sector what Stormbringer is to his.

I know her team is all shifters because she seems to have a distaste for any supe *not* a purebred animal shifter. Her behavior in our lower school was atrocious and no one did a fucking thing because she was one of the beautiful party supes. Luckily for me, Thad and Huck kept me away from their bullshit, but I remember what tangling with her crowd did to others. She's fierce and ambitious—plus, willing to do *anything*. We'll have to keep our eyes on her people.

"You saw her, huh?" Huck sidles up to me, his presence at my back comforting. "The old girl is already gathering allies. Living proof some people never evolve past puberty."

Nodding, I jerk my chin at the two teams. "We need to be careful of those idiots. Clearly, they can be swayed by a pretty face, even if it threatens their own self-interest."

"Oh, is that your Queen Bee?" Rory grins, his eyes dancing with amusement. "She's not bad, but she wouldn't survive where I come from. Mediocre in comparison to our bees without a doubt."

I frown. "That might be true, but I'm not in the habit of slamming other women to make myself feel better. If she earns my ire, I'll handle it with upfront confrontation. I don't need to hide in the shadows like a coward."

Elias joins us, his expression inscrutable. "An honorable sentiment, Sydney, and one that will certainly be tested in the future."

Unfortunately, he's spot on; no way we won't come into direct competition with Bitsy eventually.

"We should assess the others before they move us," Sebastian interrupts. "Stop focusing on a silly bobblehead when there are far more prescient threats."

"Damnit," I mutter as I walk further into the group. I hate that the vampire is also correct, but I won't fuck around and miss our chance just to spite him.

Once I'm in the thick of the supes milling around, I pretend to be bored. Being silent in the middle of a yammering crowd never draws the attention it should, so I have the time to scope out the other competitors. The teams with Bitsy are mixed shifters, but all shifters are the same. There are two teams of various magicals not far from them, then an all Fae team after that. A team that exudes mystery is in the corner, keeping to themselves, and I don't know if that means they're all vamps or not. Maybe they're all creatures based in the darkness like vamps, Cubi, and the like. I'll have to ask Huck.

The last team besides us is obviously shady as hell. I see their eyes darting around like mine, checking people out as they silently occupy space in the farthest corner from the humans. I don't know if they're all demons or Lockdowns or what, but *they* are the most dangerous beings here besides my team. Turning to Thad, I murmur, "That's who we need to find out about."

"Correct," Sebastian says and Elias nods his agreement. "They are mixed, but all have the scent of killers."

Giving him a dirty look, I retort, "What the hell does that smell like, you overgrown mosquito?"

His fangs peek out as he smirks. "Blood."

I asked, didn't I?

"Guys, cool it. The guy next to Krista is getting ready to speak."

Thad's calm words help put a damper on the embers burning inside of me and I sigh. "Fine. I'll behave for a few minutes."

"Good girl," Rory says.

My eyes narrow and I stomp his foot as hard as I can before hissing, "I'm not a girl, asshole."

His hand flies to his mouth to cover the yelp, but he looks at the other guys to figure out his mistake. They might as well be staring into the sky and whistling for all the help they give him and I cross my arms over my chest, feeling victorious. The squeal of a bullhorn distracts me and we all turn back to face front. The guy standing on a chair looks like a preppy douche —the kind I would have avoided like the plague even before The Unveiling.

"Good morning, future champions!" When no one responds, he falters briefly, but then smiles brightly to cover it up. "The FHSA has chosen you for its biggest honor since the inception and we are here to guide you through your first step toward victory!"

Again, no one says a word—the only sound in the room is a cough, then feet shuffling. If this guy thinks anyone here is going to kiss his ass for being here, he's definitely delusional. Even Bitsy is staring at him with open derision. That might be because he's not powerful enough to do anything for her, but still. It feels like solidarity when we're all quiet, so I'm going to take it.

"My name is Chad Burnett, and I lead the Wizarding Whizzbangs team over there. Today, your teams will go through the process of prep in both branding, like mine, and then the physical evals that will allow your coordinator to bid for things to help your strategy going forward. You will need to pay close attention, be honest about your abilities, and interact with your coordinator to help craft the image your team wants to project. If you think this isn't important, you're dead wrong—possibly literally once the Games begin."

Of fucking course it's a Chad. What would this circus be without one?

TODAY IS NOT THE DAY

THADDEUS

I SAW Syd's face when the douche said we'd have to name our team and come up with a 'branding strategy'. She's going to lose her mind at some point today, and I'm not sure we can afford that. We agreed to keep everything on the DL as a team so we can check out the competition, but if they're going to make us do stupid shit, it will be hard to keep her on track with that plan.

She might not be the only one, too, given the disgust mirrored by the dragon.

The trappings of this contest feel stupid and superfluous when it's weighed against the seriousness of its conclusion. Sydney is so angry about what happened four years ago—especially her father's death—and she's never processed it properly. Anger keeps her going, and she doesn't want to let go of it because she's afraid there won't be anything left to fuel her. Of course, she's never *said* that, but it's clear as day when you know her as well as I do. Her fury about the world forsaking the supes of the former America out of capitalistic greed helps her deal with the reality of our lives now.

Now we have to play to the cameras and the media vultures to ensure our survival—it's going to take time for her to swallow that injustice. The only thing Huck and I can do is help her deal with it in private as best we can while hoping the others don't push her boundaries enough to fuck up our chances in this damn competition. Sighing as I watch her stew quietly while the Chad dude continues to explain our activities for the morning, I place my hand on her shoulder gently. I don't want to spook her, but I think she needs something to ground her.

"This is such a fucking circus, Thad," she whispers. "So much money is being spent on a facade for the rest of the world when people are suffering —especially the camps ranked lower than T7.”

“I know,” I reply ruefully. “But we can only control what’s in our grasp, Syd. If we rise to the top of the barrel and gain public adoration, maybe we can put the focus on the truth of supe life in FHSA.”

She turns, looking over her shoulder at me, her eyes wide. “Holy shit, you’re right. If we use this not to escape, but to fuck up their perfect bubble of lies, we might be able to help everyone, not just ourselves.”

“Great,” the vampire says low enough that only our team can hear. “She’s going to turn into a crusader now, bear. That’s going to go badly since she can’t even defend herself with magic or supe skills, plus she’s got zero control over her emotions.”

Sydney glares at him so intensely that I think if she had powers, it would—

Sebastian starts choking, his hands flying to his throat as he scrabbles to get air. His eyes pop open, panic reflected in the red orbs as he tries to keep the noise from his struggle quiet. Our girl’s lips curve up in satisfaction, an evil glee coming over her face as she continues to stare at him. The dragon notices the problem, and I feel the air around us grow cooler, a salty tang filling my nostrils as he moves closer. He approaches Syd carefully, like she’s a rabid animal he doesn’t want to bite him.

“*Toafilemu, aloiafi natia. E tatau ona e filemu*[1].”

Huck frowns, whatever language the sea dragon is speaking, he isn’t familiar with. Rory looks similarly confused, and the vampire simply claws at his windpipe. I rumble soothingly, hoping to help her with my touch and the bear’s support. There’s no way Syd has any clue what this dude is saying, either. She’s never been out of our state, much less—

“*Ua tatau ona maliu o ia mo lana vaega i lo tatou pagatia. Ua ia faalumaina a‘u ma o tatou tagata i lona faatasi mai.*[2]”

What the fucking shit is that?!

The royal laughs softly, his chuckle rumbling with a touch of his inner beast. “That is true, *aloiafi natia*[3]. But today is not the day to mete out that punishment, and perhaps this vampire isn’t the one who has earned it. You are smarter than that, I believe.”

Suddenly, she breaks eye contact with Sebastian and he’s able to suck in deep breaths, trying to slowly get oxygen back into his body. I didn’t think vamps actually needed air, which means we’ve been taken in by a mythos probably spread by their own kind to protect themselves. A vampire locked in a coffin for revenge would die much faster of air loss than starvation—so it makes sense they’d pretend otherwise.

“Dude, what the fuck?” I say as I look at the rich moron.

He can’t speak yet, so he holds a finger up, and continues working through the injuries our girl gave him without a second thought. When he's finally able to blow out a slow, even breath, he croaks, "We don't need air, and I have no idea what the motherfucking *shit* that bitch just did to me."

Elias smirks, crossing his arms over his chest. "I believe she just showed you what happens when you fuck around with her, blood sucker."

"Well, that's for sure, scaly man, but *how* did she do that little demo, mm?" Huck pushes his cowboy hat back, his face full of confusion. "Sweet pea's never been able to do a thing in class, and bless your heart, you seem to have awakened a beast."

The dragon shrugs. "I'm not sure how I knew what to say, or that she'd be able to understand, demon. It just came out of my mouth. As for 'how', I couldn't tell you; I still don't have a read on her type, which is weird as fuck."

Sydney holds her hand up, shaking her head. "We can't deal with this here; too many witnesses, both seen and unseen. Discussion will have to be later; we have extremely unpleasant bullshit to deal with first."

She's not wrong, but what happens if someone pisses her off during our sessions?

"I don't like this shit," I mutter to Huck as the mass crowd of supes head out of the atrium back across the courtyard we used to come to our building last night. They're taking us in the back way again and Syd is keeping her distance from all of us. Probably a good plan considering, but I'm using the time to catch my other best friend alone. "How did the stupid prince know what to do? How did she do that at all? Why would the vampire admit it shouldn't have worked? There's too many unanswered questions."

The demon shrugs, his eyes darting around before he replies, "Change is seldom comfortable, my friend, nor does it come when it's convenient. You and I have had this conversation many times since I arrived in these parts; I've always believed our girl was holdin' cards we couldn't see. Obviously, I wasn't far off the mark."

"She wasn't doing it purposefully, man. You saw the surprise in her eyes at first—before it faded to happily psychotic glee, I mean."

He laughs, looking more than a little intrigued by the thought. "An attitude I find even more attractive than her normal prickly behavior, I'm afraid. The pure evil in her eyes while the vamp was trying not to die was enough to make my entire body light up like a holiday festival."

She's going to kill him, too, if he gets too aggressive with his appreciation.

"Huck, if she's coming into the suppressed power of a species we have no clue about… You might consider treading lightly with the come-ons, man." I scratch my chin as we follow the group into the building, keeping close enough to Sydney to get to her if need be. "You know how… anti-intimacy… she is."

His laugh surprises me and I arch a brow. "Oh, naive little bear. Sydney Jolie is *not* asexual in the slightest—though I would adore her regardless. She's simply terrified of being left alone again. Mommy abandonment, Daddy abandonment—even due to death—has made her create a hard shell around herself to keep from being hurt again. How can you not realize that?"

I frown, holding the door for him as we enter. "I never delved too deep out of respect, Huck. It's not my place to force her to confront shit; I'm not a fucking shrink."

The fear demon shakes his head ruefully. "I fear you've done both of you, and now me, a great disservice."

"How?"

Huck grins, his eyes swirling with the swirls of his actual magic. "Because what we fear defines who we are, and overcoming it can open many, many doors, Thaddeus. Our mind will seek to overcome them when emotions are extreme—like today. However, when there's no adrenaline forcing your hand, you are owned by them."

Groaning, I give him a frustrated look. "Explain better."

"Thad, I believe that she unintentionally used what little magic she had developed to put a shell around her that's only grown stronger over the years —especially the past four in the sector." His smug expression irritates me, but I let him go on. "I didn't notice because she kept me farther away until now. However, her true powers may be… leaking out of that shell."

"It's cracked?" I ask as we line up where the guides show everyone to stand. "What did that?"

"Fuck if I know," he says. "But I believe it has and now she's coming into her own. What I don't know is how she's able to exhibit the *level* of power she did earlier. The Marker should have prevented it."

We fall silent for a few moments, and it comes to me. "We all saw doctors separately, Huck."

"Well, I'll be a daisy, Thad. You're right." His dark features furrow into a thoughtful look and he glances at our girl quickly. "She has to know, if that's the case. Why didn't she tell us?"

That bothers me, too.

"I don't know, but it might be because we haven't really had 'alone time' with her. The others are always around. I can't imagine she'd share something that treasonous in front of people we don't know yet."

Huck scratches his head as he looks at our three additional team members. "I find myself puzzled by them, to be truthful. I don't get bad vibes from them, but the dragon and vamp are closed off to my abilities for now. I intend to work on the mage first. He's far too open for his own good."

I snort. "Hopefully, that's not a trap, man."

"I've never met a single spell sucker in my long existence who could entrap me. Don't worry your big paws about me," he says with a wink.

"Are you two done gossiping like old maids?" We look up to see Sydney standing with her arms crossed as she looks at us in consternation. "I'd prefer to have you along when we go into this... wonderful...branding exercise."

As we join her, the mage in question strolls up with a smirk. "I have news. Most of these idiots are going to use names that are both dumb and contrived. We won't have much competition in this group of teams."

I blink. "You were off doing something... useful?"

"One of us has to talk to people that aren't only our team, bear. Since Vicious isn't socially inclined enough to flirt with the guys, and you two only watch her... it's down to the rest of us. Bas over there is still finding his nuts and the dragon hates people. Again, it's all me, man."

Elias arches a brow. "I hate *most* people."

"Oh, that's helpful," Sydney mutters. "How would one know which people you might want to interact with, then?"

"I don't let them get themselves killed for strangling a vampire in public?"

Her jaw drops and she just blinks at the big supe as Huck and the mage both laugh.

Well, that's fucking fantastic.

---

1. Calm, hidden spark. You must be calm.
2. He deserves to die for his part in our misery. He insults me and our people with his presence.
3. hidden spark

REALITY CONTINUES TO RUIN MY LIFE

SYDNEY

I HAVE no idea what the fuck to do with *that* admission so I huff and turn my attention back to the morons in charge of us. How in the hell would Elias know he likes me from what little interaction we've had since *yesterday*? The whole concept is totally foreign to me—I don't like anyone until I'm as sure as I possibly can be that they aren't going to try to kill me. And in the time I've known Thad, I've barely admitted I consider him a friend out loud, much less just spouted it off in public to everyone.

Men are relentlessly bizarre and I do not have the energy for this shit.

"I think she's ignoring you," Bas says, his voice filled with sarcastic amusement. "Looks like some of that struck a nerve, demon."

Whirling around, I hiss, "Do you have a death wish, *vampire?*"

He shrugs, looking unconcerned by my venom. "Most days. But that's none of *your* business, mystery half-breed."

Thad steps between us, glaring at Sebastian before he looks into my eyes. "Syd, he's hoping to provoke you further. I don't know what nerve you hit, or why everyone is trying to dance on yours, but this *has* to wait for privacy."

"Fine," I say as I move aside so I'm not facing him anymore. "Then leave me alone to recoup my control—*all of you.*"

I grit my jaw as I pretend to listen to the rest of what's-his-face's bullshit speech, breathing in and out mindfully. Who knows if Huck is right, but the last thing I need right now is to get totally riled up when I *might* have magic or powers I have no idea how to control? It's dumb as fuck for any of them to bait me—no one's told us if losing a person from your team disqualifies you, much less if there are conduct rules outside of the assigned areas. We could all end up as lockdown losers, or worse—dead.

When Gary—or whatever the hell his name is—finally shuts the fuck up, I sigh in relief. The propaganda they're spewing at us is insane, and pretending to pay attention to the canned speeches about our 'glorious' leader are as fake as his idiotic spray tan. No one in the sectors is going to suddenly kiss that dictator's feet for locking us up and calling us terrorists and animals. But we don't have an option here, so I'm sure that's why the organizers of this nightmare are trying their damnedest to indoctrinate anyone they can.

Very few supes are that stupid and if they are, they're already acting in their own self-interest by suckling at the teat of the humans.

"Finally," I mutter as the crowd starts moving and we're ushered into yet another hallway I've never seen before. Regardless of my irritation at their bullshit, I stick close to Thad, Huck and the other clowns because the devil you know is always better than the one who might be hiding a shiv. Thad arches a brow at me and I shrug—I don't know if I'm better yet, but I can stomach looking at them, so there's that.

Huck moves closer, looking at me with an apologetic expression. "Sorry, sweet pea. Sometimes I forget you're so much younger'n me; I've been on this plane for so long it makes me accept things that newer supes haven't come to grips with yet."

I wrinkle my nose. I'd like to tell him to get fucked for mentioning my age like it's a mental disability, but I realize he's trying to explain a very prominent difference in how we look at things. Hell, likely a difference that may separate me from Elias and the damn vampire as well. Rory, I'm not sure about. Scraping my teeth over my lower lip as I consider my words carefully, I nod. "Okay. You might be right about perspective, though your damn delivery could use some work, cowboy."

His smile is almost shy for a second before it morphs into one of his normal smirks. "I'll do my best, sweet pea. Until this week, you've mostly told me to shove it where the sun doesn't shine, so I'm not quite sure where the solid footing is. But I'll get it; I'm a smart cookie."

That makes me laugh softly, and Thad bumps my shoulder with his. "There you go, Syddie girl. It's okay to say shit you feel out loud occasion-ally so we have a clue what's going on in your head."

"Perish the thought," Sebastian mumbles and I glare at him before smiling at the bear.

"Communication can be one of my areas of opportunity, but I, too, will try to do better," I promise. That earns me a snort from the dragon and a double thumbs up from the mage, and for some reason, it makes my stomach flutter with happy butterflies.

Damn it, why do I care if they're pleased? Fuck, this shit is weird.

"Team Whizzbangs, head for the room labeled Alpha-One," Gary-I-Think says. He points at the door at the very end of the hallway and I groan.

"I really hope these rooms aren't assigned by—"

"Krista, your team will go to Alpha-Two." I bang my closed fists on my forehead lightly as the idiot confirms my suspicion.

The teams are being assigned rooms by power or strength level—we have a Prince.

"Just fucking fabulous," Huck agrees as he steps forward to lead the way. Krista is waving like a tool up by our door, and a feeling of dread fills me as excitement flickers in the air as we get closer to her.

The blond woman bounces her toes, looking at us with crazy-eyes. "I cannot *wait* to figure out what your team will be called. Being in Alpha-Two is *such* an honor, and I am *so* excited for us to circle up!"

Elias and I groan at the same time, making Rory snicker. I look at the dragon, my expression relaying how much we're going to hate this shit. He mouths 'better than jail', and I have to hold back a laugh. I'm not sure he's right, but that's coming from a place of privilege, I know.

Though, I'll be the first to admit I'd rather be poked with a cattle prod than do some sort of marketing workshop—that's one hundred percent fact.

"What about the 'Alpha All-stars'? That sounds very snazzy."

Putting my fingers on my temples, I close my eyes and rub gently. So far, Krista has branded our colors in a red and blue that feels like a mockery of the flag this dumbass country used to fly and almost got herself throttled about forty times. I'm not the only one irritated with her and this entire exercise, but I'm definitely in the top two of people who are ready to end this in blood.

"Unfortunately, I would have to murder myself if I wore something that idiotic on my person," Sebastian says drily. "Try again."

This time, I agree with him—not that I'm going to let him know.

"I mean, if you're going to be that obvious, we should go with "Big Dick Swingers', right?" My head turns slowly to look at the cheeky mage and I feel my eye begin to twitch.

Elias snorts, pacing past me again as he grumbles, "You'd have to let the girl tell everyone hers is the biggest, I suspect."

"You're damn right about that," I shoot back, almost smiling for the first time in an hour. "But also, *fuck no.*"

Thad and Huck are leaning back in their chairs, watching the pingpong match happening between the new guys, Krista, and me with smug grins.

I'm sure they'll intervene if need be, but they're smart enough to keep their yaps shut otherwise. I think my temper tantrum in the hallway worried them, so they're not adding to the ribbing the others are doing.

"What about Twilight Marauders?" Krista pipes up as she looks at her tablet. "That sounds dangerous *and* sexy."

Sebastian flashes his fangs at her, his eyes red and angry. "Absolutely not. Twilight? Are you mental?"

Covering my mouth as images of the dickish vamp covered in sparkling booty dust fill my mind, I spin around so he can't see me. I hate the name, too, but I'm tempted to support it just to piss him off. The urge passes when I imagine having to wear that moniker on global television feeds. I should probably *not* get behind something so stupid to spite someone unless I'm ready to look extremely dumb in public.

Damn. Humans always ruin my fun.

"We have to decide this now so they can continue producing all of the things you'll need for branding, both in physical and digital form. Having something catchy that people will want to get behind is very important. You have to be appealing from the minute they see you; it's imperative."

Something in her voice makes me turn back to study the usually chipper human. Her brows are furrowed and I can see the tension in her frame. I don't know what she's been told, but she's definitely concerned about our success. I'm too jaded to believe that it's about my team; it's likely about what will happen to her if she's one of the failures.

I can't be responsible for anyone other than the five people I'm already tied to by this competition.

"Look, Krista. We're not cutesy people. Dante is a furloughed Lockdowner, we have a traitor and a flirty magic user, a bear, and a demon who thinks he's a cowboy. Topping it off, I'm a powerless supe. We're more the rag-tag underdog types than the 'A Team' with pretty faces."

The human looks at me in shock. "You don't see it, do you?"

I arch a brow. "See what?"

"Dear Lord in heaven, how the fuck is she so blind?" I almost respond to her but the bouncy coordinator climbs on a chair and gives me an annoyed look. "The cowboy demon is hot as hell, and has an adorable Southern boy charm. The Lockdown dragon is dark, dangerous, and looks like someone every girl *wishes* she could take a spin on. Your big cuddly bear is muscled and burly, like the blue collar boys you'd want to meet in a small town movie. The flirty, statuesque magic user and flawlessly dark vampire are also enough to make people drool. Then you have this Lara Croft meets smart girl thing going on… you guys are a *goldmine* if you'd quit being dim-witted about it."

Huck slouches more, his lips curving up as he pushes the brim of his hat up. "Why, thank you, little lady. I'm aflutter with your praise."

"Shut up, Huck," Thad and I say at the same time. His face turns red when I wink at him, and suddenly, I see the whole 'cuddly big guy' thing Krista was talking about.

My eyes skitter around the room as the guys try to avoid looking at the human with her hands on her hips. Woefully, she's on the nose. Elias is the ultimate bad boy, and his reticence only reinforces it. Rory is the popular rich guy everyone would want in a 90s high school movie, and Sebastian might be an untrustworthy motherfucker, but he looks like every emo girl's dream. Their looks and personalities being cultivated specifically would definitely help us get more… whatever the hell they want from us… to get special shit.

I don't agree with them about me, but I'm not arguing that shit in public.

"Fine. Let's say we understand what you're saying, and we're willing to figure out how to use that. What else would we need to do?"

"Pick a goddamn name!"

I wince, surprised at her vehemence. If she wasn't human, I might start liking this chick. "Okay. So it has to be catchy and simple to remember and make designs for. But it also needs to reflect us, right?"

"Yes."

The thought hits me and I smirk as I look at them all. "Then I'd like to formally introduce the 'Bite Club', Krista."

Her eyes widen and she claps her hands, looking excited as hell. "That's… oh, it's going to be perfect. Does everyone agree?"

The guys all look at each other, then shrug. Elias is the first person to speak and once he does, the damage is done.

"I think it suits us perfectly. Not one of us would allow people to come at us without taking a bite of them."

No shit, Sherlock.

I WOULDN'T TRUST YOU TO FALL OUT OF BED SUCCESSFULLY

RORY

THE BEST THING about being me is that I've learned to cover my distaste and mistrust of the species that subjugated our kind with a brilliantly handsome mask. It's kept me in a relatively comfortable lifestyle even while I endured indignities to secure it. However, watching Sydney simply face things with such honest emotion makes me wonder who I might have been if I hadn't developed my outer shell. She's not stupid—she pushes hard enough to be heard, but not so far that our chirpy coordinator feels it's necessary to report her.

Our team leader is very politically savvy, even if she pretends not to be.

It also makes me feel a tiny bit… tainted. That's not her fault, of course. Sydney hasn't once accused me of what I'm sure she and her lovesick companions know I've done. Hell, even the vampire hasn't made a fuss, but I get the feeling that's because he, too, has secret shame. It's wafting from him in thick waves of emotions that hit me like a tsunami when I get anywhere near him. I don't know what his story is, nor am I going to ask. Life in the sectors has taught me not to worry about others; I can only be responsible for myself.

"I think using black and white with the red and blue is brilliant," Krista says as she writes on a white board. "It's patriotic but edgy."

I arch a brow with the girl in question, smirking like she's won something. If I were to guess, I'd bet she absolutely did that on purpose and has some sort of devious plan brewing in her head. Since she gave in and provided Krista with the team name, she's been acting the class suck-up. "Seems like she's right, Vicious. It fits with the FHSA colors perfectly."

Huck rubs his fingers over his lips but I can see the wheels turning in his head. He thinks she's got a scheme, too, but he's not sure where Sydney is going yet. "I like it, sweet pea. The dark hues compliment my flawless complexion."

Krista looks excited as hell, clasping her hands together in front of her. "I am *so* pleased with this cooperative turn-about. Using the re-branded national flag hues, giving me a catchy name, and even being moderately less snarky… oh, we are going to give every team in this building a run for their money!"

As if that's more important than us staying alive or gaining our freedom.

The dragon and the vampire have been suspiciously quiet as Sydney took the reins for this discussion, only nodding occasionally to confirm their agreement. I don't know what that's about, either, because Sebastian definitely enjoys pissing everyone off every chance he gets. I cross my arms over my chest, watching them carefully for signs of what their game is. Elias seems to favor the tough brunette, but her enmity with the bloodsucker has overshadowed common sense consistently since we were matched.

"To sum up," Thad says, looking at the notes for a second before he continues. "We have the name, the brand colors, and Syd is our captain. Krista is going to present logo options by the end of the day to the tablets once her design team works them up. Did I miss anything?'

Our human shuffles some paper, glancing at them quickly. "Nicknames are big in sports, but I think it's better to wait until the fans give them to you so we can make hashtags to support it. When they take, we can amend your competition gear to reflect them to keep it continuous."

"Great. Absolutely marvelous. Are we done now?" Sydney asks with a flicker of her previous irritability finally seeping in. "Because if so, I'd *love* to go to lunch and not hear the word synergy again for a month."

Elias chuckles, the sound dark as his grin spreads over sharp teeth. "Eloquently put."

"No, we have a few more things to nail down and I have homework to give you for tomorrow."

For the love of Merlin's scraggy-ass beard…

"Homework for tomorrow?" Sydney scoffs as she flops backward in her chair, almost pouting at the word. "We have *two* days of this crap?!"

A flash of frustration comes over the woman's face, but it's gone as quickly as it came. "Yes, Sydney. Marketing and branding is an on-going effort. While you are preparing for the first reveal, we will have quite a few sessions, but as the Games begin it will become a minimum weekly meeting. There will be ad hoc sessions, though, if need be. Your ability to win hearts is as essential as your ability to compete in the field."

"Fuck, that's awful," Sebastian says as he pushes off the wall like a cranky cat. "I was hoping Miss Helpful took care of the bulk of this shit today."

Sydney points at him. "What the dickface said. I hate agreeing with him, but that was the point of cooperation, lady."

Drawing in a deep breath, Krista puts her hands on the table where her materials are spread out. "Look. I can't keep fighting with you the entire way through this. You are my team and more than simply *your* destiny is tied to your success. Otherwise, I could let you fuck yourselves over and get killed, *capiche*? Instead, I'm actively pushing you to do things I know you don't want to do so we all get through this with as little damage as possible. Stop making it harder than it needs to be."

I squint at her, noting she's positioned away from the camera in the corner and her voice is low enough that only supes can hear it. This is a big risk for her, and she's trying to hide her admission of the truth from whomever might review these tapes. Unless they're enchanted, she's probably covered her tracks, but the new information changes everything.

Huck scratches his face, blocking the view of his mouth as he says, "You're being threatened as well. We should have known."

"How could we? She's been an automaton since the second we met her," Sydney says as she puts her face in her hands to obscure the view.

We're all fucking spymasters now that we've caught onto Krista's gambit. Unlike her, the Confession Enforcement Zones have trained our people to do this for four years. We know exactly how to defeat the government's spy bullshit.

The question is… is she trustworthy or are we being set up?

"That was excruciating," Sydney says as we walk to the main lobby. "I'd rather they put me in a chair and pry up my fingernails with bamboo shoots."

I bet she would, actually.

I wink at her as I push the button on the elevator bank so we can head down to the level just above the bottom one where the gym is located. "I'd love to hear you scream, but that's not the way I want it to go, Vicious."

Thad smacks me in the back of the head and I glare at the bear. He doesn't flinch, simply says, "Don't rile Syd up. She's on the edge as it is, and we agreed to keep her on an even keel until we're alone."

"The bear is correct."

Groaning, I roll my eyes. "You two and the demon are the death of fun, I fucking swear. Just because this place and this reality since the Sweeps *sucks* doesn't mean we can't occasionally have a little joy. No wonder you all look like your asses are sewn shut with fishing wire all the time."

They all stare at me as I get into the elevator until Sydney bursts into laughter. I gape at her in surprise—I wasn't joking and I'm definitely right about their tight-assed misery faces. She stomps up to me, her eyes bright as she shakes her head. "Stormbringer, you're probably right. This place is meant to crush our spirits and we let it. Perhaps getting through this stupid shit with our brains intact will require unclenching, so to speak."

What.

"Very good, sweet pea." Huck's eyes flash with a slight golden tinge as he joins us, jerking his head for the rest to follow us. "I think you're learnin' how this lil' game needs to be played."

"Whatever. Let's go eat."

The irritated huff doesn't stop her from letting Thad and the demon move in close to her as she turns to face the doors, and it makes me smile to myself. She's an ice queen, but she's warming up, and that means they aren't the only ones who have a chance. I like my odds, especially compared to the criminal and the bloodsucker. I don't know why I care this much about a girl who's giving off 'get bent' vibes when I could find all too willing ones—it doesn't matter, though. My sights are set on her and I know I can win her over.

I continue plotting my approach until the doors open to the enormous cafeteria, noting it's extremely busy, and not just with the teams. Those tables are obvious—six supes crowded together as they chow down and send occasional glares to other groups. There's also a section in the back that looks like it's for the staff—everyone from coordinators to mysteriously unfamiliar humans in the branded polos that must do something here, but who knows what.

"Looks like they want everyone to know we're being well taken care of," Elias mutters. "Though damn near anything would be better than what the lockdown facilities are like."

"They won't be serving bugs here. It'll be a step up," Sebastian says and the dragon whips around to give him a dark look.

"Your existence is required for this event, but don't think I will hesitate to force you to heal yourself from a beating if you earn it." The royal scans the room for watchful eyes, then faces the vampire again. "Having the privilege of living well after The Unveiling because your kind betrayed the rest of us doesn't make you better—only more hated."

Sydney looks worried when scales appear on his arms and I dart between the two. "Look, dudes. We asked Vicious to calm her roll and now it's your turn. Bas, shut the hell up about shit you have no experience with.

Dante, back off him before you end up in chains again. It will fuck up our training."

The big guy rolls his neck, a loud crack making me wince. His angry glare doesn't lessen, but he steps back, letting me move away from them. "Fine. But I will keep my promise if he opens his fat mouth about the supernaturals kept in chains and cages because they are too powerful for them to control with Markers alone. In the five camps I've been imprisoned in since my capture, I have yet to meet a single actual criminal amongst that brethren."

His declaration surprises the entire group, and even Sydney has her jaw hanging open. When she unfreezes, she looks at Elias with a confused expression. "None? I thought only some of the ones like you…"

"Not one. They may *say* these people committed crimes, but the stories of how they were all captured and their exotic or rare species convey a much different set of circumstances. Like me, there are many royals, alphas, lunas, and other leaders who have been torn from their families and scattered to the winds to prevent them from hiding or rebelling."

Thad leans in, murmuring in a very low tone. "This is fascinating, gents, but I believe we should discuss this in a space we know isn't filled with prying ears and video. I swear, it feels like none of you remember this isn't the normal F.E.A.R. facility or open air."

I hate it, but he's fucking right again.

"Fine. These two will shut up and Sydney will let me escort her to the buffet because I've behaved so well."

She looks at me for a minute, then sighs heavily. "Fine. Let's go, Rory. We have to eat before it's time to head to training. I'm not very friendly when I have a weapon and I'm hungry."

Somehow, I don't find that hard to believe.

THAT'S A BET I'LL TAKE

SYDNEY

"I'M NOT interested in whatever plans you're hatching for my pants," I tell him as we approach the gratuitous amount of food splayed out for the teams. "You should know that going in."

Rory laughs, his head tipped back as the happy sound rumbles out of him. "Ah, Vicious. You cut me, but I promise, eventually you won't want to do it anymore—unless we're alone."

Interesting qualification.

"Being 'alone' with anyone isn't in my goals for this event," I reply as I pick up a plate. "Not dying is pretty high on the list, though."

The mage clucks his tongue, sighing as if I'm the most trying person he's ever met. "Oh, Sydney. It's not living if all you think about is dying."

"In Tempest Seven, there's not a lot to be excited about. You'd know if you lived in a less… accommodating sector, I think." I purposely don't say exactly what I'm thinking this time because while I wouldn't make his choices, I don't feel comfortable judging him for them. Some people were so attached to the lives they had in the past that they gave up valuable pieces of themselves to maintain that lifestyle.

"Things weren't as peachy as you think in my sector."

A change in his mood smacks into me like a truck and I have to press my hand against my gut as it slams into me. I don't know what the fuck that was, but I don't like it at all. Licking my lips, I take a moment to gather myself before I start looking at the cold end of the buffet. I'm not hungry suddenly, and that's a sensation I haven't felt for years. It roils within me as I pick things off the platters anyway, determined not to be weak and angry later on.

Whatever just happened to me can fuck right off.

"Okay. I don't know shit about the three El Dorado sectors except that's where the wealthiest supes went," I admit as I pile some fruit on my dish. Nice, ripe fruit is a luxury here and I'm going to gorge myself on it during this stupid contest.

Rory snorts as he grabs salad and fruit, making a huge pile on the first plate in his hands. "The only one of us *living* in an ED sector was the mosquito, Vicious. I may have been a frequent *visitor* to those camps, but it's not where I lived."

I blink as we move towards the bread, trying to summon my appetite again as the fresh smell makes me drool a little. "Um...I thought... well, I assumed maybe..."

"I know."

The handsome magic user doesn't elaborate and I'd smash a strawberry in his mug if I didn't want to savor eating ones this juicy looking rather than waste them. "Well, where the fuck *are* you from, then? You sure as hell haven't corrected anyone who assumes you're from fancy stock."

"That's on purpose," he says, shrugging as we both scoop up hot rolls and butter them. "I prefer to keep my image intact, so you'd have to earn my truth. Even shady folk like me have standards and boundaries—allowing certain things to survive doesn't change that."

Rubbing my free hand over my face, I sigh. "I didn't mean—"

"Oh, but you did. It's a shame, too, because I thought you were someone who wouldn't judge me. I guess we're both disappointed today."

My eyes narrow and I grab his shoulder, turning him to face me. I'm surprised to see a very blank expression on his features and I realize it must be a mask he wears to prevent people from knowing what his real emotions are. "Rory, I actually did *not* mean to sound judgmental about whatever it is you do. I believed you were wealthy because of your... behavior and affect... but I don't hold your choices against you."

One corner of his mouth quirks for a second, then he shakes his head. "What's sad, Vicious, is that I think you actually believe that. You're convinced of what the world was, is now, and what it will become, so you define the rest of us by those standards. It's admirable in terms of determination and bravery, but you've been sold a bill of goods about the rest. Just like Dante has a story much different than you anticipated, so do I."

I feel like such a goddamn asshole right now and I deserve it.

Pressing my lips together as we scoop meats and hearty entrees onto our plates, I gather my thoughts, picking my next words carefully. "Perhaps you're right, Rory. We've all been fed the tale about the lockdown l—the imprisoned supes and no one bothered to check it. We're all suffering, so we wrote off that contingent in our minds to make room for those closer to us. Your truth might challenge other things we've been told when you are comfortable. I can accept that I don't know everything if you can accept that I truly did not mean to hurt you."

His smile is brilliant as he winks at me, all traces of the serious Rory gone. "I didn't think you meant to hurt me. What I thought is that you'd been spoon-fed a prejudice designed to keep as many supes apart as possible to keep us under their thumbs. Now, finish getting your food and shush before we get caught talking about this shit."

I dip my chin, trying to hide my shock at his words. Stormbringer is *much* smarter than he lets on, and the himbo act is exactly that—an act he's cultivated to protect himself. "Okay. But I'm still not fucking you."

A brow arches as we approach the dessert section and my eyes widen with excitement. "Twenty bones says you'll be looking at my cock like that before these fucking games are over."

Snorting, I stack plates on my arms, desperate to maximize how much I can carry back to the table. "You're on, magic wielder. But you'd better be good for it because I kneel for no man."

His smug grin doesn't give me a lot of confidence, but I've managed to fend guys off for years before he showed up; I'll be fine.

Rory Stormbringer is going down.

"Welcome back to your first real day of training," Krista chirps from the front of the classroom.

I forced myself to eat enough to keep my energy solid for the rest of the afternoon—I think—but I have no idea what the hell these people are going to work on with us. Everything supes are taught in the schools since the sweeps is specifically *non-aggressive*, but that's not what this stupid contest is about. They'll have to assess each team's skill level person by person to figure out who was trained before that became illegal. I'm not worried about myself at this juncture; the one thing my dad *could* teach me was physical self-defense.

The magic part is where I'm going to be deficient.

"These two gents are Brick and Lancaster. They are hybrid supernaturals contracted by the FHSA to work with you because of your special physiology. Don't worry! They're very skilled and come with superb qualifications prior to The Unveiling."

Dante looks at me, his brow arched as if to say 'see what I meant?' I guess that means these guys were locked down somewhere because I know they're not from the Tempest Seven sector. I don't know if the dragon *knows* them or knows *of* them, but he's very smug right now. They don't acknowledge him, though, so I'll have to keep my theories on ice until later.

Brick is built... well, like a fucking brick shithouse. He's almost as tall and broad as Elias, but the dangerous energy coming from him tells me his physicality isn't his only strength. The vibes rolling off of him are intense as hell and some of it is frustrated fury. I can empathize with that; being locked up by these clowns and then having to pretend to willingly assist them now has to chafe something awful. I'm not sure what he is; my senses aren't developed enough to scent it, nor is my experience with rare supes.

In contrast, Lancaster is muscled, but lithe, like Rory. He exudes a dark aura, and his appearance matches it. Everything about him screams pain and vicious intent—so much so that the air gets colder when my eyes fall on him. He's glaring at Huck and Elias in particular, so maybe his kind don't like demons or dragons?

Who the fuck knows anymore?

"We're here to work you both physically and magically, though an assessment of your physical speed, strength, and endurance are on today's menu," Brick says in a gravelly voice. "It will allow us to develop personalized, rigorous training routines for each of you, plus detailed team exercises. Once we set that over the next two weeks, we will move to the supe arena to measure those skills and abilities. The process will repeat again until we have that training decided, and your real weekly schedule will be given to you."

Dante grunts and Sebastian rolls his eyes, but it seems logical to me. Deciding that being the only chick on the team means I'm going to have to be the one to ask, I clear my throat. "Is that all we'll be doing when the schedule is set or...?"

Krista waves her hand, looking amused. "Of *course* not. These are beginning battle classes, but you will have strategy courses, marketing with me once branding is set, on-off fittings or shopping trips when we're live and you gather funds and points, social media sessions, events, and more. Schedules will be *packed* if I'm doing my job right and you're doing yours."

I don't want to ask what will happen if we're not doing it, even before we hit the field for whatever trials there are.

"Performing monkeys," Elias says as he looks at me.

He's right, so I give him a slight nod when our hostess is looking away. A soft chuckle sounds from the front, but I don't see which one of the trainers made the noise. "Fine. Let's get this over with then. What do we do first?"

Brick stabs a finger at the track. "Ten laps around this. Start *now*."

I blink, looking at the guys for a split second before I jog to the marked track. The sounds of their varied footfalls tells me they're following along, but I ignore it. I run laps around the entire sector by myself at night when I can't sleep—which is more often than Huck or Thad know—so I want to be alone while I do it. It's comforting to the point of hypnotizing, so the room falls away as I simply pace myself. Ten laps around this is a much shorter distance than I'm used to, but it'll do for now.

"Vicious, wait up," I hear Rory call, but I don't even twitch a muscle to let him know I hear him.

The voice that answers surprises me when the bear says, "She's in her running zone, man. Leave her be. It's like she's in another world when she does this."

How the hell did he know that?

My expression turns irritable as I surmise he's probably followed me at least once without my knowledge. Maybe Huck has, too, and it rankles me to think they're sneaking around to 'protect' me when I'm plenty capable of it on my own. We're going to have a come to Zeus moment later on, that's for sure.

Shaking off my annoyance, I use the jogging time to muse about what we've experienced so far. This endeavor had to be at least two years or more in the making; it's got so many moving pieces and so many variables. Is it possible that some savvy human corporations used Taterman's hatred of our kind to play a long game? Capitalism is a scourge, so I wouldn't put it past them. Those dickwads use and abuse their own kind, so getting him to enact the registrations and sectors wouldn't be hard.

All they'd have to do after The Unveiling was present profit projections and stoke a senile old racist's fear of the unknown… it would slide through like a hot butter knife.

It's just as likely Taterman and his fellow crusty old white dudes and their ass-sucking sycophant women did this on their own but discovered they could profit off us, too. After all, they cut every corner on the sectors to pinch pennies, but finding a way to monetize it as well isn't outside of their wheelhouse. Spinning a positive look on the camps to the rest of the world might help keep the do-gooders who keep trying to get in to inspect from the U.N.B. from making noise.

There are just too many evil reasons for these fuckers to put us in death games; I can't decide which one is most probable yet. I'll see the board eventually, though, and that's when I will be able to plan accordingly. Magic isn't my strength at the moment, but strategy is, and I'm going to break this entire thing down to nuts and bolts to win.

Freedom will be mine, no matter who I have to go through to get it.

RUNNING YOUR MOUTH DOESN'T COUNT AS EXERCISE

ELIAS

WATCHING SYDNEY RUN WAS IMPRESSIVE. She could use a bit more endurance, but if I know the guys they picked to be our trainers, she'll get what she needs in short order. I've been moved around some since the Sweeps, so I met them during stays in places other than my most recent home in Inferno Seven. Now we're working on weight training, and I think she could use a lot more work in this arena. Her legs are fairly strong, but her arms are weak—something common in people who train for cardio to escape but not for strength to break free.

I will help her with that myself.

"Sydney, come lift with me," I say as she studies the various machines in puzzlement. "I will help with your regimen."

She looks at me for a moment, then shrugs. "I suppose since you're built like a tank, you know what you're doing."

"Exactly."

"Sweet pea, Thad and I are plenty good with weights. You don't have to—"

I give the demon a wry look. "Huck, you are not even half my size. I am not saying you are deficient; I am suggesting I might have the advantage in this one skill set."

For a second, I think he's going to protest, but the bear steps in. "He's right, Huck. I'm big, but not like him. Hell, we could all use his expertise."

That was very humble, and I appreciate supes who know their limits.

"Thank you," I reply as I walk over to a bench press to set it up for

Sydney. "It will be much easier to maximize our combined knowledge if we are not always at war with one another."

"Damn it, he's right," she grumbles. "I hate when men are right."

"Said like someone who believes it's infrequent," Stormbringer says from his spot doing bicep curls. "I see how you are, Vicious."

She rolls her eyes at him, then turns to me. "Okay, big guy. Tell me what to do."

"First, we will test the weight of the bar. You seem to have neglected this aspect, so you will do three sets of ten reps with just the bar. It will tire you out, but starting small is the best way to build a foundation."

I wait for her to comply, watching the first few before I move to a leg press where I can work as I keep my eyes on her. She learns quickly, but I was right about her being unbalanced. I'm barely through my first few sets before she lets out a groan. She's paused with the bar down, breathing slowly.

"Already, little Rebel?"

Giving me an annoyed look, she shakes her head. "Brief rest. I'm not cooked."

The corner of my mouth lifts and I go back to my presses, my gaze skirting the room to see how the rest of them are doing. Rory obviously knows what he's doing, and so does the vampire. The bear is strong, but he's not pushing himself enough. I will have to address that with him. His added bulk is very advantageous to our team, and we should not waste it. Huck is playing at the weights, but I know that's because his powers are far more useful when he's in demon form, and that does not require this sort of work.

I'll let him piddle around until I know what his other skills are; if they are not up to snuff, I will push him.

Pleased with my assessment, I finish the leg press, slurping down some water as I wait for Sydney to complete her sets. It takes longer than I'd prefer, but once she does, I repeat the process of setting up the machine and showing her the leg press, then switch to the bench. My tolerance is far greater, so I put as much weight as I can bear on the bar, then settle in. I won't have a spotter in our team—not for this kind of heft—so I whistle loud enough for Brick to hear. He strolls over, giving me a knowing expression as he stands by the bench.

He and Lancaster might be good allies, but I have to be certain before I engage in any conversations that could hurt our team. They were angry and younger when we met; I don't know how beaten down they've become in the past four years. They could have chosen to come here to get away from their captivity, or they could have assimilated into the FHSA's brainwashed supes. I won't be able to tell from this limited exposure. It will take time, and sessions where Krista isn't in the corner on her phone.

I assume she's not going to follow us to every single thing forever, but who the fuck knows?

"Leveled up since we last crossed paths, mmm, Dante?"

Nodding at Brick, I wait for him to get in position, then grunt as I lift the enormous weight and hold it up. It's not too much, which is good, so I continue my reps slowly. My eyes stay on our rebellious leader, making sure she's still doing okay, but my body goes on autopilot—up, down, up, down, repeat.

"She seems like she's pretty tough."

I snort. "So far, I'd agree."

"*She* can hear you assholes," Sydney replies. "My ears work just fine, guys."

"Actually her hearing is *spectacular*," Thad adds. "It's very annoying."

Good to know. Perhaps someone should do some research on the supes with excellent hearing.

"You two are just loud. You yammer on about dude shit and I get bored. It's not my fault you can't take objective criticism."

"Objective?" Sebastian pauses his quadriceps work to snort at her. "Somehow, I don't believe you."

"As if I give a shit what *you* think." Syd sniffs, then goes back to the leg press, gritting her teeth. It's probably starting to burn, but she's not done yet.

"Children," Lancaster says as he pushes off the wall. "Bickering will not rocket you to the top of this thing. At least, not in unrecorded pre-training sessions like this. It might be useful later on; audiences love pathos."

Oh, great. He thinks he's a fucking director, too. Just what we needed.

The rest of the physical training went quickly for me, as I worked with our trainers to help the rest of the team develop a program. In lockdown, there's little to do besides work out and sit around playing whatever broken down game is available, so we're all very familiar with the concept. It seems the rest of the sectors basically send the supes for education and sometimes, work details, then they amuse themselves until bedtime. They aren't encouraged to keep themselves fit or develop anything other than resentment.

It's no wonder the three friends in our group are brimming with anger and frustration—all they've ever done is focus on survival.

We're sweaty and tired when the session ends, and thank the swirling sea gods, Krista is gone when we head for the elevator. Sydney is particularly exhausted, and I feel for her. She doesn't have full supe abilities and physicality yet, so this regimen is very tough on her human body. Despite that, she hasn't complained about the hardship once, only stopped when she had to rest, then resumed without a word. I'm slightly impressed, but I doubt she'd appreciate anyone commenting on it. She's allergic to people commenting on her lack of supe powers and this is no exception.

"Are we eating in the suite this evening?" Thad asks as he punches the button.

The girl in my thoughts gives him a withering look. "Yes. I'm disgusting. We all smell and look like wilted cabbage. I doubt that presents an intimidating picture to all the other teams, so what's the point of being in public?"

"Good point." I nod as we walk into the carriage, positioning myself at the back. "We should be thinking about our appearances at all times, as the humans have instructed."

Huck makes an annoyed sound and I turn to face him, waiting for his commentary. "I don't know about y'all, but it chaps my ass to do all this simpering bullshit. Being from the South, I'm fairly good at hidin' my disdain behind a thin veneer of politeness, but I'm fairly certain this is going to stretch that."

"It definitely is," Sydney mutters bitterly. "I'm *not* good at masking how much these people disgust me. I admit, I'm worried about how well I'm going to survive when cameras are actively following us rather than just sidestepping the Enforcement Zones."

The bell dings, and Rory holds the doors open as we all file out, heading for our suite. He squints at the other end of the hallway curiously. "Don't you guys wonder who's at the other end? And how they're hosting all these teams but some have what are obviously nicer accommodations?"

"It crossed my mind," Sebastian says as he swipes us into the room. "My assumption was that the tests they conducted to pair teams lead to a presumptive ranking that determined where each was placed and who they received as their coordinator."

"That means Krista is likely a top-tier coach," Thad says, his voice full of surprise. "Damn."

Sydney strides into the room, her braid whipping behind her as she makes a frustrated sound. "And we'll *have* to listen to her, then. Fuck me."

Rory opens his mouth and I shoot him a death glare to keep him from adding the stress. "Yes, we will."

"*That* chaps my ass," the vampire says drily. "She makes my fangs ache."

"Finally something we agree on." Sydney turns to look at us as the door shuts. "Now I'm going to get my shit and shower first again. You should consider that standard operating procedure. Once I'm out, we can talk about dinner."

"Who made you the Queen of the Bite Club?"

She gives Sebastian a baleful look, shaking her head. "The vagina I was born with, blood sucker. Now be a good little boy and toddle off with the rest of them until I'm done."

I have to smother a chuckle at his outraged expression as she exits to her room on that line, slamming the door behind her. "You heard her, fang face. Move it along."

Rolling his eyes, the overgrown mosquito does as instructed—likely because he knows I could take him without breaking a sweat. Vampires don't have a lot of competition among the supes except mythicals and the Fae. Their fancy tricks work on shifters and humanoids like magic users, but Fae blood is a drug to them and mythicals have powers that come directly from the gods. The lesser supes do as well, but it's been diluted for so long that the power shift between rare races and more common ones is significant. That *might* be part of why we ranked so highly—a demon and a dragon, plus a wild card like Sydney, make our team an especially tough bet.

I look at the others as we settle in to wait for her, considering the possibilities. Thaddeus is pure brawn with smarts, and his bear will be fast once it gets moving. He'll make an excellent tank to clear the field. As a vampire, Sebastian will have the usual speed, strength, and bite, but depending on his lineage, he could have a wide array of powers in addition. It makes him a good 'Swiss Army knife' of competitors. I don't know how vast Stormbringer's magic is—which will need to change—but he will make an excellent long range, 'area of effect' player. My own powers lie in flight, water, magic, and armor, plus many unknown royal traits that will be useful. But Sydney… she's the real question mark. If she unleashes something powerful, it will tip the scales entirely.

"We should discuss strategy tonight once we are clean. Knowing what powers we possess before they put us in the supe arena is crucial. It would be very much in step with the humans' behavior to drop us in a scrimmage battle with lax rules to see what we can do. Without knowing what we are holding back, we may give them their own ideas about how the challenges should go."

And I'm not willing to allow those motherfuckers to put their fingers on the scales of justice once again.

I'M DYING HERE

SYDNEY

THE MINUTE the entire group is done showering, we gather in the main living area of our suite. It's quiet as Thad orders our food, but as soon as he hangs up, the silence gets even thicker. There's no trust built up yet; however, we're going to have to share basics about our powers before it becomes a public discussion. That's making the atmosphere tense as everyone retreats to their corners except for my two friends and me.

Finally, I can't take it anymore so I throw my hands up. "Look, I know we've all learned to keep secrets and protect ourselves because of the fucking humans. This is different; we don't have a choice. At some point, our lives are going to depend on having one another's backs. We can't do that if we don't know what anyone is capable of."

"I'm a bear, Syd. They know what I can do," Thad says with a half-hearted smile. "Shift, half-shift, tear things up. We move fast once we get going and are like a tank."

Sebastian snorts, giving him an annoyed expression. "It's easy for you to admit your strengths because bears don't have anything that's hidden."

"True, but I have the balls to admit that as well. I don't see you giving us a clue about what the fuck your kind actually can and cannot do."

Thad's quick retort makes me grin; I'm proud of him for standing up to the traitorous fuckwad. "You guys know I'm supposed to have some kind of magic and I don't remember or know what my mom was. I might get shit; I might not. We have to operate as if my skills call mostly towards hand-to-hand and weapons without magic for the moment."

"Again, duh."

I'm about to eviscerate that motherfucker when Rory steps forward, stopping me from speaking as he holds his hand up. "Okay, okay. I can see this will be a contest of wills and my willpower has never been great. I'm a mage, I have demi blood a little ways back and I'm able to do pretty much anything you assume mages can do, plus more. I don't have to chant to cast, and I don't need a focus item like a wand or some shit. I'm a pure magical and I have no problem using it or myself to get what I need to survive."

That's pretty goddamn interesting, and it explains why the humans have kept him like a pet. His skill set is useful in a fucking million ways from death to seduction, and he's probably never revealed the entire breadth of what he can do to them, either. His admission doesn't actually cover all of his power, but it gives us enough to work with. I'm okay with him keeping a bit in reserve for now.

"Well, I s'pose I should pony up, since the other two seem to be holdin' their cards close." Huck pushes his hat back, sighing heavily. "Y'all know I'm a fear demon an' everything that goes along with that. I've lived for a long time an' picked up a lot of tricks over that time from demons and other supes alike. Lil' bit of magic, lil' bit of mimicry, lil' bit of that sweet cross-roads persuasion… but fear is my main talent. I can get through damn near any mental shield or spell designed to keep me out if I have enough time."

Sebastian arches a brow, looking at him cynically. Huck gives him a slow, wicked grin before blowing a kiss at the vampire. His face goes even paler and he plasters himself to the wall, but his expression turns to fury until Huck chuckles. My demon friend must release his hold because the color comes back to Bas's cheeks as he cracks his neck. "Fine. You're not lying."

"I'm a lot less impressed by the mosquito and more impressed by the demon now," Elias says. "I'm a royal of the sea dragons, so that's saying something."

"Want to clue us in, oh royal one?" I ask drily. "You and the traitor are the last two to go."

He gives me an annoyed look, but nods. "Water. I can control, mutate, pull it from the air… whatever. The wind bends to my will. I can fly when not locked down and transform both half-way and fully. My dragon and I can breathe in liquid, plus expel watery blasts in various temperatures. There's more, but that's probably good for now."

Blinking, I tilt my head. "Can you breathe a hot shower?"

Thad snorts, then starts laughing hysterically. He clutches his sides as he elbows Huck, and they both snicker together as I scowl. Elias, however, looks confused as hell at their mirth. The dragon clears his throat, then turns to me. "I could, yes. That seems like a fairly simple thing to be impressed by, though."

Huck wipes his eyes, then shrugs. "Syd has been angrier at the lack of hot showers in her place because of shitty maintenance than she is about being in the camps sometimes. It's her one fucking luxury demand—not that it should be a luxury, mind—but she's very serious about how important that fact is."

Annoyed, I wave my hand at my friends. "Fine. Yes, I like a hot damn shower, and no, we don't always have hot water in this fucking hellhole. So yeah, that made me a bit excited. I don't ask for much, guys. Can we move on?"

Elias gives me a smirk, then nods at the vampire. "I believe he's the last man standing."

"Not a man," the idiot grumbles and I mock a frown.

"Wait, you're not?" My eyes dance as I pretend to be shocked. "I'd *love* another girl here. The big dick energy is killing me, especially since none of it is as big as mine."

"For fucks' sake…I'm a *male*; don't be ridiculous, human." Sebastian rolls his eyes as if I'm the biggest pain in the ass he's ever met. "I mean, I'm not a man; I'm a vampire. I can do normal vampire things, plus the extra gifts those of us from ancient lines have picked up over the centuries. Our line is very gifted with telepathic abilities, but also we're…supremely difficult to eliminate."

We're all quiet for a moment as we digest that statement.

Did he just admit to being immortal?

When the doorbell dings, Thad jumps up to get the food from the stupid robot thing and we breathe a sigh of relief. The conversation has been fairly heavy since the traitorous bloodsucker admitted his non-fatal flaw. We all had to at least hint at our greatest weaknesses, which for me is embarrassing as shit, because mine is enormous. I'm powerless in terms of supe shit and I'm going to be the first target everyone aims for.

Why the fuck my shit refuses to pop out, I don't know, and I'd like to beat the shit out of my cowardly mother for taking off.

"It has to be her fault," I mutter to myself as Thad brings the bags of food into the living room. He sits them on the table, looking at me with sharp criticism in his eyes. "I know; I know. I can't blame someone I know jack shit about."

"What's this about? The happy couple are fighting?"

I look at the chopsticks Thad just handed me and consider how hard I'd have to throw one to embed it in the nasty little vampiric shit's neck. He wouldn't die, but it would hurt, and I'd feel a great deal of satisfaction.

"Down, girl," Rory says as he walks over to grab his containers. "It will only make him more annoying as he removes them, then milks the injury to his pride for all it's worth."

He's not the fucking mindbender; how'd he know?

"You look particularly vicious right now… Vicious," the mage says with a knowing smirk. "It wasn't a magical leap, only a logical one."

"He's right, sweet pea. You were telegraphing your intent with your laser focus on his jugular and the tight grip on the chopsticks." Huck tucks his fingers into the pockets of his dark denim and shrugs. "Gotta watch those visual cues. Not everyone can read them, but when you run into people like me or others with emotion-based powers, we can."

I glare at the demon as I unwrap the wooden sticks. "Why the fuck haven't you told me this before?"

"Because you don't like to hear that you have flaws other than the magic thing and it wasn't important until now."

Damn him for being right. I can't even stay mad.

"Fine."

Thad blinks as he hands Elias his food, then takes the smaller cooler bag to Sebastian. "I'll be damned. You're mellowing with age, Syd. You hate admitting when you're wrong."

"I think everyone dislikes that," the dragon says as he settles into the big chair at the far end of our gathering spot. "I believe I was right to continue the fight against the humans, but many of my people think I should have followed them into the sea to hide from them. They think I abandoned my throne to help supernaturals who weren't even dragons, instead of focusing on our kingdom. Perhaps they're right—I can admit that now. But admitting it doesn't mean I regret what I did, just that I recognize their perceptions aren't inaccurate."

That's a lot of words for him, especially in a row. I think about it for a moment, then nod. "Sometimes, we do the right thing for the right reasons, but others don't agree with us. They make us the villain in their stories because they need one. It can be because they can't look in the mirror to assign blame where it belongs or because there isn't a clear villain, only a breadth of bad choices that no one liked."

"Exactly," Sebastian says as he stalks toward the kitchen to heat up his dinner. "A bouquet of bad options leads to a lot of assumptions from people not directly involved in a situation."

Is he trying to say that's what happened to the vamps? I don't believe him.

"The mosquito's right," Rory says from his spot on the floor. "When all the options are ugly, you make the best choice you can and hope like hell you survive it. Sometimes, you have to make that decision over and over until it doesn't bother you anymore."

Thad bumps my shoulder with his and I wrinkle my nose. He knows I need to throw in my two cents to help and I kind of hate him for making me. "My dad made what I think was a stupid choice to help the stupid meatbags and I still haven't forgiven him for it. I'm trying, but every day we spend in this place makes it harder. So maybe winning this fucking thing will… let me do that."

"We all have our darkness," Huck says as he squeezes my knee. "You, sweet pea, are doing your best just like the rest of us. It was only a matter of time before humans subjugated another race—the timing led to it being supes, but it could have been damn near anyone. Your dad wasn't the only being fooled by their platitudes."

Sebastian walks in with a large mug that he's blowing over, and shrugs as he looks at me. "You're also not the only one with daddy issues—not in history, nor in this room. The dragon has a savior complex, so it definitely came from living up to his father's legacy. Demons all have authority issues stemming from their creation and daddy rejection. The bear is lacking one and helping to fill in as one, mine is objectively megalomaniacal, and I'd wager Mr. Sparkle Pants over there is a child of divorce with adultery. Just a guess, but vampires hunt through profiling, so we're pretty good at it."

Everyone makes a noise of protest, but the vampire doesn't let it stop him as he makes his way to his chair.

That jackass just ripped the band-aid off everyone in the room's wounds and is sipping his blood like it's English Breakfast—no wonder people hate their kind.

ALWAYS A PUNCHING BAG, NEVER A BOXER

SEBASTIAN

THEY ALL LOOK at me in shock, but as one of the most hated supe races in this society, I can be a lot more objective than they can. It's easy to see from the outside looking in—their rebellion isn't driven simply by 'social justice', no matter how much they've convinced themselves that it is. The supernaturals who are the closest to human—magic users—were the most naive when it came to the regime change that landed us all here. Since they could 'pass', they believed they'd be able to hide in plain sight if anything went wrong, so they trusted the wrong people.

Vampires knew better. Being undead always made us the most human-like of the darker supernaturals, which led to being second class citizens even within the minority groups. Our leaders saw the writing on walls as we always have when the capricious and moronic beings that control this spinning rock turned on those who weren't like them. I don't agree with their decision and never have, even as a child, but I understand why they chose to ally with the inevitable dictators. We were all destined to be subjugated, but at least our people are the least uncomfortable of all the races now.

The most trusting and altruistic of the supes are the ones suffering more than they ever anticipated and it's why vampires made that choice.

"Look—"

Sydney pops to her feet with an angry expression. "I don't want to hear this bullshit from a *traitor*. Your kind are why we're here, Sebastian."

The venom in her voice is no different than what I usually get outside of the closed off undead communities, and I'm not shocked in the least. But she needs to grow up and face the truth—they all do if we're going to survive this shit. It's not something my kind likes to share, but there's a lot of reality these assholes have to face.

"I'm going to tell you things that will definitely get me killed if it goes beyond these walls at this time. You can believe me or not, but I assure you, this is one hundred percent verifiable if you know the right people with the right access. All I ask is that you let me say my piece before you interrupt. Can you at least do that?"

Thad tilts his head, studying me for a moment, then sniffs the air. He shrugs and looks at the demon and their girl, then nods. "I can; I suppose."

"Whatever."

I watch as the girl all our lives are tied to stomps to the couch and drops down in between her safety men. My eyes flit to the mage and the dragon, waiting for them to respond. I'm not worried about the demon; he's likely heard all of this well before now, but was smart enough to keep his mouth shut. The Cubi vacillate between his species and mine; they gossip like no other beings. My story won't shock the good ol' boy even a little bit.

"Speak your piece," Elias says gruffly. "But I will stop you if need be. I do not agree to allow you to abuse anyone."

That makes the half-blond girl perk up slightly and I roll my eyes before arching a brow at Stormbringer. "And you?"

He shrugs. "I'm flexible enough to give you a chance to dig your own grave."

Not surprising—he's likely flexible enough for a lot *of things.*

I have to fight to keep the smirk off my face at my own cleverness, but I nod at them. "Good. You're not going to believe what I say at first—most of you, at least—but I urge you to take the time to let it sink before you decide I'm lying. I assure you, lying would gain me nothing and telling you all this information puts my own ass at risk. I'd rather not, but it seems I must if I would like to stay undead."

Sydney glares, crossing her arms over her chest. "Just spit it out, bloodsucker."

I ignore her tone again as I gather my thoughts. "Vampires, and to an extent, demons and other hellspawn, are pragmatists. We have always been considered lesser by the bulk of the supes and their power structure because we were not originally *born* as supernaturals. Many current lines are full of vampires and dhampirs who were, but our beginnings were not the same as magic users or shifters. We are the 'other' of all 'others'. Thus, we have a very unique perspective about humans and their behavior."

"You're scavengers," she mutters under her breath.

Rolling my eyes, I shake my head. "First of all, we are *not* and I am aware you're not stupid, Sydney. We don't pick the bones of the dead like vultures. We feed on live sources who we turn if we feel it's advantageous to us or our species. No one is drinking the blood of the dead in non-war times."

"He's telling the truth about that," Huck interjects. "I've been around long enough to know the vamps are far pickier about the temp of their food unless supply is cut off. Hell, I s'pose they even did a good job of using willing donors through various businesses before the sweeps."

"Correct," I say with a nod of approval. "We learned in the Victorian era that it behooved us to keep our kills necessary and not draw attention to the supernatural world when humans started creating their own public media about us. Stoker and Shelley are to blame, but that's simply survival smarts."

Thad grunts, shifting his big bulk to let Sydney lean against him sullenly. "Okay, what does that have to do with our current situation?"

"It means we have been watching hatred of 'other' develop in those beings ever since—even of their own kind for the stupidest of reasons. They were willing to enslave their own, kill each other for meaningless beliefs, and subjugate large swaths of their own species with no compunction. Huck will tell you that their idea of 'Hell' is beyond inaccurate, as the only humans there are ones who had dealings with his kind. It's all a big con and has been since the dawn of their existence. The angels will confirm the same."

"Indeed," the demon says with a rueful grin. "We don't want them in our space anymore than the sparkling ones, but we take what we're owed. The only humans in our kingdom are ones who are serving their sentences per their agreements."

Sydney frowns. "Does everyone know that? Because it feels like they don't."

I chuckle. "Of course not. Letting the humans police their own shit with their dumb rules has helped supes survive in the shadows for millenia. You know the leaders have had a policy of non-intervention unless their idiocy will affect us. That doesn't mean all the 'heads of state', as it were, aren't watching them carefully. However, vampires and demons have always been keeping a *much* more cynical eye on the state of affairs there. We have never trusted them to do anything that will benefit themselves or us."

"Fair," Stormbringer says with a shrug. "My experience with them is vast and they are troublesome. They have no self-awareness; often, the very thing they decry is what they desire the most. Instead of embracing it and being happy, they bark bullshit and make themselves miserable. It's all service of the things Whitmore mentioned."

"You would know, I suppose," I drawl and he blanches. Sighing, I shake my head. "That was unnecessary and I apologize. I cannot cast stones at the other species who have done what they have to in order to get through this nightmare anymore than they should at most of my people."

"Most?" Elias rumbles.

When he doesn't expound, I nod. "Yes, most, and that is where my tale is going. As I said, the hellspawn species have been monitoring them more closely. They communicate with each other more than the rest of the supes speak with us, and the consensus since the humans in this country fought an entire war over enslaving their own kind was that we cannot trust them—ever. They are too easily led by their emotions—particularly fear—and it would be stupid to reveal ourselves to them. Supernaturals, despite their powers, would be the next target for them to place blame on for their woes, just as they do any faction of their own who is not homogenous."

"Demons also felt that way, which is why we increased our presence above, tempting as many of them into eternal servitude as possible. It fed our needs and helped trim the population," Huck agrees. "Not my thing, of course, because I can be fat an' happy like a hog on butcher day simply by using those feelings against them."

"Is this why the vampire numbers decreased for a few decades before the virus?" Sydney asks softly. "I remember my dad always saying that the vampires were planning something but no one knew what because they were becoming very insular."

"Your dad was a blood watcher?"

She has the grace to duck her head when she nods. That word isn't as filthy as some of the others used to denote vampire racists in the supe community, but it gets the meaning across. Her shame tells me she's only spewing hate about my kind because of their connection to the sweeps, not because she hates us for existing.

For some reason, that feels comforting and hopeful at the same time.

"We can't control the bad deeds our parents wrought. I believe that and I hope when I finish my story, you will as well." I pause, reorganizing my thought train before I continue. "So, yes, we stopped turning new vampires to prevent their hate in our community and bred more, despite the risks and long gestation times. We wanted new blood that was not tainted by human experience so our rank and file did not get as out of control as they are."

Thad blinks, then looks at me. "The bears did it, too. Many ursa leaders quietly forbid any sexual interaction with humans and have since I was old enough to understand. They cautioned us heartily as young bears."

"Demons forbid it like the mosquitoes," Huck adds nonchalantly. "They've been verboten since that Italian pretended to 'discover' this land. It's why we were only surface level for business most of the time."

Sydney frowns, looking at Stormbringer. "Magic users didn't, right?"

His smile is apologetic. "They did, but they didn't tell us why. It was poorly policed in some parts of the world like the US, where the supes typically mocked closed supe communities for being 'anti-inclusion' because they chose not to allow the beings who would hate us inside. In other parts of the world, the supernaturals were much more cautious about human interaction."

"That's probably why…"

The sentence trails off and I sigh. Definitely opening up more than one wound for our center tonight. She's going to hate me for a long time after this. "Yes, it's probably why your mother disappeared after you were born. She knew your father would have a much more difficult time raising you if people understood that you were part human. Whatever else she was likely didn't have a very accepting community and she was on her own, living outside of it."

"You think one of her parents was human and broke a law, then was cast out."

Dante saves me by saying, "Yes. Whitmore's theory makes sense. There are many powerful supernatural communities—like mine—who would not have abided that behavior as it would bring danger to our whole species. Your mother was a product of an ill-advised union and had no support. She left to protect you, it seems."

The room is quiet for a moment as Sydney sucks in a huge breath, closing her eyes and staying very still for a few moments. When her eyes open again, there's no trace of the emotion that was on her face prior.

"Finish your tale, vampire. Our food is getting cold and this night has become very tiring."

Shutting down is never a good sign, but they have to know—I'm certain of it.

THE VAMPS BEHIND THE CURTAIN

SYDNEY

I DON'T WANT to feel bad for Sebastian because his kind left the other supernaturals to fend for themselves. Even if the vampires believed humans to be dangerous and untrustworthy, they aided them in rounding up all the other species in this country. They've all been living a *much better standard* of living than damn near everyone else as a result. It's not that they're out lending a hand to the suffering, either.

Vampires only care about their own, and often, not even that.

"When the virus hit, the Council had months of talks about what to do while the humans ran around fighting their own safety measures. Many supe races felt if they were too stupid to heed their own doctors, we shouldn't intervene with our magic or more specialized technologies to save them. After all, many species go extinct on this floating rock and humans have been one of the biggest causes of that. Why not let nature cleanse the planet on her own?"

Rory rubs the back of his neck as he gives me a sheepish look. "Magic users and Fae definitely subscribed to that philosophy in large numbers in the US. They were overridden by the large numbers of overseas contingents who work more closely with the populace."

"Demons agreed that they would either save themselves or end up fulfilling their bargain, so we didn't support the movement to reveal ourselves."

I groan, looking up at the ceiling with a heavy sigh. "As much as I despise them now, I would have argued with you before the camps. My father was part of the revelation movement immediately because he thought if everything was in the open, it would make us safer in the end."

The vampire arches a brow. "Didn't work out like that, did it?"

"You know it didn't," I growl softly. "Most of the early supporters of the Unveiling were killed in the First Sweeps by *your* kind."

He has the grace to look regretful, at least. After he scratches his chin, he rakes his teeth over his lower lip. I have a feeling I'm not going to like the next part of his tale. "Yes, they were. When the dissenting factions were overruled and the Unveiling was televised, it became clear to the vampiric elders around the world that it was an enormous mistake. If you remember, for a small amount of time, the humans who were saved with supernatural methods sang our praises."

"They did," Thad says softly. "I remember singing on TV and all these hospitals bragging about their supe workers doing miraculous inter-ventions."

Sebastian nods. "But the virus spread too quickly in the most densely populated cities and the death count climbed due to Taterman's rhetoric… The tide turned on us all very quickly. His claim that *we* brought the virus in to get rid of the humans took the internet by storm. Within mere weeks, the world was on fire with infected humans and the anti-supe sentiment climbed. By the time that fool seemed to have this country fooled, my people were done with waiting."

"So you abandoned *everyone*? Women, children, elderly… all of them were killed in botched raids and in the first camps. How do you even sleep at night?"

His gaze narrows and he whips his head to glare at me. "I barely sleep and it's not because I'm a vampire *or* because there were casualties of choices made by other species who outnumbered my own."

Ooookay, then. I hit a sore spot.

"Your trauma isn't mine to ask for, but I get it."

We all look at Dante and he shrugs. "The timbre of his voice when he lashed out spoke of a deep, wrenching agony in his soul. None of us know him well enough to demand it be revealed, so I will honor his privacy until it is necessary to our survival."

"You're surprisingly emotionally intelligent for a storm dragon," Sebas-tian says, looking impressed. "Your kind are brash and blunt, with no use for touchy-feely emotional shit."

The dragon rolls his eyes. "We would all be better off if we disposed of the stereotypes our communities, the humans, and the media have portrayed other supernaturals as. Much of it is based on bias and misinformation. Dragons are no less emotional than any other kind; don't be an idiot."

Pinching the bridge of my nose, I squeeze my eyes shut briefly then nod in agreement. "That's probably a good idea. I have a lot of baggage from my insulated, myopic father to shed, and I'm sure everyone else does, too. We can't work together if we don't put all that shit in the trash and start fresh."

"Syd, that's the best thing you've said all day. I'm proud of you, sweet pea," Huck tips his hat at me and I ignore the flutter in my stomach at his praise and handsome grin.

I hate when he does that good old boy Southern shit; it makes me feel so damn weird.

"I'd be happy to, if you're still willing after this part," Sebastian says. He waits for me to nod at him, and then continues. "As I said, our elders realized that this Pandora's box couldn't be resealed. Perhaps many years in the past, as we had in Europe when one of our kind rose to fame, but not in this global media age. Supernaturals were going to be hunted, as humans do when they scapegoat a race for their ails, and we had to decide what we would do to keep our people alive. The answer was simple to the oldest vamps—we would join the humans' side and infiltrate their ranks by pretending to be on their side."

"*Wait a damned minute,*" Thad snarls as he lets go of my hand and leans forward. "If that was true, they wouldn't have joined the sweeps and killed people left and right. Stop trying to rewrite history so Sydney will like you."

"For fuck's sake, Calvin, let me finish!" The grouchy vampire rakes his hands through his hair, pushing off the wall to pace across the floor as he speaks. "I'm not saying we were heroes—though, I suspect the original intent of the vampiric conclave who made the decision was exactly that. However, as with every governing body, the wealthiest of the covens figured out how extremely profitable it was to ingratiate ourselves with the humans. The plan for the sweeps came along and instead of doing what I truly believe the elders planned to do—hide supes across the country—the local coven heads sent their enforcers and criminals to eliminate the threats to their money flow."

I blink, looking at him in surprise. "You think they wanted to Anne Frank supes, but the rich dudes decided to kill anyone who might succeed in convincing humans to free us?"

"Yes."

I fall back against the couch, my expression dumbstruck. The difference between what Sebastian knows and what the supernatural world knows is vast. "But… Why wouldn't the elders tattle on them? Why not out the bad actors and redeem your kind? Why let it go on?"

"Because the billionaire assholes—including my father—entombed them before they could."

"*What?!*"

Huck's incredulity shocks everyone. Since I have no idea what that means beyond simple extrapolation, I wait for someone to explain. The demon shivers a bit, wiggling in his seat before he turns to look at me. "Some supe species' elders are so fucking old that you can't really *kill* them. Djinns, bloodsuckers, some demon types, demi-gods, Fae.. lotta those kinds of folk. They're basically immortal once they hit certain ages and the only way to 'defeat' them is to pull a Poe on 'em."

"Like… Amontillado?" I squeak. "Wall them up somewhere *alive* and let them suffer forever?"

"On the nose, sweet pea. It's the worst non-death I can imagine and I've seen a *lot* of torture in Hell. Entombing someone also means you have to make sure no dumbfuck stumbles on the site and opens it like in that Egyptian movie. What was that the twins stole, Thad?"

"The Mummy," the bear says. "Damn fine flick even if the humans don't know their asses from their elbows."

I remember watching that when the speckled bear twins in Thad's sleuth got a hold of it—everyone in it was beautiful.

"Best movie for realizing you're bi in the entire human catalog," Sebastian chuckles as he lands in one spot and leans on the wall again. "But you're right; it's drivel mostly."

None of this is helpful and I need them to get back on track. The way Rory is looking at the others in interest is making me oddly flushed. "Okay, fine. Your father is part of the actual evil villain vamps, but most of them… are not?"

"Not willingly," he replies softly. "Coven leaders and sires have a great deal of power over vampires in their groups, especially childer. Whether by birth or by bite, your sire—and by extension all the way to the first one still living—can force you to do damn near anything they want. Our power structure is very… primal. Since the camps, covens are now geographically based and new residents *must* swear allegiance to the leader when they're transferred in. If they don't, they won't live long."

"So fucked up," Rory mutters.

"Are you saying the magic folk don't force their kind to do rituals for similar reasons, Stormbringer?"

The question is valid and the blond mage sighs. "Yeah, they do. But it doesn't give them like… mind powers over the newbies. Your people enslave each other as much as the humans do."

"Demons also—"

"Leave us out of this!"

"Fuck, guys, this isn't helping—"

Pushing to my feet, I take a deep breath then shout, "*Shut. Up!*"

Everyone stops, looking at me with wide eyes. I wait for them all to put away whatever damn fangs or claws they were sprouting, then I put my hands on my hips as I glare at them. "We will lose if we keep doing this. That's what they want, right? They've got powerful dudes with a useless girl in a mixed group that will be a golden cow for their audiences to watch fall apart and get sacrificed in the first round. They *want* us to fail even when we shouldn't based on power and skills."

The guys frown, looking at one another for a moment before finally Huck braves the silence. "Syd's right. There's a lot of same species teams in this camp and they purposefully brought y'all and many others to fill in the gaps. Those motherfuckers are stackin' the decks on this thing and they're hopin' like hell to have fireworks within the mixed teams so they get ratings. That's why there's all this media shit being set up for us."

Thank fuck someone gets it.

"Sebastian, if what you're saying is true, why hasn't the Council intervened?"

His laugh is dry as he gives me a pitying look. "Sydney, the Councils outside of the FSHA haven't been allowed to speak with those inside the borders for four years. They don't *know* how bad it is here and the ones here? Either the leaders have gone to ground to avoid capture or they've been sent to lockdown sections of camps like Stormbringer so their kind can't revolt. Those too powerful to put amongst others are kept in a secret prison somewhere in the southern states."

"A secret prison? Is that where the elders are entombed?" Thad asks, looking shocked. "Like… all of them?"

"Maybe," the vampire shrugs. "I only know as much as either my father has admitted to me directly or what I've picked up in meetings—whether by eavesdropping or being in attendance. I'm fairly certain the vampires in charge have contacts amongst other supernaturals. They're making too much money and living too comfortably to care what happens to the 'rabble' at this point. Accepting the humans' ridiculous restrictions doesn't make a lot of difference when you're perfectly comfortable in your mansions, fat and happy, now does it?"

My entire world view has just flipped upside down and I have absolutely no idea how I'm going to process this—damn that fucking vampire back to Hell.

NOT A SLUMBER PARTY

RORY

OUR FEISTY CENTER deflated after the vampire's tale. She took her untouched food and retired to her room alone, much to the dismay of the bear and the demon. After she left, the dragon and the demon threatened Sebastian, then we all parted ways. The uneasy vibe in the room from our realization is hanging around necks like an anchor dragging us to the bottom of Dante's oceans. Surmising that the most ancient leaders of any or all the various supe species in this country are being held in an unknown prison in an unknown location pretty much destroys the hope that someone will save us someday.

If you ask me, that just means we have to save ourselves and this stupid game is the way to do it.

I push the food I barely nibbled on away and roll to my feet. The rest of those assholes might be licking their wounds, but I've made certain I thrive in this depressing reality by pivoting. My life since capture hasn't been sunshine and roses, but it has been better than the people in the camps who gave up trying. The key is having goals and being willing to sacrifice every-thing for them—even your own safety or dignity. That's what I've done and our team needs to do some fucking version of it so we win this goddamn thing.

Walking over to the mirror, I check my reflection to make sure I don't have something in my teeth or shit on my face. I'm going to convince Sydney that we need to use our forced participation for more than gaining our freedom to live in some swank community. We need to use it to get to that place so we can do *more*.

I blink at my reflection, confused at my train of thought. It's not like me to worry about what happens to anyone but me. My entire life, I've never known anyone who wasn't entirely out for themselves and I always act accordingly. Why am I suddenly acting like I'm one of those do-good savior-types? My frown deepens as I spritz myself with the cologne on the dresser and step back.

I don't know what's happening to me or why, but it's weird as hell.

~

The sound of my fist knocking on her door is followed by a loud, annoyed sigh inside. My lips quirk up at the corner as I listen to Sydney stomping across the floor of her room to yank the door open with a scowl.

"Was there something unclear about 'I want to be alone' or are you just dense?"

Giving her the most charming smile I have, I tilt my head. "No, you were clear. However, you couldn't possibly have meant to exclude me. I have the absolute strongest shoulders to lean on when you're sad."

She snorts. "I believe Thad and Elias have you beat there, Mr. Wizard."

I pretend to pout, making sure I wedge my foot in the door so she can't slam it closed. "Perhaps, though for a non-shifter, I'm very well defined. You can't deny that."

"I can deny anything I want, Stormbringer. Why are you here?"

My dick twitches and I realize I enjoy the hell out of her taking me to task; who knew?

"I'm here to be supportive, just like I said." Biting my lower lip, I employ the big eyed beautiful man tactics that have served me well since the Sweeps. "My experiences since they tossed us in camps have been full of shock and upheavals, unlike your boyfriends or the prisoners. I can relate to this feeling and commiserate a little."

Her eyes narrow and she crosses her arms over her chest as she seethes. Suddenly, I'm very aware that she shed her outer layer, revealing tanned skin in a white tank top. Her long blondish-brown hair is hanging over her shoulders in loose waves from the braid she had it pinned back in all day. Other than her expression, this is the most vulnerable I've seen Sydney look since they paired us together. It makes me itch to touch her, but I'm not going to do it in the hallway.

"Rory, I'm not going to fall for your charming rogue bullshit. I've been friends with Huck for too long to let a pretty smile and long lashes distract me."

So she has *noticed how good looking her companions are. Interesting.*

"I'm not trying to distract you, Vicious. I want to… you know, empathize with you or whatever." Planting my palm on the door, I give it a little push to test the waters, and when she lets it open further my gut clenches.

Sighing heavily, she rolls her eyes. "You're not going away unless I humor you, right?"

"Smart girl," I reply with another bright smile then motion with my hands. "I promise I won't be a dick while I'm here."

"Somehow, I don't believe you," she says as she turns on her heel, leaving me to follow her inside. "Close it behind you, though. I'd don't want this to become a fucking slumber party."

Fuck, yeah. I got her to let me in.

"Understood. Sometimes, that many guys in the room can be… overwhelming." I shut the door and walk in, looking around for a place to land.

Sydney drops onto her bed, tucking her legs into some sort of pretzel as she looks up at me. "You can sit on the other side if you behave."

Rounding the end of her bed, I arch a brow. "What happens if I don't?"

The knife she flicks open seems to come out of nowhere, pressing against my spine as I pause halfway to sitting next to her. "Oh. Well, that's uncalled for."

"I don't often mince words, Rory, nor do I set unclear boundaries." Her blue eyes are dark as she says that and I wonder how many times that resolve has been tested. She pulls back, and the knife disappears as I join her on the bed.

Leaning back against the headboard, I get settled then look over at her. "That stuff from earlier put you on the reality tilt-a-whirl, huh?"

Sydney looks down at her hands, shrugging. "Sort of. I think realizing I've been sticking my head in the sand by accepting the stuff my dad told me before he died as truth was worse. I thought I knew exactly how everything worked and what wrongs I'd suffered. But…"

"But what?" I ask softly.

"My father taught me a lot of things that weren't exactly the truth, I think. He must have been more resentful of my mother's situation than I knew and that must have gotten worse with The Unveiling." She chews on her lip, then pushes her finger through her long locks as she lets out a long breath. "My behavior since I was thrown in the camps has probably been shitty and self-centered because I was so damn ignorant. I hate knowing that."

That's why she's upset? Because she might have been insensitive to a bunch of people she doesn't even know?

"Vicious, I'm gonna be gentle when I say this but… get over yourself." Her gasp and frown almost makes me laugh, but I keep it together so I can finish. "Look, you probably *were* an asshat to people. Who cares? You didn't know any better and even if you were as big a dick as Whitmore, it doesn't matter. It only makes a difference if you hurt the ones you care about. If you did that, then apologize and move on."

Her nose wrinkles adorably and I feel my entire body tense up. This hard shelled woman has a completely different side if you get her when her guard is down. "What if they don't understand? What if they don't accept my apology?"

"That's a risk you have to take when you admit to doing shit wrong." I roll to my side, reaching up to brush a lock of hair out of her face. "I know I'm not mad at you for being such a pill since we met. I'm used to people judging me for the choices I've made to keep myself alive and comfortable. It makes ignoring judgmental dumbasses pretty easy."

"I am not a judgmental dumbass!" Sydney sits up, her face flushing as I watch the shell reappear.

I am dancing around a minefield and this is not exactly my forte.—I should have brought alcohol.

"Look, Sydney. I'm here to listen and commiserate, but I won't sugar coat shit. Apparently, enough people have been doing that."

"Damn," she mutters, kicking her foot on the bed petulantly. "You got me there. Huck and Thad haven't ever tried to correct me, but they had to know. Well, Huck did, for sure. I don't know about Thad."

Nodding as I wait for her to relax again, I ask, "Are you going to apologize to the blood sucker? The dragon?"

Her snort makes me chuckle, but before I can chide her, Sydney nods. "Yeah. I mean, I've acted like Elias was a fucking dirty criminal and you were a whore. I was too rough on Sebastian because of my dad's prejudice and ignorance, too. It doesn't make me feel like a good person."

This time, I wrinkle my nose, looking sheepish. "Well… you weren't totally wrong, Vicious. I've done a lot of shit I don't want to shout to the heavens about to get what I wanted. Some of it I consented to more than other things, and I don't think it's shameful as much as I prefer to keep my choices private. I wouldn't say prostitute—even though that's totally fine— but I definitely developed what I'd call 'sponsors'. But that's about as much as I'm ready to discuss with you right now, if that's okay."

The silence hangs in the air as her features soften in a way I've only seen happen when the demon and bear comfort her. Very slowly, Sydney lifts her hand and places it on mine. "Rory, I was being a nasty, sanctimonious bitch. The camps are awful, everyone is terrified when they arrive, and people make decisions they don't want to in order to survive. I didn't realize I'd been using some sort of litmus test to decide who was worthy when we're *all* victims of this regime."

Holy shit. She's touching and asking for my forgiveness.

Suddenly, I realize this isn't what I came here to talk about, but that doesn't matter. No one has ever heard this much of my truth without being *more* disgusted rather than less. "You were, and we are. So I forgive you and I'm pretty sure everyone else will, too. It's obvious you're meant to be the leader of this circus and to do that, we have to keep letting each other in."

"Fuck," she mutters as she leans back against the headboard, too. "I'm not good at… emotional things. Dad trained me on strategy, fighting, and tried to get me to use magic, but he didn't give me a lot in the way of social graces."

I smirk at her, arching a brow. "You know who's pretty good at that shit, right?"

"Uh, everyone but me?"

Laughing, I shake my head. "No, I am. Whitmore, too, I suppose. Maybe even the—okay, everyone but you."

Her hand shoots out to sock me in the gut, the speed amazing as her fist makes contact. Grunting at the force, I rub the spot with a pout. "Damn, Vicious. I think you're actually getting faster. That's insane."

"Don't make fun of me, Stormbringer."

"Fine, but that means you have to stop being so mean to me when I lighten the mood. That's *my* way of using emotional intelligence to smooth shit, by the way."

She gives me a small smile, rolling her eyes again, but I can feel the change in her mood. "Sure, that's why you do it. We'll pretend I believe it if you tell me why you *really* came to see me. You might be telling the truth about commiserating, but there's something else, too. I can't explain why, but I *know* you had other ideas."

I'm sure as hell not telling her about my cock's plans, so sharing the 'saving supernaturals' thing it is.

THAT THING NEEDS A PERMIT

SYDNEY

RORY BREATHES a heavy sigh and I squeeze his hand lightly to encourage him. The mage doesn't know why I'm so averse but I want him to believe me when I say I don't judge him anymore. He chose the path to an easier life with the one I avoided, but he's a victim just like the rest of us. I won't be able to live with myself if I don't fix the ugliness I've been nurturing like a fool for the past four years. So despite the fact that I'm not a huge toucher, I'm making an effort.

"Whitmore's story made me realize something," he finally says. "This fucking shitshow could be more than the propaganda tool they want it to be. We can *use* it, and not just to get ourselves to safety."

That's… unexpected.

"You mean we should… like *Hunger Games* these bitches?" My expression is doubtful, but he nods eagerly. "I don't know, Rory. They've set up all the accounts, they monitor all the feeds… it will be almost impossible to cultivate anything rebellious without getting caught. And you know what they'll do then—arrange an 'accident' during the Games."

He looks thoughtful for a moment, and a small coin-shaped energy ball appears in his free hand. Rory rolls it over his fingers like a poker player as he makes small sounds that must mean he's thinking. "True. But if we hijack their shit for our purposes, we can do it under their noses. We have to win the followers, get the fans, and dominate the ratings. All the accounts and the contests and whatever the fuck—we take it as seriously as a goddamn heart attack."

"I'm never going to be able to pretend to be a shiny, happy Barbie doll when they're making us fight for our lives on camera." I tip my head back on the headboard, groaning at the thought of it. "It won't work and I'll fuck everything up."

"Then don't do that. Play *yourself*, not a role they want to assign you." He chuckles and I arch a brow curiously as my head lolls to look at him. "If you're the lion, we'll all play your tamers. Flirting, softening your verbal blows, and being accessible in ways you aren't. It might kill Dante and Whitmore to do it, but I think it's the right gambit."

Narrowing my eyes, I frown. "You want me to be a sarcastic, biting bitch as usual while you jackholes charm and woo everyone? *And* I'm supposed to also pretend that I might be falling for said charms slowly, too?"

"That's it on the nose, Vicious." He laces our fingers together and I flinch, which only makes him clasp my hand tighter. "But you'll have to work on your reactions in private 'cause no one's gonna believe you're attracted to us if you pull away like that."

Fuck. Me.

Not literally, of course, because *no one* gets to do that. But I'm sure going to have to pretend I want them to eventually. I bite my lip, letting the feel of his big warm hand settle over me as I consider what he's suggesting. The push and pull will probably be very good for ratings, especially if I draw on the enemies-to-lovers thing with the bloodsucker. Thad and Huck will hit the softie and the country boy lovers, especially since they've been my best friends. Dante is a big scary dude, and Rory is the flirt. We can play on the audiences by exaggerating their natural behavior, and I'll be able to stay mostly true to myself.

"Damn it." I growl softly and the handsome magical chuckles at my frustration. "I really *hate* that you're right about this. It makes my ass clench just thinking about you guys fawning all over… whatever you have to… just to further some cause."

Rory sighs and shrugs. "I've been doing much worse for a long time. If I can avoid having to seduce anyone, I'll be happy to playact just about anything."

Not going to happen.

I blink at the snarl in my brain, surprised by the weird feeling of possession inside when I think about any of them having to do such a thing. There's no reason for me to feel like that, even in reference to Thad and Huck. None of these dudes are anything more than friends or teammates. Maybe it's getting close to when I should have cycle? I get a bit weird around that time, despite the implant, but life in the camps is so fucked up that it hasn't been predictable for almost as long as I've lived in them. I never know when that's going to happen, and the only reasons I know I'm not pregnant is the device they put in and my complete *lack* of sex.

"Woooooo, that is *perfect*, Vicious!" The grin on Rory's face distracts me for a second before I scoff. He shrugs, curling his fingertips into my palm. "No, really. You giving the folks cozying up to us that kind of look every once in a while will definitely sell it, especially if it's sort of sneaky."

I pinch the bridge of my nose with my free hand, trying to calm the tingling spreading through me as he strokes my palm lightly. This plan has disaster written all over it, and I need him to realize that before he takes it to everyone else. "Rory, I don't know if I can pretend to be hot for you guys. Even if I can, I don't see how courting the romantically inclined people watching will get us to a rebellion."

"Come on, use your imagination! Think about all the movies and books where the rebels get the masses on their side, *then* they start the revolution. If we win over the world, we can sneak in signals and symbols, things to get the actual resistance in this stupid country to pay attention. We can use anything they do live to get messages to the rest of the world. There are limitless opportunities for us to gather our forces. We just have to be ready for them all the time."

His enthusiasm is contagious, but I'm not a naive young girl anymore. Unlike when I was growing up with my dad, I'm not willing to believe a handsome music man convincing me to follow him everywhere. At least, not yet, and not without everyone else weighing in. I need other perspectives to balance the fragile flicker of hope that I keep buried deep inside of me. I don't know how Stormbringer knew it was there, but if I let him stoke it, I'll be consumed.

Licking my lips, I wait until the emotion passes, then respond. "Look, I'd love to jump on the guillotine train with you, but we can't make decisions for everyone. And-and… I still don't think I can pull off anything other than being me. I'm no actress and that makes me a weak link *again*. You guys don't want to risk your lives for a chick with unpredictable magic *and* terrible acting chops."

"What *specifically* do you think you won't be able to do, Vicious? You've been doing fairly well so far, but for a few things we softened. Seems to me like you're making excuses."

I'm not, you idiot, and I will get you all thrown in jail or worse, killed.

"You saw me flinch. How the hell am I going to let Sebastian touch me? How will I be able to 'pal around' like you want me to eventually? I can definitely nail the bitchy, standoffish stuff. But flirting? I don't have a goddamned clue about that shit." Pulling my hand away, I clench my fists on my lap as I look down at them so the fear rippling through me doesn't show.

"Holy shit, you're scared," Rory murmurs as he reaches over and tips my face up. The coin he's been sliding over the knuckles of his right hand disappears and a zip of magic pings around the room before coming back to him. "I'll be damned. I never would have believed it if I wasn't seeing it myself."

I suck in a deep breath, clenching my jaw as he forces me to look at him. "Fine. I'm worried I'll get us all killed for yet another reason. And *yes*, I'm worried about my lack of experience in this arena. I chose not to be distracted by that particular pursuit, but… I'm mad that it might be a problem now."

"Ohhhhhh."

Glaring, I yank my face away and cross my arms over my chest. "Yeah, oh. Now stop fucking with me."

His hand comes up, turning me back to look at him again. "Ah, Vicious, I didn't say you were wrong. We're going to need to practice with you—all of us. The fans won't buy what we're selling if you can't get comfortable."

The fans? Poseidon's seaweed pubes, just kill me now.

"I'm not fucking any of you, Stormbringer. Get that shit out of your head."

His laugh is undeniably male this time as he scoots closer to me. "Interesting that you went right there without any prompting, Sydney. That makes me think you've been having not-so-innocent thoughts about someone already. Mmmm. I wonder who, though?"

"Don't be ridiculous." I lean away, but he follows until we're centimeters apart. Swallowing as I stare back at his mischievous blue eyes defiantly, I wait for him to back off. When he doesn't, a ball of indignation forms in my gut. This is Rory's way of calling me a chicken, and while I won't be bullied, being challenged is an Achilles heel. "Get out of my face."

"Nope," he says with an easy grin. "Prove to me that you look at us all like Ken dolls and I'll accept it. You'll still have to play nice for the cameras, but I'll believe you when you say it's acting."

"Why the hell would I care if you believe me? You're not my hero, nor my mentor. I don't need your approval." I hold as steady as I can with him in this close proximity, but he's right about the effect he's having on me. I won't admit it, but it's not just him and it definitely worries me in regard to this damn fool plan of his.

"I don't want to be your hero or your teacher—well, not in the traditional way," Rory tsks, his smile getting wider the longer we stay like this. "I'd prefer Daddy, but I'm going to guess broody bondage loving vampires and giant dragon dicks will claim that."

Oh, gross! No fucking way.

"You're mental if you think I'm ever going to—"

Before I can finish the sentence, Rory's face darts forward and his lips are on mine. I make a muffled, half-hearted sound of protest that even I don't believe. He doesn't stop, though; he just slips his tongue past my lips and dominates the kiss without pause. Lifting my hands to his shoulder, I tell my brain to push him away, but it ignores me completely in favor of grabbing onto his shirt. A small growl rumbles in the mage's chest, and his hands land on my waist, yanking me into his arms.

Our lips break when we have to breathe, and I pant softly as I look at him. This isn't me, and I never do this kind of thing. In fact, I've never done *this* before. My entire body is filled with tingling sensations that make me want to ask him to show me what he can do. But I can't do that—this situation is too fucking tenuous as it is. I sure as fuck can't let a nice kiss and some stupid hormones convince me to make a shitty decision that will change everything.

"We can't do this, Rory. Not because of your past, but because… this isn't me. I'm not… This isn't right."

He bites his lower lip and I have to grit my teeth so I don't take back what I said. That expression is hot and the heat rising in my frame wants me to give into it. Finally, he pulls back, sitting against the headboard again as he lets out a long, frustrated snarl. My eyes roam over his tense form and I see why he sounds like he's going to lose his shit.

Damn. Now I know why he was so popular… that thing is freaking huge and I have no idea how it fits inside anyone.

"Stop that."

I tear my eyes away from his sweats, a guilty expression on my face. "Stop what?"

"You're not even fooling yourself, Vicious, but I'll let it go because I'm trying like hell to respect your boundaries. But if you think I believe that this isn't you? That you aren't curious about what we could do together? You're full on delusional, woman."

He's got me there, and that terrifies the shit out of me.

YOU'RE A DAISY IF YOU DO

HUCKLEBERRY

SOMETHING about the story the vampire told is tickling my senses. I know our leaders don't tell us shit at my level, despite the fact that I'm older than a good deal of demons living on the surface. They used to communicate more than they have since the fucking sweeps, but I figured it was because they'd managed to peace out to the homeland in time to avoid that shit.

But what if they didn't make it?

I can't imagine the kind of power and continual supply one would need to not only imprison, but *keep* the elder supernaturals from multiple species for years. It would require a strenuous, difficult to maintain kind of magic and power, plus beings who can withstand the effects of being around that for a lengthy amount of time. They'd need day-to-day sustenance and care, which means a lot of black market shit is being funneled to the location without anyone being the wiser. The operation has to be massive, very secret, and overseen by knowledgeable supes—humans wouldn't know the details we keep from public knowledge and those things could kill ancients like the leaders.

Digging my fingers into my hair, I pace back and forth in the room as I consider how I can find out more about what's going on in the Underworld. We don't have the ability to contact one another in the camps because the necessary materials for summoning a messenger are hard to come by, and therefore, expensive. I've relied on incoming demons and gossip along the criminal grapevine to get what I need for a while, but that may not be enough. I'm going to have to figure out some way to contact demons who aren't constrained by the humans' dominance on this continent.

It will have to be hidden in the social media or TV shit—that will be tricky.

"Some days, I wish I'd fucking skedaddled like a lot of the other old guys. Others, I realize that would have prevented me from finding the person who will eventually make my long-assed life bearable." I pause in my pacing, blowing out a breath slowly. I haven't told Thad, much less Sydney, what I know about her and me. We both have a thing for her and that's about the extent of what we've discussed—and not much about it, either. He'll be pissed when he finds out, especially since he's mentioned his own thoughts on the matter and I stayed quiet.

This sort of thing for shifters isn't the same as it for demons, though. Besides the *very* different things that will happen in the acceptance of that— physically, magically, and biologically—his claim won't involve immortality. It won't require the sacrifices mine would, and I'm not ready to talk about that with our girl a'tall. *She's* not ready to hear it, either, which is why I've kept my interest through flirting a bit.

But Sydney Jolie is most certainly my mate—even if she truly is Thad's as well.

My brows furrow as I consider the belly-ups I've seen from the other supes in our new clique. I don't get why any of them are complying with her demands other than wanting to survive this shit. However, they could easily have stayed clammed up and made underhanded deals to fuck the three of us over during the team-wide events. They didn't and that makes me wonder why—have they, too, figured out something about my sweet pea that would benefit them? Is that why they're accepting this far more easily than I would ever have expected?

"Thad and I need to get them alone and try to ferret out their intentions, especially the vampire. His stories have rocked my world, too, and I didn't think that was possible anymore."

I'm not going to solve this without some help, but I don't want to involve people I don't trust yet. Frowning, I walk out of my room, heading to the living area to pour myself a hefty drink. Once I've got mine and a second for Thad, I walk back to the rooms and knock softly on Thad's door. We've had a secret pattern for years so we could visit one another at night if we felt we needed to chat without our girl in the middle. He opens the door in sweats, his big frame taking up most of the doorway as he tilts his head curiously.

"Huck? What the hell, man? It's getting late and those alarms are fucking brutal here."

I roll my eyes at his whining, handing him his whiskey as I push inside of his room. "We need to talk about the shit that's gone down without the new faces and Sydney clouding the discussion, friend."

Thad closes the door, sighing heavily as I walk in and flop on one side of his bed. "How did I know that was why you came tapping at my door at this time of night?"

"Don't be such a grumpy old bear, Thaddy. You love when I come tip-toeing to your room." I wink at him playfully and he looks up again as if I'm the most trying thing in the universe.

"Huck," he says as he joins me on the bed with his glass. "You're being ridiculous. Just tell me what the hell you want."

My lips quirk as I eye the big guy. I know he's *a little* interested in my flirting, but has no idea what to do with it. As a demon, I'm as pansexual as they come, and he's definitely one huge hunk of beefcake, so I'd happily teach him a few things if he responded. Based on his responses, though, Thad isn't ready for that conversation any more than he is when I bring up Sydney.

The poor dude is repressed as fuck because his sleuth leader is a stodgy dick when it comes to sex.

I blink as it strikes me that the gorgeously bulky bear next to me might be a virgin in *every* way, not just the dirty thoughts I've had in the past. That's… well, appealing isn't the right word, but the vision of my sweet pea and me initiating him together makes my entire body sing with excitement.

"Why do you look like someone just handed you a 'get out of jail free' card?" he says as he eyes me suspiciously.

"No reason." I beam at him, shrugging as I take a sip of my whiskey. "I just enjoy your company, brother bear."

"*Huck*," Thad grinds out as he gets comfortable. "Come on, man."

Touchy, touchy furry man.

"Fine." I grin and take another sip before I continue. "We need to know more about the new guys. They're definitely trying to worm their way in with our girl and the shit they're sharing puts our lives at risk even more than the Games themselves do."

Thad taps his fingers on his stomach, his expression turning thoughtful as he contemplates my words. "You're probably right. I didn't expect the vampire to unload that much truth ever, much less so soon."

Pressing my lips together, I think about how much I want to share with him after the shit dropped this evening. The bear can handle more than Sydney, but most of the lesser supes have a limit. Sebastian's information was a *lot* to process for the beings who really didn't pay much attention to global hierarchy and systems. Shifters aren't known for doing so, which means Thad won't have a damn clue about any of this shit. When I'm ready, I look over at him.

"I knew *some* of his shit—not all or even a lot. Demons, deities, Fae, and demis stay pretty dialed into global supe politics. Non-mythical shifters don't and only the most connected of the magical humanoids do. So, yes, I knew a fraction of that, but the vamp shit? No clue, man."

Thad frowns, groaning softly in a way that makes my cock twitch. "Syd is gonna *murder* you when she finds out. She'll be pissed at all of us because you held back."

"What good would it have done to tell you two what was going on before the sweeps. Before Taterman, and before I came to live in a camp? How would it have helped either of you?" I shake my head, scoffing softly. "It wouldn't. There was nothing we could do about the bigger picture once we were imprisoned, and frankly, species groups can't communicate between camps. And I didn't know shit about the assumptions made about her father. He's dead, so pissing on his memory wouldn't do her any good."

He nods slowly. "I suppose that's true. Until the Games shit came about, we were living in this massive bubble where hurting her wouldn't have done any good. Whether she was mad at the world in general or mad at them plus her dad wouldn't change the situation. But now… Now, we have to be more honest because the secrets could get us fucking killed."

"I know," I say as I sip my drink again. "Which is why I'm here in the middle of the night chatting you up about how we're going to keep our girl safe now that the others seem to be sniffing around her."

His growl tells me exactly how his bear feels about that and I wing a curse to the depths before I broach the harder topic. I'm going to have to talk to Thad about what he and I feel, what we believe, and what might be the truth in the future. If he's having trouble while we're alone, he's going to need to get his shit together. I know what I'm afraid of, and what I believe to be possible. He needs to know it, too.

"Thaddy, I know this is gonna make you madder'n a wet hen, but we gotta beard the lion."

"That's a lot of metaphors, Huck. What the fuck are you talking about?"

Swallowing hard, I blow out a long breath then continue. "Thad, I know you think Syd might be your mate and fuck knows, I didn't think I'd *ever* have one, but the minute I met her, I did, too."

Thad sits up straight, his eyes flashing with the gold of his bear, and he grips the comforter with his big fists. "Shut your mouth, Huckleberry Monroe."

I chuckle, giving him a sympathetic smile. "Thad, she doesn't know, but I'm far too fucking old to pretend with you. I can tell when someone is pining, and even more, I can see it written on your face now. We have to be honest, remember?"

"Fine."

That's all I'm getting, I suppose, but he's a stubborn son of a bitch sometimes. "Well, our fighting group is about as disparate as one could get. It's full of strong, even royal, dudes and centered on a girl who we can't verify the lineage or species of. Doesn't that *sound* like something only destiny or Fates or some shit could plan for? I mean, it's like a goddamn plot line on a TV show or in a book."

"Yeah, maybe."

Ignoring his pout, I go on. "Which means that it stands to reason that the others are here for a reason, too."

His eyes widen and he snarls, "No fucking way. The vampire? The playboy mage? A *sea dragon royal?*"

I shrug, looking at the bottom of my glass as it gets closer. "If she's even more special than we thought, she'd need fierce protectors around her. Her destiny might be to break the supes free. There's probably a reason why she hasn't been able to access her powers, why she ended up in our camp, and why we were drawn to her immediately, man."

"She's going to fucking *hate* the idea that her life might have been planned by something out of her control."

"Uh, I don't know that we need to tell her *that* just yet. Maybe we just need to check these fuckers out before she gets closer to them?"

"Why does that matter if you think they could be fated?"

I forget sometimes how dense the shifters can be.

"Look, being fated is great, but if their damage on the way to her is so bad that they won't keep her safe and not sell her out? Then I don't care what the universe says. They're not getting within an inch of the vulnerable side she doesn't show people. I won't let some jackasses hurt her more; will you?"

He flashes me a smile full of ursine teeth and I chuckle.

I guess that's a 'no'.

YOU CAN RING MY BELL

SYDNEY

I MADE Stormbringer exit stage right eventually, and oddly, I was able to get decent sleep. Once I got up and dressed, I headed for the kitchenette to find *all* of the dudes in there having coffee. The conversation stops the second I walk in, and I glare at them. That definitely means they were talking about me, which sets my teeth on edge.

Are they trying *to piss me off? What the shit.*

"Whatever you chucklefucks were discussing before I showed up had better not be me. I'm warning you—today is not the day and I am not the one. I've got a lot of things to come to grips with, while pretending to be a good little automaton at this goddamned training."

Their expressions don't change and I sigh internally. Men are fucking exhausting and I'm really not in the mood to push this after last night. I roll my eyes and stomp over to the coffee machine, pouring myself a mug and taking a long, restorative sip. Coffee this rich and full is definitely a perk of this stupid place; in the camps, it's usually watered down to almost eagle piss because of the need to make it last. The bitterness helps me curb the fury roiling inside of me for a moment, and I open my eyes to see every one of them looking at me with a stupid grin.

"What the fuck are you all grinning like dumbasses for?"

Thad clears his throat, scratching his chin as he tries to get his face under control. "It's just nice to see you look so damned ecstatic for once. I had no idea a good cup of joe would do that."

Smug asshole.

"How often do we get shit like this, Thad? It's heaven in a fucking stupid cup." My frown is hidden by the edge of the cup, as I take another fortifying drink. "I don't know about the two fancy pants guys, but our version of these hellholes doesn't allow for such a luxury."

"Mine, either." Elias says mildly. "But he's not wrong, little rebel."

Mollified, I continue sipping the delicious brew as I mull over what I learned and what I think we need to do. "Anyone concerned about the fact that we haven't been given a start date or real info about when we go from training to the real thing?"

"Me," Sebastian says as he licks a spot of red from his lips. It reminds me of what he is and I have to suppress my long encouraged urge to sneer at him. He arches a brow like he's read my mind, then continues. "I believe they will soon, because this 'warming up' period was more about figuring out what we can do and how our minds work. They likely had shrinks watching videos and taking reports from the coaches and trainers to analyze every word and move, so that they can create marketing based on each team."

"Awesome," I mutter. "Love feeling watched everywhere I go for years on end, only to be shoved in the world's biggest fish bowl until I get to fight to the death to amuse people."

Elias chuckles. "Perfect way to describe it. I like it."

"Privacy died long before the sweeps, sweet pea," Huck comments as he returns his mug to the sink. "The humans gave it up as a trade for games in their pockets and our leaders gave it up hoping to prevent the exact bullshit we're living through. This is just trading a prison for a trophy case."

Goddess, I hate how right that demon always is.

"Okay, so we're fucked and people watch our every move like we're in a terrarium. You guys are supposed to act like you're lusting after me and I'm supposed to fight you off and be a snarky rebel. Got it—yay team."

Thad dumps his mug as well, walking over to me and standing so he's all I can see. His kind eyes meet mine as he does what he always does when I'm clearly going to go off the rails in a snit. "Syd, I know all of this shit is so far beyond your boundaries that it probably chafes inside and out. Your world has been rocked so many times in a few days that you're on the edge of spiraling. But we don't have the time for you to do your normal 'disappear into a black hole' somewhere for a week act."

I suck in a deep breath and blow it out in annoyance. The damn bear knows me so fucking well that it irks me on a good day, but now it's so much worse, especially because he's right. In the past, when my impotent rage welled up like this, I'd ditch everyone and go hide out away from the academy, my friends, and my life in the darkest parts of our camp. Neither of the boys ever found me, because I made sure I disguised myself well enough that I could blend into the darkness of that quarter.

That kind of emotional indulgence isn't possible here and now; I have to get my shit together.

"Okay," I finally mumble to my towering best friend. "I'll do my best not to react the way every cell in my body is screaming. But it won't be easy."

"Sydney Jolie *never* takes the easy way out," he replies with a grin. His arms reach around me, crushing me into a tight hug that makes me grunt as he squeezes. If anyone but Thad was doing this without warning, I'd probably go for a nut shot, but I know he's trying to ground me.

The problem is that suddenly, I don't feel very grounded and it's like even my comfort zone has morphed into something I didn't expect—just fucking fabulous.

"Good morning, faithful competitors!"

I blink as Dean Wallace-Brickman stands on a platform in the area just outside of the cafeteria and booms the greeting via microphone. We haven't seen her since we were moved into this facility, and I'm not certain why she's here now. The teams aren't students at F.E.A.R. anymore; we're basically property of the fucking FSHA. What's a feckless administrator doing here disrupting my digestion after I eat?

"Who's that, Vicious? You look like you'd happily gut her and wear her intestines as a feather boa."

Rolling my eyes at Rory, I shake my head. I'm not explaining my complex history with camp schools and the way our academy allowed the guards to be abusive and skeevy, even at the college level. "She's the dean of the college Thad, Huck, and I had just started when they yanked us for this shit."

He makes an interested sound as he nods, then says, "I take it this place wasn't very fun."

"Is *anything* in our world right now fun?"

His brows bob and he winks at me playfully, obviously putting on a show for the people around us as instructed. "Oh, I can think of a few fun things they can't take from us."

I want to smack the smirk off his handsome face, but also… I don't. Not because we're playing the roles assigned to us, but because the idiot kissed me the other night and still doesn't realize that he's the first person to ever do so. That little act of rebellion on his part has awakened something I repressed for so long that I don't remember when I started to, and I have zero clue how the fuck to stuff that shit back into the box.

"Fuck off, Stormbringer," I growl loud enough to be heard. "Don't be a perv."

A loud blast of sound echoes in the room, making every single supe grab their ears and wince. Dean Wallace-Brickman gives us all a bland, happy look when the room is silent as a tomb while we all struggle with the pain. "Very good. Now you understand that this is *not* all luxury, yes? You will be required to comply with our edicts and the punishment for not doing so will be far more severe than what I just used."

I knew these motherfuckers were gaslighting us with this royal treatment.

"We have finished assessing your teams and thus, have created specific schedules and lessons you will attend during the training. These are mandatory and your progress will be reported by coaches, professors, guards, and all applicable advisors. You will not skip any sessions that are not approved by your main coach or medical staff. Nothing we instruct you to do is in any way a request."

Thad has his big hands over his ears, but he gives me a knowing look. Our gazes drift to Huck, who seems to be having even more trouble with the effects of the weird noise. I frown, checking on the other three. The dragon and the vampire are doubled over like Huck, while Rory is about equal to Thad and me. I wonder for a moment if that means I'm going to turn out to be like them or does my ability to withstand it better than any of my team mean I'm something else entirely? The thought of revealing that to whatever spies are in this room makes me nervous, so I amp up the theatrics on my 'pain' while the bitchy dean continues her tirade.

"Your coaches will escort you to the first session of the day and provide you with your schedules. You will program them into the tech we have provided, and you will complete any and all work given to you by these skilled instructors. Compliance is mandatory and failure is not an option— not if you want to survive to see the actual Games. Am I understood?"

Everyone stays quiet, either unsure if the question is hypothetical or trying to deal with the effects of her crowd control device. The lack of enthusiasm makes her face turn bright red and she lifts her hand to do something about it. Enough supes get the picture and start the shouts of 'yes, ma'am' before Brickman deafens us all again.

I'm not sure if doing that a second time wouldn't bust some people's eardrums, honestly.

I know she thinks we're lower life forms, and it makes my stomach churn with hatred. No living being should be treated the way humans have treated supes since Taterman's rule began. The disconnect between 'humanity' and how they see us as less useful than the animals they consume is puke-worthy. Not a single employee of the camps and F.E.A.R. would give a damn if her stupid noisemaker actually harmed one of us. They'd just go steal a replacement from the college and keep going.

"Calm down, little rebel. This behavior is not unexpected."

I look at Elias as he looms over me. He's quick for a big ass motherfucker, and even though I know he's hurting worse than me, he's at my side trying to keep me from getting everyone punished with a snarky remark. "It isn't. But I'll never be numb to cruelty, Elias—never. I'm not perfect and I'm obviously learning the world is very different than I knew. At least I'm willing to admit that and learn, rather than operate from a place of hate and fear. They will never be able to say that."

His darkly handsome features turn amused as he cracks his neck. "You're right, but beings like this—human or supernatural—do not *care* what we think of them. They are so brainwashed to believe the rhetoric that confirmed all their biases and resentment, that logic and truth will not sway them. Their one tiny scrap of power in this world is attached to abusing those 'below' them. They don't realize that they're no better off now than when the terracotta tater ascended to his fake throne."

I have to cover my mouth when a giggle almost slips free. This is serious and the announcement was another abuse mechanism; I shouldn't be laughing. But the big guy gives me a proud grin that looks so gorgeous on his bad boy face that I can't help it, even if I feel terrible. "Elias, that was bad."

"Who cares? If we cannot laugh, we are truly lost. I believe that."

"What are we laughing at?" Huck asks, his voice a low rasp as he moves to stand by the dragon. "I could use a chuckle or two after that horse pucky. My bell's been rung like a lightweight boxing heavy, and all I can see is blurry shit."

Fuck. I have a bad feeling about this.

MAKE THEM WANT TO DRINK THE KOOL-AID

ELIAS

SYDNEY IS OBVIOUSLY ANGRY, but I believe it's her permanent underlying state of being at this point. I can't say I blame her; she was raised with a false story that made her suspicious of trusting anyone by some weirdo supernatural rebel who thought he could keep her safe. Then the world fell apart, he was killed, and it just reinforced all his bullshit. She lived with that through the trauma of his death and supernatural imprisonment, only to find out everything she's been using to get through the days is a lie and no one told her.

It's a recipe for one sizzling cauldron of hate and resentment, but she has to pretend to be happy and excited to be paraded around like a zoo animal.

"If it helps, little rebel, everyone has problems with their parents, and most are more serious than they let on to others."

She snorts at my words, shaking her head just enough for her long braid to whip back and forth at her waist. It won't be difficult to fake being flirtatious with a woman as subtly beautiful as her, especially since she has zero clue that she's attractive. Putting a wall between her and the world led to Sydney viewing herself like an asexual Barbie doll, and it makes me chuckle to see her two 'best friends' trip over themselves trying to get her to notice them. It's like she has blinders so opaque that she's lucky she doesn't run into shit when it comes to anything resembling sex or emotions that aren't related to anger.

"Vicious, you're going to hate this class and who the fuck knows who this second instructor is so… maybe breathe before we get into this classroom?"

My gaze darts to Stormbringer as he attempts to assuage Sydney's fury at the announcement and the woman who made it. I'd like to know what their history is, but I know this isn't the time to ask about why she looks like she wants to rip the dean's head off and piss down her neck. "He's right, for once. I can only surmise that 'Cultivating A Cult' will be tiresome for everyone but the mage and the demon because they are the most extroverted of us. We have to listen to their methods in order to be successful as a team."

"I'm not stupid, you know," she grumbles as she finally responds. "I've been listening to everyone's perfectly worded stroking since we were paired. I can do this."

Huck grins at her, tilting his hat back a bit in his slow, country boy style. "We know you can, sweet pea, but when you're fit to be tied, sometimes your brain takes a vacation by the river."

Interesting way to put it, but not inaccurate.

"Are you going to wear that thing everywhere today?" Sydney asks as she narrows her gaze at him. "This stupid paper they handed us says we have battle training after lunch."

"Sweet pea, I wear my hat *everywhere*, including—"

"Oh, for fuck's sake, Huckleberry…" Thad says with a groan. He stops in front of the door marked 'Tech Classroom BC' and gives the demon an exasperated expression.

"I'm just preparing her for the great fake-out we all agreed to, Thaddeus. Our lil' sweet pea has to get comfy with the strapping young men of this group flirting like mad with her, even if her reaction is derision or sarcasm. That's the plan, isn't it?"

"I hate it already," Sydney growls as she reaches for the door and yanks it open. "But he's right, so if he wants to tell me I'd be riding the demon D with his Stetson perched on my head like Annie Oakley, I suppose I'll have to get used to it."

My eyes widen and my jaw drops as she stalks inside. The others share my shocked look, and every one of us has to adjust a bit based on the picture she just painted without a whit of emotion.

We're all fucked if that woman actually starts calling us on our shit.

"The basis of forming a cult following lies in finding out what your super fans want and giving it to them over and over. In psychology, they'd call it 'love bombing' and each of your team members *must* learn how to do it both individually and as a team. You will need to pay very close attention to the comments, messages, and posts of the first fans who follow you, especially those who are frequently liking and sharing your content. Once you do that, you can identify the ones who are most susceptible to our methods."

My gut recoils at the thought of manipulating the most vulnerable psyches of the supernaturals and humans who will view our show. While it's clear this stuff would work on anyone, Chantelle is instructing us to watch them closely and find those with the weakest minds. She wants us to use the same things abusive assholes do to keep their prey and minions in line to create a rabid core of our fans who will be easy to control. Evil tyrants and bad royals across the globe have done this, including the fuckwit Taterman, for millennia in order to get and consolidate power.

I hate it with a passion that makes my skin crackle with tiny jolts of electricity.

A hand lands on my forearm and I look over to see Sydney squeeze it gently. Her eyes meet mine and they are full of the same impotent outrage I feel, but neither of us can do a damn thing about this. She moves her hand when the little shocks stop, and I blink in surprise. It's not normal for someone to be able to calm my storms once they start, especially with something as small as a light touch on my skin.

"Mr. Dante, are you paying attention?"

The woman's hoarse, haughty voice brings me back to reality and I glare at the new instructor. "I am capable of listening without keeping my eyes in one place. Don't be ridiculous, human."

She bristles immediately at the moniker and I roll my eyes internally. I'm not making a big deal of the fact that she should be calling me His Royal Highness, Elias Dante, first of his name and king of the Storm Dragons, but she's pissed that I referred to her as a human. Chantelle is *definitely* a human and they don't believe that to be a slur as far as I know. I have no idea what her fucking problem is.

"You will address me as Professor Chantelle, and I take exception to your tone. If I want to be educated on something, I will *tell* you, lockdown scum. However, you don't have a single iota of knowledge I'd consider useful to me or my class, so that will never happen."

Whoa. What the fuck just happened?

This woman just went from mostly normal to flat-out speciesist dictator in two seconds flat without any provocation. She wasn't really *pleasant* before, but she certainly had a mask on when we first arrived to class. No wonder they picked her to teach this fucking topic; Chantelle Moakle is an expert at hiding her true self behind the disguise of a polite, cheery exterior. Her entire persona is a complete fiction and she just fucked up by showing us her hand too early in the game.

"Of course, Professor Chantelle," I reply mildly, leaning back in my chair as I think about how we're going to play this game two days a week for however long the training period is. People like this deteriorate quickly when questioned, especially if they're hiding their complete lack of knowledge and expertise. While the demon, bear, and mage will be able to play along easily, I fear the vampire and the little rebel will struggle. For me, it will depend on the day; I was trained for diplomacy from birth, but I'm also a dragon.

"Can we get a move on with this? I think we're all smart enough to understand that you want us to lie, cheat, steal, and abuse the people who follow us until they are so brainwashed that they will believe anything we say to them. That about sum it up?"

I knew *the vampire was going to fuck up; I just knew it.*

"Ah, yes, the vampire lord. Well, I'd expect you to know how to do this, given your kind's betrayal of the rest of their world." Chantelle gives him a smug grin, primping her messy rat's nest as she bats her lashes flirtatiously. "Plus, you have such *useful* skills in this arena when up close and personal."

I have to swallow a laugh when Sebastian gets a greenish-tint to his skin, obviously catching the less-than-subtle hint that this woman would let him fuck her into the next available surface if he so chose. "Good luck, man," I mutter under my breath. "You might be the sacrificial vamp."

"Absolutely not."

Blinking, I look over at Sydney, her fists clenched on the desk as she grits her jaw. I might have expected that reaction for her bear or the demon—hell, maybe even the flirty mage—but never Sebastian. "Huh?"

"That is never going to be on the table—for any of us. Understand?"

Sebastian clears his throat and I notice that he's done something to the room to keep this conversation from being overheard.

The motherfucker just slowed time and we had no idea he could do it.

"While I appreciate your concern for my mental and—by the looks of her—physical health, you cannot give our enemies this kind of weapon to work with, Sydney. If she'd been able to file this tiny conversation away in her mind, or worse, her official notes, you can bet that sex would be used as a weapon as soon as possible. Whether it's leaked to other teams to divide and conquer or... uh... *harm* someone without their consent, sex is and has always been a major weapon of war. And make no mistake—this competi-tion is a war between the teams *and* the staff."

Her expression darkens and I see a faint swirl of black in the little rebel's aura. "I will *not* allow that and you can mark my words, Bas. The first son of a bitch who tries to force *anyone* in my presence, even on other teams, will die so messily that they will be using vacuums to pick up the pieces."

"So... fucking... hot," Stormbringer groans as he looks up at the ceiling. "*Goddamn,* I think I'm gonna blow in my damn pants if she doesn't quit saying shit like that."

Sydney whips her head around and gives him a withering look. "That doesn't bode well for your sterling reputation as a sex god, Rory. Plus, you'll walk around in dirty pants until after lunch. Maybe pinch it off or something?"

That gets a snort out of the demon, then a bark of laughter from the vampire, and soon, we're all chuckling as the mage pouts. "Vicious, you're wounding me. If only you'd give me a chance to prove myself…"

"Mother of mayhem," Sebastian mutters as he catches his breath. "This idiot and his fucking ego are going to get us killed."

I tilt my head at him, my eyes serious as I ask, "Why keep it a secret that you can slow time? It's a fucking baller power for strategy; was that purposeful?"

Clearing his throat, the vampire sighs. "We can do a lot of things and some of them are closely guarded secrets within our species. Using this ability would normally be followed by wiping the memory of those who knew it happened—which I don't want to do to my team. It causes… mistrust."

"So does lying—even by omission," the bear says as he shrugs. "So quit doing it or we'll never believe the shit you spew, even the stuff that makes perfect sense. Syd will lose her shit every time and we'll continually take steps forward, then backward."

The half-blond girl nods, turning back to the vampire. "He's right. Stop hiding shit."

"Fine. But everyone get back into place and look forward at this nasty bitch. I need to let go and she'll notice if we're not in the position her brain expects us to be."

I face forward, bracing myself for whatever tirade the scattered, two-faced woman teaching is in the middle of.

This day is going to suck.

DON'T MAKE ME OVER

SYDNEY

THE REST of the cult class was as revolting as before Sebastian shared his little secret. I have no proof that it will be the one I hate the most, but given its topic, it's highly likely. I recognize the value of keeping secrets when needed and I also understand that our team has to market itself for popularity. I'm just not happy with using such disgusting techniques to get ahead. Unfortunately, if the conversations we've been having about revolution are truly the goal—we're going to have to get in bed with dogs and deal with the goddamn fleas.

Absolutely against my nature and it rankles me to the core.

Walking into *Strategy & Planning* has me on edge; I'm ready for this to be as onerous as the previous session, and I'm getting hungry again. It seems to be a growing problem since my secret removal by the centaur doc, so it must be part of the powers I'm supposed to have breaking free. I can't ask anyone, though, even the guys. That one piece of information feels dangerous to share, even with Huck and Thad—I don't want them to be punished if it's discovered. If only I know, they can only torture or kill me for the offense. I'm okay with that, but not with putting my friends in the crosshairs.

"Welcome to *Strategy & Planning*," the human says as he writes his name on the whiteboard. "I'm Brantley Westlake and before you decide to hate me for who and what I am, I'm going to share important information. I am *not* here of my own volition, nor am I free. My sentence requires teaching classes at schools or programs until the day I die, which will be far sooner than any of you, so lucky me."

I blink, gaping at the studious-looking guy incredulously. What the hell did a human do to earn that sentence? I thought they were all free as birds. My gaze shifts to the others who seem similarly surprised, and that makes me feel marginally better.

Brantley grins at us. "Shocked, right? You probably weren't ever made aware of how many educated, liberal-minded humans were rounded up in the sweeps and put to work for the new administration because they did not agree with their policies. Social media was used to locate us, along with our precious technology, when we were foolish enough to speak out in public. Again, something you probably wouldn't have seen, as it was covered up as quickly as other atrocities I cannot speak about. So I'm here now and I am invested in making sure that your team is given the tools to succeed. I *want* your team to win your freedom, because I believe you deserve it as much as any other human."

Holy fucking crap buckets.

"As if we're going to trust that," Rory says with a snort. "I'm fully aware of how devious your kind can be when they want research on subjects. You're just as likely a spy as you are to be telling the truth."

The human nods, his expression serious. "Good. You *should* question everything you are told by every single being in this building in every situation. Not only will other teams try to manipulate you based on their Cult professor's teachings, but the employees and prisoners working here will as well. However, I plan to show you *why* I am telling the truth, though you may not believe it until we've spent more time together. Are you ready for that?"

I arch a brow. "Do your worst."

Westlake walks over to the door, shutting it firmly before coming back to the front of the classroom. He takes a deep breath, then slowly tugs the polo he's wearing over his head. My eyes widen as he reveals his arms, neck, and torso, simply *littered* with scars. Everything from burns to gouges to whip marks cover him from top to bottom marring his tanned skin and thin frame. He holds up his wrist, gritting his teeth as he shows us the cuff-like band on it. "This is currently shocking me, as it does every time I say something I'm not supposed to. It's enchanted, unremovable, and incessant. That burden was placed on me the moment I was captured during the Second Sweep, and has remained, even during the many, many sessions they put me through trying to find my contacts. I almost died twenty-three times in the first two months."

The horror reflected on my face is unpreventable as I stare at the mess that was once Westlake's skin. "Is that all?"

"Nope," he says with a grimace, "but I'm not sharing what lies beneath my lower half. That is my own personal pain and shame, which I do not share with anyone. It might seem extreme, but I assure you, what happened to me was done to *vast* numbers of sympathetic humans who looked just like the architects of the FSHA who dissented. We thought we were safe and the old rules applied, but once Taterman and his goons steamrolled the rest of the hapless politicians in this land, they came for the humans who didn't share their views. Just like the poem said, yet somehow, no one ever saw it coming."

"What happened to you is a tragedy. However, I have seen far worse on supernaturals; things no one should ever experience or witness." We all look at Elias as he stares back at the professor with a blank expression. "It was not only men, or women, but even children and babies in my first camp. Your kind committed atrocities that will haunt those who witnessed them until the day *we* die and, as you said, it's much further away than your last days."

The dragon's flat affect doesn't surprise me, but imagining what he must have seen almost breaks through my walls to make me emotional. I have to look away so I don't lose my grip on my control. Elias may harness stoicism to that level, but I am not immune. I can almost hear tiny cries of pain and it's making my hands tremble. Huck catches my eye and I feel a small push of strength zing through the air to slide over my skin.

That son of a bitch is trying to help me, but it only makes me feel weaker not to do it on my own.

Clearing my throat, I finally speak. "Fine. You've suffered and you might be an ally. Let's get this lesson over with so we can move on to the next horseshit we have to endure today."

"I like you, Sydney. Your spirit may earn you serious consequences, but if you pay attention here, I might teach you to be strategic about how you use it. After all, we can endure the pain when it benefits us, yes?"

Whatever you say, human.

The rest of the day went fairly quickly until the session I was dreading most —until I met Chantelle, of course—*Beauty Maintenance.*

I cringe the second we walk in the door and see six curtained sections that obviously separate us while the bubbly looking redhead with perfect teeth and a filler-worthy smile claps her hands. This is going to be the absolute fucking worst; I was mistaken earlier. Not only do I have *zero* interest in being primped and pampered, but it's impractical for the stupid games, anyway. How will we fight with fake nails? Be for real.

"Welcome, my new creations!"

Ugh, no fucking way I'm letting that *stand.*

"I'm no one's 'creation' and I resent you suggesting it," I bite back as I wait for the others to file in. "What a stupid way to ensure we all despise you."

Huck chuckles as he stands next to me, tucking his thumbs in his boot loops. "My sweet pea is right, little lady. Humans damn sure didn't create any of us; all you did was abuse and imprison us."

"So dour!" The woman tsks, wagging her finger as she looks at each of us with an assessing eye. "That will make the 'grumpy alpha' lovers swoon, but it will also give you wrinkles. Be careful how often you do it."

"Supes don't get wrinkles—well, most don't," Thad corrects himself as he crosses his arms over his broad chest. "Don't be ridiculous."

Rolling her eyes, the redhead walks over to the wall, pulling an armful of robes off of hooks, then coming back to us. "You will need to go behind your curtains and put these on with your undergarments. Today, my assistants and I will work on the following treatments to get you camera-ready: waxing, trimming, plucking, injecting, buffing, and modifications. Based on my initial assessment of your team, I realize you're all *very* well proportioned and physically fit, so we are going to really lean into the team name by making you fit the 'rebel' image completely. I'm going to message Krista to let her know you'll be quite late for free time in order to get a good jump on the work we need to do."

"Wait a minute, lady—" I protest, but she shakes her head.

"Nope! Not your decision and if I have to strap any of you down, I will, but this is *my* canvas, and you will behave so I can give you the best chance at winning. I understand you may think, 'But Gemma, you don't own my body' and you'd be right—except unfortunately, the FSHA owns every being in the camps and you all know it, even if you hate it."

Sebastian looks ready to rip her throat out, and Elias seems similarly affronted, while Rory just sighs. He's used to this sort of treatment, I suppose, which makes me sad. The mage won't fight it and his expression is telling the rest of us we shouldn't, either. The woman won't hesitate to make good on her threat by his defeated gaze, so we'd best get this over with.

I hate this fucking timeline.

"Fine," I reply before any of the guys get us tied up like we're criminally insane. "We understand what you're saying. But we don't have to like it or you, nor do we have to be happy about it."

Gemma smiles brightly. "But I promise you *will*. My gift—though nothing like supernaturals—is to imbue your spirits into the looks I craft and I am well paid for it because I am *that* good. If you want to regain your freedom in victory, Miss Jolie, I promise your image is a large part of that. I will give you the power to draw followers and diehard fans with the crook of a finger. You've lucked out in getting the absolute best tech in the entire program, and I will prove it to you if you simply let me do my job."

Thad grunts, tilting his head as he watches the woman plead with us, then finally nods sharply. "Fine. You're good and we should listen. How does that translate to a twice a week class?"

"I'm glad you asked, Mr. Calvin!" Gemma beams as she hands him a robe. "This look will require several sessions of prep work—getting you to the full vision I have for you—and then maintenance, just as the name of the session suggests. We have to keep colors, sculpting, and all the small pieces that aren't as permanent as body art and other modifications fresh for the cameras and media. You will, of course, destroy some of my work during events, which my team will correct as needed. It is *work* to be the avatar of your themes, and we will work all the time."

"Does that mean there's *homework*, so to speak?" Rory asks in amusement. "Things we have to do outside of class?"

"Without a doubt, Mr. Stormbringer. We will provide you with kits containing everything you need for daily care of our artwork, and you will make certain to do as asked. If you don't, we'll know and that would be… unfortunate. Please don't force me to notate files that way. I don't want to end up covering far worse things than what I plan to do to your bodies."

And there's the threat of torture—what a great way to end our day.

I WONDER HOW YOU COMB YOUR HAIR SO THE HORNS DON'T SHOW

RORY

THIS IS GOING to be one of the most difficult classes for everyone but me and maybe the vampire. Vicious and her guys have been living this place, surviving off the scraps, and Dante was imprisoned. None of them are used to being pampered anymore, nor having people expect you to look like a picture perfect avatar of their species. I, however, spent the past four years being a well-taken care of concubine to more rich humans and powerful supes than I can count. Maintaining the 'look' of upper crust beauty was part and parcel for me; it wasn't even an option to run about looking any less than fuckable.

They won't have to do a lot of maintenance—I haven't been traveling that long and many of the surface adjustments they'll need to make on the others are normal upkeep for me. I'm shaven, tattooed, and pierced in plenty of places as it is… though I could use a little time under a sun lamp to help my glow, I suppose. I won't fight whatever else they want to do, because I learned a long time ago that being appealing kept me in relative comfort and safety.

Mostly.

Sydney will give them hell in a handbasket when they pull a Miss Congeniality on her. I'd love to watch it, but I think if we all leave her alone, she might actually acquiesce begrudgingly when the ladies servicing her transformation explain why they are doing each thing. I can't be certain they'll treat her kindly rather than strap her down, but the attitude of Gemma as she spoke led me to believe she will reserve that for extreme issues.

The girl is naturally beautiful—not that she knows or recognizes it—but they're going to make her shine like a newly cut diamond. That will hook the population of femme presenting worshippers in a blink, and if the talented assistants here do the same for the rest of this crew, we'll have those who love males as well. There's a cunning strategy at play in this set-up by our fascist government, one that allows them to distract the world from their cruelty with well curated content.

We're likely pawns in some ploy to prevent sanctions or alliances from gathering against Taterman's regime.

That's more than I can worry about in our current predicament. If our rag-tag team of misfits is going to incite a revolution, we have to focus on winning their hearts first. The first lick of flames will light a slow burn that will start the wildfire—but only if we're able to do it without anyone realizing our true aim. Getting primped today is just one tiny step towards that goal.

"Ow! By Lucifer's shiny hooves, woman!"

I chuckle, laying back in my chair as I hear Huck getting feisty with his technician. The demon is making a gut wound out of a wax strip, but I know why. Vicious' men are outwardly friendly, but inside, they're as suspicious and careful as our girl. They hide it better, and this is the demon's way of making sure he seems prissy just in case any of these chicks have flapping lips. It's not a bad plan, but more believable coming from someone not as groomed as me or as intimidating as the dragon.

"Mr. Stormbringer, Gemma is pleased with the level of care you've been taking with your appearance. She would like me to catch-up on the basics, then begin working on a few more essential procedures to enhance your current look."

My eyes open and I look at the dark-haired girl. "Do what you will, dear. I'll behave and I won't kick up a fuss. I'm quite used to being sculpted, poked, and prodded until I'm a masterpiece. Hell, I might even fall asleep; don't be shocked."

Her expression is doubtful, but I'm not lying. "Okay. Well, we're going to start with the maintenance now. Would you like eye covers, nose plugs, or headphones?"

Fancy.

"The eye covers, please. I'm enjoying listening to the rest of my team learn that beauty is often painful. It amuses me." I wink at her, getting a bright pink flush and accomplishing the distraction I intended. I don't want to be blind *and* unable to hear what's going on, much less deprived of scent as well. That's plain stupid and it leads to… less than desirable outcomes. Of that, I'm very aware.

"Alright," the tech replies as she hands me small soft cups to cover my eyes. "Let me know if you need me to pause briefly at any time. I'll get everything warmed up and mixed while you relax."

Yeah, whatever, chickadee. As if I have a choice in the matter.

It's late by the time they finish with me and when I meander out of my little cubicle, the rest of the guys are dressed in the loose garb they gave me afterward. We're all carrying bags that contain our previous clothing and to my surprise, no one looks as if they've been drugged to behave. That's a good sign in my book; I was definitely concerned about the dragon fighting the treatments. Since they're upright and conscious, I breathe a soft sigh of relief.

"Time to head back to our suite, yeah? I doubt the cafeteria is open," I ask as I look at them.

Sebastian grunts, his expression dark as he nods sharply. "I believe taking our meal in our quarters would be optimal, mage. Comfort and security is our prime need after this nonsense."

My lips quirk as I stare at the vampire. They've tamed his shock of white hair, making it curl temptingly around his face to soften the sharp lines of his visage. He's obviously the avatar of all things evil and broody now, and it makes me curious to know what they did to him that I cannot see in the long sleeved, high-necked outfit. "I'm definitely sore, if that's what you're getting at, Bas."

"Stop calling me that and quit gawking," he mutters as he looks at the others for agreement. Letting them weigh in is another step in the right direction for the pissy bloodsucker, and I wonder if they gave him a tranquilizer, too. It wouldn't knock a vamp out, but it might mellow his ass a bit.

"I agree," Dante says as he scratches his chin. The dragon already had the 'big bad' look going, but they've razored his dark hair into an enticing yet masculine style and changed out some of the visible jewelry to things that look far more roguish than hoops. There's a claw through the pierced eyebrow and the one in his septum looks like a curved lightning bolt. He's still scruffy, but it's artful now, which I hope like hell he can maintain. He'll be in trouble if he can't; I know it.

The boy-next-door bear, however, is now clean shaven, but roughed up a bit in terms of what style elements I can see. I suppose he's meant to be the 'working class' nice guy to offset the haunting vampire and the bad news dragon. I'm the golden boy, I know, so their theme is becoming readily apparent—all the men you'd love to have in your bed embodied in one team.

"Sebastian is right, Stormbringer," Thad grumbles. "The staring is weird."

I shrug, not really worried about their crankiness. Of all the people in our group, I understand this bullshit the best. "I'm assessing their visual strategy, gummy bear. None of you are qualified to figure it out, so unfortunately, you'll just have to deal."

"For fuck's sake," Huck says as he tilts his Stetson back. His dark hair is hidden by it most of the time, but I can sense they've done things to him we can't easily see when he's dressed. It wouldn't surprise me, but I was hoping to be able to discern more than just 'country boy' from their efforts.

"He can't help himself. It's how he copes with this shit."

We all whirl around to see the center of our team step out from behind her curtain. I have to force my jaw not to hit the ground when I see the woman joining us. I said Sydney was naturally good looking and I meant it, but they've transformed her from angry waif to stunning bundle of fury. Her expression speaks to the feelings of violation she's feeling after her session, so I just swallow rather than comment on the changes. After all, I know how I felt the first time I experienced this sort of thing and I'm not nearly as rigid as Vicious.

"You look amazing, sweet pea," Huck says softly as he holds out his arm. Her jaw grits and she shakes her head, making the demon shoot a concerned look at the bear. "Well, alright then. The magic man says we should eat in our room and I'm inclined to do so. How 'bout you?"

"Fine." Sydney lifts her chin, her hand grasping her bag tightly as she walks past us to the open door. "Let's head for the dorm before we miss the room service window."

Not good—she's barely talking and she refused to let her closest friends touch her.

Striding toward the door, I follow the perfectly highlighted blond woman, watching her braid swing down her back as she makes a beeline for the main atrium where the elevators are. Her spine is rigid and posture stiff like she's ready to pounce on the first thing that crosses her path. It makes me look around carefully as we move, trying to suss out what might be an issue before it gets anywhere near her. I don't want there to be a scene when our girl is this volatile.

Sydney stops at the elevator, stabbing the button with her finger a few times, as if that will make it come faster. Thad and Huck flank her, staying within reach but not close enough to touch her on accident. She huffs and crosses her arms over her chest, wincing slightly as she does so. Again, I wonder what they did to her that's making her this furious.

Unluckily for all of us, watching Sydney to ensure no one approached her left everyone else unguarded. A chorus of giggles erupt behind Dante and Sebastian, announcing their presence before any of the gaggle of girls speaks. Vicious doesn't turn at the noise, but I do, groaning internally as I note the wolf girl and her pack of shifters staring at them.

This is going to suck.

"Oh, look! It's the loner girl. How the hell did that weirdo get put with these smokeshows?" The canine grins toothily as she primps a bit, thrusting her chest out as her friends laugh. Sydney doesn't respond and I almost think we're going to get out of this without a giant mess. "She can't keep hotties like this satisfied. I'm asking to be transferred. Men this fine *deserve* a woman who knows how to take care of *all* their needs."

That gets our team leader's attention and her head turns slowly as if she's in that human movie about demon possession. Sydney's eyes are dark and hollow as she looks at the group of girls without a flicker of recognition in them. In a blink, her hand shoots out, grabbing the wolf by the throat and whirling to slam her against the wall by the buttons. Her move was swift and brutal, leaving the girl gasping and squirming in her grip as she tries to get away.

"I will only say this *once*," Sydney says in a flat, calm voice. It's eerie, and I almost shiver at the lack of emotion behind it. "Women who thrive on punching down other women are worse than the human scum enslaving us. I will *not participate* in stupid, childish games with you. Take your syncophants and get the fuck away from my team or I will rip your goddamn arms off, beat you to death with them, and make my first selfie a picture of your corpse with #lessonlearned in the caption."

"But… but… you lived in the same house…" The girl wheezes and chokes for a moment as Vicious tightens and releases her hold again. "And we're supposed to—"

"I don't fucking care. Bite Club is *off-limits* for that shit. Do. You. Understand?"

"She does, she does," sobs one of the other girls. Her friends nod, looking deathly pale when the wolf girl turns redder and redder in Sydney's hands.

"I didn't ask you."

I sigh, knowing that her bear and the demon aren't going to do a damn thing. It might be fine for her to end this bitch later on, but doing it here and now will have consequences we can't predict. Leaning in, I place a feather-light hand at the small of it and murmur softly, "Let her go, Vicious."

Her eyes cut to mine and the emptiness in them is startling. But she turns back to the pinned canine and growls, "Say it or you die in this lobby."

"I understand!"

Sydney nods, removing her hand immediately and letting the girl drop to the ground in a crumpled heap. The elevator dings, doors opening, and she steps over her former prey, looking at us. "Are you coming or not?"

Honestly? I almost fucking did in my pants, thank you very much.

YOUR CLOTHES WOULD LOOK BETTER ON MY FLOOR

SYDNEY

SURPRISINGLY, Rory touching me didn't set me off even further, though I expected it would. Going through the humiliating process of being waxed, shaved, sculpted, tattooed, pierced, primped, and every other damn thing in their playbook for hours put me well over my personal violation lines. I didn't even want Huck or Thad to lay a finger on me afterward, because I felt so out of control in my skin. For four years in Tempest Seven, I've managed to at least keep autonomy over my physical form by not engaging in any of the mind-numbing substances or casual sex other supes did, and what was it all for?

Nothing. It was for nothing because they finally took the last shred of my freedom away with that stupid session.

I swallow hard as I stare at the floor of the elevator silently. My emotions are all over the fucking place because I'm grieving the loss, while raging at the system and the people everywhere who allowed us to become little more than cattle for this fucking government full of crusty old losers who have to step on others to make themselves feel better. Oh, and enrich themselves, of course—we can't forget how obscenely wealthy the humans who backed Taterman have become in the following years. Global corporations who staff and supply the camps, mercenary teams who capture the stragglers, corrupt politicians, companies that make their propaganda reinforcing merchandise, books, and media—all of them are rolling in the profits soaked in blood.

Closing my eyes as I work to regulate my breathing, I tell my brain to stop proselytizing and get a grip on the feelings, making it difficult to function. Life in Tempest hasn't been easy, but compartmentalizing as much as possible works. I should divvy up all this shit and shove it into the appropriate boxes for later—whenever that is. But I'm not, and I don't know why. Instead, the spread of those pesky emotions is making my skin tingle and my veins pulse with weird sensations that I cannot ignore.

What the fuck is wrong with me?

"Sweet pea…"

"Vicious…"

"Little rebel…"

"Syd…"

The sound of everyone but the snarky vampire saying my name feels like it's at the end of a tunnel. There's a light there, too, but it's so far away, and getting smaller by the moment. I'm being consumed by the intensity of my violation slowly; I can't seem to crawl out of the hole that fury and sadness are pulling me into.

Suddenly, my chin is yanked up and I open my eyes to stare into the crimson orbs of Sebastian Whitmore. They're pulsing as he stares at me silently, his mouth moving to form words, but no sound is coming out. I want to fight his grip, and maybe I could if I were totally in control of myself, but right now? I have to endure the touch of someone I definitely do not trust nor want forcing their way in when I'm feeling this dirty.

Then, like a bolt of lightning, the trance snaps. My chaotic inner bullshit quiets—though it doesn't go away—and my mind can bring the world into focus again. Breathing heavily, I look at the vampire as he studies me carefully. "What-what are you doing?"

"Bringing you out of your spiral," he says in a very matter-of-fact tone. "Your powers, whatever they are, are slowly emerging. Heightened emotions like you're experiencing now can cause a break with reality if you do not learn to manage both the feelings *and* your supernatural abilities. I assume you must lock your emotions down fairly tightly on a normal basis, which means you will struggle with this quite fiercely."

Is he saying no more boxes? How the fuck will I handle shit?

"It's going to take a lot of work, and likely, some painful moments where you finally deal with things you long sealed up and never dealt with. But you *cannot* leave this undone, Sydney. Outbursts like you had at those girls are dramatic enough to be acceptable here—even if you had killed her. But what happened in this elevator is not interesting to a viewing audience and will *not* be acceptable. Plus, it's an enormous weakness to be exploited by others."

Thad clears his throat and says, "She's not stupid, Whitmore."

"I know that, Calvin, but she's one of the most stubborn people I've ever met—and I've only known her a little more than a week. This is important to *all* of us, as she could get us killed by falling into one of these K-holes of past trauma."

Shaking his hands off, I glare up at the vampire. "Okay, I get it. Thad's right; you only have to say it once. I need to work through some shit so I don't fuck up. Now back off, okay?"

Huck pushes through them, looking at me with that fond softness he has sometimes. "Sweet pea, no one wants to make your problem worse. We want to help, and as much as I don't trust the bloodsucker, either, he just used his mojo to bring you back from the brink. Probably could muster a 'thank you', don't you think?"

Damn this demon for his Southern bullshit; it works every time.

"Fine." I sigh and look at Sebastian, my expression grumpy. "Thank you for helping me. But if you pull that mojo bullshit on me when it's not an emergency, I'll gut you like a fucking trout."

His lips curve up in satisfaction, and he arches a brow. "What about if it's with your consent? I'd like the lines to be *very* clear if you're going to draw them so publicly."

"When the fuck would I ever consent to it willingly?"

Rory waves his hand, winking at me before he says, "I know; I know! Vamp sex is hot as fuck when the 'look into my eyes' shit is part of the play."

I make a horrified face at the mage, and all the guys laugh in this masculine, dude way that makes me want to bludgeon them all. "I refuse to answer that question based on how disgusting you are."

"Mmm, not an adjective I'm used to hearing regarding that subject," Sebastian says, shrugging as he turns to release the elevator doors. "More's the pity for you."

Did he just offer to fuck me in front of all of them? And no one protested? What the hell is going on here?

The random thought from earlier has consumed me since we got off the elevator and headed for our suite. The guys watched me closely because I was so quiet, but I wasn't spiraling into another incident, so they didn't push. We simply headed inside and went to our rooms to get cleaned up— something I think everyone quietly agreed on.

But I can't stop my brain from whirling around the idea that the five dudes in that small metal box seemed perfectly fine with one of them slyly propositioning me.

Sex isn't a topic of conversation I allowed with Huck and Thad. I knew they were probably 'dating' people or maybe just relieving tension some- where, but I didn't want to know about it. I'm not a prude, per se, but I'm vastly uncomfortable with the surrounding discussion. Growing up with a father who did his damndest to keep me from forming any lasting bonds with others makes me suspicious of relationships, and so I've never tried. Now I suppose it was because he thought someone would find out about my mixed lineage and we'd have to run, but I guess weird patriarchal bullshit was part of it, too.

I don't think he wanted to have any 'womanly' chats with me and I definitely figured out my period on my own. It didn't seem odd, but then, I wasn't questioning my entire childhood like I am now. That's not really an issue after being shunted into the camps; they made certain we're all implanted and kept from reproducing without permission from those who run our prisons. At best, I bleed every couple of months, and it's not much. I'm not due for a while, either, since it happened right before my last re-up a month ago.

But it will at some point, and I'm going to have to contend with that—just fucking lovely.

All of this simply underlines the fact that I have a biological understanding of desire and physical intimacy, but no actual experience. My decision to keep my body to myself as the last vestige of personal autonomy has left me floundering with the situation at hand. Not only did the FHSA take that last remaining bit of dignity by primping me into oblivion today, but they've made me question what the hell the point is. Denying myself the ability to get lost in things that would take my mind off this nightmare feels a lot less important now that my very skin isn't even my own.

The worst part is that nothing they did—no matter how violating—looks horrible. All the bullshit I had to give into makes me more human, not less. That's a general term, obviously, since I'm not remotely human now that the supernatural parts of me are waking up. I simply mean that I look healthy, well-groomed, and like I could smile for a toothpaste commercial unironically. From the girly bits like waxing and lashes to the practical things like teeth bleaching and bronzing, the techs Gemma directed took my basic natural gifts and enhanced them into blessings. Even the 'bad girl' additions like tattoos, injections, piercings, and other shit are perfectly in tune with the image they want me to project.

I hate that, but I can't lie to myself anymore.

Walking to the mirror, I look at my reflection, examining the coiffed perfection the artists rendered. I'm expected to keep this up between appointments, so they had to teach me quite a lot. That's why I came out last—I've never been shown how to shave my legs or wield a mascara wand before. Gemma was appalled at how little I understood, but I had no explanation to offer other than it was never something I had access to, nor cared to get for myself.

It's easy to stay basic when you purposefully keep everything with a pulse as far from you as possible. It took a long time to get comfortable with Thad, and longer to allow Huck in my sphere. They're the first friends I've had, and I was determined not to fuck it up by letting typical boy-girl hormones shit come into play. Hence, the brush off of talk about sex or dating in our interactions. Keeping the topic banned made certain that I wouldn't be questioned about my participation or lack thereof.

Unfortunately, the change in the tenor of our group with the addition of our new members makes that almost impossible. Rory is a very flirty, sexual being—even though much of that is a personality he's developed specifically to survive the camps. Dante is broodingly hot and alpha with this oddly gentle way of shepherding us to the right conclusion. And Sebastian… Well, that goddamn vampire knows how beautiful he is and he definitely knows who thinks so.

I'm trapped in a seething cesspool of testosterone and pent up hormones that I have zero experience fending off.

Worse yet, now that Gemma's people have inadvertently removed my barriers about my body, I don't even know if I *want* to fend it off. The stubborn refusal seems pointless and the magic inside of me is giving me subtle hints about what it would prefer me to choose. I notice more about the guys and their attractiveness than I've ever noticed about men in my life. My body *feels* more about their naked forms than I've ever felt. Everything inside of me is haywire and I'm struggling to keep up with the onslaught of newness in every form.

To top it off, not a single one of these jokers—even my best friends— knows that I'm a fucking virgin. Antiquated as the term and idea are, it's the one phrase that will cause a mini-uproar in this dorm for certain. I'm not stupid enough to assume that if they find out, it won't cause a chain reaction of either *very* interested or *very* disinterested dudes to sniff around me. I'm not ready for that, especially right now, so I can't let them know until I can wrap my head around how to deal with it.

But that's a problem for Future Sydney, as they're waiting for me to come out and discuss today's assholery while we eat—hopefully, without losing my goddamn shit.

NOBODY IS SAFE
FROM THE MONSTERS
INSIDE THEIR HEAD

SEBASTIAN

I WASN'T SURPRISED by the level of detail the techs went into at the 'beautification' session. They're grooming us like prize livestock to show the world that the FSHA isn't the big bad dictatorship oppressing supernaturals. Every inch of the competitors will be scrutinized by anyone who has been on the fence about resuming relations with the country, and if we all look presentable, fed, and shiny, it might convince them to cave. The nations who are staunch enough and have their own intelligence to contradict this razzle dazzle won't budge, but if Taterman can get even a few countries to give in, it will appease his base.

This kind of machination is far above his intelligence capability, especially since he's been whacked out on drugs since he popped out of the womb.

Getting people to follow a revolution will be a lot harder if the assholes here can trick the globe into believing that everyone is being treated like we are now. I frown as I consider the alternative—we won't win them over if we're not picture perfect and worshippable, either. Humans are the most naïve and easily led species on the planet, which is how we ended up in this mess. I just don't know if everything we're being taught is going to be enough to do what *has* to be done. It's infuriating, and I have no way to muddle it out when we're trapped in this holding pattern.

"There she is!"

My head turns when the mage cheerily announces the woman in the center of this messy rebellion. Sydney changed into comfortable clothes, but the work they did on her remains. She was pretty beforehand—even I'll admit that—but now she's absolutely stunning. It's a fact that works heavily in our favor, but she will need to stop making a face like she's swallowed a pound of lemons. The grumpy badass trope works well for her, but it can't be her only image.

People need to root for her… to love her. That's how we'll gather the troops.

"Yes, yes. I'm here, hurrah," Sydney drawls as she heads for the couch, dropping in between her two sidekicks. "I look ridiculous, given the state of everyone in this damn camp, and I'm pissed as fuck about having to give up the last vestiges of my personal freedom for this. *Don't* make me lose my shit, dickheads."

The demon tips his hat back, looking at her fondly before he murmurs, "Just because they did some shit on the outside doesn't mean they touched the inside, sweet pea. None of the polishing they did changed who you are and it never will."

"I *know* that, Huck. I just…"

Her voice trails off and there's something in the intonation that catches my attention. This truly upset her, and it's deeper than being told what to do. Something about the session has wounded her in a way that is significant and she doesn't want to share that—even with her friends. Allowing them to re-make her into their vision has violated our sassy leader, and it's trauma-tizing her as we speak.

"Sydney, no one is going to push you to relate how you feel. However, we should all be familiar with what they did to us so we can use it to our advantage. It's more than hair dye and makeup, so the information could be useful."

She looks at me defiantly, but the spark of sorrow is still in her eyes. "If you say so, Bas. I don't know how recounting tatts or piercings or implants affect a damn thing, but hey… Who am I to protest?"

That's concerning in so many ways, but the others keep looking at her encouragingly—except for the mage. His eyes are narrowed on Sydney and I think he's figured out the same thing I have. I'm not the person to help her work this shit out; she's still working out how she feels about me after the revelation. But someone needs to talk with her—that much is extremely clear. I tilt my head, hoping the blond mage will notice, and when he does, I nod a little. Luckily, I think he gets it. That or he's just grinning because he's perpetually a fucking golden retriever, I'm not sure which.

"You're a member of the team, obviously, and that's important," I reply smoothly. I don't want to get into a piss fight with her when she's clearly vulnerable, so I cloak my irritation at the flip response behind my normal detachment. "And if anyone disagrees with me, we can discuss it."

Thad frowns, then shrugs. "Your premise is sound, I think. The target audiences are meant to form attachments to us and possibly ship things, so knowing beforehand what we can use to feed those rumors isn't a bad idea."

"Agreed," Huck says as he drapes an arm along the back side of the couch. I think he's watching the unusually quiet woman, too, but he's obviously an expert at hiding his concern. "And I'm not shy, so I'll show and tell if need be."

Sydney's eyes widen, and she slaps his leg immediately. "Huckleberry Monroe, you will *not*."

That makes both the demon and the bear laugh, so it must be a normal reaction for her. It was adorably schoolmarm-ish, but I can't see why a woman her age would be so—

Oh, fuck me raw with a spiked strap-on. That's why she's so on edge.

Now that I've realized what I absolutely never should have missed in a million years, Sydney's reticence about her session makes sense. Her body is the one thing she's kept for herself—for whatever reason—and now she's lost control of it. Probably puts her entire worldview in yet another free-fall like my story did, and she wasn't done dealing with the fallout of that yet.

"I think telling one another is probably sufficient," Dante finally says. "But I will agree as well."

Navigating this now that I have the knowledge of why Sydney is so touchy will not be easy. Stormbringer may well help her come to terms later, but for now, I'm not sure how delicate her psyche is. Normally, I wouldn't give a flying fuck about this kind of shit, mind you. But getting the rest of them to see me as a part of their team rather than the enemy is important if I want to stay alive and get the fuckheads like my father out of power.

"Who's going to start?" I look around the room, brow arched as I study the others. I'd wager they did very little to punch up the dragon's 'bad boy' aesthetic; hopefully, Dante volunteers to ease the rest into this.

"You all know I don't give a fuck," Rory declares as he stands and spins in place. "Tanning, sculpting, waxing, tattoo upgrades, including the team one I assume we all got." He points to the bandage at the base of his neck near his collarbone, then continues. "They changed out the jewelry in my ears and added nipples, plus a special new piece in my PA. Bleach to keep my highlights nice, and shots that I assume contain who the fuck knows what to strengthen muscles, etc. Nothing out of the ordinary for maintenance in my previous life, so I'm not pressed."

Sydney's face gets red at the mention of his steel, and I'm fairly certain that it's only going to get worse. Stormbringer is the flirtiest out of our group, but unless my typically accurate assessments of people are incorrect, he's definitely *not* the most bent out of the group. I doubt he comes anywhere near the demon or me. The bear's likely the most vanilla about sex, so he'll be uncomfortable when he figures out the spectrum of deviancy represented in this room. I believe our royal dragon falls squarely in the middle of the two camps, which I'll admit, interests me. But the girl in the middle of this mass of testosterone has faked her way through these questions for a while without being caught; that means she has the knowledge, but no experience.

My inclination is to show her, and I know that's never going to happen.

Thad saves me by sighing as he stacks his hands behind his head and looks up at the ceiling. I have to hide the smug smirk on my face as he finally says, "Tanning. Highlights. Wax—which fuck that, by the way—and the team tattoo on my pec because it blended with the ursa clan tattoos. They touched those up; I'll have to explain that massive breach of bear protocol later. They also stuck a fucking hoop where it doesn't belong in my dick. There."

His blunt admission makes the rest of us guys look at one another, amusement flittering over our faces briefly before we burst into laughter. This guy is absolutely their icon of 'boy next door' and the fact that they had to add a Prince Albert—I assume—to give him a little 'edge' is pretty hysterical. His reaction is even better, and the look on Sydney's face is giving me more life than a blood bag at the moment.

"Yes, well. Okay, that's two." I say after I cough. "Next?"

Dante shifts his enormous bulk, crossing his arms over his chest before he answers. "I had tattoos all over prior. They did not touch them up as I specifically explained the magic of dragons tattoos and what would happen if they tried. Since it is not *my* magic that controls them, the implants we have would not have saved their lives."

"Holy shit, that's cool," our girl says with the first tiny smile she's flashed all night. "Good for you."

The dragon shrugs with a nonchalant look. "I felt I should be honest with them about the consequences of messing with a royal alpha dragon. So they gave me the team ink on my neck." He points to the bandage on the left side of his neck with an eye roll. "I had a ladder already, but they added a bolt to the forks in my tongue. No dye or injections—another thing that works poorly with my kind. They did rip hair with their wax and it wasn't nearly as fun as better uses for wax. That's about it."

I lied—the dragon had the least done to him, even though he was living the roughest of us all.

Before anyone can respond, the demon jumps in. "Highlights, wax, and the team tattoo on my arm. They already had the rings in places, but they added nipples and a belly button for no good reason. My tatts weren't in need of touch-ups—that's a demon thing a lot like the dragon's—and they tried a few shots that I suspect won't do a damned thing to demons. We're highly resistant to… just about everything humans have ever come up with."

"Except holy water?"

"Aw, sweet pea, you know that's a dad gummed myth. Don't be ridiculous." The demon pushes his hat up and gives her a slow, fond smile I can tell is making her squirm. "But you're welcome to try throwing some at me if I can get naked first."

Her eyes widen, and the joking atmosphere is sucked away as Sydney shakes her head. "No… no. That's, um, okay. Thanks, Huck."

Looking at her, I arch a brow as I ask, "Do I have to go before you will admit what we need to know? I'd think you would be less than eager to hear about my modifications."

"You'd be right, but here we are." That statement is followed by a very sarcastic looking smile and since it's not the sad face she's been making since we left the session, I'm going to allow her the victory.

"Fine, but note that this process for my kind is… less straightforward than the others." Sydney frowns, but nods, and I clear my throat. "First, they hooked me up to an IV to infuse various blood and whatever else they wanted to use to… mutate the nutrients within it. That's nothing new and happened at home frequently. I'm not going into vampire lore entirely, but it wasn't surprising. They did not opt to add piercings, as I have enough as it is. Tattoos are tricky for us as well, so they applied the team logo differently."

"What way?" Sydney asks curiously.

"By branding." I hold up my forearm with the bandage wrapped around it and shrug. "Not the worst thing I've survived, but not pleasant, either. Waxing and the rest as with most of you. However, whatever they've used the blood to induce will take a few days to have an effect. We'll know better what they hoped to achieve once it's absorbed into my system fully."

"What does that even mean, Bas?"

I give her a shrug, shaking my head. "It will be more easily understood by seeing the results than by spending time lecturing you on specific supernatural biology. Now, tell us what we need to know so we can order food. This little tête-à-tête has been a trifle exhausting."

Her head dips and she looks at her hands before sucking in a breath and letting it out slowly. I'd bet she's counting in her mind. When she looks up, her expression is blank again. "Highlights. Injections. Team tattoo. Implant renewal. Teeth whitening. Injections. Tattoos. Pierced nipples and genitals. Tanning. Makeup. Waxing. Stitching. Lashes. Exams."

That said, she pops to her feet, glaring at us. "Someone order me a pizza. I'm going to my room."

Well, that ended well. Hopefully, food and the mage will bring her out of this.

WALLOWING ISN'T PRETTY

SYDNEY

CLOSING the bedroom door behind me firmly, I lean against the wood and suck in deep breaths. I don't know why I'm so upset or why this—of all things—has sent me right over the edge of sanity. All the indignities, the deaths, the subjugation in the camps… None of it is as violating as losing control of the one thing I thought I'd kept for me.

I guess I know why I'm freaking out, but that doesn't help me deal with it.

"There's just nothing left for me," I murmur as my eyes slip close and I tip my chin up to the ceiling. "Everything is theirs."

A soft knock makes the door vibrate behind my body, and I jump, then freeze. The voice is low, but gentle as it says, "Vicious, let me in."

I don't open my eyes as I consider Rory's demand. Of everyone in this suite, he's probably the one who would understand how I'm feeling the most. But he's also dangerous to my focus, especially when my jumbled psyche is ready to admit defeat regarding my convictions. My brain also wants to shoot back that I can take care of myself—because I can—so the rest of them don't think a pretty face can sway me.

"C'mon, Sydney. I get why you're losing your shit. I can help."

I'll just bet he can.

Snorting, I blow out a long, slow breath, then say, "I want to be alone, Rory. I can't… deal with being perceived right now."

He's quiet for so long that I can visualize the question mark dancing around his head. Eventually, he says, "Sometimes, you think way too hard, Vicious. And while I'm not stupid, I don't let my logic brain override my ability to experience emotions. You *need* someone to help you with that right now."

I wrinkle my nose, not liking his implication. "I feel plenty of things."

"You know I didn't mean you're emotionless. I meant you push too many things down to your toes for later, and today, your shoes got full. You need to open the release valve or you won't be able to do what we want to do."

Damn it, he's right and I want to punch him for it.

"Fine," I murmur as I push off the door and step away so he can open it. "You can come in. But no one else. I can't… I need space."

His handsome features are fixed in a very sympathetic expression when he enters. It makes me feel silly, despite knowing that he's not trying to be a jackass. So I stomp over to my bed, flopping myself on it with a huff. "Now, Vicious, that's almost pouting. I find it quite adorable, but I doubt it reflects how you really feel."

"No, it doesn't."

Rory rounds the other side, sitting on the edge carefully. "I've been trading bits of myself since capture to stay sane. Sure, I could have lived as rough as everyone else and not died. But the tiny illusions of comfort I've bargained myself for are what kept me going, Sydney. I sacrificed myself purposefully so I could stay deluded."

"I did the opposite; I guess," I mutter as I wrap my arms around my chest, hugging my torso. "The jack-booted fuckheads took everything away from us, but my own body. I mean, someone could have and I bet they did to a lot of girls, but it's what I had left. You know?"

Rory tilts his head. "So you made that part of your identity? Seems risky in this environment, Vicious."

"I know. But that was all I had, Rory!" I cover my face with my hands, feeling emotions and weird vibes shooting around inside of me. "My dad was gone; the world was upside down. The absolute only thing I could mostly control was me. So I just did everything I could to learn stuff, to stay healthy as much as I could, and to keep people the fuck away from me."

I will not admit the truth to him; it will be way too annoying to get knowing looks from him.

"I get it." I hear the bed creak a bit as he scoots to lean back against the headboard—I think. "But that's kind of a dangerous thing to hang all your… strength on, isn't it? We're not safe from anything in the camps, and the fucking humans can do a lot of awful things just by accusing supes of random offenses. They don't have courts or appeals—anything could have destroyed this image you built at any time, Sydney. You know that."

Lifting my hand off of my eyes, I look over at the mage sadly. "You're right, but I guess I figured I could keep myself safe. I mean, to be honest, I did until now. That's nothing to wag your finger at, you know."

He snorts, crossing his legs at the ankles. "The bear and the demon probably helped. That's *not* me saying you didn't do a good job, but those two have definitely been running interference behind your back the whole time, Vicious. If you're having a 'come to Zeus' moment, you might as well go whole hog with it."

I blink, blanching as his words sink in. "What? Seriously? Those dill-holes were running around threatening people when I wasn't looking?"

"Fuck if I know for sure, but I would have in their place. They're both guys and they care about you. It's no stretch to assume they wanted to make certain people didn't break you simply because they could." His lips quirk as he shrugs, then puts his hands on his toned abs. "I'm not saying no one respected your choices without their meddling, by the way. You definitely seem like the type to reinforce your own edicts in a pretty firm way when crossed."

His words make me smile a bit, and I sigh. "Well, yes. But I hate thinking that I didn't earn my reputation. How many things can this fucking timeline take from me? After this… modification, I thought I'd lost the last bit I kept for me. Now you're telling me I could lose more."

Rory gives me a sour look, then rolls to his side with his cheek in his palm. "Self-pity doesn't look good on you, Vicious, and I thought everything did."

Ouch. That one hit me where it hurt—my pride.

"Not pulling punches tonight, huh?" I say ruefully. Rory winks at me, and I bite my lower lip. "Okay, maybe I am being a bit self-centered and definitely kind of whiny. It's just that I feel rocked by this 'vampires aren't all evil', followed by 'the leaders aren't lazy; they're imprisoned', then we got shuffled in classes and basically transformed into living Barbie dolls. I'm not great with change as it is, and my world is completely off-kilter now."

The mage nods, tapping the fingers of his freehand on the bed as he thinks about what I said. "Yeah, that'll do it. And I'm not saying you don't have a *right* to be upset, Sydney, but… We also don't have the luxury of indulging in our pain anymore. No supe has since the sweeps, and being put into these damn games makes that even less possible. The only way out for us in this scenario is through it—which you can't do if you're mopey and self-pitying."

"Your pep talk needs some work, Stormbringer," I chuckle softly.

He shrugs, giving me a smug grin. "I think too many people have been coddling you as it is. You don't want me to do it, too; that much I know."

Rubbing my fingers over my lips, I nod. "You're right, but that doesn't make this any easier. Being so attached to my previous beliefs is making it really hard to process this stuff, especially all at once. I spent so long using it to help me survive and protect myself that I'm just… struggling."

Rory nods, his fingers drumming on his tight abdomen. "I get it. When I got to my first camp and I figured out how everything worked, I had to do some serious soul-searching to decide what I would give up to survive. It wasn't like I immediately flipped a switch and became a character of ill-repute, you know."

My grin is tiny as I ask, "No? You seem like the type to make rash decisions."

"Look, I will not claim I enjoyed nothing. Of course, there were liaisons that were…tolerable and even some that were enjoyable. Not every 'supporter' of my lifestyle was a shitty sadist or a creepy asshat—in fact, I had some regulars who were quite kind and actually treated me like a real person. That didn't change *why* I had to do what I did, but it helped balance out the less pleasant relations."

I frown, not liking the sound of this at all. Knowing Rory had to give up so much of himself to survive when I walked around being a naïve dumbass while people cushioned my mental health behind my back makes me realize I'm luckier than I thought. "I'm sorry, Rory. Having people fuck around with my body clinically isn't nearly as bad as what you had to go through."

"Violation is violation, Vicious. It's not a contest." He scoots closer, wriggling across the bedspread until he's within reach. "Whether I gave up sexual favors for an easier lifestyle or you gave up the sanctity of your body to this damn game is irrelevant. The humans running the FHSA see us *all* as cattle, much like the dictators in their checkered past. It takes long-term planning and a lot of strategy to create a timeline where the masses in this damn place forgot how horrific that was simply because they want to feel superior."

Rolling onto my side, I look at him earnestly. "It was decades in the making, I think. They don't let us study that kind of information anymore, but I vaguely remember world history being taught with an eye to this kind of fascism when I was in lower schools. Our leaders made desperate decisions, I suppose, hoping to save everyone by rallying the rest of the world."

He presses his lips together for a moment, then says, "If the rest of the world actually gave a shit, there was a lot more they might have done. That's my opinion, of course, but I'm far older than you. You could ask the demon, the dragon, or even the vampire. The power of the global clans, covens, sleuths, what-the-fuck-ever… all of it was greater than what any powerful human military could achieve. They let us be subjugated because they feared humans across the globe joining Taterman."

"This is such a depressing fucking mess," I groan. "We've gone down a conspiracy rabbit hole now, but the further we go, the clearer this shit becomes. Is that dangerous? I don't know. What I know is that *no one* is coming to save us, Rory. Even with this damn show, even if we court a worldwide audience who loves our team—they're not coming to help."

"Duh." The mage chuckles roughly, shaking his head. "I've never believed that anyone—supernatural or human—was coming to save the folks here in Dick-Tater-Land. I made bargains with myself because I knew better than to expect it. *But…* I believe it's possible to use them all to save ourselves. If I didn't believe it was possible, I wouldn't be doing my damndest to get this team's shit together."

The sincerity in his voice is comforting, and while I still feel gross from head to toe after letting them breach my final boundary, I know that he's probably right. No matter what we do in the Games, the revolution will have to come from within the communities here in the camps. All the species will have to believe what Rory does—that our combined power is far greater than Taterman's weapons and enforcement squads. We will have to save ourselves when the time is right, instead of praying for others to don a cape and fly into battle.

To do that, we need to figure out how to fuck up the Markers—and I know someone who figured it out.

I'M NICER THAN MY FACE LOOKS

ELIAS

SIPPING MY COFFEE, I wait for the others to rise. Last night was irritating for me, but as a royal, I frequently had to give up my personal needs for the good of my kingdom long before the idiotic humans locked me up. If it weren't for their miraculous invention that keeps us from accessing most of our powers, I'd still be reigning over my people off the West Coast, unconcerned with their bullshit insecurities.

However, that ship sailed four years ago and as much as it chaps my spikes, I'm beholden to their whims.

The vampire was sure the magical Lothario could calm the little rebel down. He practically had to hog-tie the demon and the bear to keep them from joining in, but in the end, we allowed Stormbringer to shoot his shot. The rest of us took care of getting dinner, and when it came, I walked theirs down the hall to her room. The secretive thumbs-up I got when I delivered it made me hopeful, and now I'm simply waiting to see if things have been smoothed over. Our first class is one about social media with Krista, so we all need to be in sync.

"You get up this early every morning, dragon?"

Turning to look at the bloodsucker, I nod. "Force of habit. My kind like to greet the sun over the waves and though I haven't been able to since my capture, it's been ingrained for too long to change now."

Sebastian walks over to pour himself a mug of the caffeinated brew, eyeing me with an amused expression. "That's a lot of words for you."

"Sometimes, more words are necessary; sometimes, they are not."

"Communication is much smoother when everyone is sharing as much as possible, but then, I'm a demon," Huck says as he stumbles out to join us. He's still in his joggers, but the damn hat is on his head like it's glued there permanently.

Shrugging, I take another sip before I respond. "Unsurprising."

"That's more like it," the vampire says with a smirk. "Though you two being on opposing ends of the spectrum isn't a stretch. Demons enjoy twisting words like the Fae, while dragons have made grunting a language unto itself."

"Please don't provoke anyone, Whitmore." Thad walks out of his room and into the kitchen area with a yawn. "We need to be calm and united for Sydney. She'll be in a mood for a couple of days after that bullshit yesterday. Trust me, I know."

We all look at one another, sharing a grimace as the other two pour themselves morning joe. I hope he's mistaken; the mage was sent to help her come to terms with her anger. If he failed, it will set us back for as long as she rages at something that cannot be changed. I understand *why* someone raised like a human might attach such significance to a thing that can be taken away at any time—don't mistake me. But I also know that this will not be the last thing they force on us as we move through this cocked-up contest. That much became clear when they added piercings to places that audiences should never be able to see; they intend to play up our sexuality for popularity, as much as any other skills or attributes.

There may not be lines these fuckers refuse to cross, and we need to slowly prepare ourselves for that.

"Good morning."

The soft voice catches me off-guard, and as we whip our heads toward the hall to see Sydney coming toward us, I'm struck by the difference in her posture from last night. Her hair is twisted into the long braid again, and she's got makeup on, though not as much as the humans put on her. Unlike the rest of us, the little rebel is dressed in her uniform, every inch of her looking like she's ready to face the nonsense downstairs. I have to cover my surprise with my mug because I don't want to spook her.

"Hey, Syd," the bear says with a broad grin. He walks over and squeezes her shoulder with a smile that you'd have to be an idiot not to recognize as smitten. "Want a coffee?"

"I think so. Thanks, Thaddy," she says. Her gaze flits to each of us and she ducks her head as he walks away. "So… I'm sorry I was so sharp. I needed to work through some shit—which I guess you know—but I also needed to get over myself. I didn't know that, but I do now."

Sebastian blinks, tilting his head as he stares. "Huh?"

I'm kind of impressed that she shut him the fuck up.

"Rory came to talk to me. He helped me sort through all the shit, although I was pretty determined to feel sorry for myself." Sydney sighs heavily, fiddling with the buttons on her shirt. "Because of that, I forgot that you guys and every other damn supe in these places have all had to suffer indignities as bad and worse as I did last night. And that perhaps I'd been sticking my head in the sand about how shitty others have it, especially since no one ever called me out on my bullshit."

Huck and Thad look at each other guiltily, which almost makes me laugh. It's obvious who was helping her stay angry and focused only on her own injustices. I can't fault them for it, though; I probably would have wanted her to stay oblivious to the darker side of the camps, too. Sydney looks at them with a stern gaze, her arms crossed over her chest as her posture stiffens again.

"Don't do that anymore. I know why you did it, and I appreciate you wanting to protect me. But I have to be aware of everything if we're going to succeed. And I can't be above criticism, either. Rory called me to the carpet on being self-absorbed and he was right to do it."

"I am occasionally quite erudite," the mage says as he strolls down the hall with rumpled hair and a smirk. "People miss it because I'm so damned hot. But the old noggin is just as sharp as yours, guys."

Huck rolls his eyes as the bear gives our woman her coffee. "But you don't mind being spoiled as a prize piggy, I assume."

Sydney shrugs and takes the drink with a grateful smile. "You are supposed to pretend to be courting me. That's the plan, isn't it? I don't know a damn thing about dating, but everything I've seen says this kind of thing is part of it."

"It is."

Sebastian rolls his eyes at me, and I consider throttling the sarcastic asshole until he nods. "For some of us, it will be easier than others to play the role."

"Oh, I'm so sorry you have to deal with someone who repulses you." The little rebel snarls into her cup, her brows furrowed as she makes sure not to meet anyone's eyes. Her posture changes ever-so-slightly and I realize that reading her isn't just about watching her face. She learned to control the amount of emotion shown there, but her body is full of clues if watched closely enough.

We'll need to work on that, and I may be the one person who can teach her about it.

"Welcome to Social Media Savvy, team!"

The chipper human in charge of our team makes my teeth grind, but you'd never know it. I find the ones that pretend everything here is completely normal and not a horror show of the worst behavior in any species' history to be the most egregious. At least the overtly evil guards who relish using cattle prods or the creepy types that Stormbringer likely serviced wear their lack of humanity on their sleeves. People like Krista are vacant automatons that accept the awful deeds of their kind because their own lives are more comfortable with it.

I want them to suffer even more than the others, because their apathy helped enslave every race that wasn't theirs with a wink and smile.

Sydney bristles a little, I can tell, because her spine stiffens at the woman's tone. Hiding the curl of my lips as I lean back and stack my head behind my hands, I clock the reaction of my other team members. The vampire is sneering—not at all unusual, so he's off the hook to maintain deception in irritating environments. Thad looks bored as he, too, adjusts his bulk to fit into these stupidly small desk things. His indifference isn't perfect, but easily honed. Stormbringer is flashing her his megawatt smile as a distraction, but I bet his eyes give him away. Of course, the demon is the very picture of relaxed, uncaring, good old boy lassitude.

Two skilled liars out of five aren't unworkable. I'll have to work with the ones who aren't used to keeping things buttoned up, even while being physically harmed, like I am. Being in the 'lockdown' quadrants of every camp I've been in makes me an expert on that, especially because the humans who chose not to hide their cruelty loved to focus their efforts on anyone with lineage in leadership. They believed it would keep us from rising up when it only encouraged a simmering hatred that lay dormant, waiting for a time like now.

Hence why I'm perfectly willing to be part of this miniature resistance, even if we are all destroyed by it.

"As we discussed in the last, more informal session, you are being groomed by your full slate of professors and techs to fit images that will allow you to gain as many raving fans as possible in the quickest time you can. Those numbers—both individually and as a team—will be important for many reasons. You have to be obsessed with them in order to succeed; there is no other way to climb the ladder in this situation."

"That sounds... healthy," Sydney remarks wryly.

Krista frowns for a second, then continues. "Your focus, when not on camera, needs to be nurturing, maintaining, and cultivating those fans so thoroughly that they will do anything, say anything, and give anything for your attentions, even from afar."

Rory chuckles as he runs a hand through his hair, rumpling it perfectly. "You want us to create followings that would literally go to war for us if anyone were to attack, yes?"

Cute, mage. That smartass remark was awfully close to the fucking line.

"Yes!" Krista claps her hands with an excited expression. "We want you to whip them into such a froth that they will even go after *other* competitor's fans if they *dare* to speak ill of you. The crazier they are, the more likely they are to believe everything you say and do—without question. We don't even want them to *think* about it, only echo your every word."

I watch the vampire pinch the bridge of his nose as the cheery woman describes the brainwashing Taterman used to get all the scared and dissatisfied humans to support his rise to dictatorship. Sebastian knows how easily led unhappy people are, especially when people perceived to be powerful pay attention to them. That's the blood bag vamps don't even have to use their mojo on.

"Isn't that dangerous, darlin'?" Huck drawls as he stretches his legs out in front of him. "Whippin' people into that level of obsession always gets the truly deranged on board. I assume we won't always be in this camp as we're promoting this little venture."

Good fucking question, demon.

"It's true that there may be off-campus events at some point, but there's no way any of your devotees will get into the camps, the competition arenas, or slip past the military escorts you'd have for any non-camp based events. President Taterman, in his infinite wisdom, has decreed that all the players in the games will always be protected by both human and contracted magical means as they honor their species in competition."

I want to snarl in frustration. Monroe was definitely testing the boundaries of our confinement and the possibility of slipping communication out of the dragnet. Krista's eagerness to show that we'll be 'safe' from any of the mouth-foaming loonies we're supposed to court also illustrated how difficult it will be to get the true message into the world. Whoever they have planning their strategy for this is smarter than anyone in the administration has been before.

WHAT YOU SEE IS WHAT YOU GET

SYDNEY

NOTHING about this training is making me feel any less apprehensive about the assholes in charge. It's laughable that they're sharing their fucking playbook for taking over America with those they put under their boot, but I've never assumed the people at the top had any self-awareness. In fact, I question that most of them even have a goddamn clue what most of these words mean. No, this strategy was developed by educated, slick puppet masters, especially since it was used to fool leaders of species that should have damn well known better.

I guess even supernaturals can have a blind spot with dangerous idealism.

"Syd, you okay?" Thad murmurs as we head for the next session. "Lunch is coming soon, if that's what's eating you."

Arching a brow, I give him a stern look. "I'm not hangry—well, not *just* hangry. This manipulation stuff makes my skin crawl."

"Prefer the blunt 'in your face' honesty approach, mm?" Sebastian smirks at me knowingly. "That will work well in some situations, but a lot of this will be very Machiavellian. If the Games were simply 'to the death' fighting, it wouldn't matter. But adding in this popularity aspect makes everything much more difficult. They're giving us just enough training to get through the first round, I'd say. After that? We're probably on our own."

Huck nods as he lopes alongside me. "Reckon I agree with the mosquito. They won't bother giving much in the way of training once the shitshow is up and running, sweet pea. That will leave us to fend for ourselves—total Darwinism in every aspect."

Pinching the bridge of my nose, I sigh. "I know, guys. I'm not naïve enough to believe these dickheads are going to be helpful. In fact, I assume they'll do all sorts of dirty shit to sway opinions in the direction they choose. I'm just adjusting my entire worldview to include everything I've learned since we were tapped."

"Let her have the time to process when we are not in front of them."

Turning to look at Elias over my shoulder, I give him a small, grateful smile. The dragon often interjects when the others are being too over-bearing or too demanding. I didn't expect it, but I appreciate it more than I can say out loud. "Exactly. I'm sure I'll get my shit together soon, but I have to let this stuff simmer until it's cooked."

"Speaking of which," Rory pipes up. "Putting these bullshit classes before lunch makes me want to stab myself in the eye with a fork."

"Agreed." I reach for the door to the corridor, but Thad gets to it first, smiling as he holds the door open. "Stop that shit."

"I can't. We're supposed to pretend to dig you," the bear replies cheerily as we find the classroom the schedule lists for *Style & Flair*. "Stormbringer, what the hell is this going to be about?"

"Why are you asking me? I have no idea." Rory huffs and the rest of the guys just stare at him. Finally, he wrinkles his nose, grumbling, "Probably something to do with clothes and attitude. We got made over, and this is probably about how to put together looks if we get access to wardrobe. That's a guess, but it would be a good marketing strategy. They don't know how much natural ability any of the competitors have in presentation."

Just fucking great. Another torture session I'd trade for an actual *torture session.*

"There will be events where you are provided *basic* accoutrements to take part. *However*, it is always in your best interest to cultivate your fan base so well that they are eager to sponsor or support you by getting you better equipment, fancier clothes, or other upper tier necessities. Your classes on creating the rabid fanbase are all in service of swaying the audience in your favor so that they will trip over themselves to take part in your journey this way."

Scratching my chin, I keep my eyes on the paper as I take notes on what Shoshana is telling us. She's a snooty dilettante, and her attitude makes me want to strangle her on the spot. Unfortunately, doing so won't help us win this damn thing, and she's more annoying than she is evil. I'd wager she grew up with money, never worked a day in her life before the Sweeps, and her family probably made a fortune off of confiscated supernatural lands or businesses. Everything about her screams entitlement that cannot be hidden beneath a fake veneer of professionalism.

Some people spend way too much time drinking their own delulu juice and it's plain as day when you listen to them rant.

"So we're supposed to stroke their egos until they give us stuff?" Rory asks, his expression amused.

"That's it exactly, Mr. Stormbringer!" Shoshana claps her hands like she's teaching toddlers how to write their name. "We want them to send you fabulous clothes, accessories, weapons… anything you can desire. That's why it's so important to focus your team on the branding and follow the planned roles as closely as possible. Giving the audience what they want always leads to easy conversion."

"I *hate* feeling scripted," I mutter at the desk. "It's fake and gross."

Shoshana clicks her way over to me in the towering heels, and I look up when she clears her throat. "That attitude will not help your team succeed, Miss Jolie. But I suppose it's not surprising from someone who lacks powers entirely."

My eyes narrow as I look her up and down. "Rich coming from a human with no conception of how supernaturals' powers manifest, nor any powers of their own."

She crosses her arms over her chest, looking irritated as she flips her chestnut hair. "I don't need to know how you people work to know you're the anchor that will weigh this team at the bottom of the lake."

Elias snorts, his bulk flexing as he mimics her arm movement. It looks *much* more intimidating on him and I have to cover my grin with my hand. "Humans never develop *any* powers. The Markers are the only thing keeping you in the position you're in. Without them, this situation would look very different."

The woman gapes at him for a moment, then screws her face up as she smacks the edge of my desk. "You can thank the assistance of your own kind combined with our superior technology for your dog collar, prisoner."

I'm about to shoot my mouth off, but Sebastian moves so quickly I barely register it until he's standing toe to toe with the chick. He looks down at her with a blank expression, but his eyes are a deep ruby that indicates his fury. "You will *not* be violent in her direction—ever."

What the fuck.

"You can't—"

The vampire tilts his head, his brow arched elegantly. "I can't? Vampires have more connections and privilege than other supernaturals. You've probably heard of my father… Astaroth Whitmore?"

Shoshana's face drains of color completely and she steps back shakily. "I…"

"I'm here for a reason, and if I report your insolence back to him, I'm certain it will be ill-received."

I don't like being defended by a vampire using the slimiest vampire in existence to threaten an enemy. But I can't undercut Sebastian when he's drawing a line; even I'm not so socially inept. He's clarifying that my team will not stand for the professors doing certain things—which isn't a bad thing. We haven't had a human male instructor yet, but I doubt they'll be any better than the females. The guards at F.E.A.R. certainly made every day a challenge with their abuse of authority; I don't want to think about what the shit weasels in this place will do.

"Sebastian, I think she gets it, buddy," Huck says as he smirks at the woman. "Miss Larson knows our girl isn't to be trifled with, so we can get back to dressing for success now."

The brunette woman backs up carefully, tottering as she puts space between herself and the intimidating bloodsucker. "Understood, Mr. Whitmore."

Sebastian's serial killer look fades to a pleasant smile as he nods, then goes back to his seat. "Good. I abhor miscommunication."

For fuck's sake.

"Ahem." Shoshana coughs as she rifles through some papers, obviously still trying to get her bearings. "Your assignment for the next class will be to use the software on your tablet to plan fake looks for several scenarios. Obviously, you will not always have access to such an array of items as the app provides, but the point is to judge how instinctively you can combine them."

Thad groans softly, looking up at the ceiling as if pleading for help. "Barbie fashion creator shit? Come on, man. Can't we just fucking stab things?"

I blink, my lips quirking up as I smother a laugh. Thad can smash things, especially in his bear form, but he's more of a cuddly teddy bear than a killer. I think he hates this shit as much as I do. "Apparently not, Thad. We have to learn to work the runway *and* gut our enemies to win this thing."

Rory laughs, tilting his chair back precariously. "I would pay good money to watch you do a supermodel walk, Vicious. It would be the highlight of my month."

"Good fucking luck with that. Sydney won't be caught dead strutting around in heels and a ballgown," Thad retorts. "She's all bad ass and no frills."

"That won't matter if they make us go to some big ass party or dance," the vampire cuts in. "Then we'll *all* have to show our style and flair—or whatever the fuck they say to do. Right, Shoshana?"

The terrified human is sitting at the desk now, her posture rigid as she keeps it between her and us. When no one continues, she finally nods. "Yes, that's correct. We have been told there will be many scenarios—fighting, formal, sporting, hunting, social, and more. You could very well be put into formal attire for a social event that is televised and incentivized in various ways."

Incentivized—just fucking peachy.

"I assume that means every single time we're filmed it's considered an opportunity to build that relationship, then?"

Rory's question is on point, but I think we all know the answer by now. He's making the human say it out loud on purpose, though. We all need to hear her confirm we are expected to sell ourselves at every turn to survive this and win the FHSA, the goodwill world-wide they so desperately need.

"Yes, Mr. Stormbringer. Winning requires a great deal of focus, sacrifice, and humility, but the reward will be worth it."

Dante makes a disbelieving sound and I grin. Of course, none of us truly believe the dictators who control our lives to keep their fucking promises. We hope, we wish, and we dream—but the truth is that we're planning the revolution because they cannot be trusted. Supes tried that before the Sweeps and look where we all are now. But humans like Shoshana don't have any real context for the seething hatred or mistrust we have for them because they don't think they did anything wrong.

"Just wanted to make certain I understood you correctly." He looks at me and I jerk my chin up, getting his point. "Because I, too, despise a lack of clarity."

Gee, guys, why don't you just hold up a blinking 'do you get it, now, Sydney?' sign and be done with it.

"Excellent. Now, before class ends, pull out the tablets so I can go over the program you'll use to create your portfolios for the next class." Shoshana waits for everyone to follow her instructions, and I stifle the groan before it eludes me.

YOU GOT PLAYED, PLAYA

THADDEUS

LUNCH WAS A FAIRLY quick affair because we had to get as much energy generating food into our bodies as possible before our next class. This one is bound to be easier than the last few—for one, the instructors aren't sniveling humans looking down their noses at us.

The bigger plus is that we get to fight and wield weapons.

I'm not violent by nature, though my bear is certainly protective enough of those I care about to decimate anyone who deserves it. My sleuth leader has always wanted me to embrace the animal side more, stand up to things to help the cubs, and be ready to take his position someday. I'm just not that guy, though. Being the leader wouldn't be horrible if they didn't expect me to fend off new alpha bears or fight with other species for shit when needed. I can do it, and I'd probably win, but I simply dislike violence as the solution to problems.

The only exception to that is sitting next to me inhaling her tray of food like they're going to go back to limiting our rations later in the day. Sydney's never been girly, though I wouldn't mind if she was. From the moment we met, I've felt this pull to her that makes every cell in my body hum with satisfaction. So I honestly wouldn't care if she was covered in pink from head to toe, poured into leather, or wearing a fucking purple dinosaur costume. She's just the best girl I've ever met and I'm happy to be in her orbit, even if she barely realizes I'm a dude.

Which is pretty accurate most days, unfortunately.

"I'm looking forward to fighting with you guys again," Rory says, as he sucks down a protein smoothie. "The dragon is pretty fucking great at the physical angle. It's like I actually learned shit."

Elias grunts, shrugging as he leans back in his chair. He just ate enough meat to feed a small family for two days and didn't look full in the slightest. "We are trained to battle from the moment we can walk, especially those of us destined for leadership and the defense forces."

"Imagining a small dragon toddler wielding a sword bigger than him is kind of amusing," Huck drawls before he belches a smoky puff of air. I have no idea what he was eating or how demons digest, but the weird smoke is interesting. "Is that accurate in the slightest? Please tell me it is, Your Highness."

A heavy sigh escapes the dragon's mouth as he gives the playful demon an annoyed look. "They had appropriate gear for younglings. We didn't look like cartoon characters, Monroe."

Sydney coughs, covering her mouth as she tries not to choke on her third sandwich. Once she's got it under control, she grins at the grumpy lizard. "I don't know, big guy. That image is pretty fun. You sure it's not right? Like really sure?"

He frowns at her, then shakes his head. "It is not, little rebel. Even if it would please you, I cannot lie about it. If it will suffice, I will instruct you on using a broadsword as I did when I was young."

Damn. That's a solid offer and we should all *strive to get him to extend it.*

"Hmmm. I think I might enjoy that, Elias. Offer accepted."

Sebastian mutters something under his breath, and I smirk. He knows how to fight with that weapon as well, and the dragon has undercut him. I watch the bloodsucker sip from his innocuous mug carefully, unsure how I feel about his barely contained interest in Sydney. Huck and I aren't stupid —we know these dudes find her attractive. We also know she's been intentionally sheltered from dating and sex by her own choice the entire time we've lived in Tempest Seven. I'm not sure she gets that they're gunning for her for real anymore than she understood how obsessed the demon and I have been.

"I'm better with magic, alas, sweet pea. However, I believe the mage and I will be downright indispensable when the time comes." Huck gives her his best country boy smile, the Stetson tipped back on his forehead as he smiles at her.

That son of a bitch is good *at making himself look adorable and sweet when he wants to.*

"Have you guys noticed the atmosphere in here?" Rory interrupts as he leans forward on his elbows. "It's oddly quiet, yet I feel like there's a thousand eyes on us."

I blink, thinking about his question as I pretend to leisurely sweep my eyes over the room as I turn to Syd. The mage is right; there's an ominous feel to the cafeteria and the lack of noise around us is weird. People are talking, but they're keeping it quiet in their various groups. Occasionally, I see someone's gaze flicker to our table, then away quickly. Something is going on, and I was too busy overthinking our relationship with Sydney to notice.

"Yes," Sebastian says as he continues drinking with a bland expression. "I've been monitoring it, but I haven't caught the whispers. Apparently, our fellow competitors are using their skills to obfuscate the surrounding sound. That's not a good sign."

Grimacing, I look over at Dante, then Huck, who both nod. They haven't heard anything, either, then. "They could just be strategizing. It wouldn't be a good idea to let everyone hear what they're planning."

"One does not plan in public places, bear."

The dragon is right; I was just hoping this wasn't actually a problem. "Fine. They're purposefully gossiping behind spells and whatnot. Since the teams have barely interacted, what the hell is their problem?"

"I don't know. Maybe it's because we're all so pretty?" The mage chuckles, then frowns when we all roll our eyes at him. "Look, I wanted you guys to pay attention, but I doubt it's anything serious. If it was, whatever it was would have made its way to our feet long before the end of lunch. Right?"

Sebastian nods, setting his mug down to steeple his fingers together as he leans in. "Stormbringer is probably correct. Violence would have erupted quickly, rather than simmering for an hour. We will need to keep our ears open as we head down to the gym. Someone will be stupid enough to let it slip outside of their safe zone. We're not surrounded by evil geniuses, after all."

Perfect. Just add another thing to the plate—why not?

As we head for the elevators, my entire body is on alert. I hate this kind of tension; it makes everyone and everything in the vicinity feel like a threat. That riles up my bear, and he's a grumpy fuck when he gets territorial. It's why I try to stay calm and placid all the time—I don't *want* to be on the edge constantly.

"I'm useless with this shit," Sydney mutters as she stabs the elevator button with her finger. "If I don't get whatever I'm supposed to have before these things start, I might lose my fucking mind. I hate feeling like the weak link even more than I hate being violated by my captors."

This way, madness lies; time for a subject change.

"Syd, you're great hand-to-hand. Even Brick and Lancaster said so," I say. She rolls her eyes at me, and I smile guilelessly. "Come on. You're doing well with accepting the changes; don't backslide."

"Ugh." Sydney wrinkles her nose and crosses her arms over her chest as we wait for the ding of the doors opening. "Fine. I'll try not to let this bother me because I get to beat on you dicks soon."

"That's the spirit," Rory chirps and her arm snakes out to punch his arm before he can blink. "Niiiiiice speed there, Vicious. See? You're getting *some* powers, just slowly. That was fast as hell."

"He's right, sweet pea." Huck winks at our girl, holding his hand out when the bell signals the elevator's arrival. "Now let's go. We need to get changed before class begins."

"You know, forcing us to wear different uniforms to various things is a waste of time and money." Sydney walks into the car, waiting for the rest of us to join her. When Dante blocks other teams from joining us with a snarl, she chuckles softly. "I guess that's one way to keep people talking about us, big guy."

"I see no reason to allow them in our space if they are plotting something."

His shrug is nonchalant, but I recognize the protective spark in his eyes. The dragon might be pragmatic, but he's also quite good at keeping his natural instincts under wraps. Out of the entire team, what I know about his kind—besides their legendary tempers and tendency to hoard things—is that they are fiercely possessive of what they consider theirs. It feeds into the hoarding, I'm sure, but it extends to other beings as well. Elias showed his hand just then, and I bet the others saw it, too.

"He has a point," I offer, hoping to show the enormous man that I'm on his side. The knowing smirk on his face tells me he understands, and I reach out to push the buttons. "But we're not going anywhere if we're all too distracted to remember simple shit."

"I'm stuck in the middle," Sydney complains. "How am I supposed to get through the wall of muscle and testosterone mist?"

Chuckling, Rory reaches out to tug her braid lightly. "Very true. Point to you this time."

Her eyes narrow as she pulls her hair closer to her body. "If we're keeping score, you're all in the negative. Keep that in mind."

"No fair, darlin'. I've been accommodating as hell. Where did I lose points?"

"Hey, wait!"

"Excuse me, but—"

They all scramble to correct her and I just stay quiet, smiling smugly as she growls. I'm smart enough to know she was baiting us and if we protested, she was going to use that to deduct more fake points for being annoying. Sydney turns to look at me, her lips curved fondly. "Thad wins this round. He knew better than to irritate me by whining. You all need to take your cues from him."

Ha. Suck it, losers.

"Judas, Lilith, and Lucifer…" Huck grumbles as he smacks his forehead. "I walked right into that one like a damn freshly summoned darkling, I swear."

"Sure did, buddy." I wink at him, waiting for Sydney to turn away and then make a victorious face at my friend. "Classic blunder, really."

"I thought that was starting a land war in Asia," Stormbringer mumbles as he rakes his hands through his golden locks. "Alright. Don't irritate Vicious is rule number one—got it."

The vampire taps his fingertips against his lips, looking thoughtful. "Seems like that rule is rather open to interpretation. I'm not sure it's an achievable goal."

"Maybe for you, fang face. The others might be able to do it," she counters. "I like this points thing. I might just keep it. It's like a demerit system for jackasses."

I groan softly and she whirls around to look at me reproachfully. My smile is sheepish when our eyes meet. "Syd, I'm not saying it's *impossible*, but I am saying it's not really an objective measurement. You can be a little… volatile sometimes."

"Ten point deduction for you, Thaddy. Nice job canceling out your victory, man."

We all look at one another over her head, our expressions equally grim as the ding of the elevator announces the bottom level. Huck moves aside, letting Sydney walk past him with her head held high, then shrugs. "Looks like we hoisted ourselves by our petards, gentleman. This should be interesting."

ROLL TIDE, BABY

SYDNEY

"BE FASTER, Calvin. Get those feet moving!"

I wink at Thad when Brick yells at him, then duck the punch he throws in frustration. "He's right, you know. You need to work on foot speed for hand-to-hand when you aren't shifted."

The bear growls in irritation and I dance away, moving out of range, so he has to follow me. Thad and Huck have sparred with me many times during the past several years, which I told our professors. We're all too familiar with one another's moves, and it's obvious when we're able to anticipate what's coming next.

"Thad, switch with Whitmore. You two are doing more circling than landing blows. That won't help anyone."

Thank fuck Lancaster sees it; I need to be challenged if I don't have supe powers yet.

The vampire strolls over slowly, bare-chested in low slung black joggers and sneakers. I swallow hard as my eyes rake over his muscled yet lithe form up to his red eyes. Of course, he's bone dry, unlike the rest of us, because his kind doesn't sweat. It's unfair as fuck and I hate him just a little more for it. "You won't be fast enough."

I snort, getting into position as he switches with Thad. The bear looks disgruntled as he moves to take Sebastian's place with Rory, and I don't blame him. Rory is quick for a decent-sized guy, and he definitely has had some formal training. He's not as good as Sebastian or Elias, but he's good competition. "That remains to be—"

Before I can finish, Sebastian has me pinned to a wall with his hand on my throat gently. Our bodies are pressed together in a way that's absolutely sinful, and I look at him indignantly as he smirks. One brow arches as he says, "You were saying?"

"That's cheating. You didn't even call it," I growl as I try to ignore the throbbing in my body as his frame grips mine.

Rolling his eyes, the vampire flashes a fang, licking it with a smug glee. "Enemies in the Games will *not* warn you before they attack, Sydney. Fairness is not mandated in our world, and the other players will *not* behave with honor."

I hate when this asshole is right.

"Fine," I grit out as I push at his chest. The skin under my palms is cool, but the muscles are firm as fuck. It makes me heat up from head to toe, and I glare when he doesn't let go. "Let me go and we'll go again, dickface."

Sebastian chuckles, his expression still full of pleased egotism as he looks me in the eye with his crimson stare. "You're not scared. That's interesting."

Definitely not frightened, but I'm sure as hell not telling him *what* I'm feeling in this position. "Of course not. We're just sparring, Whitmore."

His fingers flex against the column of my neck, squeezing a tiny bit until I feel the pressure. "Not even now?"

I can't respond; I'm too busy tamping down my response, so I just give him a dirty look. When he finally lets go, I give his chest another shove and move away. "You're such an asshole. I don't know how you stand yourself, much less how anyone else does."

"Oh, I have skills people enjoy," he drawls as he wanders back into the sparring area slowly. "They more than make up for my occasionally abrasive behavior."

Somehow, I believe him, but he doesn't need to know that.

"Let's go again," I reply as I drop into my stance again. "And this time, let me work up to your stupid vampire tricks. I'll get there if you actually work with me."

"I highly doubt that," he counters as he grins. "But we can try."

Now it's a challenge and I'll get there if it kills me.

By the time the class is over, I feel like overcooked spaghetti. That damn bloodsucker stayed with me the entire fucking time, pushing me past every limit I thought I had. He was intent on driving me up the goddamn wall with his taunts and lack of exhaustion. Worse than that, he successfully beat me so many times that a lesser person with no pent-up fury would have given up. I, however, let the eruption of heat he made simmer inside my body with every one of his purposefully intimate dominations fuel me to continue fighting back.

The hotter he made me, the harder I fought back—I don't know if he realized that or if it was just a side benefit, though.

When Lancaster tells us to check our devices for the post-session break downs, I groan audibly from my spot on the bench. I'm drenched in sweat, feeling disgusting, and definitely not ready to read about my abject failure to beat that jackass even once. We have an all team lecture after this, so I'm definitely going to make use of the showers before we get crammed into a room full of other supes.

"I'm headed for the showers. No way I'm going to that shit without a quick rinse," I mutter dejectedly. No one responds, so I limp to the locker room to grab my toiletry basket out of my locker. Once I have it, I grab an embroidered towel, sneering at the FSHA logo angrily before I choose the first stall I see.

It's clean and obviously newly installed, as there's a bench for my basket, hooks for my clothes, and fancy looking showerheads. The suite has a bathroom like this and it was quite an experience using it for the first time, compared to the communal bathrooms in my apartment before the selection. I sigh, shaking my head as I feel guilt at the pampering we're receiving while others suffer in this camp and all the others. Logically, I know that's nothing I can control, nor can I refuse to bathe or eat in protest.

But it sucks and I feel like a traitor sometimes, despite our grand plans to fight our way to a revolution that will save those people.

"Stop blaming yourself for things you have no control over."

My eyes widen when the voice echoes in the shower area and I hear another rainfall start-up next to me. I'm definitely bare-ass naked now, so I clutch the curtain to my front and peek out into the open area where my clothes are hanging. "What the hell, man?"

The vampire chuckles, then I hear several other laughs as feet slap against the tile floor. "Sydney, we're all getting rinsed off. You can't have thought we were going to the lecture smelly, right?"

I didn't think I'd be naked in the shower inches away from all of them, that's for goddamn sure!

"I suppose that makes sense, but I wasn't prepared for you all to come in here while I'm showering, Sebastian," I retort. "Talking to you while I'm naked isn't my idea of a comfortable situation."

"True. I'm not usually doing a lot of 'talking' when I'm naked with people," he muses, and I hear Elias snort. Soon, Huck and Rory join him, and I wait to see if Thad does as well. He might be too far away, but that doesn't matter to the vampire. "However, I'd prefer a less pressing timeline than what we have before the coaching. That's why we're all in here together, obviously."

Wrinkling my nose at his perfectly acceptable answer, I step back into my hot as hell shower and start scrubbing myself quickly. We don't have time to waste, so I'm moving this along, but I'm not happy about it. "Fine. Keep to your little chambers, and I'll keep to mine, boys. I can nurse my pride on my own."

"Improving your skills is not something to feel ashamed of." The dragon's voice is loud enough to be heard over the water, and a few hums of agreement reach me as well.

I know he's right, but losing to Sebastian makes it smart more. Being the non-super power gal in the middle is hard enough without the snarky guy I want to throttle whooping my ass. That I was turned on by it rubs salt even further in the ego wound, and I'd sooner run a sword through my gut than let anyone find *that* out. So yeah, I'm bitter and I'd prefer to brood in private.

Yet another thing I won't get because we're fucking chess pieces, not people to these fuckers.

"Vicious, the dragon's got a point. Your bear may not be fast, but he's got a killer right hook. I'm gonna bruise," Rory whines as the rest of them laugh. "It's not funny, you guys. I'm the prettiest of the bunch, and that's an important weapon. Don't mark the face next time."

Thad snorts from what must be the farthest shower. "Then don't make cheeky remarks to rile me up, mage. You asked for it."

I frown. "What cheeky remarks?"

"Nothing!"

The word is a five-part harmony chorusing their reluctance to tell me what made my teddy bear friend get rougher than usual while sparring. I don't believe it for a second and if they weren't naked, they'd be standing in front of me with pie plates for halos, I bet. No woman alive would be dumb enough to let that bullshit ride. "Fine, keep it to yourselves, jerks. But if you step over the line with this macho horseshit, I'm going to be really pissed. Pushing one another is okay—we need that. Tormenting one another into being too rough is another. Rory and Thad lose ten points."

Their groans make me smile as I scrub off the rest of the workout grime and rinse the conditioner they provided out of my hair. By the time I'm opening my stall to grab my towel, the grumbles are finally dying down. I dry myself from head to toe, then use all the stupid lotions and sprays to ensure I'm smooth and smell like flowers.

"What is that scent?"

My brow furrows as Sebastian asks his question in a strangled tone. The scents of the perfume are gardenia and currant with jasmine and citrus. He's smelled it before, so I don't know why he's being a weirdo. "My shower gel and lotion? It's the stuff they told me I have to wear. Nothing new. What's your problem?"

"No." His voice is low and dark as he snarls at me. "Something else. You need to… check your towels."

What the fuck?

"Stop being creepy, asshole. How did you know I'm drying off? Are you looking? I'll gut you—"

A loud cough echoes off the walls of the shower room and I hear Elias say, "You turned your shower off, little rebel. But… the vampire is correct. Do as he suggests. *Now.*"

I roll my eyes, irritated at their apparent need to tell me what to do. When I look down at the white, fluffy cotton, my eyes widen. There's blood on it and since Sebastian didn't injure me, I've somehow gotten my first period in months. Luckily for me, I made certain to put the supplies they provided in my bedroom, but that was supposed to be an 'emergency' rip cord.

Why the hell is this happening now? I'm not due for my implant change, nor the magic renewal yet.

"Motherfucker," I growl as I look around carefully, then deal with the situation. Pulling my clothes on quickly, I gather up my stuff and stomp to my locker to put my kit away. This is the most annoying thing that could have happened and here I am, trying not to die of embarrassment that a fucking vampire had to tell me about it. The existence of my period doesn't make me upset, of course; that's normal for women. I just didn't want to share it with a dude I want to punch ninety percent of the time.

"Are you okay, sweet pea?"

Huck is trying to be kind, but it just makes me more upset. "I'm fine. Finish up and meet me at the damn lecture. I need some space."

Before any of them can protest, I sling my bag over my arm and speed walk out of the locker room. Brick and Lancaster try to speak when I rush out, but I ignore them to get the hell away from this entire situation. As I stride down the hallway towards our next session, my emotions threaten to overflow and I have to take deep breaths to push everything behind the mask again. I'll need to go see the damned doctor today; that's a given when the things I used to control seem to fail much earlier than normal.

Just what I wanted to do during my dinner and free time tonight—fuck my life.

KNOW WHEN TO HOLD 'EM
HUCKLEBERRY

OUR GIRL'S rapid departure from the locker room wasn't shocking. In the time I've known her, I've only detected her cycle once, and I suppose it was some kind of early decline of whatever method she's using to keep herself from being fertile. Thad said nothing that day, so I followed suit. Nothing about it is shameful; in fact, much like the vampire, it smelled like heaven in liquid form to me. But my sweet pea grew up without a mama and a father so concerned with keeping them away from the rest of the community that he failed to support her.

It's not shocking that she's so tightly wound about sex and the other mechanisms of procreation.

"You know, if that bastard wasn't dead, I'd gladly ring his neck."

The words come from the mage's shower stall, and I hum my agreement. None of us want to press the issue, but Syd's hero worship of a borderline neglectful father is a bitter pill to swallow. It doesn't take a fancy degree to see that his rhetoric and paranoia damaged her in ways she hasn't even figured out yet. As her only friends in the camps, the bear and I didn't see the need to bust that bubble she lived in if it helped her survive our daily bullshit.

Now it's vital that she accept a lot of hard truths about the world and her past that she's not had to face. I hate that, especially because I know it's hurting her and it won't get easier along the way. But we need to survive, and I'll be damned if I'm going to let some tinfoil hat whack job who's been dead for years keep us from achieving what his rebels couldn't. This ragtag group of supes is going to start, lead, and finish the revolution that will end these fucking prisons, that I guarantee.

"Agreed, Stormbringer, but we cannot push too hard."

I feel Thad's bear prickle from the next stall and it makes me smile. His voice is rumbly when says, "Sydney is strong—stronger than she thinks, even. She'll be able to get through all of this… new reality… if we give her time and space. I don't think I'm over-assuming when I say that we've come to terms with almost everything she never dealt with. Other than her shitty dad, of course."

"Hmmm," Sebastian replies. I hear the water turn off at his end and the slap of wet feet on the tile. "That may be true, ursa, but we have precious little time to get her up to speed. We have no idea how long they plan to 'train' us, and the minute the actual competition begins, her blind spots become weaknesses. We can be respectful, but we also must be realistic."

The dragon makes an annoyed sound that is somewhere between a huff and a growl. "I dislike forcing people to face things they are not ready for. It is not our way, mosquito."

"Mine, either," Thad admits. "Though I suppose the vampire and Huck are more inclined to do it by their nature. And Rory is just pushy."

"Hey!" the mage says indignantly. "I'm not pushy, but I know how to convince someone when needed. That's what I did the other night, and you assholes didn't complain. Don't hate the player, hate the game, buddy."

"Do you think Sydney would appreciate being called a game?" The vampire tone is amused and I hear him rifling through his stuff to get dressed. "I'd put money on 'no' being the answer."

Bets? Now, that's my kind of action.

"Dependin' on how much you're willing to lay down, I'll—"

"For fuck's sake. Betting is no better than using the term 'game'. Stop being so juvenile."

Elias thumps his big fist on the wall of his stall and I swear the damn lights shake in response. Probably best not to upset the storm dragon, I suppose. Sighing, I concede before he shorts out the electric and leaves us wet in the dark. "You're right. I was only joking, anyway—about betting on sweet pea, anyway. I enjoy the fuck out of wagers otherwise."

"Unsurprising," Sebastian remarks drily. "However, I suggest what we say between us stays between us as long as it is not detrimental to Sydney's progress and the team. If we are to bond in a group setting, some friendly interaction like this may be necessary."

"Why do you sound like such a damn robot?" I shake my head and turn my shower off, exiting into the small dressing area to pull on our ever-present uniform. "You need to lighten up as well, Whitmore. If your ass gets any tighter, it's going to shit out a diamond the next time you hit the head."

That gets a laugh out of the rest of the guys, and I grin to myself. The bloodsucker isn't wrong in his assertion, but he needs to say it in a less formal way. We do need to bond as guys and as a full team with our girl. Otherwise, the plan will not work, and neither is the suspicion I have about where this is going. None of us can hate one another forever; that much, I'm completely certain of.

Trick is, Syd can't hate us, either, and right now, she's probably hoppin' mad.

We leave a spot for her between the mage and me in the back row of the lecture hall. Krista is at the front with all the other coaches, and I can't help wonder what in the merry fuck this session is going to accomplish. There are too many cooks in the kitchen down there and way too many groups of suspicious supernaturals looking at one another as if a poison dart is going to materialize out of thin air.

Everyone is fixin' to get ugly, no matter what their beauty sessions accomplished earlier this week.

The room is just barely filled when I feel Sydney enter. I turn, looking for her gaze at the back of the large hall, and when she sees me, she hurries over to slide in between Rory and me. Our girl doesn't say a word, but I notice her scent is drowned under a *lot* of perfumes and sprays. Of course, she likely doesn't realize that most supes can scent her underneath that mess, and I sure as hell don't say a word. Her face is a bit pink as it is, and her discomfort is radiating from her frame.

"I didn't miss anything, right?" she mutters as she pulls her tablet out.

Wisely, the jokey magic user doesn't comment except to say, "Naw, Vicious. You got here in time."

My eyes cut over to the vampire on the far end, then the dragon, and finally, my chosen brother bear. I try to communicate the need for discretion to each, hoping we can hold this shit together in the last class of the day. If I were a bettin' demon—and I am—I'd say our girl will make a beeline for the doctor's bay after this. The only way we'll be able to convince her to let someone come along is if we behave here and now. Otherwise, she'll fight us and waste a lot of time that could be better spent re-fueling and knocking out our damn 'homework'.

"Attention, competitors!"

The voice from the front isn't our cheery coach. My head whips around to see which one projected that well and I roll my eyes when I see them using what has to be an infused item to accomplish that range. Humans hate all of us with every fiber of their being—enough to imprison or kill every supe they find in this country—but they sure as shit love using our powers for their own gain. It's infuriating, and I want to throw a ball of terror at the jackass doing it to teach him a lesson. I can't, though, so I slouch in my chair and pull my hat brim down so I'm unlikely to be called on by this tool.

"Thank you for attending our first Intrigue & Socialization seminar."

"As if we had a choice," Syd mutters in the lowest tone I've ever heard from her. Her shoulders hunch as she keeps her eyes on the tablet, waiting for the dummy to say something she can add to her notes.

My lips curve up at her indefatigable spunk. It's my favorite part of this woman and has been since we first met. No matter how angry or upset or happy she is, Sydney Jolie always has that sharp edge. She doesn't tone it down for anyone or anything, though I've seen the softer side peek out occasionally. Her sarcasm makes her funny, but it also makes her real, and I adore it whether it offends others or not.

Leaning in slightly, I murmur, "Easy there, filly. Don't want to start a brawl we can't finish."

She frowns at her screen, but nods quickly. I know she's embarrassed about her period starting unexpectedly in the locker room, but getting control of her more volatile emotions is important for this stupid training. I tilt my head, considering her behavior since we were chosen, and it occurs to me that since her powers—whatever the hell they are—started emerging, she's been like a yo-yo.

That might be a side effect of emergence, but I'm uncertain what it means. Shifter like her dad possibly?

I yank my device out of my bag, turning it on. The others need to know my thoughts about the ups and downs of Syd's moods, and I will not say it out loud.

"This class will address both friendly and not-so-friendly interactions between the teams competing in the Games. You should seek to form alliances, as they may be needed, but also to gather information that might be used as leverage as well."

Their advice is contradictory and I can't imagine that anyone listening hasn't figured that out. Every one of these sessions will be a huge fucking waste if this is what they're 'teaching'. I might as well use it to take notes on the teams and individuals based on their reactions. But for now, I'm going to hit up the other guys via this lovely technology they provided—carefully. I open the chat function, creating a room titled 'Dude Bros' and swallow the chuckle before it escapes. Adding each of them from the pre-populated list, I consider how I'm going to say this in a way that won't give away our shit if someone is actively monitoring this shit.

> DocHolliday: I believe I've discovered a foundation for the roller coaster.

I wait for one of the others to respond, hoping they get what I'm trying to say. After a few minutes, the bubbles on the screen turn into words and I sigh in relief.

Vladthelmpaler: Discuss.

DocHolliday: Perhaps it is linked to the rising sun.

I know I'm being cagey as hell, but I don't trust the humans pitting us against one another for sport as far as I could throw them.

YogiBear: That may be accurate. It wasn't common in the past.

MrWizard: Also, the new information.

PuffttheMagicDragon: Both are likely.

DocHolliday: Clues to origins?

Vladthelmpaler: Multiple, not singular.

YogiBear: Probably. Unusual.

Their agreement makes the wheels turn in my head for a few minutes and I'm totally absorbed until a sharp elbow hits my ribs. I automatically click my screen closed as I look over at the woman sitting next to me. She's finally meeting someone's gaze after the incident in the shower, so I wait for her. I don't want to spook Sydney, so she withdraws again.

"I… I have to go to the doctor."

Nodding, I scratch my chin. "Okay, darlin'. No problem."

"Will you go with me, Huck?"

I blink, a little surprised by the request. The dumbass upfront is still droning on about how to socialize with other teams and when we'll be tasked with doing so, but I couldn't care less about that. I figured she'd tap the mage because he's been doing so well of late. "Well, of course, I'll come, sweet pea. You know I'd walk through Hell barefoot if you asked."

Her nose wrinkles as she whispers, "You're a demon, Huck. You can walk through Hell bare-ass naked and it wouldn't hurt you."

"Ah, but the thought still counts."

She rolls her eyes, then shrugs. "Okay. But I won't ask you to drink holy water or whatever. Just come with me, so no one gets worried and sit outside the med bay until I'm done."

I grin, pushing my hat back a little so I can see her better. "Absolutely. Nothin' I'd rather do."

That might not be exactly true, but anytime I spend with Sydney is better than every other minute I spend without her.

DON'T WORRY, I'M A DOCTOR

SYDNEY

AS SOON AS the stupid coaching lecture ends, I stand up, looking at Huck as I gather my shit. The other guys are still quiet, which surprises me a little. I clear my throat, not meeting their eyes as I say, "Huck is coming along to the infirmary, so I'll see you upstairs in a bit?"

When my eyes skitter upward, I see Thad nodding. He's not looking at me like I'm the odd person out, and I'm grateful. Rory and the other two do some sort of dude thing with their eyebrows at Huck, but he ignores them to offer me his arm.

"Ready, sweet pea?"

Normally, I'd balk at his chivalry, especially when I'm feeling less than strong, but the small spotting from earlier must have increased during class. I'm cramping pretty badly, and it honestly aches to stand upright. So I grit my teeth and take his arm with a fake smile, letting the demon lead me up the stairs of the hall and into the corridor. "Thanks," I mumble as we start towards the main wing.

He pats the hand on his arm lightly, not saying anything as we walk at a slow pace through the classroom hallway. You wouldn't know anything is wrong by his posture or expression, and I add some points to his mental tally. I don't even want to discuss this unwelcome visitor with my team, much less some dill hole from one of the other teams. Listening to them answer questions and act like unruly high schoolers in the class was bad enough. Having one of the unenlightened dudes milling around us start shit about a normal biological function would send me over the deep end, I fear.

Not that it takes much, especially lately.

Huck opens the door for me as we exit the education wing to the main area, and I sigh in relief. "I think it's this way, right?" Pointing across the atrium to a set of doors diagonal from us, I squint up at my escort. Hopefully, that ingrained spatial memory of his is working because I didn't pay enough attention when we were being shuffled around on arrival.

"Yep. That section has all the medical and administrative offices, I believe." He winks at me, obviously realizing I haven't mapped this giant eyesore of a building yet. "It's not like you to skip over knowing your surroundings on day one, Syd."

He's right; being unemerged forced me to develop a lot of habits to help keep my ass unharmed while moving around Tempest Seven. Not memorizing every inch of this place as if my life depends on it—and it might—is a huge failing on my part. I chalk it up to having to learn to live with a bunch of people in my space and continually getting smacked with reality I had no concept of before being sent to this circus. It's thrown me off my game and I need to get my shit together before I pay for my distraction.

"After we eat and get this stupid ass homework done, we'll work on it together. You're the best at it, anyway." I grin a little, ignoring the radiating pains from my gut as we enter the double doors to the correct wing. "Will you help me, pardner?"

His face lights up at my request, especially because I teased him. "Sydney Jolie, I would gladly help you learn to walk over hot coals if you asked."

I frown, giving him a pinched expression. "You're a demon, Huck. You can walk over hot coals with zero issue, I bet. That's not saying a damn thing."

"Sounded pretty, though, didn't it?" He puffs up a bit and I laugh softly at his antics. He's purposely keeping my mind off my situation, so I think he's realized I'm hurting. "But if it makes you feel better, I'd let you wear my hat and put pink sparkly bows on my horns if you asked. How's that?"

That sounds like a lot of fun—not that I want to admit it.

My eyes dance as I look up at him when we stop at the door to the infirmary. "I'll hold you to that, Huckleberry Monroe. Don't play with me."

Leaning back a little, the devilish demon smirks and pulls his hat off, plopping it on my head. "Cross my black heart and hope to be exorcised. Now get in there and see this doctor before I decide to find a use for those ribbons you're not ready for."

My eyes widen and I squeak, making me want to die of embarrassment on the spot. Hurrying inside, I head directly to the desk, looking at the witchy nurse from our medical inspection when we first got here. "I… uh. I need to see the doctor, please."

Her eyes narrow behind a pair of black wire rimmed glasses. "Name and team?"

"Sydney Jolie, Team Bite Club," I reply quickly, not wanting to look back at Huck after that flirty exchange."Is there a wait?"

I don't see anyone else in the small waiting area, but this isn't the same place they checked us out back then, so I have no idea how many patient rooms there are. The inspections were done in quickly thrown together suites and this feels like a real medical office. I guess the people responsible for running this joint have been busy while we've been getting orientated. The nurse shakes her head, bringing my focus back to her as she clicks at a tablet on a stand in front of her.

"No. Dr. Moreau is here this evening and he's very efficient. There's rarely a wait when he's working. Follow me, but your friend has to wait here."

Huck frowns, about to protest when I hold my hand up. "That's fine. He has excellent hearing, so if I need him, it won't be long before he comes for me."

"Hmmph," the nurse says as she rises from her chair to grab a well-protected tablet from a charging station. "If you say so."

I follow her down a short hallway to a door labeled 'four' and when she opens the door, it looks exactly like a normal exam room. They've been busy as fuck in this place and I've been too worried about my own shit to notice. She points to the exam table, then walks over to pull out a smock. Once she lays it out, she hands me the thick cased tablet with another squint.

"Fill out everything on this. Then change into the gown and push the button by the door so we know you're ready. Make sure you don't forget or fake any information—doing so might lead to bad diagnosis and treatment which can disqualify you from the Games and possibly open you up to punishment."

Blinking at her, I take the device and watch her leave without another word. Of course I realize that the government fucks who run this place don't want bad PR, but punishment for fucking up a form is a new low. Though I suppose it shouldn't surprise me. They think of us like widgets in their asset portfolio or show ponies. Messing up our health would decrease both our value and the value of our team.

I hate this fucking timeline.

I blow out a slow breath, calming my nerves as I sit on the edge of the table and work through the questions on the screen. I do the best I can with what information I have; it's not like I had time to bring medical records when they did the Sweeps and I haven't had to see a doc since I got here. That's probably why I'm here now, though my understanding is this is happening about a year early. Hopefully, this is good enough for the doctor and what he needs to get me fixed up.

Once I'm done, I take off my uniform and fold it neatly on the chairs across from the table. I feel gross being this naked when I'm on my period, and it's cold as fuck in here, but it's not like I have an option. I have to get this taken care of before I make any decisions about my body while I'm here. Plus, I *really* need to make sure I don't smell like a fucking buffet to a bunch of species slinking around this damn building. That's the number one goal, to be honest, because while I can keep my legs closed on my own, I can't control their noses.

Walking over to the door, I push the big green button and move back to the exam table. Hopping on it, I groan softly. I don't know that I've ever had cramps this bad before and I don't like it *at all*. I feel heavy and smelly and really irritable—none of which are good for my temper. Lying back against the slanted back of the table, I sigh as I look up at the bright lights on the ceiling. Being a female is a certified pain in my ass sometimes, and men do not have the slightest *clue* how much work it is just to exist some days.

"It's you!"

I turn my head, looking over at the centaur as he enters, kicking the door shut behind him with his hind leg. His expression is happy, but it turns to a frown when he looks at the tablet I left on top of my clothes. He's scanning the information quickly as he moves closer, and I should feel apprehensive, but I don't. This doctor removed the Marker and I've wanted to know why ever since. I'm lucky this damn birth control failed on the night he's working. If I believed in such a thing, I'd say it was kismet.

But I don't, so I'm just going to hope it's as fortuitous as it seems.

"Hello, again," I say carefully. My eyes dart around the room quickly, hoping to identify any monitoring devices that might be stationed in here. "I'd say it's nice to see you again, but… given the circumstances, it's not."

The handsome doctor winks at me, then jerks his head backward. I follow his inclination and see a small thing tucked on top of a cabinet. It doesn't look like a camera—though I wouldn't put filming us naked past the FSHA assholes—so I suppose it's an audio recording thing. "I certainly didn't hope to have you as a patient again so soon, Miss Jolie. But according to this, it seems your contraception has expired early? That is a problem for a young woman like yourself."

I don't want to respond with any information that can be used against me, so I nod. "Yes. I need it refreshed so I'm safe and also because I seem to be in more pain than normal. It's escalated quickly since I noticed spotting this morning. I guess it really went kaput."

His eyes widen and he holds a finger up to stop me before saying, "We can certainly help with that, Sydney. It's a fairly quick little procedure, and once we do it, you'll need to wait at least two weeks for effectiveness. I'm going to get Nurse Ames to help with the insertion and anesthetic, then afterward, we'll discuss the rest of your concerns. Okay?"

I nod, not sure why he's leaving rather than simply pushing a call button or something. However, I want to talk to Dr. Moreau about our last visit, so I say, "Yes, doctor."

The room is silent as I wait for a few minutes, then the centaur comes back with the grumpy witch in tow. She bustles over to the cabinets, pulling out a bunch of jars, then a mortar and pestle, and finally, a small thing that must be the replacement. It doesn't look like the one I had when I was dumped in the camps; that one was put in by a human doctor and it was more painful than I'd been led to believe. I frown as she does a bunch of… witchy… things while the doctor raises my gown to fold it up under my breasts.

"This isn't like they did when I first got to Tempest Seven," I say as he arranges me just so on the table. "Is this something new?"

Dr. Moreau gives me a reassuring smile, his eyes full of understanding. "Normally, the camps have human doctors who practice medicine in human ways. Luckily for the competitors, they get supernatural medical practitioners who do things in a far less unevolved fashion."

"Whether they deserve it or not," the witch grumbles as she brings the mortar full of something smelly over. "This will take away the pain, but it will not make you loopy, dear. Mind, it's cold."

I don't have time to absorb that before she slathers it on my lower abdomen liberally, making me squeak in response. That's twice people have made me sound like a hiccuping mouse today and I'm going to punch someone if they do it again. The salve is cold as fuck, but my entire lower half numbs nicely within moments. Nurse Crabbypants huffs at my glare, then toddles over to grab the small shiny thing I saw before and brings it back to the centaur.

"Dr. Moreau will hold you still while I get it situated. Don't wiggle," she growls as she palms the thing and hovers her palms over me.

How the fuck are they getting that thing inside me without… tools or whatever?!

The witch chants a bunch of foreign sounding words and a blink of light flashes, blinding me. When I finally get my vision straightened out, I see her back at the cabinet, cleaning up her mess while the doctor smiles down at me. I shake my head to clear it, not understanding what the hell just happened. The doctor waits for the nurse to finish up, wiping the gunk off of me and pulling my gown down as she finally brushes past him. Once the door closes, he grins a little.

"I suppose you have questions about your… procedure, Miss Jolie. Don't worry; I'm happy to answer anything you need to know." The centaur hands me a pen and piece of paper on a clipboard, winking as he keeps his back to the audio device. "Fire away."

Oh, buddy. I'm going to make you pay for this shit even if you did just perform the most painless IUD insertion known to womankind.

THAT'S COVERED
BY THE CODE, BRO

SEBASTIAN

THE INCIDENT in the showers has been playing in my mind on repeat since Sydney ran from us to deal with it before class. Given my age in vampire years—which is far more than my appearance on the outside—I have an iron-fisted grip on my hunger. Being able to control one's self takes a few decades for those who are turned, and less if you are born into our kind, like me. However, the second that tiny trickle of fluid escaped, the scent had me struggling to hold back like a fledgling. I was so shocked that I didn't handle it as well as I could have and I know that frightened and embarrassed her.

I need to apologize, but I'm still replaying it in my head and I can't do that until I'm completely under control.

That's why instead of heading straight to our dorm with the others, I waited until Sydney and the demon left to peel off from the group. I didn't give the other guys an excuse, but I think they were smart enough not to ask why I took the second elevator down to the gym level. The only thing I'm able to do here, in this stupid facility, to burn off this oddly pervasive blood-lust is beat the living fuck out of something until I'm too exhausted to think about anything else.

Even grabbing a blood bag from the hydration area down here didn't fix the problem, so I've been sweating out my mental obsession ever since. My hands have been re-taped several times, and I've pulled half the weapons off the wall trying to push away the inner demon that defines my species, but so far, it hasn't worked. I can feel the burning that tells me my eyes are deep crimson without looking in the mirror. My fangs are still dropped in my mouth, and I have the dry sensation there that indicates my demon wants to feed. Unfortunately, he's fixated on a single source that is *absolutely* not available for more reasons than I can count.

"What the fuck is wrong with me?" I mutter as I slam my fists into the bag in a blur of motion. "I'm too old for this shit."

My only answer is silence, and I snarl in frustration. Perhaps it's simply the allure of forbidden fruit… even vampires fall victim to unattainable desires. I frown as I consider that, then discard it because I've run into shit I couldn't have before. I've even run into *people* I couldn't have before and I just re-focused on something else without an issue. No, this is something entirely different that I don't understand.

If only my species weren't so goddamn closed off since the human coup, I might have been exposed to more lore than the remaining coven leaders allowed us to learn.

I sigh, pausing my fury to put my hands on my knees and breathe deeply. The mage and the bear are far too young to understand my concerns about this situation. I may need to speak with the demon and the dragon—they're in the same age range as me and have a lot more knowledge of the ancient ways. They're also species that are less tamed and mingle less with the humans, unlike shifters, magic users, and the like. Given their unique perspectives, we might dissect the extremely unlikely theory I have regarding our reluctant female.

"Or they'll laugh me out of the fucking room, but it wouldn't be the first time that ever happened," I mutter as I stand up and peel the tapes off of my hands. The wounds will heal this evening, so I don't bother bandaging them. "This damn team might be the only beings I haven't *killed* for mocking my legitimate questions, but I can live with it."

Hopefully, these clowns don't set me off and start a fistfight in our damn room.

"Syd, is that you?"

I roll my eyes when the bear calls out. No surprise that he's worried about her; he and the demon are the closest to her. It was obvious they'd only run into the situation briefly in the past by the way they both behaved in the locker room, despite not knowing them well. I didn't have to think hard to figure out that they probably ignored it until she did whatever she needed to rectify the problem, then never mentioned it. The amount of coddling they did with our team centerpiece has become more and more apparent as time goes by, and I'd love to ask why the fuck they thought keeping her in the dark helped keep her safe.

"No, dipshit, it's me," I say as I shut the door and stride through the kitchen to the living area. "You'd know that if you were using the gifts your animal gives you, by the way. What's with you avoiding your non-humanoid side so much, anyway?"

I'm greeted by the sight of the dragon sprawled in the big armchair and the mage sitting in lotus position with his eyes closed on the floor. The bear is trying like hell to imitate him—though he's failing—and I arch a brow questioningly. When no one responds, I roll my eyes and head for my room to change. Cleaning up before Sydney and the country fried hellspawn get back is my goal, so I drop my bag and strip off my shirt quickly.

I won't be able to cover up all the damage I did, but at least I won't scare the shit out of her when she's already upset.

My brain clicks, and I suddenly realize that I know how those two dimwits ended up hiding all the ugly stuff from our girl. Even *I'm* purposefully covering up normal shit for my kind to prevent her from being shaken. Something about the vulnerability tucked under her hard shell snuck into my consciousness, and I'm behaving differently so she will be less likely to need to confront basic truths. I am a vampire and we are very primal—violence and hunger are integral parts of who we are, though it's not always a negative thing. That same primal instinct is at the core of Thad's grizzly and definitely Huck's demonic side, but they consistently tamp those parts of themselves down.

"Someone has to normalize accepting their supernatural species, and if she hates me because of it, I will deal with it," I mutter to myself. "Sydney *has* to get comfortable with people using and embracing their powers or she'll never be able to handle these stupid classes, much less the damn competition."

I kick off my shoes and socks, tossing them into the basket for laundry pickup later in the week. Pulling a pair of sweatpants out of the drawer, I replace the stinky, sweaty ones, but I don't wipe off the telltale signs of my spent fury in the gym. Once I'm done, I step out of my room and head for the kitchen to pour myself a large mug of blood. I don't make a big deal of my secondary nourishment when we eat, but today, I'll be less decorous.

Sydney will face other vampires and worse supes than us amongst the teams—she has to develop a callus for it.

Sauntering into the living area, I plop into an armchair and cross my legs at the ankles as I sip my food. "Why is Thad trying to injure himself with the mage, anyway? And why aren't you joining them, Dante?"

"Because I want to find my Zen, bloodsucker," Thad says without opening his eyes. "Not that I owe you an explanation."

"True enough, but inner Zen isn't exactly a normal trait for a grizzly shifter, Calvin. I'm curious; sue me." I grin a bit as he cracks one eye and gives me a dirty look.

Rory's eyes open next and he smirks. "Just because you aren't a master of kama sutra doesn't mean our ursine boy can't be taught, Whitmore. Don't be a hater."

I suppress the urge to sigh heavily as I go back to studying the dragon. He actually looks pretty zoned out, so he might be meditating in a manly fashion in his chair. "Not confident enough to answer, dragon?"

Elias grunts, glaring at me before he shakes his head. "My kind meditate better in our other form, vampire. I was simply reviewing the information and things I saw today to prepare for our meeting during dinner. I find those small details I noticed, but thought little about, jump out when I'm quietly examining the day internally. That can lead to valuable intel."

"What the hell could you have picked up today? It was a total shitshow, if you ask me." I take a long drink of my blood, then shrug. "The first session was useless—we're not stupid enough to need someone to tell us we need to pick apart the other teams for weaknesses. The flair thing will not be helpful until we're out of training. Combat was good, though it took a nose-dive at the end, which is where we all lost the ability to focus for the rest of the day. Tell me I'm mistaken."

Thad sighs and looks at me with an annoyed expression. "You're right, but that doesn't mean Elias didn't notice things subconsciously. Hell, it doesn't mean any of us were too distracted to pick up on interesting shit."

I snort, tilting my head as I look at him. "Then, by all means, please enlighten me as to what you gathered during that last session. Tell me what you picked up while trying not to worry, that Sydney would be angry with us as a defensive mechanism for being embarrassed about what she likely considers to be a weakness."

I guess I'm not coddling them, either.

"Yikes, Whitmore. What did he do to earn you going for his throat like that?" The mage leans back on his palms, still twisted into a pretzel as he stretches. "Thad did nothing to piss you off; take it easy."

Setting my mug on the side table, I push to my feet and glare down at them. "See, that's where you're incorrect, Stormbringer. Tap dancing around *everything* is why Sydney is woefully behind on information about our world before *and* after the purges. It's why she's totally naïve about normal supe behavior and embarrassed about her own biology. Between her weirdo father, the fucking humans, and her two besties, she's been sheltered so thoroughly that if she'd landed with anyone but us, she would have already had a tragic 'accident' so the team could replace her."

All three of them stare at me as I cross my arms over my chest. I'm not backing down, and they *should* be more concerned. When no one speaks, I throw my hands up in the air. "I'm *not* saying we should be less understanding, but we have to quit masking all the shit that comes with being a supe of our particular kind. The only way to prepare her for less… human presenting teams… is *not* taking up yoga to calm your horny-ass bear.”

Thad turns bright red, and the dragon bursts into laughter, slapping his knee hard as he howls. Rory gives me a sly grin, his expression knowing as he finally untwists himself. Once he's upright, he walks over, looking me over head to toe, before he makes a soft 'tsk' sound.

“Methinks you project too much, Sebastian. You hit the bricks fast enough to leave burning trails behind you after Vicious and the demon left.” He looks at the various bruises and scrapes from my gym tirade slowly, then shakes his head. “Especially because you retreated to the basement to demolish the fuck out of what looks like half the equipment. Hopefully, we've got weapons left for class tomorrow.”

Rolling my eyes in irritation, I huff. “Vampires always work out frustration with physical exertion. There's no way that you're unfamiliar with that, especially given your life prior to coming here.”

He shrugs, his eyes dancing as he moves away, dropping onto the floor with the bear again. “I am aware of that, thank you very much, which is why I know you were riding high on bloodlust. Since you were down there for a pretty long ass time, I'm betting it wasn't easy to get rid of. So don't act high and mighty with our poor cockblocked friend—sympathize with him like I do.”

Everything stops when the door opens, and we all look at one another knowingly.

'They're back.' Thad mouths and we wince.

This conversation definitely falls in that 'bro code' area we discussed before—no way we're explaining it to Sydney, even if she's not on the warpath anymore.

WHY DIDN'T I GET A HANDBOOK?

SYDNEY

WHEN HUCK and I walk into our dorm, the quiet makes me suspicious. The guys don't get into crazy fights, but the lack of sniping feels off. We make our way through the kitchen to find the four of them sitting in their usual spots as they focus on their tablets. I arch a brow, not believing this shit for a second, and Huck lets go of my arm to bow playfully.

"We've arrived, darlin'. Why don't you change quick-like so we can order food and get this bullshit done?"

The demon gives me an innocent smile and though I don't trust that, either; I nod. Truthfully, I won't complain about him giving me a brief out so I can gather myself. He wasn't in the exam room when the centaur and I spoke, so he didn't realize how much was racing through my brain. "That sounds good, actually. I wouldn't mind a Chinese buffet if you guys want to order while I'm gone."

"I'm on it," Thad says with a cheerful smile. He motions for Huck to join them so they can use one of their devices to order, and I turn on my heel to head for my room. The bear's easygoing attitude is part of why I let him in so long ago, and definitely why he's one of my closest friends now. Thad never stresses me out because he's the calm in the storm.

"Don't be long," Rory calls out, and I raise my hand, waving at him over my shoulder as I walk to my room.

Too bad for him; I'll take as long as I want after the completely FUBAR day I just had.

~

The clothes I took out of the drawer are still sitting on the comforter next to me when I blink back into consciousness. It takes me a minute to realize that I came in, got my shit out, sat down, and spaced out entirely for… Frowning, I look around, then give in and say, "Irina, what time is it?"

When she replies, I'm relieved to find that it's been ten minutes—not a short time, but definitely not so long that I'm going to have men breaking down my door. I kick off my shoes with a rueful grin, then peel off socks, pants, and the rest to toss in my laundry bin. It's not a normal thing for me to blank out while my brain processes like that, but damned if I don't get why it's happening. The past weeks have been so packed with emotional overload and world rocking new information that I can't always handle additional shit being piled on.

Which is without a doubt what happened in that fucking office.

Once the nurse left, the first thing I asked him was why the woman seemed like she wanted to gut me for making her do her damn job. He laughed, explaining that she's been pulling extra shifts to cover all the 'problems' cropping up as teams figure out their dynamic. I arch a brow and the doc turns his back to the microphone corner, hastily scribbling on his clipboard as he elaborated on various minor injuries.

They're hiding the major injuries and two deaths. Not all the supes have been able to gel in their groups.

His secret clue made my eyes widen as I thought about how often that might happen before the actual competition starts. It seemed likely there would be some issues, but it still shocked me to find out that things escalated that quickly without the humans intervening. That solidified my opinion that they really care less about us than the show animals they race or own. Supes dying or getting maimed wasn't even a blip on the radar for the people running this shit. After that, I took the pen from the mythical, writing my own question for him to answer.

What did you do to me at intake and why?

Dr. Moreau pressed his lips together, writing a different response than he said out loud, "The implantation will not be completely safe for two weeks, Sydney. You need to be careful until after that date."

I removed the Marker to give our people a chance. You were the first supe to feel like I could trust you not to get me caught or to abuse it.

I caught his game, nodding as I scribbled my next query. "Got it. Two weeks. How long will it last? This one went bad at least a year early, which is why I'm here at the last minute."

How did you know that? I haven't even emerged, which you had to know.

The low neighing sound that tinged his chuckle made me smile. He added his secret answer and tapped the point on the last word. "It should last five years and this time, not fail early. The way we did this for you is much less painful and more effective than what their doctors put you through when you first arrived at the camp."

The nurse and I sensed it. We're both gifted in assessing beings of various types through their bodies and the impressions of their spirit. It's how we diagnose.

Our conversation lasted almost a half hour, but the kindly centaur helped me understand that the human birth control likely failed because of my physiology changing with emergence. I'm still in the process, but as much as it's playing havoc on my powers, it's doing similar to my body. He didn't know what I've got running through my veins without doing a test that might cause me more problems than not. I didn't like accepting that, but I also don't need the humans declaring me persona non grata so they can execute me.

Sighing, I turn to look in the mirror, examining the various additions the beauty folks did, then the small, magical tattoo Dr. Moreau's procedure left on my lower left abdomen. I can't fault the guy for hoping he could create a hero, but I don't know if I'm that gal. Obviously, I've been allowed to live in the dark for most of my life, and I've got anger issues that would cripple an elephant. There's nothing special about me I can see, even with all the upgrades.

Why would anyone think I'm a 'chosen one' or whatever?

"Because we're all so goddamn desperate," I mutter to myself as I head back to the bed and tug on my tee shirt. I pick up my pants, then frown, deciding to change my undergarments as well. Walking to the dresser, I grab a fresh pair and quickly deal with that before I put on the sweats. "Everyone is praying someone is coming to save them in the camps, but that hope should have died years ago. I don't get why there are supes still thinking the elders or anyone else is going to fix this mess."

Frustration fills me as I wad up the previous dirty stuff in a ball so I can get rid of it in the bathroom before I join the others. Whatever my powers are, they aren't unfurling quickly enough, and shit like the birth control randomly failing keeps putting me at a disadvantage. I've never wished I was a guy more than today in that damn gym. The look on the guys' faces made me want to crawl under the floorboards even though I *know* what happened is completely fucking normal.

"Get a grip, Sydney," I say as I set the ball of pants on the dresser and reach up to undo my braid. The relief I feel when I let the tightly woven strands loose is palpable, and I carefully run the brush through it until the golden waves fall over my shoulders. "You can survive almost anything if you've lasted this long. No way are you going to let the goddamn humans best you."

My eyes narrow and I realize that my hatred for what they've done to our kind definitely outweighs my doubts and fears. Even if I wasn't meant to be the savior or whatever, I can still help fuck up their precious order with the help of my teammates. We can spark the flame of revolution and the supes can save themselves, for fuck's sakes. That's how we can win—not that it will happen quickly or without sacrifice.

Am I willing to be that sacrifice if it comes to it?

I ponder that question as I slap the stupid creams and drops on my face like Shoshana's people instructed. Do I believe in this cause enough to risk my life? Pressing my lips together, I stare at the array of cosmetics while my mind races. I do, especially because so many women and children died during Taterman's fucking sweeps. People who weren't resisting were slaughtered along with the rebels, simply because they were in the same general area. They could have sent those without weapons to the camps; they made an unforgettable, unerasable mental picture they broadcast across this country so we all knew to surrender.

"If I'm being forced into this kind of bullshit, and I'm reluctant to give up my life for freedom, what chance do supernaturals have? No one will risk it if they don't have examples of others who are putting it all on the line to unshackle themselves."

Heavy-handed rhetoric, of course, but that doesn't make it untrue. If I stand for nothing, I'll fall like everyone else—and anyone who thinks simply winning this damn competition will earn them the right to live peacefully hasn't been paying attention for the past four years. There's no option for the supes on the teams now, but I can help others, even if I don't get to see the result.

Suddenly, a smirk comes over my lips when I realize how mopey I sound. "Those damn hormones are hitting me like bricks to the face today. I'm angry, emo, hungry, cranky, and ridiculously poetic. I hope this shit doesn't last for long or the guys are going to wish they could be on a rocket to Mars."

One more glance in the mirror confirms I don't look like a scarecrow, so I pick up the bundle of pants. Opening the door, I quickly scoot from my room to the bathroom, disposing of what I need to and stuffing the clothes in the hamper there. The last thing I want to discuss with anyone is the nightmare that has been my personal hygiene today. I pick up an extra perfume spray sitting on the counter and douse myself, then sigh in relief.

Okay, now I think I'm ready to face the firing squad.

I take a deep breath and exit the bathroom, heading down the corridor to the living area. The guys are still pretending to be engrossed in their homework, so I drop down on the far end of the couch and tuck my feet under me. "Thanks for letting me decompress for a few. It's been a long ass day."

Elias' gaze flicks to me, and the quiet dragon rumbles, "We all need space sometimes, little rebel."

"Not me," Rory says, as he leans back on his elbows, his eyes dancing as he grins at me. "I like to be as close as possible. However, since I'm a gentleman…"

I frown, tilting my head as I glare at the mage. "That's not true. The other night you barged into my room despite my apparent discomfort, and I'm fairly certain the rest of these goons put you up to it."

He blinks, looking confused for a moment. "When I didn't let you close the door? Vicious, I didn't mean to push your boundaries with that. I just… I knew I could help, and no one wanted you to be hurting."

"Next time, keep your body parts to yourself and wait until you're invited, then," I whisper. "I'm not saying you were wrong, or that you didn't help—you helped a lot. But it would have gone a lot more smoothly if you'd waited until I was ready to let someone into my space."

Rory is quiet for a moment—a minor miracle, to be sure—and then he nods. "Message received, babe. I'll be more conscientious from now; cross my heart."

Thad clears his throat, looking at me seriously. "While we're on the subject, it would be good if we all try not to huff off and leave the rest wondering what the hell is happening when we get upset."

I blink, surprised at the blatant insinuation and that *Thad* is the one who said it. It's not like my gentle, laid-back bear to call me out so publicly. He's *right*, of course, but I'm just shocked to hear him say it. "Um, yeah. I'm sorry about that. That's my bad habit to break, I suppose. Product of being on my own with my dad for so long, I guess, but that doesn't excuse making you guys worry. I'll work on it."

Surprisingly, I actually mean that, and the relieved expressions on their faces are making me warm all over.

YOU CAN'T SIT WITH US

RORY

I THINK *I'm the grease that makes all the wheels stop screeching.*

Making nice with Vicious last night calmed her down, and while we waited for food, she even helped the others with their fashion homework. Well, she tried, and in the end, Sebastian and I had to step in. But it's the effort that counts, right? She was so upset when she fled the showers and then our last class… I expected a lot of head butting when she got back. My well-thought out belly up made her feel heard, and then she gave me back the same consideration. That allowed everyone in the room to quit holding their breath—though the vamp still looked pained most of the time.

It's probably because he could smell the blood—from her, from whatever the docs did in her dirty clothes—and it's pushing buttons he didn't think he had. I'm a flirty disaster bisexual, but I'm aware of when people are trying to pretend they're not attracted to someone. He's probably got it in his noggin that she'll never truly like him and while that's fair, it's also discounting the fact that Sydney is actually taking all this change better than she thinks. A few dust-ups here and there, but mostly… she's riding it out.

Most of the people I've been stuck with since the Sweeps wouldn't have been able to navigate through nearly as much without major blow-ups—worse ones than a few emotional outbursts. But I also know that females—even supes—have been damn near trained from birth to give one another shit about externalizing emotions, especially in public. I bet she's worried that people will think she's acting like a child or being selfish—which is why she hides shit at first. That's dumb as fuck, and men *never* think about that shit when they lose their tempers.

No one calls them toddlers or immature when they have public meltdowns—it's such a weirdly internalized misogyny.

Luckily, I'm here to be the sexy, jolly buffer and I can help talk all these pent-up assholes in my group off the ledges. It's a bit of emotional labor I didn't ask for, but for once? I'm happy to do it. For some reason I haven't pin-pointed yet, I'm very on board with creating a weird, misshapen Addams Family with our team. I want us to overthrow the fucking government, yeah, but I kinda want to retire to some luxury house and bicker until we're ancient. I'm multi-layered like that.

"Why is he smiling like a stoned pink cat?" Vicious says as she joins us at the door. Her crankiness isn't because of yesterday or even the morning—no, we have that damn shitty set of classes again, starting with the cult one.

Winking at her, I yank the door open so we can file out and head downstairs. "I am just pleased with our development as a team. We barely even argued this morning; it's a real accomplishment."

Huck snorts, draping an arm around the girl's shoulders as he drawls, "I have to agree with the magic man, sweet pea. We're doin' a right fine job of communicating and working out problems together. Few bumps in the road, but that's nothin' we can't overcome."

I like him; despite being a demon, he's got his head on straight.

"The question is, can we maintain that with the second session of our worst day of the week?" Thad grins as he falls into step with Sydney and the demon. "Because even I admit this day is going to suck."

Sebastian jabs his finger at the button, and when it opens, we cram into the box. "The only thing we can do is control our tempers and glean any useful information they might offer. Even if we are not using their methods exactly, there will be small gems we can adapt to our plans. Rory is the only one with enough natural charisma to do the 'attract a following' bit without training; the rest of us should focus on finding the tricks we can live with."

"Thanks, Fang Face," I say as I grin at my other teammates smugly. "Like we did with the fashion homework last night, we all just need to work together. It doesn't matter how stupid you think the assignments are, guys. They're presenting this shit for a reason."

"Driving me fucking insane," Vicious grumbles and everyone laughs.

At least she can joke about it.

~

"Now, if we're trying to implant an idea in your target audience's mind… How do you think we would do it without *directly* saying it?" Chantelle asks as she leans against her desk.

We all look at one another, and finally, Huck answers, "I'd use magic, but that will not work across the digital landscape, I fear. You can try, mind, but the farther the distance, the more likely it won't do diddly."

The impeccably dressed teacher nods. "Exactly. So you'd need options that would work for those without that skill, especially ones geared toward visual and auditory presentation."

I think about it for a moment, needing to come up with an example that will make sense to my teammates. "You need research on demographics first —who are you trying to reach? Once you've narrowed it that far, the next step is to gather data on everything about that target, from location to favorite foods. If you're pressed for time, you can try relying on generalizations like these people like wine or beings from this realm can't touch iron… but more specific means you have a better chance of luring them in."

"Excellent, Mr. Stormbringer," Chantelle says as she claps her hands. "Data is key to marketing, and it's why companies and governments hold focus groups or have analysts. What comes next?"

"If you don't want to be blunt, you would want to use that information to place phrases, images, or sounds that trigger the emotions in your media." Sebastian tilts his head as he interrupts and I shoot him a thumbs-up. "For instance, if the person enjoys a specific band, you could include lyrics or song titles from their catalog in written or verbal conversations. Playing the songs just loud enough to be heard in the background would work for video. Using visual indicators that tie to their identity *and* that data will reinforce it."

His response makes our professor look even more delighted, and I sigh in relief. The better mood she's in, the less likely she is to repeat her performance from Tuesday. I'd prefer not to stomp out of every session of every class with our team fractured, so keeping the less… palatable trainers solid is key. "I agree with Sebastian. It's all part of subliminal messaging and that's a good way to hook folks without them realizing it."

"You are spot-on, and that's what we'll be discussing for the rest of the session. Use your tablets to open the examples and we'll discuss the photos and videos I've assembled. Our focus will be on dissecting them and then plotting out how to replicate the methods used in them to convince your fans of something that may or may not be accurate."

I frown as I look down at the device, realizing this is the part that will get messy.

Batten down the hatches, Rory, it's about to get rough.

"I don't see why people are so dumb that they'll eat up an unconfirmed story," Sydney says as we leave the class to head for Style. "Especially when it's so *obviously* biased. Why would everyone follow along like sheep when contradictory information is easily accessible?"

The vampire snorts and shakes his head. "The supernatural world watched this happen in real time four years ago. It's not hard to believe that many beings are happier when they feel superior to someone—anyone—and giving them that tingle of acceptance can net you very useful acolytes."

She rolls her eyes and growls, "I get humans fell for it. They were scared and afraid for their lives, so a scapegoat was comforting. That's… different."

"No, it's not," I reply as I push open the double doors. "The stakes were higher, but things don't have to be life or death for people to make shitty decisions, Vicious. The need to be safe, to belong, to feel wanted, to be loved…are all powerful emotions that will aid you in getting what you want. Evoking the core feelings everyone shares is what most advertising is about."

Thad frowns and I follow his gaze to the group of chicks who gave our girl trouble before. "Conversely, that applies to making others feel excluded, wrong, abandoned, or disenfranchised. It's often how petty dictators and self-centered assholes gather their minions. It doesn't matter if anything they say is true or even if what they claim they'll do happens. Manipulation is a gray area filled with pockets of opportunity when you're working with desperate folks."

"Very good, bear!" I say with a big grin. "Now you're learning."

"It's like a rumor mill in school, sweet pea." Huck tucks her arm in his, patting her hand lightly. "Remember in the lower school when the girls would talk shit? Even though I wasn't part of it, I heard a lot of shit from the shadows. I'm a smart man, so I could figure out that most of what they were spreadin' around like butter on cornbread was false or edited truth. But the girls they were using to do their dirty work? Lapped it up like kittens and cream. Why? Because the popular, powerful person was payin' attention to them for once."

We hit the door to Style, and Sydney stomps her foot, looking irritated. "I don't like it—not any of it. Lying and scheming to use weak minded fools is what the bad guys do; look at Taterman for that shit. I don't want to be part of it, but that stupid class makes me think I won't be able to avoid it."

Dante chuckles and we turn to look at the muted dragon. "She's right, but I enjoy her indignation. It takes integrity to know what is right and wrong—and even more so to fight for that integrity when it's difficult."

"*Yes*," I reply as we shuffle in. "However, sometimes morals have to take a back seat to survival. Ask me how I know."

Vicious frowns, letting go of the demon to walk over and place her hand on my arm. "We know what you had to do, Rory. And I know I'm not being asked to do… that. But this feels like petty, waspish, mean girl shit like Huck said. It bothers me to shade the truth simply so people will think I'm cool and vote for me or whatever."

Shoshana clears her throat as we enter, her perfectly coiffed appearance making even me feel frumpy. "Ah, the philosophical discussions I get to witness when my students come from Chantelle's class. It's amusing to listen to—especially because so few are of the opinion Miss Jolie just voiced."

I'm not sure if that's her being an asshole or if she's trying to warn us, but I don't get the chance to parse it before my group sits down. Once we're in place, the talk from the hallway is tabled because we know Shoshana will expect us to stay focused on her assignments.

"I've been eagerly awaiting the design work you were to complete," the professor says as she dims the lights in the room. "We're going to put them up on the smart board, so I'm able to highlight where you have done well and where you made mistakes. Get your tablets out and connect to the signal so you can drop them to me."

Sydney makes a grumpy sound and I tug her braid lightly from my seat behind her. "Don't worry, Vicious. Your stuff is definitely going to make the grade; I guarantee it."

"I'm not worried about that," she hisses. "I'm worried she's going to make me *wear* it at some point."

Oh. I didn't fucking think about that—they're all going to kill me if that happens.

WHAT'S IN A NAME?

SYDNEY

THE REST of Flair went as slowly as I feared, but lunch was mildly useful. Rory declared the table we've been using as our 'permanent' location for the mess. Staking a claim on it will reinforce our strength, he explained, and since I'm not used to having to use this type of behavior to intimidate, I let it ride. Dante looked pleased when I didn't complain, and I don't know why that made my stomach flutter, but I enjoyed it. The vampire took it in stride with my best friends, though I think he wanted to question my complacency.

I'm not sure how to read his quiet watchfulness, but I know he's up to something.

If I tell Huck and Thad, they'll chide me because we need to extend trust to all the group, not just everyone but the bloodsucker. And I *am* trying, but it's hard to erase the indoctrination from my teen years and then the start of the Sweeps. Until the day he was killed, my dad swore the vamps were all evil and had sold us out to the humans for special treatment. Sebastian says that's only partly true and he might not be lying—but I have to work at believing him just the same.

I guess that's the same sort of ingrained fear and hatred Taterman used to get the humans to turn on us. Realizing that makes me very unhappy with my brain and I'm fighting against it with every fiber of my being. That doesn't make it any less work, nor does it make it painless. True growth is not as simple as a plant striving for the sun unencumbered—no, it's finding a path to the light through all the obstacles in your way, like weeds in cement.

"Jeez, Syd, what is with the poetry today?" I mutter to myself as we leave the elevator and head for the locker room. My gut tightens and I grit my jaw as it nears, remembering the embarrassing event from the other day. I can't have a hang-up about this facility, so I take a deep breath and stride in with fake confidence. I'll be damned if I'm going to be frightened of a fucking *room*; there are bigger things to worry about.

Thad stops at my locker, looking at me with his soft, soulful eyes. "Are you cool, Syd?"

I give him a bright smile, batting my lashes playfully. "Just peachy, Thaddy. I can't wait to beat the shit out of the mosquito for a couple of hours."

He gives me a dubious expression, but nods and heads for his locker. When he's not looking at me anymore, I sigh silently and open my storage to place my bag there and grab my uniform. Shutting it with a click, I walk over to the shuttered changing area and peel off my clothes. Everything they did to me in Beauty is healing well, and the mark from the new 'supernatural' birth control is also looking good. Rolling my eyes at the irritation I feel about them, I tug on my physical activity uniform and shoes.

This is the only class where I feel like I'm useful, even with the vampire besting me because of his speed; I don't want to ruin it with melancholy.

Once I stow my other clothes, I turn to look at the guys, blinking when I realize they're in various states of undress. While I used one of the closed off units, they're all whipping shit off in the middle of the aisle as if it's perfectly normal to be naked together. The view is breathtaking, though I'm sure as fuck not going to admit that to them. Instead, I frown as I slam the door shut. It makes Huck jump, and he flushes beet red under his hat as he recovers.

"What was that for, Vicious?" Rory looks like he could play a fucking Greek hero half-clothed in his sweats and bare feet. I swallow hard as I take in the small additions they made to him, and his perfectly cut chest and abs, then up to his classically handsome face and blond hair. "Hello?"

"Uh," is all I manage before I shake my head. "You're all—"

"Naked? Or sort of?" Sebastian muses from where he's standing clad only in skin tight boxer briefs that I'm glad I can only see the back of. That view is definitely *enough* and if he turns around, I might actually keel over dead.

I nod, clearing my throat as I retort, "Yes. You're stripping in the middle of the room like it's your job!"

Thad tilts his head, drawing my attention to the large, broad-shouldered bear with his hulking build. "No one's *fully* bare assed, Syd. Don't get twisted."

I'm not sure how that's *supposed to comfort me while I'm having what feels like a heart attack.*

"But… but…"

Huck chuckles as he pulls up his sweatpants and moseys over to me. He's only wearing that damn sexy hat and those indecent pants as he looks at me with a beatific smile. "Sweet pea, we're trying to get you used to all this so we can believably flirt and shit. You know that."

I do, but I didn't realize I'd be seeing every single perfect line, curve, and dip of them this soon—especially not all together. Licking my lips nervously, I fight the urge to press my hands to my face to feel the heat rising there. "Yes, but this is… a lot at once."

"We don't know when things will begin."

My eyes flick to the biggest guy, almost popping out cartoonishly as I note his huge thighs and enormous build. I shouldn't be surprised that a dragon—a royal one, at that—is built like a brick shithouse. Every time I look at Elias, I'm struck again by his sheer size and solidness. It's other-worldly and strangely makes me want to see how dwarfed I'd be if he hugged me.

Sweet baby Hercules, Sydney, you've jumped the track completely.

"Well, that's true. So, um, I'm glad you guys started getting me ready. See you out there!"

They don't answer before I beat a fast retreat from the locker room, beelining for a treadmill to do cardio.

Cowardly? Maybe. Necessary? Without a doubt.

"Come on, get your hands up," the vampire growls, and I huff as I dance around with him in the corner.

Brick and Lancaster allowed us to work with cardio, weapons, and endurance today, so I'm not dodging anything I can't counter, but I'm still exhausted. Sebastian, like all his kin, never seems to lose energy and moves so fast that even though I *know* he's slowing it down, it's insane. I'm occasionally able to get him with good feints or clever tricks, but head-to-head? I'm fucking toast. To add to the humiliation, he's not putting his full strength behind his jabs, nor using any really special talents.

A vampire is definitely going to be my end in these games; I can feel it in my aching bones.

"I've had enough," I groan as I shake out my noodley arms and try to stand without swaying. "You've been using me for a light workout for hours now. If you were trying to make a point, it's taken, Bas."

He pauses, dropping his fists to study me. "What did you call me?"

"Bas?" I say in confusion. It's not the first time, I don't think, and it's definitely easier when I'm so out of breath. "Why?"

"No one calls me that. They only use my full name or title." His lips purse as he thinks, then he nods. "I like it. You may commence with your nickname."

Squinting at the weird ass supe, I ask, "You think you get to *approve* people's nicknames of you? That's not how it works, buddy. People just… give them to you. Like… Thaddy. I gave that to him and that's just how it is."

"I call you Vicious," Rory shouts from his sparring match with Elias. The dragon gets a good one in and the mage grunts in pain. "When I can breathe, that is."

Nodding at him, I turn back to the vampire and shrug. "The big guy uses 'little rebel', which if he'd drop the 'little' portion, I'd dig. But I don't get to decide, you see. It's not my nickname for me." No one else corrects me and I give Sebastian a smug grin. "See? I'm right."

His expression slowly morphs into one of supreme satisfaction as he looks at me and my skin gets hot. "I understand your ritual now. I'll consider what I am going to select for you very carefully. And you will accept it, as everyone has agreed upon the rules of this custom. That makes it a bargain, right, demon?"

Huck's eyes widen as he's tugged into the fray, but I can't help him. If he says 'no', then my statement isn't right. However, he looks very concerned about agreeing with the bloodsucker. "Uh, well, technically…"

I fear I've made an error now, but as usual, I've discovered it far too late.

"Be careful, Huckleberry. You know we are telling the truth to one another," Sebastian warns with an evil grin. "You wouldn't want to set a bad example for our girl, hmm?"

The demon takes his hat off, running his hand over his dark hair before he puts it back on. It's a tell for him—a physical sign that he's getting ready to give into something he wishes he didn't have to. "Shit fire and save the matches, Syd. I can't say he's mistaken. You really stepped in it this time."

My face drains of color; I can feel it. We're all being a lot nicer to one another as we learn to get along, but I just handed the fangy fuck a free pass to make me look stupid. I'll have to accept whatever he chooses as long as it's not objectionable enough to tweak the other guys because I ran my mouth. I really need to stop trash talking to people when I'm tired; it just never ends well for me.

"Fine. You win, *Bas*." I grit my teeth as I glare at him, and when he grins even wider, I want to punch his ridiculously perfect face. Fucking gorgeous half-dressed idiot has been distracting me or kicking my ass all session and now I handed him yet another victory. It's enough to put me in a foul ass mood for the next lecture.

And *it's the Intrigue & Socialization bullshit, and I'm already not looking forward to that.*

"If you're all done bickering…" Brick says as he arches a brow. We just stare back at him and he shakes his head. "Whatever. Hit the showers so you aren't late to the all teams' lecture. Those coaches bitched to high hell on Tuesday because some of us who have subjects where we have to work hard made people late."

I give him a sympathetic look—this is the one training I truly enjoy— and turn on my heel to do as asked. The guys follow, their heavy footsteps and dude sweat smell filling the air as we go into the room where I almost had an episode two days ago. When I open my locker with a bang, they all look at me with varying expressions of concern.

"This is fine. All taken care of," I say as I wave my hand. Grabbing my shower stuff and my clothes, I beat a fast exit into my stall, yanking the curtain closed. As the water warms up, I feel the sensation of someone trying to test my aura, and I blink in surprise. I'm normally not sensitive to others' magic until I have an issue—this is like a small tickle at the base of my spine telling me I'm being clocked.

I don't say anything out loud, but my lips curve up as I toss my gym clothes on the bench and get the water running three times as hot as I could get it in my old apartment.

It might not be quick, but my magic is coming and when it does, everyone needs to get the hell out of my way.

STEP BY STEP, ONE BY ONE

ELIAS

IN MY LONG LIFE, I have seen many courts, armies, and groups form and dissolve. There's a natural flow to that process, particularly if the members are disparate in backgrounds and have been forced into banding together. Any beings that are harmonious normally will have a small period in which they require trust building, and then it will gel as one. However, if those conscripted into action are not that lucky, then it takes longer and the progress is incremental. It's also filled with bumps and bruises as the individuals struggle to overcome what their minds and hearts want them to believe, despite the logic of their union.

Royals are schooled in this type of thing in societies where they lead their troops on the battlefield, such as the sea dragons.

I know that is not the case for many species in this modern age, and it is hard not to take charge to force them to do what we need to. Since the Sweeps and allowing my capture to facilitate my people's escape, I have had to let go of many things to survive the treatment of the humans. One of them was my pride and my inclination to lead—those sentiments only got me in trouble when I first arrived in the lockdown section of my first camp. I also learned to distance myself from my title and my destiny so that I could exist in the ignominy of my circumstances without my dragon causing me to be thrown in solitary so severe I would try to kill myself. The other powerful supernaturals who could not do such a thing are long dead, and I took their lessons to heart as I watched them wither away.

As I scrub the remnants of our hard work off of my skin, I listen carefully to the others. We followed Sydney to the locker room, and she seemed to handle being there despite her unnecessary shame from the other day. However, my new brothers are being very subdued as we get clean, and I believe it's because they hope to avoid triggering that emotion in her again. The only one who is determined not to treat her with kid gloves is the vampire and while I am currently staying in the middle on purpose, I believe he's right to do so. Sydney is quite strong and will be even more formidable once she has fully acclimated to reality.

Unfortunately, that adjustment is required on the heels of a lot of other jarring changes in her world and it's very stressful. Centuries of evaluating warriors and comrades tells me she will rise above it all and that Sydney is going to be extremely powerful. So I am doing my best to balance the scales as our team becomes a unit—genuine leaders know when to step back and let their soldiers make decisions they can learn from. That's my goal in placating both sides until we're copacetic, and I will continue until it no longer works.

"This class is going to be a snooze fest again," the mage says loudly. "I don't see the point of it. They can lecture us on this stuff, but with so many people in one room, the message gets lost."

My lips curve as I wait for someone to correct him. I know why they are holding this class in the fashion they chose, but I want to see if any of the others have figured it out.

Sydney coughs, then replies, "Uh, I think… Someone tell me if I'm off-base, but I think they're only pretending to teach this stuff in the lecture. I think it's actually a lab."

The bear makes a confused sound and I grin quietly. "A lab? Like in high school when we had the lecture part and then we had labs to do the actual experiments live to test things?"

"Yep," the little rebel says, her voice getting firmer as she goes on. "I think this is like a… psychological lab? And they're lecturing about similar stuff to what we learn in stupid Chantelle's class, but they want us to *use* it when we're all in forced proximity with the other teams. You know, to prepare for what we'll have to do in social situations when this bullshit starts."

Bingo, little rebel.

"Sweet pea, that's downright devious," the demon says. His voice breaks the silence that followed her statement, and I'm pleased that he's the one who gave credence to her theory. Sydney will listen to him more easily than she will the vampire or mage, and if she is to be our center, we need her to be confident in leading.

"I agree," Sebastian says, and I hear one of the showers shut off. "It is a practical application of many of our sessions, and they cloak that intent by lecturing. What they really want is for us to gather as much information about how the various teams and their members behave as we can."

Thad sighs and I know the big shifter is probably frustrated. He doesn't have a disingenuous bone in his body, but our current circumstances are forcing him to learn that as much as they are making Sydney find her way. "I will not be useful for that. I just don't see that shit the way some of you guys do. But if you're all right, then we need someone to help build profiles of the teams and players as we find things out."

Ah, very true. More strategic than I would have expected from him.

"We should have some of us watching and taking notes and others in charge of building that into a database outside of the session." My statement is firm, but with just enough flexibility that it doesn't sound like an order. That will make it easier for the more aggressive members to get behind.

I hear softer steps leave the tiled area, and I know Sydney has completed her routine. "I think Elias's idea is good. Who wants to do what? We all need to learn the 'watch and dissect thing', but I'm not sure this is the best place for someone who isn't good at being in charge."

"Does that mean we should have people who read others well watching others and the others collating data?" Rory asks, as his spray shuts off next to me.

He's the second one to finish, and I believe Huckleberry was the first. They're good choices to face the little rebel first as we head to the class; it won't bring up the memory of her blood being scented last time. The rest of us cannot pretend we didn't know simply by virtue of our biology and she knows it. It's a delicate balance, helping her move past the minor issues that she runs into because her neglectful father and the humans taught her absolutely nothing about life.

Turning off my spray, I make certain to be loud enough when I move that Sydney knows what's coming. Then I say, "We should have Rory and Sebastian watch people. Perhaps Huck as well. Then the bear, the little rebel, and I can put it all together for us."

When no one argues, I smile to myself, pleased that I am successfully using my skills as a Prince once more.

"The best way to infiltrate a group is to make yourself indispensable to them."

I arch a brow at the coach for the all magic user team skeptically. Perhaps that works if you have things the targets will need—influence, materials, wealth

—but it will not work with those you cannot service. There are always people you need that do not need you, and often, they are the ones who will benefit you the most if you can turn them. It's simple asset evaluation, and the handler for the spell jockeys is ignoring a very important subset in his statement.

Sighing, I look over at the vampire and he, too, looks irritated with the claim. His kind definitely know how to influence others, even without using their given powers. I have never met a bloodsucker who wasn't extremely skilled at manipulation, both verbally and non-verbally. Obviously, having the ability to use compulsion helps, but I believe they often grow bored with the lack of challenges that skill provides.

His voice is low as he murmurs, "That is one way, but there are many others. Infiltration is an art, and it has as many techniques as there are beings on the planet. This joker is explaining it from a very human perspective and we should remember that we are *not* human."

"Gee, I hadn't noticed," Sydney cracks and I grin.

The demon pats her hand, leaning back in his chair as he scans the room surreptitiously. "You can tell the supes in here that are closer to that line than others. They all nodded eagerly at that little gem o' knowledge while the less human-adjacent folks looked a bit huffy."

"They should," Thad says as he carefully prints notes with his stylus pen. "Even I'm aware that was, at best, misleading. Getting into a group has to do with emotions and using them to evoke reactions. Once they've labeled you as one of them, keep pushing that button."

That came out of nowhere, but it is very astute.

"How do you know that, Calvin?" the vampire asks curiously as he continues eying a group of demons and shifters at the front of the room.

Thad shrugs as he continues writing things down. "There are not enough bears in Tempest Seven for individual sleuths by actual type. The alpha that runs ours has to use some of this stuff to help integrate different bear species into one group. We're all very different, especially the lesser known kinds, so…."

Sydney looks surprised, frowning at him briefly. "You never told me that."

"Well, you didn't have a group except for Huck and me. It always seemed to make you sad, but you didn't want to talk about it. So I tried not to discuss political stuff, you know?"

Her expression is shocked, then sad as she sighs. "Okay, yeah. I get that. You guys were doing the whole 'protective' thing, and I was too caught up in my shit. I'm going to feel like a real idiot as this stuff keeps getting revealed to me, but… don't stop telling me, okay?"

That I am quite proud of her for saying—it is a big step in the right direction.

"Good girl, little rebel."

I don't know why I said it like that, and my brain freezes when I think she's going to be angry as hell. But surprisingly, she gives him a half-grin that makes my dragon lift his head and bellow happily inside of me. "I can behave sometimes, big guy. I'm getting better."

She's definitely telling the truth with that statement, so I nod at her. The mage leans forward, pausing his assessment of the teams to hold his fist out for Sydney. Our girl bumps it with hers, and the sensation of positive emotions flows from end to end in our group. That is a very powerful weapon in getting a group to become a unit, though negative energy can work as well if aimed properly. I want the former to be our guide, so I let a small trickle of sweet ocean air escape me to help continue the calm, good energy of my roommates.

Sydney inhales for a moment, then turns to look at me with a shocked expression. "I've never been to the beach before, but I know that's how it smells. How do I know that?"

I find that egregious, but I let it go to reply, "My dragon's magic is tied to the seas and when he is pleased, I can share it with you. He finds our current energy pleasing, thus... the ocean comes to you."

I don't know how to describe the way she looks at those words, but I am definitely committed to making it happen repeatedly—that is a promise.

SOMETIMES YOU NEED TO UNPLUG

SYDNEY

AS WE HEAD BACK to the room for dinner, I'm irrationally pissed that my dad never took us anywhere—including the ocean. The scent Elias shared made my senses sing with pleasure, and I'm angry that despite certainly having the ability to travel, I've never been over fifty miles from where I grew up. My father used to claim it was because we had to stay under the radar, but I'm beginning to believe that, too, was bullshit. In fact, I have no idea what percentage of the things he told me were true, and it's been freaking me out since the guys clued me in.

But I'm remaining calm, and let my brain do the processing it needs to, just like Rory suggested.

It's not easy, but I know he's right about presenting a united front and keeping weaknesses under wraps. However, right now? I want to stomp my foot in frustration like a child, and that's probably because the child inside of me is pissed about things we missed. I bite my lip as we all get into the elevator, considering what to do to help burn this emotion off. I can't go down to the gym because I spent so long getting my assed kicked by the vampire earlier. I'm just too sore and tired to even contemplate it.

"Vicious?"

Rory's voice pulls me out of my head and I frown over at him. "Yeah?"

"Have you been paying attention to anything we said?" The mage grins knowingly and I blink at him. "I thought not. You're all tangled in your brain again."

Feeling ashamed, I shrug and look away from him as I say, "Maybe I'm just plotting things. You never know."

"Point of fact, sweet pea… We actually do. Your overthinking face is pretty obvious to anyone who spends a good deal of time with you." Huck's smile is sheepish, but fond as he interrupts, so I can't be mad.

"Okay, you got me," I sigh. "I was rehashing shit about my dad because of Elias's scent earlier. But you don't have to worry, I'm handling it. I mean, I'm *trying* to handle it without being an uber bitch. I just ran into a wall when I realized I'm too blown to go beat up a bag."

The vampire's brows furrow, and he shocks me when he looks concerned. "It was too much?"

I shake my head vehemently, not wanting him to go easier on me in the one area I can attempt to compete. "No, I'm just sore. Whatever stamina and strength I'm supposed to get with emerging hasn't increased yet. So I get tired or bruised more easily than you guys; however, you shouldn't adjust because our opponents won't. We don't know the timeline for my stuff to come into being, so I have to be prepared."

"That is a very wise statement," Sebastian says, and I see the hint of pride in his eyes this time. "I think you've done exceptionally well today from beginning to end. It probably deserves a reward, don't you?"

Is he asking me? How the fuck should I know?

However, Rory nods his head, his typical smile growing to epic proportions as he responds to the vampire. "Hell, yeah, she does! I'm totally in, mosquito. Good call."

His reaction is so enthusiastic that I shrink back a bit, worried that I have no idea what the hell they're going to use for this 'reward'. Thad must sense my wariness because he holds his hand out to me and I grab it like a lifeline, letting him tug me forward into the middle of the circle again. "Guys, I don't know…"

"Syd, no one is going to do anything to upset you when I'm around." The bear squeezes my palm gently. "I have no idea what the fuck those two are so eager to do, but I promise, it won't be something you don't agree to."

"Seconded." Elias meets my gaze resolutely. "No boundaries will be crossed, little rebel. However, I will help treat you to any agreed upon reward."

It takes a *lot of* my remaining energy to screw up the courage to look at the surrounding men before I say, "Okay. I trust you."

Hopefully, I'm not wrong about this—we'll never come back from it if I am.

～

"First, it's time for relaxing and getting clean." I arch a brow at Rory as he hands me a clean towel and the basket from my bedroom. "You didn't really shower for long because you're still aflutter about that locker room. I've swiped some of the stuff from your bedroom that you hadn't opened yet to make the bathroom nice and relaxing. Everything is ready, and while you soak, we'll order food."

My eyes narrow at the mage as I open the bathroom door. They made me wait in the living area while he did this part, and I'm less than thrilled that he was rooting around in my room. "Where did you find this stuff?"

His grin widens as he sighs. "Vicious, you have boxes of shit that Gemma had sent to our room that you haven't even opened yet. I just rifled through them until I found some stuff that would work for this. I didn't look through your undies drawer or anything. Dante said no boundary breaking, right?"

He did and I'm relieved to hear that despite his excitement, Rory is trying to stick with that.

"Alright," I reply as I move to turn the light on, and Rory shakes his head. "What? I can't see."

A small ball of fire pops up in his hand, and I shrink back. "Don't worry, Syd. I'm gonna light the candles with it, not set shit on fire. It's all good."

My face turns red and I'm glad he probably can't see my embarrassment in the dim light. I watch as he moves from the sink to the toilet to the edge of the tub, lighting each one of the small candles carefully. "This feels so extravagant," I murmur. "I mean, I'm here soaking in this big tub and smelling candles and whatever the hell else you have stacked along that back ledge… but people are…"

Rory's expression is firm as he turns back to me. "Don't do that, Vicious. You're right; this is a lot compared to what you're used to and maybe even more compared to what the dragon experienced in lockdown. But we didn't ask to be chosen for this shit and we might die trying to save people. So… we're going to enjoy what we can when we can, because without *some* joy, life just isn't worth the pain, you know?"

I hate it, but he's right. Without little pleasures, you have nothing to hope for.

Swallowing the weirdly strong emotion sticking in my throat, I nod at the handsome magic user. He puts out the flame in his palm with a cheeky wink, then futzes with a few more things before he claps his hands. "There we go. One very soothing, calming bath to soak away some of the pain and frustration. Then when you're nice and relaxed, you can come out to eat and be further pampered, milady."

"Uh, milady? I don't think so, Rory." I snort at him and he just bats his lovely, thick lashes at me. "I'm not that kind of girl and we all know it."

"Sydney, you can be any kind of woman you want now that you're free of the past shit. And whoever that is, I guarantee every asshole in that front room will be okay with it. Some things, you just need to take on faith."

I open my mouth to protest, but the mage takes my momentary surprise to duck out of the bathroom. The door clicks behind him and I frown at the space he was occupying a moment ago. Why in the hell wouldn't they care who I become if it's not the 'me' they all met? What kind of male bullshit is this whole 'reward' thing they're so into? I peel my clothes off, placing them in the basket as I walk over to the very frilly bathtub with my basket of girl crap.

This feels like a trap, but also, it feels like a moment in time that I have to pay attention to. The guys didn't have to suggest this—especially Bas—and I definitely didn't earn it, no matter how much they say I did. All I did today was hold my shit together and survive the classes without punching anyone or starting an argument. I have no idea why anyone would think those things merit this kind of treatment.

Do they think such tiny achievements are worthy of this kind of… kindness?

Lowering myself into the warm water carefully, I groan as I sink into the silly bubbles Rory insisted on. I lean back slowly, allowing my skin to adjust to the odd fizzing around me and the temperature he set. "Rory and Thad would think so little is deserving; they're both very soft despite their muscled guy-ness. I can see them talking Elias and Huck into it. But Sebastian? He's all sharp edges and disdain, yet he was the one who spoke up."

Obviously, the empty room doesn't answer, so I reach up and undo my braid to give my scalp a little relief. I sigh again as the tight hair-do is released and I'm fully able to relax. My eyes close as I replay the day, still puzzling out what might have triggered their offer. I'm fairly certain I'm the biggest pain in the ass of the entire group for so many reasons, and they're constantly having to deal with my bullshit. That was fine when it was just Huck, Thad, and me, but it feels different now that there are three more people who didn't choose my bullshit as their load.

"You can only do your best, Sydney," I murmur to myself as I let the atmosphere and the bath calm my jangling nerves. "If you're trying, it doesn't matter if you stumble occasionally. The effort counts and that's important."

My father used to say that when he'd run me through the paces and I'd fail to come up with any magic—which was worse than because I didn't even randomly do shit, I just fizzled out. With the discovery that most of his teachings and behavior were abnormal, it's strange that I'm thinking about aphorisms he used to use with me. But brains are strange and emotions are unpredictable and… This damn relaxing bath thing is making me soften like butter in the microwave.

I wonder if that's why they were so eager to let me prune up? They figured I'd be less bitchy?

It makes as much sense as anything else, but I'm uncertain I believe it. Huck and Thad have put up with my moody shit for years; they wouldn't play into some scam the others dreamed up if it was negative. Possibilities race through my mind and I draw in a slow breath, then blow it slowly as I sink further into the water. My muscles are relaxing and the aches from earlier are ebbing as I lie back in the serene setting Rory created.

"It's probably about the freaking period," I muse. "Men are really squicked out by that, and even though Huck took me, they were all there when Mr. Sensitive Nose scented my problem before I knew about it. They're probably just doing this because I'm a fragile woman with bloody shorts and they think I have to be coddled because of it. Yeah, that's gotta be it."

I wrinkle my nose in irritation as I decide that has to be their motivation. Knowing why makes me realize they've talked about the damn incident and, for a moment, my Zen fades as my temper flares. But my eyes are closed, and the room is quiet, so I inhale deeply and push that anger away like the guys have suggested. Even if they discussed the stupid failure of my previous implant, they weren't doing it to be jackasses. They probably just wanted to make sure I'm okay.

Right?

Again, there's no answer to my mental meanderings, and I growl softly. The mage was right when he said it helps to talk shit out to someone who can respond rather than bitching to myself with no affirmation. I'm not sure how he's wriggled his way so far into my head and my damn personal space, but I have to admit he's accurate with such an unerring frequency that it's spooky.

Hell, he's even right about this stupid bath—not that I'm going to tell him when I go out there.

WE'RE ORDERING THE SAMPLER PLATTER

RORY

I DIDN'T REALLY THINK the vampire's idea would work, especially given our girl's resistance to anything that might mark her as 'weaker' in her mind. But it did, and now I'm so full of kinetic energy that I don't know what to do with it. The others are looking at me like I've lost my marbles and maybe I have—but this is our *chance*. Getting Sydney relaxed enough to be comfortable and bond a bit rather than have her hackles up is a big step towards the unity I can feel in my bones is coming someday.

With her consent and approval, of course, because I have never *been that kind of guy, nor will I be now.*

"Okay, sports fans, listen up," I say as I clap my hands. "We've had a few conversations about protecting Sydney and helping her, but we all need to be real fucking honest right now. I mean, with ourselves and each other; otherwise, this will go south quickly and it will be forever fucked. Got it?"

The vampire's expression is droll, but he nods. "What, pray tell, are you babbling about, mage?"

Raking my hand through my hair in annoyance at his careful response, I sigh. "We all know that woman has walls a million feet high and has been put in a fucking fake bubble for most of her life. Whether or not that was for legit reasons, this is like… a moment in time for us. As a team, yeah, but also as more than that. So… lay it out while we get this place ready, you absolute donuts."

Thad blinks, chuckling softly at my insult. "Right. Okay. What are we supposed to do while we confess our sins, Rory?"

Thick as bread dough sometimes—this is why dudes have so much trouble.

"Make this room comfy, relaxing, soothing, and warm, you oaf. Get blankets, pillows, candles… Order finger foods and drinks. Dim the lights. Move the furniture. You know, shit you'd do for a bear girl in her heat or whatever, man. Don't be so dense."

"I think he means to make a nest as dragons would for their mates."

I beam at the reticent lizard. "Exactly! Let's make this the safest, homiest living room in the universe. We want Vicious to know that this—and us—are her escape and her home now. Everything else in the world can fade if we're all together."

"Why would we do that?" Sebastian says as he pretends to yawn.

"Fuck, man. Stop that aloof vampire nonsense. Do we all like this woman or what?" I ask bluntly. "Cause if we do, then *this* is the moment to show her how much. It will lead nowhere unless she wants it to, but that's fine, right? Because we actually *like* her, not just want to nail her, yes?"

Huck blinks, then tips his hat back and sticks his thumbs in his belt loops. It's a quintessential cowboy pose and I'm not sure if it's for effect or if he simply does it blindly. "Hell, yes, I do. Have since the day I met her when they shipped me here. It'd be stupid to deny, I s'pose."

"Same," Thad admits as he pushes the furniture away so there's a wide open space in the middle of the room to build. The bear is the most obvious fan of Sydney, of course, but he's hidden it so long that it surprises me for him to flat out say it like that. "I haven't been an angel or anything, nor has Huck, but our hearts have always been with her. She's just never noticed, I guess."

"I don't think that's true," Sebastian muses as he walks to the kitchen and rummages around in the drawers. He pulls out a bunch of taper candles and brings them in, handing them to me for distribution. "She's purposefully shut away the part of her that feels things like romance and sexual attraction to keep herself safe from loss. At least, that's my read on it. It's not my truth, nor am I reading her mind, so I cannot be certain."

As I find places to settle them, I hum my agreement. "I think so, too, based on the conversations we've had privately. I'm not repeating any of that, of course, because it would be a violation. But what I *can* say is that if we want her to be our girl eventually, we need to show her we can be trusted and we're safe. That's why I want to set this all up; I want to do it right."

"Our girl?" Thad echoes as he tilts his head. "Who said this was a group project?"

I snort and roll my eyes at his naivete. "I just did. Plus, it's clear you and the demon have agreed to share or one of you would have scared the other off long ago. Since you didn't and I know that both of your kind are fine with polyamorous relationships, I didn't worry about you protesting. I'm all for sharing and lots of other things; vampires are, too. Dragons love a hoard —even people."

Elias tilts his head, then says, "We do. I have not had one for a long time in the camps. I find myself fond of the little rebel and my dragon agrees. We will take part."

That's one very definitive 'yes' for forming a group.

"It's not the first time you've mentioned courting her for real, mage. But you didn't make everyone state things so plainly before. Why now?" The vampire's gaze narrows on me as I light the tapers, his arms crossed over his chest.

I sigh, frustrated with the push-back on something I know they actually want. "I'm making absolutely *certain* you're all on-board so we don't set ourselves up to fracture the team if someone changes their mind. Worse than that, I don't want anyone to hurt Sydney just as she's finding her true self now."

"Oh," the bear says as it dawns on him what I'm doing. "I get it. This is your way of keeping her heart from being broken by someone being an asshole suddenly."

"Bingo." I point to the hallway and look at the demon. "Go get blankets and pillows and shit, cowpoke. We need to make this big open area very cozy and comfy before she finishes soaking. Get along, little doggie."

The demon rolls his eyes, but does as I ask. He heads into their room first, then the others—except for Sydney's—to gather the necessary linens. When he comes back, he looks at me seriously. "I'm all in for the family idea if my sweet pea is. Because that's one detail you've forgotten in this pact, magic wielder. Syd has to agree to it, too."

Groaning as I stoop to arrange the blankets first, I arch a brow at the vampire and the dragon. "You two need to help. Order food. Fix drinks. Set up the TV." Once they move, I turn back to Huck. "I'm aware of that, and I don't plan to coerce her. I want her to come to the conclusion on her own, then discuss it. But it will never come up if she doesn't trust us as people, then as men."

"You missed a career as a fucking therapist," Sebastian mutters as he peruses the menus for room service. "This shit would have made you serious money."

Leave it to a vampire not to understand that as an upper tier sex worker, I was not only very highly compensated, but functioned as a therapist, priest, friend, punching bag, and much, much more for years.

"I'm going to leave that statement alone for now because I don't think you truly understand my former world," I reply in an even tone. "But the next part of this discussion is that we can snark and be playful with one another—especially in public when we play roles—but we have to support and be good to each other. Sydney never needs to feel like she has to choose one over the other because we said stupid shit like that. Got it?"

The dragon walks over to the counter between the kitchen and the living room with a serious expression. "The mage is correct about that. I think we have very different pre-Sweeps histories and even more varied post-Sweeps experiences. Judgement and condescension will not aid us in forming a team or a family."

"You've said more tonight than, like, ever, man." I grin as I fluff pillows and form a big ring on the floor where everyone will fit. "I appreciate the support."

Thad pulls cushions off of the furniture and starts pilling them around the pillows, his brow furrowed as he makes the 'nest' even more comfortable. "He has, and I think that's good, too. No one's saying it, but if we're all going to date Sydney and she agrees, we have to discuss some other things."

I arch a brow at him curiously. "Just what are those, Vanilla Bear?"

"I think that's what he means," Huck chuckles as he drops to his knees and crawls over to help us with the pallet. "We need to discuss our own boundaries, so to speak."

Unexpected—not upsetting, but definitely not the topic I thought the bear would broach.

"I'm up for almost anything," I say with a shrug. Sitting back on my heels, I fiddle with the linens next to me before I continue. "I'd prefer not to get too close to my past in terms of the pain threshold, but otherwise? I'm good with top, bottom, sub, Dom, most equipment, men, women… Virtue of my experiences, I suppose."

"No."

I turn my head to frown at the vampire. "No, what, Whitmore?"

He sighs heavily, as if I'm being the most trying person he's ever met. "No, you will not simply accept things because you're 'okay' with it in this situation, Stormbringer. That would not please Sydney, nor am I happy with it. I'm not one of the vampires who uses our powers to manipulate people in the bedroom, nor am I one to allow past damage to do the same here. You will tell us what you actually want and like, not just what you're allowing."

"Yes," the dragon says as he turns to the fridge to pull out the refreshments. "The bloodsucker is correct. We will explore anything the participants are happy to experience, but no one does things to simply make someone else happy. I believe there is much curiosity among this group and many things we can mutually enjoy without sullying it that way."

When this guy talks, he really fucking goes all in.

"Okay. I get it." I rub the back of my neck, my face heating in a way I haven't felt in a long time. "So… to be honest? I prefer submission. I like a soft Dom, and I'm definitely pansexual. I don't want intense pain. I enjoy biting, I like marks, and I'm not shy about what makes me hard once clothes are off. Is that better?"

They all stare at me, and I grin to myself. I'm very experienced in discussing limits with people—hazard of the previous job—and though I blushed a bit unexpectedly, I'm not uncomfortable doing so. They're all hot guys and I'm slowly finding myself enjoying their company. I could definitely see us all in a group with Sydney and each other—and it makes my dick hard. I don't know how willing the rest of them are, and that's part of why I started this chat.

Sebastian clears his throat. "Well, that was very helpful. My kind likes a bit more pain than him, obviously, but most of his statements are true—except I am certainly dominant and not submissive. I will not be silent about what I am comfortable or not comfortable with as we explore."

"Gentleman, you know I'm your Huckleberry," the demon says with a chuckle at his own reference. "In so many ways, because I'm very versatile and even more vocal."

I have to suppress the urge to rub my hands together in glee. This is even better than I hoped and the more our family is open to, the easier it will be for us to form a tight-knit, unbreakable unit. That's not me being manipulative; it's just a fact. Plus, I don't know that any of us have had a support system like that in a long time—or ever. It will strengthen us and become more stable for the danger ahead.

"I, um, don't know much about all that stuff," the bear says as he stacks more cushions industriously. "But I'm interested in finding things out."

My lips curve up as I look at the biggest dude in the room. "What about you, big guy? Where do you fall on the scale?"

"Wherever I want, mage. But not on the bottom, nor as a submissive. Perhaps it's from growing up royal or maybe my dragon, but I need control. Anything else is up for grabs."

Smack my ass and call me a bad boy—I couldn't have asked for a more perfect group if I tried.

I WANT THE ENTIRE BUFFET

SYDNEY

LICKING MY LIPS NERVOUSLY, I stare at the bathroom door. I know once I open it, things will change somehow. I'm not sure *why* I feel that way, but the notion has settled deeply in my guts as I soaked away the aches from earlier. My mind is arguing with my heart and body—something that hasn't happened in the past. I don't know if that's healing or just a natural progression of aging that I'd fobbed off for the past four years. Either way, it's unsettling and a lot like standing at the edge of a cliff to look down.

I'm terrified of free-falling to my doom.

The carefully crafted image of Sydney Jolie I've maintained since my father's death is *not* scared of shit like this. She scoffs at it and at people who are terrified of it. Relying on others only leads to betrayal and pain; my father taught me that over and over during my life. People leave and you're devastated; it's an absolute in life.

But I'm tied to these men, two of whom I do trust, and it's not just by selection. This team is inexorably connected to surviving these fucking Games. If I cannot allow them to get close enough to anticipate things, to know me, I'll put all of our safety in peril. That's not a smart move, nor is it going to make anything easier. The small steps I've taken in the past weeks are making a difference—they were right—and to continue working towards our shared goal, that has to continue.

"You are stronger than you think, Sydney," I murmur softly. "They are not the men you've seen in the camps, nor are they your father. If nothing else, the newer members of the team want to live, and to do so, they have to keep their word. Trusting in their instinct for self-preservation isn't naïve; it's logical."

My brain knows this, but my heart isn't done fighting for protection, obviously.

I swallow hard, looking down at the loose tank top and sweats I put on, then over at the mirror to see my long hair unbound on my shoulders. Not braiding it is a sign that I'm trying to let them in—I am pulling off the hardened mask I wear in public. This is the side of me I refuse to allow others to know—a woman whose entire world has been upended so many times I can't find solid ground. This version of me is in the middle of redefining herself to reflect the tumultuous revelations about my powers, the world, my father, and everything in between that being picked for this event has wrought.

Sucking in a slow breath through my nose, I put my hand on the doorknob and twist. My mind is repeating the mantra of 'you can do this' and my skin is prickling with anticipation. The way I respond to all of them is insane; it's like an electric wire is sparking inside of me, especially when they touch me. I don't know if that's normal for attraction or if it's something else because, in a low-level way, I think it's how I reacted to Thad and Huck when we first met. But I locked that down with my vow to ignore the body as a currency atmosphere many supes my age were adopting. Nothing the humans could give me was worth that compromise—for me—and I shut down my reactions completely to avoid it.

When I walk into the hallway, the suite is quiet. The lighting is dimmed, and my feet dig into the soft pile of the carpet as I pad through the kitchen to the living area. My eyes widen as I see all the work they've put into making the space look welcoming and comfortable. Candles, pillows, blankets, cushions… everything is on the floor, including trays of food and drinks that are close to each of them as they watch the muted TV. My appearance gets their attention without fail, and I bite my lip as I give them a nervous smile.

"Um, this is… really… nice," I say, feeling shyness overcome me as emotions riot inside my chest. "I didn't think you'd do so much work."

Rory grins at me, his expression pleased as his eyes move up and down my frame. "Vicious, you look positively radiant. Come over here so we can help you get even more relaxed. You're going to love it."

Anxiety rockets through me, but the expressions on Huck and Thad's faces help me push my limbs to move onto the big pallet they've constructed. I lower myself down in the center, where it's obvious I'm supposed to sit. The mage quickly shifts pillows until I'm propped up, and I watch them move in concert to surround me with just enough space to make sure I'm not being crowded. That graceful dance confirms my mind's insistence that allowing them access to the real me will help us form a better team, and I sigh softly as some of the tension seeps out of me.

I wasn't just fooling myself; they really are working together.

"We have an extensive selection of finger foods, so it's easy to munch while we work," Thad says as he puts his enormous hands on my shoulders gently. He pauses, giving me time to protest, and when I don't, another sliver of worry fades from the atmosphere of the room. "I'll work on your shoulders with this stuff from your beauty baskets, and Huck will help you with that."

My eyes widen and I have to swallow past a lump in my throat when I realize that means the demon is going to feed me. He's smirking at me fondly, but it's not in a creepy way. I nod my consent to them, and Thad lifts his hands again to deal with whatever weird cream he's going to use. I watch as the other three wait, curious what they're going to do while my two friends pamper me.

"I'm gonna work on your feet, Vicious. It's one of my tier-one skills, and that's not because I have a fetish or anything. I'm just *fantastic* at it," Rory says, as he scoots down while keeping his eyes on my face. "You'll love it; I promise."

"Okay," I murmur as he picks up one foot. "I mean, you guys don't have to—"

Huck leans in with a piece of fruit, smiling that adorable down home grin that makes him damn near irresistible. "Sweet pea, no one is forcing us to do anything. We want to take care of you an' believe you me, we want *you* to want it, too. So tell us if anything is bothersome, and don't be shy about sayin' what makes you feel good, either."

How does that honeyed voice always activate the calming sensors in my brain? It's fucking magic.

"In fact, I particularly enjoy sounds that tell me what feels good," Sebastian says as he lounges in the spot between Huck and Rory. "I bet the dragon does as well."

"Very much."

Elias's quiet agreement, so typically succinct, is a balm on my nerves. Knowing that they're all behaving exactly as I would expect, without changing who they are, is more evidence that they are willingly doing this stuff. This isn't just a feint or a trick—they mean it when they say they're all happy to be here with me. That helps me relax a little more, and Thad rumbles happily behind me as he kneads my tight shoulders.

"That's perfect, Syd. Relax, so I can get all these knots out for you."

I finish chewing the fruit Huck placed against my lips, then feel my face heat as the guys who can see me chewing stare. "Did I do something weird?"

"No," Rory says with a chuckle. His thumb digs into my arch and a straight-up moan escapes my mouth before I can stop it. He ducks his head, hiding his expression, but I can see the others as their faces go from soft to intense in a blink. "Damn, Vicious."

"Sorry," I mutter, then drop my gaze to my hands in my lap, not able to look at them when they're staring at me that way. "That, uh, was good."

"No shit," Sebastian grumbles as I feel him moving next to me. "If we couldn't tell that, they should send us all back to the factory to be reset."

Damn him for making me even more self-conscious without being mean; now I can't snark at him.

Thad leans in, his lips against my ear as he continues massaging my shoulders skillfully. "It's okay to feel good, Syd. I know you've been fighting it, fighting happiness for a long time. But even in the darkest times, we're allowed to find joy and peace. That doesn't make us bad people."

"Good point, my ursine friend," Huck says as he holds up a piece of cheese. I accept it, my eyes fluttering at how tasty it is, and he groans. "Look at how well you're adaptin', sweet pea. You didn't even look like you were going to bite my finger off this time."

His praise does funny things to my stomach and I scowl at my hands. I don't need dudes to tell me what I'm doing well at; I'm perfectly able to gauge my skill sets. But even as I frown at the weird sensations, the rest of my body disavows that thought. Hearing Huck's sweet twang compliment me has my nerve endings firing and the heat in my face racing down my torso to blossom in places that aren't normally this involved. I swallow the cheese and lick my suddenly dry lips, realizing how thirsty I am suddenly.

"What can I give you, little rebel? I sense you need a drink. We have water, juice, and soda."

Turning to look at Elias, I force myself to meet his gaze. It's still intense, but there's a determined softness to it that immediately helps me accept his offer. "Water for now, please."

The dragon brings a cup to my mouth, tipping it enough for me to get a cool drink of icy water. I take one more, then nod, so he pulls it back. His pleased expression makes me shiver, and I'm about to say something when Rory unlocks another groan of pleasure as he wrings my toes between his fingers. I've never enjoyed someone touching my feet as much as this, and I have no idea how he's doing it. He wasn't just bragging; he's a goddamn *master* at foot massages as far as I know.

"Your face when you make that sound is *delicious*," Sebastian says with a languid smile. "It's enough to launch ships, and I have no idea how these two have managed for four years."

Huck chuckles, bringing a piece of meat to my lips that keeps me from shooting back at the vampire. Once I take the bite—which is insanely good

—he responds. "It wasn't like we had a choice, bloodsucker. Our girl here wasn't ready to share and now, I believe, she's in a place where sharing is workin' out very well for her."

Oh. My. Goddess.

I know my face is flaming and I can't stop it. Hopefully, they can't see it so well in the candlelight, but my entire body is rapidly following suit. I'm flushed and warm, but also feeling comfortable and safe in a way I haven't in—-my entire life, maybe. It was their goal, I'm sure, but as Thad and Rory continue making my muscles go from knotted to puddles of goo, I can't control the rest of me. Everything they're doing and saying works together to melt my mind and body in ways I couldn't have imagined on my own.

"Is that true, Sydney?" The vampire looks at me, his red eyes boring into mine as he queries me. "Are you accepting the benefits of sharing our abilities in non-Games related ways? Is it making you feel good enough to melt in place?"

I have no idea how I'm going to answer that without revealing the truth—I'm almost melted as it is.

IT'S NOT HOARDING
IF IT'S MEN

SEBASTIAN

I DIDN'T ACTUALLY NEED to ask that out loud because any supernatural in the world could smell how much she's enjoying the treatment. But I also realize that this girl is as delicate as she is strong, and part of being able to accomplish our goal of sharing her is making certain she's okay every step of the way. Of all the things she's had *no choice* about since her birth, we need this—us—to be something she chooses without question. Otherwise, it will never last and we will all end up burned.

"Ummmm…" Her big blue eyes look up at me with a mixture of desire, uncertainty, and bliss, but I make sure she can tell that I'm not using any of the vampiric skills I have available to me. "I *am* enjoying this. I don't think I've ever… you know. Felt this relaxed before."

Baby steps, but still progress.

"That's good, Vicious," the mage says from his spot at her feet. "But I think they need more than that."

Elias leans in, whispering to her in a low voice. "Are there other things we can do for you, little rebel? More… tension… to be relieved?"

The air around us shifts and I feel a tiny spark of anxiety flicker through it. It makes me chuckle softly because it confirms something I've wondered about. Sydney's powers aren't tied to sexuality like a Cubi, but that she's this age and hasn't gotten them had to be stunted maturity of some kind. Perhaps this is part of it—which tells me the assumptions about her lack of experience are also probably accurate. I'm not sure having five men surrounding her for this is the best introduction, but we're also not going to go that far tonight.

Sydney swallows hard, then pulls her lower lip through her teeth. "I don't—I don't know?"

That's not a 'no', so we can work with it. My expression is sincere as I reach over and brush a knuckle over her cheek. "Perhaps Rory can move to your legs to see if he can relax them as well, then?"

She looks down at him, and he lets go of her feet to slide his palms upward slowly. "What happens if I say yes to that?"

Stormbringer wraps his hands around her ankles as he switches the position of his body to sprawl out on his stomach like a lazy cat. Sydney watches him nervously, but she doesn't balk as he moves his palms to her calves. I feel he's adding a little magic to his ministrations, because yet again, she groans low. "How does that feel?"

"Really nice. I didn't know I worked them that hard," she murmurs. "I didn't know anything else was so overextended, either. I just thought I hurt a bit from Bas beating me up."

I roll my eyes, tsking at her as I tip her chin up. "You, Sydney, need to learn that you cannot just spew bullshit because you want the others to chastise me. I did not beat on you any more than you and the instructors asked —you specifically accused me of holding back as it was."

Her pout makes me want to bite it, and I wait until she responds. "I can say whatever I want—"

Moving quickly, I let go of her chin and place my hands on her cheeks. My eyes catch the dragon's, then the bear's, the demon's, and finally the mage's before I smirk at her. "Listen, you infuriating little brat... if we're going to help you relax, there will be a few... rules. I know that's not your strong suit, but I think the others will help you navigate it."

There's a spark in her eyes for a moment, then she adjusts as we stare at one another. "Is it going to be 'brat'? Is that the name, Bas?"

Of course, that's the part she'd focus on.

"I don't know, Sydney. What I know is that you have to trust us to take care of you in private. That's what tonight is about. You can go toe-to-toe with all of us in public, but here? This is where you need to believe that we have your best interests at heart."

"Which we do," Thad rumbles as he continues working her shoulders. "You know Huck and I have always had your back, and we trust the others to do so now, too."

Sydney pushes against my palms with her face, obviously wanting to look at him, but he's not in charge, so I keep her focused on me. "Let me—"

"What did the bloodsucker say, little rebel?" Elias chides as a long, thick scaly tail snakes over his shoulder to brush along her neck. "He and I are the only ones giving orders at the moment. If you want something, the point is for you to ask."

Her body tenses and I can tell she's trying not to panic about the dragon's casual use of his tail to trail over her. "We all have unique tastes, Syd. You're going to like some things, and not like others. Declaring who's in charge does *not* ever mean you have to suffer things you don't enjoy. In fact, sharing what makes you feel good and cared for is exactly what we want you to do. Does Elias's tail upset you?"

"N-no," she whispers as it tickles her ear. Her instinctive scrunching makes me laugh, and the bear joins me. "It's just… different."

That's when the demon holds up another piece of cheese and I let go of her face so he can give it to her. "Very good, brat. And you're right—many things about each of us will be different, especially because you've insulated yourself from damn near everything."

"Like what?" she frowns, and I sigh.

Let her move slowly, Sebastian. She needs to feel steady before she continues.

"Well, I doubt you could tell me any of the specific differences in anatomy for the supes in this room, much less across the board." I wait for it to register and her eyes go wide like a cartoon character. "And that's saying nothing about what powers we have that can enhance the experience."

"Piercings," Huck adds as he picks up another piece of fruit to hold up for her. Sydney takes it—surprisingly—and chews as she tries to parse our statements. "All the special things will be a little shockin' at first, sweet pea. That's what Sebastian is tryin' to say."

When she swallows, she clears her throat, then says, "You're right. I'm not—I never thought about any of this because I… Well, I purposely pushed all this stuff down and stuffed it in a box. The reasons aren't really important and they feel silly now. I don't want to say them, either. I was woefully misinformed and um, a lot judgy."

Stormbringer blinks as his hands inch past her knees, carefully watching her expression as he works the muscles and joints. "Oh, Vicious. You thought controlling your body meant they didn't own you, right?"

Her head bobs, and she looks away from us at her hands. Tension is seeping back in; I can feel it. "Yes."

"Ohhhhh…" the bear mutters and the demon looks similarly clued in. "Now, I get it."

"Shut up," Sydney mutters as she worries her bottom lip with her teeth. "You all know I was working on bad information growing up. I was mistaken, but I didn't know it, and I'm sorry."

"Vicious," Rory says softly. She doesn't look up, and he puts a little more sound behind it. "Sydney, look at me."

She lifts her eyes, looking guilty as hell and I think she might have done or said things she's regretting now. "What, Rory?"

He squeezes her knees with his hands, his expression earnest as he holds her gaze. "It's okay that you had a skewed view of what defined people because you didn't know better. Should you have sought new information when your life changed drastically and you weren't beholden to that influence? Yes. But you really had nothing but a poor substitute for education provided by the FSHA and a lot of rage about your circumstances. Plus, you BFFs were scared to break your brain, so they didn't bring you back from the brink."

"That's true, sweet pea," Huck says as he tilts his head at the dragon. "Give her a sip, Your Highness. She might need it." Once she's taken a drink, the demon continues, "Thad an' I were worried that your psyche was so fragile after your dad died that revealing who and what he was would have damaged you in a way the camps don't have treatment for. I'm sorry we didn't try it; we really thought it would hurt you more than help."

Thad stops the massage, his cheek brushing hers as he nods. "Huck isn't lying. Tempest Seven doesn't have mental health stuff, Syd. You worshipped your dad and were so angry about the Sweeps. Maybe we should have tried as the years went on, but the longer it went, the harder it was."

I'm kind of impressed with these assholes—this is a lot of truth for one night.

"Regardless…" I interrupt before anyone starts up again. "The point stands that we realize you don't have experience or knowledge in this area. And… that you're still coming to terms with the rest of the shit dumped on you since this started."

"But," Elias rumbles and his tail flicks up her torso to rest just under her chin. "We want to teach you. That's why the vampire is setting guidelines— it will be important for all of us to agree on them so we can take care of you."

Sydney makes a very girly sound when his tail brushes back and forth over her, the tip moving to her collarbone. "I… um. Taking care of me… It includes… um, this?"

The uncertainty is unexpected; I thought she'd puff up and get angry, breaking the comforting quiet of our little nest. "We would like it to; would you like to explore with us?"

"*All* of you? Like, all five?" I feel the heat in her frame and it makes me grin broadly. Her body likes the idea, even if her mind hasn't wrapped around it yet. "Doesn't that… bother any of you? Sharing me, I mean?"

That gets a chuckle from the magic user, and he slides his palms to her thighs to massage gently. When she doesn't protest, he looks thrilled and I have to keep my own face from reflecting my excitement. "Not in the slightest, Vicious. Polyamory is very common amongst a lot of supe communities, including all our species. And we're getting along so well that we think it will only get better when we're focused on supporting you."

Her brows furrow, and Sydney looks at me seriously. "I don't know if I could handle this if you guys are going to… you know. Use your skills for, um, other things with other people in the Games. It would probably end up hurting me and I can't really ask you to—"

This time, the demon puts his finger on her lips gently. "Sweet pea, if you agree to this, I promise you that Thad and I will not play those kinds of games. We've wanted to be with you for a long time. You already had us, darlin'."

Somehow, she looks completely shocked, and it makes me laugh. Everyone in this room knew those two were head over heels for her—the object of their affection—and they weren't being sneaky in the slightest. The bear and the demon were ready to form this little alliance long before the rest of us got here.

I study her for a moment, letting it sink in before I add, "Sydney, no one in this room wants to harm you. In fact, despite your best efforts, we're unable to do anything but orbit around you like fools. It's very annoying, if I'm honest, especially since the three of us have known you for a short time in which you did everything you could to push us away."

She licks her lips, looking at me through her thick lashes as she murmurs, "So… you're saying just us? Like all of us? Only us, together?"

I open my mouth to answer and stop when she lets out a groan of pleasure that makes every eye move to the mage. He's dusting small kisses on the skin above her knees, and I suddenly realize that her scent has filled the room while we've been talking. My eyes darken, and I know they're a deep crimson as I inhale deeply.

That son of a bitch has been slowly getting her ready, carefully monitoring her reactions while we all gabbed, and now we're past the point of no return.

THOSE PANTS WOULD LOOK BETTER ON MY FLOOR

SYDNEY

THIS ENTIRE EVENING IS SURREAL—I didn't expect them to propose a night dedicated to making me feel better, but I also didn't have them asking if we can all… date… for real on my bingo card. That's supposing I had a bingo card, which I don't. But if I had one, this would absolutely *not* be on it.

Is this for real?

Five men who almost everyone would consider top tier choices for boyfriends are surrounding me in a soft, warm nest with treats and gentle touches that make my body sing. And they want me to agree to letting them guide me through experiences that I should have had much younger, but didn't because I was being a jackass. My reasons are actually offensive to one of them, but instead of chastising me, they accept that I am redefining myself on the fly now. Every single one of these gorgeous, powerful guys is pledging to share me even though I'm nothing special, especially compared to some men and women in this competition. They want me, flaws and all, and they're willing to make our family exclusive.

I didn't ask for any of this, nor did I consider it being possible. This situation hasn't been a blip on my radar until we ended up in this dorm together, and I have no idea how to do any of the shit required in a genuine relationship—sexual or emotional. They seem to know what they're doing, and it's not a problem that I don't. In fact, they're offering to teach me. It should seem weird and creepy, I suppose, but it's also… a little sweet? Like they somehow care enough to make certain I am not being pushed into things I'm not ready for, even if they are.

But what do I do? Saying 'yes' gives them power I've stubbornly withheld from everyone on the planet for the length of my brief life.

Rory's hands are still massaging my thighs gently and it's making me melt in ways I've ignored in the past. My skin is hot and my pussy is leaking fluid as steadily as it would for a period—but this is different. I'm turned on by what he's doing, and by the rumbly vibrations of Elias's voice behind me. Thad's hands are magical as they push me forward a tiny bit to work on the muscles of my back. It's yet another delicious feeling, and while I'm trying to get a grip on my emotions, Huck is bringing another piece of food up for me to sample.

"Sweet pea, I know this is a lot all at once." He presses the piece of meat to my lips and I open up dutifully, surprising myself as I take it and chew. "It will take a lot of trust that's in short supply in your heart. Finding out the world differs completely from what you thought makes that even harder."

"Yes, it does," I murmur when I'm done with the bite. "How can I trust people I've known much less time than my father when he was lying to me for almost two decades?"

This time, it's Elias who answers. "Your father had something to gain by lying to you—a devoted companion, a daughter who stayed safe, and someone to give credence to his beliefs. We don't know how much of his rhetoric was true because we're stuck here instead of wandering the world to confirm it. However, at this moment, you *know* we have all agreed to work as a team and to use this event to help start a rebellion. We don't need you to say you want to date us to achieve that goal. Since it's the only thing we can focus on and it's not a motive, you know we're being honest."

"Holy shit, Dante," Rory says, as he looks up from his spot between my legs. "That was a fuckton of words for you, man."

My lips curve up a little as I turn my head to look at the dragon. "You know I like when you talk more."

"I do, little rebel. That is why I put in my two cents."

Sebastian pulls my face back, looking into my eyes seriously. "The mage has been making you feel relaxed, but he can do so much more, kitten. Those light kisses are just the beginning. If you would like, he can show you what we mean."

"Um…" I lick my lips as I stare into his crimson eyes, my brain warring with my body inside my head. "I don't… I don't know?"

Thad presses his thumbs into the small of my back and I moan as the knot on one side loosens slightly. "Syd, you smell like citrus and flowers; it's intoxicating. I've known you for four years, and I've never caught this scent on you before. You have no idea how hard it is not to sniff you until I get drunk on it."

Oh, my.

"If you say no to more, no one will be upset, Vicious," Rory says hoarsely as he pauses. "We can still have the food and be comfy and make sure you don't have muscle aches. You can do that with the option to reconsider later on without it being an issue."

Turning to look into his beautiful blue eyes, I see the truth in them. He's serious, and since no one is correcting him, the rest of them are, too. But I can smell things, too, and when I inhale, the mix of their own arousal is heavy in the air. I don't know if I noticed shit like this before or if the ability is new because I'm slowly 'emerging'. Either way, I know Thad has the smell of cinnamon, amber, musk, vanilla, and other spices coming off of him. He smells tasty, too.

"We want this, but we can wait until you're ready—if you're ready," Sebastian says when I look at him again. I breathe in again, smiling at the smell of gardenias, jasmine, and the wings of the night. His scent is exactly what you'd think a creature of the night would smell like, and I hate admitting that it also makes my whole body tingle happily.

"You guys… um. You guys smell fantastic, too," I finally say. Sebastian looks surprised, and his head tilts as he looks at me curiously. "I can tell the difference, I think."

Rory punches my thigh lightly as he smiles prettily. "That's a really good sign, Vicious. It points towards a shifter in the mix, which we sort of ruled out. You're an enigma, baby."

Hearing his raspy, eager voice say the word 'baby' regarding me hits me right in the needy bitch button. I clench everything for a second, trying not to give in just because my sorely neglected sexuality is bursting at the seams. "I, uh… I'm not sure. I just know my mom had magic, and he didn't, and it was forbidden for them to be together."

"It's probably forbidden for us, too, by that standard, kitten. But I don't give a fuck." Sebastian dips his head to get closer, and I can see the tips of his sharp fangs between his lips. "The longer we're all together, the more I think nothing about this entire set-up is coincidence. You've done nothing but smack me around, and I can't do shit without keeping my eyes on you. It's not normal."

I frown, unsure how to take that. "I'm sorry?"

That gets a laugh out of Elias, and his tail flicks over my collarbone lightly. "It's nothing to be sorry about, little rebel. Being obsessed with you has been infinitely more interesting than anything I've done in the past four years."

"You, too?" My eyes widen and I turn for a second to glance at the dragon, but Sebastian brings my face back again. "Hey!"

"Focus, Sydney. You don't need us to repeat what we said in order to stall. If you do not want to continue, you can say so. But you will need to decide that before the mage has to hump the blankets to deal with his… problem.”

He's baiting me and it's working—I want so badly to see what he means now.

“I… I think I…” my voice cuts out and I have to clear my throat before I can speak again. “I want him to continue.”

The collective groan from the men around me makes my stomach flutter, and Rory drops his head to dust more kisses over my sweats. I feel the heat of his lips even through the fabric, and for some reason, I wish I'd picked shorts. Thad starts on my back again as Rory's hands slip up my hips, and Elias's tail traces along my torso, studiously ignoring every spot that seems to ache for his touch.

“We're teasing you, kitten, but not in a joking way,” Sebastian whispers to me. His breath is warm on my face and I have to lean back a little to watch him as he talks. “It's the best way to get you excited, and sometimes, you'll find that it's both pleasure and punishment.”

“Punishment?” I breathe. A not-so-subtle grip on the hem of my sweatpants makes my heart rate kick up, and I don't resist when Rory's hands wiggle them down on my hips. “Why would I want… um… that?”

The vampire chuckles. “Oh, you won't. But you're a brat, Sydney, and I guarantee you will earn it. Am I right, dragon?”

His tail flicks over my nipples and I make a strangled sound when the gesture sets me on fire internally. “You are, Whitmore. But I also think she will enjoy some of it. She enjoys irritating you far too much not to savor the sharp edges.”

“I don't know about—”

I have to swallow hard when I realize Thad is now lifting my hips so Rory can tug the sweatpants down. He drags them down my legs, then tosses them aside to leave my legs bare in front of him. “Vicious, all you have to do is say the word.”

“You didn't set the word,” Huck drawls as his eyes rove over my skin.

“Good point.” Rory stops and looks at me again. “You need to pick a safe word. One you won't say by mistake if you're moaning or writhing. When you say it, everything stops, we get you cleaned up, and you rest. That word will never cause a discussion or argument. It's final.”

I guess I've heard of this before, but I wasn't paying attention. Are they setting me up for bondage stuff?

“Is this like… bondage stuff?” I ask carefully. “I don't know if I'll be good at that. I mean, I don't even know what most of it is.”

“Pick a word, little rebel. It only gives us a clue when you truly mean stop.”

Elias's reassurance helps; he definitely won't let me get into things I'm not comfortable with. “Okay, how about kumquat?”

They all have amused reactions and for a moment, I wonder if I'm too naïve to handle one of them, much less all of them. Squirming in place, I feel the fear of disappointing people well up inside me, and I consider using that word even though I just set it. Before I can do it, Elias's tail wraps around my waist and squeezes. The gentle gesture makes my chest tighten and I realize that I definitely do *not* want to stop them—at least, not yet.

"Are you ready, Vicious?" Rory murmurs against my upper thigh. I feel the evening's slight stubble sting as he moves along the inner curve of my right leg. "Because you got to eat, but I'm still hungry."

Holy fuck, I'm never going to survive this.

JUST DON'T CALL
ME LATE TO DINNER

HUCKLEBERRY

THIS IS *the hottest fucking thing I've seen in a long time, by far.*

Our girl—the one Thaddeus and I have been trying to get to notice us for years—is spread out like a nervous little buffet, and she's actually *allowing* us to touch her. Not only that, but I'm pretty damned certain she's going to agree to the vampire's terms by the time we're done making her sing for us. My imagination hasn't done this moment justice and I have an active bloody imagination—I'm a demon, for hell's sake.

Sydney's long blondish-brown hair is unbound, spilling over her shoulders and onto us as she watches the talented mage slowly makes his way toward the promised land. I can smell her desire, which is intoxicating as is, but there's also a bit of fear and worry leaking through her aura. For most, that wouldn't be ideal, but for a fear demon like me, it's the spice that makes everything taste like ambrosia. I'd be concerned about that if I didn't know that it's not connected to us as much as her deep-seated terror about letting people in. The world gave her that phobia, and we're going to teach her that sometimes people stay.

The thought of her relinquishing that fear is almost as delicious as the scents surrounding us.

"Darlin' girl, you're gonna need to part your legs for him a bit," I murmur as I reach over to stroke her cheek. "I know this is new and you're feelin' shy, but you won't feel like that for very long."

Rory looks up and winks at me before diving back to his task of nibbling and marking his path up to her soaked cunt. I know she's practically drippin' by the look in his eyes and the dazed expressions of all the other males forming the circle around Sydney. Each of us is affected by the smell and strength of her need differently—the vampire with his fangs, the dragon's tail teasing, my ursine best friend's tension as he relieves hers, and the mage barely keeping the ravenous hunger off his features. I'm delighting in my versatile role in the middle because being amongst the chosen is fueling me like no other rush before.

"You heard him, kitten. Open up for Rory," Sebastian says in a firm but gentle tone.

I didn't expect him to pull off soft Dom, but here he is, shocking the shit out of me.

"Are your sure that you want to—*oh my fucking…*"

My entire face lights up when Stormbringer finally reaches her neatly shaven pussy and licks the most sensitive spot eagerly. Sydney trembles in our embrace, her head falling back against Thad as her eyelids flutter. The timbre of that exclamation was throaty and breathy like a noir ingenue; I want to hear it again immediately. It made my dick twitch like a Mexican jumping bean and I guarantee I'm not the only one.

Thad's big hands grasp her thighs, pulling them apart a bit more as the mage goes to town. His own moans tell me she tastes as good as she smells and I'm jealous as fuck that he gets to go first. But our girl will have a lot of firsts, and we'll all claim ours, eventually. My sweet pea deserves to feel pleasure and since he's wormed his way into her graces better than anyone else, it makes sense that she didn't protest his exploration.

"Little rebel, relax…" Elias's tail flicks over her breasts through her tank and my eyes zero in on the pierced nipples begging for more. "This is all for you. Let him show you a preview of what we will make sure you feel whenever you are aching. Your pussy will weep for us, and it will be our honor to drag every ounce of pleasure from you until you cannot move."

Damn, the dragon's a good dirty talker when he's not being a silent statue.

"Elias, I…"

Her voice trails off on another moan and Thad curses under his breath. "Motherfucker, Syd. That sound makes my cock try to tear through my fucking pants. Do it again."

Her eyes crack open and a huge shiver runs through her before she speaks, "I… Is that what… I can't…"

The mage lifts his head, his lips and lower face *coated* in shiny juices. "I like when you can't remember how to talk, Vicious. Want me to continue?"

That gets her to open her eyes, and the look in them reflects the exact emotion his nickname refers to. She reaches down and grabs his hair, panting softly as she growls, "Don't you *dare* stop."

Sebastian laughs, his rumble dark and satisfied as he leans down to kiss our girl roughly. When he pulls away, his forehead is ridging with the physical manifestation of the vampiric demon inside of him. "That's perfect, kitten. Demand what you want... what you need. I enjoy seeing that spirit. That's what makes *my* dick hard, if you're wondering."

Sydney narrows her eyes, looking like she's going to mouth off, but Rory goes back to eating her out and that stops the brat from exiting her lips like an entirely different magic. She buries her fingers in his hair and tugs, earning a few little snarls from him. I know he has to be humping the blankets like a madman down there because the veil has fallen on everyone's tippy-toeing around their words.

"Are you overheating, sweet pea?" I ask, trying not to sound as desperate to see her bare as I am. "I can help with that."

Her eyelashes flutter as she arches her hips, grinding them instinctively into Rory's face, and then she looks at me with an expression resplendent with pleasure. "Um, I... I... yes... yes. Hot."

I grin happily, enjoying her intermittent speechlessness. Rubbing my hands together, I let the magic flow to my hands, and push it to the tank top covering her. It disappears in a blink and I say, "Abraca-naked, darlin' girl."

"Son of a bitch," the vampire hisses as his crimson eyes rove over her tanned skin. "Where the *fuck* have you been running around *naked*, kitten?"

That earns him a lazy, knowing grin as her fingers dig into Thad's legs and she whimpers. She must be getting close, and I'm honestly surprised she's held out this long. Since I'm not worried about how she got an all-over tan, I slip a hand under the bear's arm to cup her right breast gently. It fits in my palm perfectly, soft and sexy like I always imagined. My thumb brushes over the pierced nipple and she shudders hard, my name escaping her lips like a prayer.

A sharp smack breaks the silence and I blink as I realize the dragon used his tail to spank her other breast. "Answer him, little rebel. You promised."

She's still wriggling against all of us as she stammers, "They... ohhhhh... they... Rory, *please*." Sydney pants again and I watch the redness spring up on her skin where the whipped tail caught her. "Tanning... bed..."

"No more. They're unhealthy," Sebastian rasps as his eyes stay focused on the flushed skin of her boob. "Only spray tans from now on. Understand?"

"Yesssss," she hisses, and I realize she absolutely *loved* that tiny blow from Elias and has no idea how to handle that knowledge.

"Yes, what?" The vampire grabs her chin and forces her to look at him, his tongue sliding over his fangs as he waits for a response.

I chuckle at her confused look, soothing the anxiety roiling off of her by tugging on the piercing. It distracts her enough to make her relax again, and she bites her lip. "I think you forgot to tell her what you wanted, blood-sucker. She doesn't know how to answer and she's too lost in the moment to ask."

Sebastian blinks, dumbfounded by his own omission, and before he gets his shit together, the dragon responds, "She will call us king when we mate."

That's his little kink, but it has a nice ring to it.

"I can live with that," the vamp says as he looks down at our girl with an arched brow. "Yes, what, kitten?"

"Yes, my king," she mumbles, just before another strangled sound escapes her lips. "Rory… what the.. helllllllll…"

"Does it feel good, sweet pea? Are you ready to fall apart yet?" I ask. My fingers pinch her hard nipple and I grin as Elias does the same with his apparently talented as fuck tail. "Because I gotta be honest… I can't believe you've held out this long the first time."

"Don't be stupid…" Another rap on her left side with the tail gets her attention and she moans. "I mean… I have had… orgasms."

"Serving a party of one, mmm? Had to be pretty inconvenient living in that hovel and getting time alone, Syd." Thad dips his head to kiss her neck as he squirms against her back. The bear is having more trouble than the rest of us, but to be fair, he's the youngest supe besides Sydney.

She doesn't answer, but I can imagine her having to relieve her own tension sneakily in the shower and it immediately morphs into joining her there. "Damn, sweet pea. We're definitely going to give the bathroom a try sometime. The vision of you naked and slippery is fuckin' hot."

Not that this is anything to shake your fist at.

"Bet it didn't feel like this, did it?" Sebastian leans down, kissing her again before he lets her respond and Syd shakes her head vehemently. "Do you like Rory's tongue in your pussy, kitten? Do you feel how much we all want you? Do you smell it?"

She swallows hard as she bobs her head, then keens low and I wonder what the mage did to draw that sound out. Her limbs are visibly trembling now, and I almost hold my breath as the vampire waits for her to respond verbally. "N-no. It was not… like this… Never like this."

"Good girl," he murmurs as he casts his gaze down to Rory's blind head. "Answer the other questions, Sydney. Tell us what we want to hear."

"I…" She sucks in a breath and I see her jaw grit as she does her best not to do what I *know* she needs to. "I love it. I didn't know I could feel… unnghhhh. You all smell delicious and I don't understand it. It's like I want to *devour* you and I don't even know what that *means*."

He blinks, stymied for a moment as his eyes cut to everyone but the mage for confirmation. We all heard it; it was impossible not to. But it doesn't make sense—the likelihood of her being a dual hybrid is low, but the hunger speaks to something entirely unprecedented. I know what he wants to ask the dragon and me, but he's not going to. Not when Sydney is accepting us as a team and in her bed—it will be too much for her to contemplate.

"Kitten, what do you mean 'devour'?"

She shakes her head, gripping Rory hard as she writhes under his mouth. "I don't knooooooow. *Please, please…* Sebastian. I need…"

Her throaty pleas knock him out of the trance her previous admission put him in, and the vampire grins fangily down at our girl. "That's not how you ask, Sydney. If you want release, you ask for it, and you tell us what you want us to do. If you're behaving, you will get it."

My heart almost skips a beat when she lifts her head, looking at him with lust-filled eyes and pouty lips. "I want to come, my Kings. And I want you all to feel good, too."

"Poseidon's seaweed pubes," Elias curses as his tail whips over her. "Your mouth is getting dirtier and I like it, little rebel."

"*Please*, Sebastian. Let Rory make me come and the scent of you all fills the air. I want it."

If that son of a whore doesn't let her, I'm going to—

"You may come, kitten. Scream the roof down for us, and it will send everyone over."

I don't know about the logistics of that, but a tingle hits me like a bolt of lightning and I have to clamp down on myself so I don't blow my load before she does. "Holy fuck," I mutter, but it's drowned out by the wail Sydney lets out as her body locks in the middle of us. The heat of her skin doubles and I twist the nipple I've been toying with hard, hoping to wind her up more, so she yells again.

Luckily for me, that's exactly what she does and, like magic, an orgasm smacks me in the face like a ton of bricks. The shouts from the other guys join the chorus with hers, and I hold on tight as the entire room is one vibrating climax that rocks us until we finally calm. I pant as the fluid fills my fucking pants—something I haven't done in so long that humans drove goddamn coaches—and flop backwards on the pallet when my limbs cannot hold me aloft.

"What in the three faces of Eve was *that?*" I ask as I damn near melt into the blankets. "Did you do that, sweet pea?"

A low chuckle breaks the silence and I look at Sebastian as he smirks, despite also having destroyed his sweats like the rest of us. "No, that was *me*, demon. Vampires can do much of what our Cubi cousins do if we use the voice."

"Son of a bitch," Rory mumbles as he finally sits up, his face looking like a glazed donut and his pupils blown to hell. "I forgot about that shit."

Thad leans back on his elbows, his eyes hooded and grin goofy as he comes down from the ride with the rest of us. "We promised to clean her up. We should do that when we can move."

I think that's going to be a group activity now, and I'm looking forward to it immensely—Happy Thursday to me.

LAST THURSDAY NIGHT

SYDNEY

THE INCESSANT BEEPING that wakes me up is an unwelcome intruder. I stretch carefully, my brain committed to believing I'll be sore when, in fact, I'm more relaxed than I've been in… ever. My muscles are loose and there's not a single hint of the aches and pains present when I walked in the door of our dorm last night. My face flushes when I think about the way the guys relieved that issue, and I roll to my back to look up at the ceiling as my mind races with the implications of what happened.

I let them touch me, kiss me, even command me—and I'm surprisingly not sorry.

Because of my father's rigorous dislike of the world—both supernatural and human—I was isolated and indoctrinated to think that withholding myself strengthened me and made me morally superior to those around me. I wore those convictions like a superhero cape, even when reality crashed into that belief so hard that it knocked me flat during the Sweeps. Sure, my father was killed trying to 'work' within the two groups for peace in the end, but now that I'm able to see his rhetoric clearly, I don't think it was for heroic reasons. He was part of the peace brokering supes because he wanted both sides to fuck off and leave us alone.

I don't know *why*, of course, except that he was adamant that my mother left because they were forbidden. Yet he vacillated between trying to develop my magic and keeping me focused on the more human ways to defend us when it wouldn't work. My understanding was he was simply magical, and I *thought* my mother was human, then maybe a shifter. But neither makes sense when you add to his insistence that intermingling was so taboo that we had to stay on the fringes of all the societies.

Was he just crazy or was there an actual reason he was the supe version of a doomsday prepper?

Unfortunately, I don't know and I also have no idea how much the rumors of the elders of the major supernatural species being confined in some secret locale plays into his nuttiness. Was he on the 'we can all live in peace' side because he feared such a thing happening? He wasn't religious; he didn't encourage me to believe in higher beings skewed toward any pantheon or species' favorite deity. That means his absolutely feral conviction that we weren't safe and I would be hunted if people knew about him and my mother didn't follow some Flavor-Aid drinking, body of a holy man eating sect scripture.

Sighing, I close my eyes for a moment, pushing away my concerns about why I was so rigorously taught to avoid everyone, to keep myself strong by not allowing others access, and most importantly, why withholding things that gave me joy or pleasure were such a huge part of honoring myself. I've been able to enjoy things here and there since I was tossed into Tempest Seven—my two best friends, books, embarrassing assholes, etc. But even the occasional physical 'boost' I gave myself wasn't enough to truly bring me more than physical relief, which is simply biology.

Living like a monk without faith in anything didn't do me any favors, but that's what he wanted for me.

The lingering questions will not be answered this morning, and certainly not while I'm lying in the ridiculously luxurious sheets of the comfy bed provided by my true enemies. No, I need to get my ass up and go face the men who just showed me what kind of true elation can come from defying my father's whacked out bullshit. And, of course, to make sure that they haven't changed their minds about what they said now that I'm not naked and willing to help them slake their own desires.

I frown at that knee-jerk reaction, sitting up to scoot off my bed and onto my feet. That's my internal trauma talking, I guess, but it's hard to push away. It was drilled into me that my mother left to protect me, and then my father died claiming he was trying to do the same. The truths I held to be part of my core being are in question, and I already didn't trust people not to leave. Now I have to contend with my brain's desire to insist that they will also lie to me and I'll be left floundering for purchase after they're gone.

"Get it together, Sydney. Why do you keep having to tell yourself that? For fuck's sake, stop letting intrusive thoughts ruin everything. You're doing fine and the guys will not abandon you after one session of oral sex and magical hand jobs. Stop thinking about how you will gut them and get dressed."

The last part is necessary because the trickles of unfamiliar blue and red and black inside of me whisper, too.

I pull the stupid uniform out of my drawer and don it, then braid my hair in the tightly wound coil that serves as armor. It takes a few moments to do the basic skin care and makeup routine I've been advised on, then I load up my bag with the things I need for today's sessions. Stopping to look in the mirror before I go out, I note that I don't look any different, but I feel like a slight weight has been lifted off of my shoulders. I don't know if that weight is named self-denial, oppression, or anger because none of those are small enough to completely lift. It might be a tiny slice of all of them, and as I navigate the world as it truly is, more will flutter away.

Regardless, I check myself one more time, then something catches my eye. The damn tattoo for the team they scarred me with looks a little brighter. Not totally, but just a smidgen brighter than it was before. It might be the scarring healing, and I'm just imagining shit. My brain is so crowded with questions and worries that it's possible I'm hallucinating a little. Even after the guys took me to the bathroom last night and helped gently get me clean and warm again, I still felt fuzzy from the strength of that release. I was barely awake when Rory—I think—carried me to my room and tucked me in.

Maybe I'm still high on orgasms and their attention that fed me like a starving stray on the streets?

Who knows what crazy shit I'm going to have run through my mind today as I come to terms with yet another major change in such a short amount of time? I'm a woman on the edge, and trying to predict what will happen as I process life-altering shit day after day is like trying to predict the weather accurately. There might be sciences dedicated to it, but they're mostly pattern recognition and data-backed guesswork. No one can tell me how I'm going to react, not even me.

I let that deep thought go as I open my door and stride to the kitchen. My stomach flutters with fear as I face them for the first time since last night. I'm trying to be strong, but I can't stop the lump from forming in my throat as I wait to see what they're going to do. Before I can open my mouth to speak, Elias comes over to me, handing me a mug of coffee and a burrito with a stern expression.

"Eat, little rebel. Our days are long and we were quite late when we retired last night."

Nodding, I take the breakfast he's offering and, like a good automaton, I take a bite. It's better than saying something stupid as I wait for the others to respond to my presence, especially since the room is quiet as a tomb right now.

Sebastian puts his tablet down, then rises from his stool to stand in front of me as I mechanically consume the tasty breakfast food. "Excellent, kitten. You need the protein for the amount of energy your body is using to push you toward emergence. The caffeine is simply to off-set our lack of rest—though, by the look of you, I believe you rested better than normal. Is that right?"

I wipe my mouth on my hand before I take a sip of my coffee. The bitter burn of the drink is soothing and I savor it for a second before I answer. "Yes, I slept very well—surprisingly so, in fact. And, um, I—"

Rory bounds over like the overgrown puppy man he is and elbows the vampire aside with an eye roll. "Idiots, both of you. Come here, Vicious. Let me breathe you in for a minute, hmm?"

Blinking as he tugs me into his arms and just hugs me with his face buried in my neck, I carefully put my coffee-holding hand around him. "I have hot java, you know."

He snorts against my skin. "Don't care. Taking care of you means you don't get up wondering if we give a shit or if we were lying to get in your pants, Sydney."

Holy shit, that asshole is reading my fucking mind, I swear it.

"I'm not reading your mind," he says as he pulls back with a soft chuckle. "Not even right then. What I'm doing is remembering how I've felt in the past—and despite being right in my case, I want you to know that your panicking brain is *not* right in this one."

"It's gonna sound bad when I say that I thought you were about as deep as a spit puddle when we met, mage, but I'm awful impressed with your emotional intelligence now that we're gettin' to know you." Huck pushes his hat back as he gives Rory a sheepish grin. "I was a bit of a snob, too, I suppose. Sorry 'bout that, man."

The others look at each other, then Thad coughs. "Yeah, me, too. Sorry. I just… you know."

Rory pulls away from me, his face resigned as he faces the group. "I play a role when I first meet people. It's easy, safe, and gives me time to figure out who's real and who's not. If they don't go beyond the surface, I don't worry about showing them anything deeper. Clearly, all of you felt safe enough for me to show the real me. That's also how I know what's going through Sydney's head when she's getting caught in her trauma."

I consider that for a moment, then hand Sebastian my coffee mug. He takes it and this time; I turn to the mage, wrapping my arms around him to squeeze him tightly. He seems surprised and I guess that's fair, but I swallow my fears to say, "Thank you for trying to make sure I don't feel like you did. You're a pretty decent man, Rory Stormbringer."

"He is, and we will help him remember that as we do for you."

Elias's support makes me grin as I squeeze Rory again, then I let go so I can face them all again. "You're all pretty decent. And I'm going to try very hard to not be a jackass when things are overwhelming me. I promise."

"That's fair," Thad says as he stands and clears his plate. "I accept it; how about you, Huck?"

The demon gives me a slow, sexy grin as he nods. "You know I'm in, sweet pea. Always have been."

"While this repetition of commitment is touching," Sebastian says with an oddly amused expression. "We need to get to the first session. If we don't leave now, we'll get caught waiting for the elevator and have to hustle to get to that stupid social media thing—"

A loud squeal echoes throughout the room and my eyes widen as the Irina speaker in the living room makes a long wail like a siren. We all stop in place, concern etched on our features as we wait for the sound to stop. Sebastian moves to stand behind me and Rory grabs my hand, both looking resolute.

I don't know what's coming, but I knew yesterday went far too well for it to last.

DISASTER? I BARELY KNOW HER.

ELIAS

THE ALARM IS ear-splitting for the bear and me, so it was certainly set to a frequency that would make shifters take notice. I don't know if that was intentional or if the humans believe all species are affected similarly to that tone. Thad is holding his ears, his palms pressed tightly to them because he hasn't had the lifespan I have, nor the power of a mythical in his bloodline. He isn't weak, simply weaker than someone like me.

"This is hurting him," Sydney says, her eyes reflecting the fear and upset we were trying to chase away by admitting our desires to her. "When is it going to fucking stop?"

As if she willed it into being, the siren stops and I let out a long breath of relief. I can withstand it better than the bear, but not forever. The vampire's jaw is locked as he glares at the ceiling in fury, then he turns to the demon, his expression determined.

"I want you and Stormbringer to figure out how we can block that kind of shit like you are in our conversations when the device's name isn't said. That will never incapacitate one of us again—I'd tear it down if that wouldn't bring the wrath of Krista on us."

My lips curve when he avoids calling attention to the fact that it was painful for me as well. The little rebel is worried enough about Thaddeus; she doesn't need to know I was white-knuckling it in order to remain staunch for her. I do not aspire to be dishonest with her; we promised not to coddle her. However, I believe this small omission is simply counterproduc-tive, nor is it necessary at the moment. She's tensing up to prepare for whatever bullshit is coming and that's totally fucking up our efforts from last night.

I am unhappy with this turn of events and if I can punish those responsible, I will.

"What the hell do you think they're—" Rory's question is interrupted by another squeal, then the sound of a throat being cleared.

"Good morning, Competitors! On this wonderful day in the Federate States of Human America, we have a most exciting announcement for you: the honored, the selected, the venerated supernaturals of the very first Supernatural United Challenge of Endurance."

We all look at one another, the chill of the unknown flowing through our group at those words. There's far too much insincere flattery for whatever is coming not to be awful, and we've barely had time to train for this nightmare, so if they're moving the start date up, we're definitely in trouble. We hoped we could get *some* measure of Sydney's powers to come out before the beginning of the insane competition, and this is making me worried we will not have time to do so.

"The organization of this event has been over a year in the making, and we have worked hard to transition from residents of the re-education camps to all-star competitors seamlessly. Corporate sponsors from all over our great nation have generously poured money into making the Games Complexes in the camps selected for the Supernatural United Challenge of Endurance the best accommodations possible and to recruit the most talented coaches and leaders for your training from all sectors of business, education, and sports."

"I don't think they did a very good fucking job of *our* staff," Sydney mutters as she lets go of the mage's hand and starts pacing. "Except for Brick and Lancaster, our damn people are full of shit."

Rory tilts his head, looking regretful as he replies, "Honestly, Gemma isn't bad. You hate her because her job violates your person, which is fair, but she and her team are objectively talented."

Her look could wither the balls on a Yeti; that's how cold it is. "Not the point."

I wave my hand at them, dismissing the spat. "We must listen."

They stop talking, and I grin happily. I like the rules the vampire set last night and am amused that everyone seems to follow them even outside of the bedroom, which he did not request. I don't know if that's instinctual or if the others actually prefer having someone else in charge, but couldn't say it out loud. Pride is important to many species and definitely to someone as independent as our woman.

"In that vein, we are continuing the training program for another six weeks to ensure that all teams in all camps are prepared for the start of the Supernatural United Challenge of Endurance. This event is important to our government, our businesses, our people, and, most of all, our glorious leader, President Richard Lorcan Taterman. It will signify our

recovery from the bio-weapon that was unleashed on humanity by the supernatural elders and their operatives to the world at large. You, challengers, will restore honor to your species by reforming the image of this country as one still plagued by the remnants of global plague your kin released in their attempt to overthrow the human governments worldwide."

Sebastian looks as if he's going to burst into flames on the spot; that's how angry his countenance is. "None of that drivel is remotely true. The virus was natural and jumped from actual animals to humans in Asia. Did you know the vampiric counsel were the ones who suggested Taterman's lackeys use that insane internet theory from the tin foil hat brigade to bolster their reasoning for the first Sweeps, right?"

I did not, and by the looks on the faces of the rest of my new family, they also did not know that. "Why would they do such a thing, Whitmore?"

He snorts, shaking his head as he clenches his fists at his side. "Our elders believed we could make the rift between supes and humans widen and it would allow for a leadership change in the Supernatural Councils that would favor vampires, demons, etc, who have the longest lifespans. They believed that shifters, magic users, and the like who are more plentiful had too much influence on the way we were governed, especially since they don't have the wisdom of our ages."

"I'd like one day to go by where my world isn't up-ended," Sydney mutters as she continues pacing. "But I don't think that's going to happen soon."

"As a treat for you, we have arranged an important event this weekend. Part of it will be recorded and packaged as promotion for the event, so there will be schedule changes today in order to get the teams ready for it. After this message, a schedule for today will be flash messaged to your tablets, and you will follow it to the letter. It is imperative that no resistance is given to the changes and that you do not object to the tasks laid out for you. The event tomorrow will go off without a hitch and it will be the public sneak peek for what is coming in six weeks."

I frown, looking confused as I try to understand why they are stating this in such explicit terms. Huck shared his experience in the doctor's office, noting that he believes unlike our team, others are having issues that have caused injuries and perhaps deaths, but nothing in his statement indicated that there were strong enough issues for the assholes running this circus to speak in this fashion.

What the hell are they preparing us for and why has the cheery tone changed so suddenly?

"I don't like this," Thad says. I see the energy of his bear rippling along his skin, and I know the others cannot. My dragon is also quite close to the brink as concern wars with frustration inside of me and they cannot see that, either. It takes a full shifter or strong hybrid to sense the animal of others and its moods. "They've changed how they're talking to us."

Sydney turns, walking over to the counter and placing her palms on top of his. "You're having trouble with control, Thaddy. Breathe."

He blinks, his eyes flying to mine. That is certainly a sign that magic is not her only gift, and one the others will not recognize. "Yeah, I am. I don't like the shift to more authoritarian phrasing. It feels like the broadcasts before the Sweeps."

"He's right, little rebel."

I don't know how much her father sheltered her before she was brought here when it came to the media. Keeping her so ill-informed probably required that, and she might not realize that the former US government broadcast and posted insanely fascist nonsense for months before they were comfortable enough to enact the first wave of public kidnappings that would eventually become the Sweeps. Supernaturals innocent of any crime were secretly accused of something criminal and whisked away—first in the dead of the night and then in broad daylight—in acts reminiscent of the humans' own great shame from the 1930s.

No one paid enough attention, and the Councils sat impotently while it happened, so the local leaders of species figured out quickly that we were on our own.

"Yes, he is." The demon is leaking dark shadows filled with fear, and no one seems to react, so I wonder if they can see it or if they're simply pretending not to notice. "This is the way the speeches and online presence turned before the squads Sebastian's father was part of forming began their reign of terror. Demons fled the earthly plane like rats on the ship during this time, as did Fae."

"Do you think they're going to do something worse than put every supe left in the country in prison camps and reform the government into a racist, fascist, authoritarian regime that's been cut from the world?" Sydney arches her brow as she waits for the damn announcer to continue their speech. "Exactly what can they do that's worse?"

"Schedule this damn challenge every six months until they kill us all," Sebastian mutters around his fangs. "Including the idiots like my father and the elders and the Councils they can reach. They can use it to complete a genocide, if they get the entire world hooked on the brain candy of reality TV paired with internalized discrimination against supernaturals."

"We are hoping the next announcement will be the most exciting thing you've experienced in your lifetime, as it certainly is for your staff and administrators!"

Frowning, I stop paying attention to the various issues amongst our group, zeroing in on the speaker with intensity. Somehow, I know this is the most important part of their morning interruption, and we all need to focus on it. "Shhhh."

"This weekend, Tempest Seven's competitors will receive the highest possible honor in the Federated States of Human America. Tomorrow evening, when we film the rally to

kick off the Supernatural United Challenge of Endurance, we will host our most generous and benevolent leader, President Richard Lorcan Taterman!"

That statement freezes us all in place, and we look at one another in shock. Since the last Sweeps, Taterman rarely leaves the Capitol and never appears in places where his support network in the military and law enforcement communities do not have everyone locked down like a super-max. Even the human population doesn't get to see him in person for fear of rogue rebels attempting to assassinate him and cut the head off of the snake. His major political staff, supporters, and donors have all used their clout to have surgically altered dupes for their own appearances in non-secured areas.

Despite Taterman's claim of a national and global mandate, he and his people haven't been truly safe since the first Sweep, and he knows it. Unfortunately for his closest advisors, he's too egotistical to have doubles like the others who helped him rise to power. If they say he's coming, it will absolutely be the most corrupt, morally bankrupt, and hated leader of this country in its brief history. He will stand on the dias in our complex, in front of our teams, and spout his vile bullshit coated in gilded words to entice the rest of the world to pretend they don't know he's imprisoned over half of his own people because he's a bigoted opportunist.

"Your day is being altered because each team will have an audience before the President and his most honored guests so he can decide which groups he will follow closely and eventually support publicly. You are strongly urged to remember the executive orders issued in the past four years when you present yourself, as there are many ways to be permanently removed from this challenge before it begins. Those consequences will be dire at best and deadly at worst. You have been warned."

"We're not ready," Sebastian says, his teeth gritted in frustration. He picks up a coffee mug and throws it, watching it smash against the wall with a growl. "The first time in *years*, and we're not *ready!*"

"Then this is our one and only opportunity to figure out how to be ready," our woman says as she squares her shoulders. "We can't do what we'd like tomorrow, but we can use it to launch our plan. If that waste of flesh takes a shine to us, his support could play either way, but it still puts us in the middle of a media frenzy. And it will keep us from being eliminated too early if that washed up druggie that helped Taterman rig the votes for all his crimes against us hasn't overdosed yet."

"We have to control ourselves from the moment we wake up in the morning to the second we come back to this room, and today will be important, too. No one can get us on a list; is that understood?"

"I promise I'll behave," Sydney says earnestly. "This is too important to fuck up."

"Truer words, little rebel.... truer words.."

Unfortunately, I'm uncertain the people organizing this are planning to play fair and that might be a problem…

WHAT IS GOING TO HAPPEN?!!!
Order your copy of Book Two in the F.E.A.R. Academy series now!
Join my REAM to read along as it's written here.

GET A SECRET BONUS SCENE!

For a secret bonus scene that follows this book, *click the link below, sign up for my newsletter, and get your freebie.*

Get your bonus scene here!

REVIEWS, PRINT, AND MERCHANDISE

If you have enjoyed this story, please review it.
It helps other readers find my work,
which helps me as an indie author.

Thank you!

Reviews are appreciated on the following platforms:

TikTok
Instagram
Facebook
Bookbub
StoryGraph
Threads
Tome
Lemon8

To purchase print copies or merchandise, go to The Worlds of Cassandra Featherstone

TEMPEST SEVEN ROSTER

Sydney Jolie (sid-NEE JOH-lee) hybrid supernatural who lost her dad in a sweep and her mom left when she was a kid; her goal is to get out of the sector; she's part magical, but no one knows what her mom was

Nicknames: Sweet Pea, Syd, Vicious, Little Rebel, Kitten, *aloiafi natia* (hidden spark), brat

Scents: Truffle, Gardenia, Black Currant, Ylang-Ylang, Jasmine, Bergamot, Mandarin Orange and Amalfi Lemon

Piercings: nipples, ears

Special equipment: none

Safe Word: kumquat

Thaddeus Calvin (THah-dee-us Cah-L-VIN) grizzly bear shifter who is friends with Sydney and Huck

Nicknames: Thad, Thaddy, big guy, cub

Scents: cinnamon, amber, vanilla, musk, cedar, sandalwood, cloves, bergamot, neroli

Piercings: lots of tatts for his ursa clan, prince albert

Special equipment: baculum, knot

Huckleberry Monroe (huck-uhl-bear-ee MON-roh) fear demon who was brought into Tempest Seven after a problem in his last sector; country boy

Nicknames: Huck, Rustler, cowboy

Scents: saffron, black rose, truffle, patchouli, vanilla, agarwood, oakmoss, fruity notes, floral notes

Piercings: nipples, Prince Albert, lip, tattoos

Special equipment: shadows he can control, small spikes that vibrate, size control

President Richard Lorcan Taterman (Rich-urd lore-CAN Tay-ter-man) human who got elected and imprisoned all supes in sectors because he blamed them for COVID; bright orange spray tan and dictator vibes

Angus McSherry (ang-US MICK-SHare-ee) leprechaun that leads a gang of Fae spies

Guard Wicker (Wick-er) front door guard who is a creep; human

Guard Bishop (BISH-up) front door guard who is decent; human

Professor Ashley (Ash-lee) teaches Human Literary Masterpieces; human

Dean Patrice Wallace-Brickman (pah-trees wall-ass brick-man) human who runs FEAR Academy; obnoxious ass kisser in ugly clothed

Tucker Calvin (tuck-er cahl-vin) Thad's uncle who took him in; alphas of the bears

Jingo Calvin (jing-OH cahl-vin) panda bear Tucker took in after a sweep

Penny Calvin (pen-nee cahl-vin) grizzly bear Tucker took in after a sweep

Patsy Calvin (pat-see cahl-vin) spectacled bear Tucker took in

Andromeda Calvin (an-drom-ih-duh cahl-vin) polar bear Tucker took in

Saleos Ignia (sall-ee-oh-s Ig-nee-uh) pit demon; part of Huck's past

Nurse Ames (ay-mess) witch nurse at Games inspection

Dr. Moreau (more-oh)centaur doctor who seems to be a rebel at the Games inspection

Sebastian Whitmore (seb-ass-tee-en whit-more) vampire; lives in upper class portion of Supe sector; vampires made deals as most humanoid supes did. His father is the rep on the sector leadership—jerk, mom died in the first sweeps, lives in El Dorado One sector

Nicknames: Bas, Bloodsucker, Mosquito, King

Scents: truffle, gardenia, black currant, ylang-ylang, jasmine, bergamot, orchid, lotus, patchouli, amber, sandalwood, vanilla

Piercings: Jacob's ladder and magic cross, tongue

Special equipment: fangs, transformation, aphrodisiac bite, knot

Rory Stormbringer (roar-ee storm-bring-er) mage; parents are considered lower class because they were part of the supes who wanted to negotiate with the humans. Any of them left were sent to the sectors and stripped of all money and titles; lives in Inferno one

Nicknames: Spell sucker, Spell caster, Pup, Sparklepants

Scents: cardamom, pepper, bergamot, leather, cinnamon, sage, lavender, amberwood, musk

Piercings: ears, nipple, Prince Albert

Special equipment: magical aphrodisiac, euphoric cum

Elias Dante (ee-lie-us dahn-tay) dragon; found abandoned and contained in the units of this sector. certain species are locked down due to the humans fear of their powerful traits; lives in Inferno Seven

Nicknames: Smokestack, big guy, lizard man, King

Scents: sea salt, Sicilian lemon, bergamot, iris, mandarin, musk, woodsy, fruity, ocean water

Piercings: forked tongue piercings, Jacob's ladder

Special equipment: knot, electrical stim, ribbed with special extras

Krista Philbert (kriss-tuh Phill-bert) human, team coordinator for the Games;

Astaroth Whitmore (ass-tuh-roth whit-more) Sebastian's father, vampire, in tight with the human government in El Dorado One sector; traitor to supes

Bitsy Carlyle (bit-see car-lie-uhl) Chimera shifter; HS bully; shady dealings to get comforts in their sector

Brick (brick) trainer, big dude

Lancaster (lan-cast-er) trainer, dark dude

Shoshana Larson (show-SHA-NUH LAR-son) nosy, smarmy fashionista working with Krista on the Style & Flair class ; thinks she's bigger than she is in her arena; always causing trouble

Chantelle Moakle (shan-telle moh-k-lee) human helping Krista with Cult class; ridiculously egotistical and self-centered; teaches them dirty tricks and ways to lie to their followers to manipulate them into attacking other teams

Brantley Westlake (bran-t-lee west-lake) human teaching Strategy class; conniving and cunning; uses war based strategy to discuss how to break down opponents on the field and in the media

Gemma Bolero (jem-muh BOH-lair-o) beauty technician assigned to their team for weekly appearance maintenance

LOCATION GUIDE/TERMS

Tempest Seven: the supe sector Syd and the guys are living in

F.E.A.R Academy: the college level university they attend

Federated Human States of America: also called FSHA; changed from the United States after Taterman took over

Shrieking Succubus: bar in the seedy part of the sector

Victory Hall: new dorm area for all competitors

El Dorado One: sector Sebastian is from; one of the wealthiest and most comfortable of all sectors

Inferno One: sector where some of the lowest supes are housed; there are seven Infernos and the seventh is the worst

Inferno Seven: worst sector in the country; most dangerous supes housed there

U.N.B.: United Nations of Beings, formed after sweeps from former U.N. and supernatural councils

TERMS IN THE FURY OF THE FORSAKEN UNIVERSE

Marker: placed on supes to control their powers; includes a tattoo

Confession Enforcement Zone: section policed by whisper drones

First Infected Being Sweep: the name for the first (second, third and fourth) sweep of the US used to rounds up supernaturals and imprison them

The Unveiling: the big moment supernaturals revealed themselves to humans on TV

Secret Supernatural Enforcement Agents: the secret police used to gather supernaturals by Taterman

Bite Club: Sydney and the guys' team name

STALK CASSANDRA FEATHERSTONE IN THE DARK CORNERS OF THE WEB

JOIN MY FACEBOOK GROUP AND FOLLOW ME EVERYWHERE!

WANT MORE?

SIGN UP FOR MY BI-WEEKLY MANIFESTO FOR A FREE SERIES SAMPLER:

Join my Ream as a FREE follower or exclusive subscriber to get access to cover reveals, WIPs, Serial Stories, and personal chats from me!

SNEAK PEEK:
COME OUT & PREY

JUST A GIRL

Delores

Sighing, I look around my bedroom at the posters and decorations covering my walls. My obsession with pop music, musical theater, and high school rom-coms sickens my parents. They would prefer me to be into heavy metal and horror movies like the other kids my age.

Being the only child in a family as prominent as mine is difficult when you don't fit the mold. My parents—like their parents and all my friends' parents—are apex predators. Preds rule our world, and the division between

361

us and prey is so severe that we regulate them to a completely different echelon of society. Prey shifters are weak and beneath our lofty abilities. The ruling class of elite predator families stretches back generations, and they've evolved into a bunch of assholes who only care about succession and greed.

My animal has not manifested yet, but it will soon enough. Luckily for me, none of my friends have manifested their inner animals, either. I'm part of the in-crowd at school, and my boyfriend, Todd, is the most popular guy in my class. While he and I aren't officially engaged yet, we've talked about it enough that I know it's only a matter of time before he puts a ring on my finger. I should be on top of the world, but I can't help but feel like my life just doesn't fit me the way it's supposed to.

Every teenager wishes their life was different, but I dream of becoming an entirely different person. Not inside, mind, because I'm pretty comfortable with who I am. I don't want to be part of this legacy, this society, or even this family. They are all focused on competing to be the richest, the deadliest, or the most powerful, and I want no part of it.

I walked over to my closet and pulled out the outfit that I had chosen for my tour of Apex Academy. My mother hired her personal designers to create a custom school uniform for today and expects me to present the 'appropriate' image of the sole heir to a Council seat.

I hate having to pretend to be like them because I'm nothing like them.

Regardless, I pull on the short, pink pleated skirt, three quarter length sleeve blouse, knee socks, and Mary Janes that comprise the uniform for my exclusive private high school. Since I'm using a 'college visit' day to tour the Academy, I'm expected to represent Shifter Secondary as well.

Shifter Secondary is the most exclusive high school for unmanifested shifter teens on the East Coast. Unfortunately for me, it was not my parents' first choice for my education. They hoped I'd follow in their footsteps by choosing to force my animal to emerge early. If I had done that, I could have attended *Apex Academy Lower School.*

I didn't have the stomach to use my body in that manner at fourteen.

Their heirs followed my lead, which made my mother and father furious and their hoity-toity council colleagues angry. My closest friends, the Heathers, also refused to force their animals to emerge, as did Todd and his friends. That was the first time the adults in our circle decided I was a bad influence. After that, I had to toe the line at every turn, ensuring that I followed all the strict rules and regulations that govern the heirs to council seats.

Everywhere I went, I had to dress in a manner befitting the next Drew to sit at the table. They forced me to take dance lessons, piano lessons, diction lessons, and other more humiliating tutorials to prepare for the day that I became a true predator. In our society, teenagers have no say in how we prepare for our animals to emerge.

Your parents make all the decisions, choose your friends, choose your mates, and decide every detail of your life down to what you eat every single day. At least, that's how it is in my family, because my mother is from the old world.

She came over from Slovenia when she was incredibly young and met my father on the society fundraiser circuit. Her idea of preparing her daughter for the future involves lessons in makeup, clothing, jewelry, and on how to keep your mate satisfied. Lucille is completely unconcerned about whether I end up happy, only that I attend to my council seat and my husband's *needs*.

Once I get dressed, I grab my vintage Vuitton bag and peek at the mirror for a last check before I head downstairs. I tuck my perfectly high-lighted blonde tresses behind my ears, and the smokey eye and winged liner are on point with this year's fashion trends. I apply a quick swipe of cherry red lip gloss and open my mouth, inspecting my teeth to make sure they are pearly white. Even though once I develop threatening incisors or sharp fangs, something will inevitably cover them in blood, my parents want my smile to look like a toothpaste commercial.

It's all such utter bullshit.

I take a deep breath and turn on my heel, heading for the door. I can already hear my parents yelling in a Scotch and vodka induced rage in the drawing room. It's only eleven thirty in the morning, for Hera's sake.

Lucille and Bruno don't fuck around with cocktail hour. They are nicely sauced by ten a.m. every day, without exception. I can't remember a time when my parents didn't get drunk off their asses at an event or party, much less in our 'home'. They liquor up and fight until they part for the day, and then start again once they arrive home from their daily commitments.

I brace for the barrage of criticism my mother will subject me to when I cross the threshold. Closing my eyes, I whisper words of encouragement to myself via lyrics to some of my favorite songs, desperately trying to hype myself up before she can tear me down.

"Delores! I hear you breathing at the top of the stairs, darling. Come down this instant and let your father and I inspect your presentation."

My mother's purr *sounds* friendly, but believe me, it's not. I roll my eyes as I make my way down the stairs, knowing my mother won't hesitate to send one of the staff if I don't acquiesce to her command. Most of their staff would gleefully jizz themselves with being chosen to drag me down-stairs for inspection.

At this time of day, the only servant in the drawing room will be Matilda—my ex-nanny turned personal assistant—and that request would test her loyalties. As the only person in my household who has my back, I don't want to put her in that position, so I answer. "Yes, Lucille. I'm on my way."

I'm not allowed to refer to her as 'mother' because it makes her feel old. 'Lucille' is always what I've called the woman who supposedly gave birth to me. I'd be tempted to disbelieve we shared any DNA at all if it weren't for our similar bone structure. She's about as nurturing as a rattlesnake, and if it weren't for Matilda, I might have died as a child. If the kitchen staff whispers are accurate, I have to accept that my mother neglected to feed me much of the time.

"You coddle her far too much, Lucille," my father growls. "As the heir to our family seat, Delores will come without being instructed to do so. We will not tolerate her insolence after her animal emerges. She will behave as I command or suffer the consequences."

The last of Bruno's rant echoes off the marble walls of the foyer as I step onto the hideously expensive, endangered teak floor. Schooling my features into the mask of indifference I wear whenever I have to deal with them, I enter their den of drunken fights with my spine steeled for an emotional assault.

"I apologize for my tardiness, Father. I only wished to perfect the image I will present during my tour of Apex Academy. I realize it is imperative I impress the Headmistress and her staff."

The humanoid features of his face shift seamlessly, and the hungry crocodile inside of him gives me a toothy smirk. "You will impress them, daughter, or so help me... I'll send you to Bloodstone Isle."

My stomach drops like a stone as I barely suppress a shiver.

Bloodstone Isle is a reformatory school. It's surrounded by spells and enchantments to prevent students from escaping—a feat that has only happened once in its one thousand years of existence. The most feared cat group in the shifter world—the Khan ambush—runs the school, and they're rumored to consume errant students when the Council allows it.

It's the threat both rich and poor shifter parents used to keep their children in line. Wealthy parents like mine use it as a method of controlling any heirs that refuse to conform to the rigid structure of our society. Predators don't value the lives of those who are weak, and they label heirs who refuse to take their rightful place at the top of the food chain weak. Everyone knows Bloodstone is full of criminals, miscreants, and psychos, and even they don't seem to survive.

Bloodstone is a death sentence—pure and simple.

"Y-yes, Father. I understand," I croak out. As if the pressure of touring my new school isn't enough, now I worry the Dean will relay something to my parents that gets me shipped off to Death Island.

"Bruno, darling, if you scare her, she'll frown. That causes wrinkles. Delores, chin up and smile for us."

Swallowing the lump in my throat, I flash my mother my brightest smile. Her blood-red lips curve, and her leopard fangs burst free as she all but purrs. "I will not have you sullying the family name, Delores. It's bad enough that your education gave you ideas about your value beyond breeding stock. You will take the seat on the Council when it is time, but the husband we select will control the business—as nature intended. Do you hear me?"

My eyes narrow briefly, and for what is possibly the millionth time this week alone, I nod at my mother to appease her temper. "Yes, Lucille."

"Excellent!" The leopard fades as she claps her hands. "Matilda!"

The tiny woman steps up, her eyes wide behind her glasses. She's a pred, but the smaller size of hawk shifters puts her in the servant class. I believe she genuinely lives in fear of one or both of my parents deciding to eat her. "Yes, madam?"

"Fetch Bruiser. He will accompany Delores to the academy for her tour. Tell him to take the Escalade—it won't do for her to arrive in a tiny car—it will draw attention to her extra weight. We must make an impression."

Matilda nods, and I feel the fear radiating from her, and I don't blame her. Bruiser is one of my parents' bodyguards and our frequent chauffeur. He's a Komodo dragon shifter and the house staff are terrified of him. It's hard not to be, given that he prefers to play with his food, then eat it after it's dead. The kitchen crew believes he 'handled' the gardener that looked too long at my mother when I was ten. He disappeared without a trace.

Once Matilda scurries away, I watch my parents drink and bicker about their plans for the day. Bruno is going golfing with a congressman, and Lucille is going to the spa. We all know that both outings will include stops at the homes of their current pieces of ass for a quickie, but no one talks about it. The appearance of the loving couple has to be maintained, although neither of them has slept in the same room since I was a baby.

They don't give a damn about fidelity; I learned that at an early age. Children often discover things they shouldn't because of adults discount their ability to understand the conversations happening around them.

I stopped keeping track of who they're boning long ago, because I'd need an assistant to keep the affairs straight.

While my parents' marriage is a sham, I remind myself that my boyfriend, Todd, isn't like them. Yes, his parents only own half the live entertainment industry, but my father allows me to see Todd. The other parents will force the Heathers to accept an arranged betrothal, and I'm grateful I'm lucky enough to have found the perfect match on my own as my high school sweetheart.

"Delores, Bruiser is ready to escort you to Apex. He's pulling the car around now," the hawk shifter says softly.

Snapping out of my reverie, I smile at the trembling woman. Bruiser must have scared the living hell out of her. For no other reason than it amused him, I'm sure. He's as much a brute as his name implies, and I don't look forward to riding alone to the academy with him.

Something about that shifter gives me the creeps…

SNEAK PEEK: VEILED FLAME

LOSER

Kat

The little blue icon on my app has been glaring at me all day, but I'm too damn nervous to open it. Everyone at Woodlawn High has been buzzing all day with their notifications and the squeals of joy and moans of despair were too much for me to take. My anxiety is through the roof—this is the moment I've been waiting for since middle school, but I can't seem to force myself to bite the billet and check.

Maybe it's because I don't have the support system most of my classmates have?

That's probably true, given I've always been a loner and I don't fit into any specific 'caste' here. It's hard to make friends when you get shuffled from foster home to foster home over the years. I've rarely stayed anywhere long enough to make a friend, much less a group of them.

I'm not delinquent or anything—the families I've been placed with just return me like a pair of pants that doesn't fit after a year or so. The case-workers click their tongues sympathetically and hunt down a new place-ment, but I've never been given a reason *why* people don't want me around. One lady said I must be born under a bad sign and hell if I knew what that meant other than I'm not good enough to keep around.

It would be different, almost understandable, if I misbehaved or got bad grades. But I don't—I'm always in the top five percent of my class and I do everything I'm asked. I don't even lord my smarts over the other kids or adults. Being presentable and unassuming was something I adapted long ago to improve my probability of staying in a home long term.

Unfortunately, it never worked and though I should be a shoo-in for scholarships and acceptances galore, I can't bring myself to be rejected yet again.

So I wait for the last bell of the day, slinging my bag over my shoulder and trudging home to the latest in my temporary housing. I can't even contemplate looking at the possible heartache waiting for me in the college application system WHS insisted we use. The fear is too great and despite knowing I'll be on my own for good at the end of this year, I'm unable to risk the pain.

I hate being this way.

My court mandated therapist says it's some sort of attachment disorder that's common in foster kids, but I think that's bullshit. The problem isn't *me* not forming attachments; it's asshole adults not forming one to me. Being left at a safe haven in a fucking basket as a baby wasn't because *I* did anything wrong—again, fucking adults couldn't handle their commitments.

As usual, I arrive home to an empty house. There are two other kids who live here—Bryce and Blake—but they're at football practice. Of course, the Jamesons *love* them; they get to strut around at games because their strays are the stars of the team. I'm not mistreated, but I'm definitely an afterthought. Both of my 'parents' are still at work, so I drop my bag on the couch and head for the kitchen to get a snack:

Don't get me wrong. I *could* have been placed in far worse homes than any of the seven I've been in since elementary school. None of the ex-fosters starved, beat, molested, or abused me. They were all decent folks with jobs and houses that weren't hellholes, but they never liked me.

I have no idea why. I tried to be everything they wanted.

But when the end of each school year came, I was handed in like a textbook and off I went to some group home until the next contestant stepped up. It baffled everyone, not just me, but that's what happened every single time.

Sighing, I pull some fruit out of the fridge and grab a soda. I have homework to do and if I want to have time to work on my stories, I'll need to get it done before the house is full of people at dinner time. Bryce and Blake will have gotten messages about their applications, too, and I'd bet my pinkie toe those idiots got into some big sports school. Brett and Allison will be oozing happiness for them and I don't know if I'll be able to keep food down if I have to admit my failure when they ask.

Being eighteen sucks ass.

After I grab my books and tablet, I head down to the den. I have to give my current parents credit; they set up a very nice workspace for us to study in the converted basement. By the time they took me in, the Jamesons created a cozy room down here where the three of us could relax and do our work for school without being interrupted. It might have been more for the boys than me, but I appreciated it all the same. Desks, a couch, big chairs, and bookshelves fill the space, making it almost seem like our mini-library. They even put a small fridge for drinks and snacks in case we had to be up late to cram.

It's my favorite place in the entire house and I spend most of my time here.

I sink into the huge armchair, putting my drink and snack on the side table. It only takes a few minutes to arrange myself in the soft cushions and I pause to tug my headphones out of my pocket. Music always soothes my jagged edges and I need it to stay focused on the bullshit AP Calculus I need to keep my average up in. My course load is heavy, but I applied to tough colleges. I wouldn't have a chance to get in, especially on a scholarship, if I wasn't taking equally challenging classes in comparison to all the prep school kids.

As always, the sounds of Vivaldi carry me away as I scrawl equations on my screen and before long, thoughts of the blue notification completely fade away.

"Kat!"

The shouts barely register as I continue working on the problem set, gnawing on my lower lip in concentration.

"Jesus fuck, where is she? I could eat a hippo!"

"Kat!"

Thumping followed by what could pass for a stampede of elephants jerks me out of my math filled trance when Bryce and Blake come down the stairs. They smell as bad as the aforementioned pachyderm's cage, so they must have rushed home right after practice. The blond twins glare at me as if I'm the offending element despite being sweaty and covered in dirt and grass stains.

This doesn't bode well.

Usually, they're tired and hungry after practices so I'm used to cranky ass boys, but tonight, there's a light to their faces. That had to mean they've gotten their letters and dinner will be a gush fest in honor of their perfection. I'm going to need all of my strength to fake smile and nod as Brett and Allison fawn over them.

I don't begrudge them their success—not really. They work hard and play even harder on the field. It's not their fault they're the American dream teens and I'm the nerdy basement troll no one wants. But it's awfully hard living in the shadow of their bright light, especially when I'm no less intelligent or talented.

"I'm finishing the AP Calc, guys. What do you want?"

They roll their eyes at me before Blake scoffs. "It's not due until Monday. You're so hyper."

Duh. I take anxiety meds, douchebag; of course I'm 'hyper.'

"I can only be who I am, Blake." That earns me a snort from Bryce and I know it's because he thinks that's the problem. "Is dinner ready?"

"Almost. Get upstairs and set the table so we can shower—Brett's orders." Blake grins smugly.

The two of them seem to always arrange it so chores get passed to me for some half-assed reason and this is no exception. Sighing, I put my stuff aside, fully intending to hide down here after the dinner mess is cleaned up. Likely by me, but like I said, I could definitely live in worse foster homes so I let it go. Doing some chores isn't worth risking the group home for the last few months of my high school career.

They take off running up the stairs and I wait for them to disappear before I follow suit. My phone is tucked in my pocket and I feel like it's a stone of shame I have to bear. I know once the adults make over the twins' success, they will remember me, and I'll be forced to find out what disappointment lies in wait for me. The dread weighs on me, but I head into the sunny kitchen and pick up the pre-prepared pile of plates, silverware, and napkins on the counter.

Allison looks up from the stove and gives me a half-smile, nodding as I take the dishes into the dining room. Like I said, no one is mean or horrid, they just seem…obligated. After a while, it makes it hard to waste time trying to be bright and sunny. Being reserved makes it a hell of a lot easier not to feel rebuffed when they don't pay attention to you regardless.

"Make sure you include champagne glasses for your dad and I!" she calls from the other room.

The twins definitely got acceptance somewhere big. Brett must have gotten the bubbly on the way home.

Once I set the table, I return to help Allison bring out the roast and sides. I'm a little amazed at her efficiency when it comes to getting the housework done while working full time, but I suppose it's something people with real parents get taught as they grow up. My home life has been so fractured that I haven't learned how to cook more than very basic shit from YouTube videos. That may be a problem after graduation, but I've never felt comfortable enough to ask Allison if she'd teach me. I'm sure she would try, but it doesn't feel right.

"How was school, Kat?"

I look over my shoulder, seeing Brett in the entry to the dining room. He's already changed from work and smiling, but I see the distraction in his eyes. He's waiting for the boys to come down. "It was fine. I've got a Calc test at the end of the week. I'll be studying a lot to get ready."

"Good, good. No matter what happens with applications, keeping your grades up will ensure no one pulls any offers," he says.

Those words aren't for me. They are for the two wet haired boys who just appeared behind him.

"Kat's too much of a geek to ever let her grades slip, Dad," Blake says as he pushes past his brother and drops into his usual chair at the table. "Grab me a Powerade since you're in the kitchen, mouse!"

Both Brett and Bryce stare at me and I turn around, heading to the fridge despite the fact that I was *not* closer than the other twin. Out of habit, I take two of the drinks and a soda for myself. I've been here long enough to know Bryce will send me back to get him one as well. It would feel like typical sibling stuff, but for some reason, I just *know* they do it to fuck with me. I have no idea why I feel that way, but trusting my gut has been the one thing that helped me get through all the upheaval in my life over the years. It's a good gauge for knowing when I'll get booted or if people are being earnest in their reactions.

The therapist says that's some sort of trauma induced early trigger warning shit, by the way.

After I hand out the drinks, I sit down on my side of the table and we wait for Allison to come out. Brett is at his seat at the far end of the table and the twins are punching each other as they look at something on their phones. I know where this is all going but I drop my gaze to the table, swallowing the coppery taste of fear as it courses through my body.

I'm going to be exposed and there's nothing I can do to stop it.

Read the first three episodes free on Kindle Vella: https://www.amazon.com/kindle-vella/story/B0BSTMB1X3

SNEAK PEEK: BLOODTHIRSTY

QUEEN BEE

They dim the lights in the club, and the spots click on as the curtain slides open.

It's a full house tonight in the little burlesque club off the Rue Pierre Montaine.

Chez Arc En Ciel is not well known compared to the *Moulin Rouge* or *Le Lido*, but the wealthy from both sides of the Seine gather here for shows four nights a week. If you pass the various layers of security checks to even be permitted to book a reservation, you also have to be able to afford the two thousand Euro per guest cover charge. If you don't eat or drink anything, that's all it will cost; however, that would get you blacklisted.

Intro music pumps through the speakers and I stand on my mark in the opening position. My cane is resting on the wooden boards of the stage by my front foot as I pretend to lean on it. Roars of applause echo through the room as our troupe of dancers catch the lights, sequins sparkling like diamonds when the stage lights rise. We're dressed in pinstriped black pant suits and fedoras to match the big band style opening to the song. As soon as the horn-filled intro finishes, the dance begins.

I follow the routine with precision, snapping and popping my hips to the beat as we spread out across the stage. You wouldn't know by the fake smile on my face that I'm scanning the crowd. Two fan kicks later, I've rotated past the proscenium, and I think I've found my mark. Twirling, I stop in the place I need to be for the bridge, singing along as if my life depends on it. It might, to be honest, because I need to sell my cover tonight, so no one notices me.

The Guillotine moves in the shadows, but tonight, she's in the spotlight.

My ass shakes as I dance my way through the song, swinging the prop cane I'd replaced with one of my design. You wouldn't know by looking at it, but it's not the painted balsa the other dancers have for a very specific reason. I need it to complete the mission that forced me to spend two months in Paris working my way into this job at *Chez Arc En Ciel*. If I can't strike tonight, the surveillance, counterintelligence, and time spent building this cover are wasted because my mark is leaving for Asia tomorrow.

Tonight, the Cobra dies for his sins.

The break of the song slows the music and the dancers pour into the crowd to wiggle around the rich assholes. It's choreographed, but it's also to advertise each girl for private dances in the lounges upstairs. We're not strippers—not that there's a damned thing wrong with a woman using her body to support herself—but we do bare more skin in the closed rooms. The *laissez-faire* attitude of the owners means as long as we kick them thirty percent of the fees for those dances, they don't care what any of the girls do in the rooms. I'd find it sleazy, but the girls who work here are highly skilled performers who choose to make thousands of dollars a night rather than peanuts in some ballet troupe or chorus line.

By the time I've flirted my way to the VIP tables, the Cobra is staring intently at all of us. Spotlights pin each one of us on the floor at the bass hits, and I swivel my hips as my free hand slides down to the secret spot on my jacket. In unison, we tear the jackets off to reveal rhinestone studded bras with straps crisscrossing our waists like shibari ropes. A lift of the fedora and pop of my hip, along with the beat, draws the fierce-looking brawler's eyes directly to me. I pout prettily and stalk towards his table with the swagger of a tiny dicked asshole that owns a monster truck.

His thin lips pull back over the famed curving fangs he had implanted. Dark, glittering eyes follow every move I make as I approach, and I pretend to whip my hair from side to side as I check for his guards. They're here somewhere, but I need them to be far away so I can beat my escape before they notice. When I get within inches, I tap his leg with my cane and spin around to shake my ass in his face. The grunt of approval makes me want to heave, but I turn, holding onto the prop with both hands. My feet click on the floor in a soft shoe step as I make 'fuck me' eyes at the dirty bastard. He leans back, his pants tented as he gestures towards his lap.

Fucking gross.

I don't care about his weapons trade or what happens when people get the shit he moves. I have no clue why I have to take him out. The reason they have sentenced him to death isn't part of my contract, and I'm nothing if not a dispassionate observer of the darkest parts of human desires. Twelve years at *l'Academie* ensured I care very little about anything that isn't directly related to my ability to complete my jobs.

Sighing, I dance closer and drop onto his rather unimpressive erection and wiggle. There's plenty of cloth between us to prevent him from doing anything I'd make a scene over, so I focus on the task at hand. I slip the cane behind his head, resting the wood against his neck as I tug him forward. The move reads as playfully bringing his face to my breasts, but at the last second, I click the release built into the custom weapon. One end slides open to reveal the razor sharp garotte and before he can say a word, I yank it through.

Faint gurgling is the only noise besides the end of the song, and I carefully slide the sides of the cane together. Climbing off the nasty fucker, I put my hands on his cheeks so I can pretend to flirt with him while I arrange the head so it looks as if he's leaning back in the booth. It needs to look realistic to allow me to return to the stage with the others. When I have it settled, I back away from the booth, blowing fake kisses as I walk backwards through the crowd. I almost collide with a dark-haired guy with his collar pulled high as I head for the stage, and I roll my eyes. Whatever celeb that is trying to keep their face away from the paps is doing a shitty job of it.

The entire troupe takes a few bows and shuffles off of stage left to the wings. I exhale a sigh of relief when the next group enters on the opposite side. I haven't heard shouting yet, so I don't think the Cobra's men realize he's down. Now I take this emetic pill, have a vomiting episode, and I'll get sent home.

That's when Arabella Montaigne, the burlesque dancer, will cease to exist, and Remy Arsine Benoit will re-emerge.

I smile to myself as I chew on the tablet that will have me retching my guts out in a few moments. This is a more complex extermination than I usually prefer, and I can't leave my normal calling card behind. The Cobra's head had to remain in the booth rather than get delivered to his home in a basket.

Such a shame, that. I quite enjoy the reactions my little gifts engender when they're discovered.

Walking into the dressing room, I carefully strip my costume off, putting all the pieces in my bag. Every item in the locker room that belongs to gets placed in the duffel carefully as I wait for the effects to hit me. It won't do to leave loose ends, even if my prints have never touched a single surface in this place. My gut roils and I turn, facing one of the other dancers as the vomit finally comes. Gracelia screams like she's being skinned when I hurl on her and it's everything I can do *not* to smirk through the chunks.

"*C'est la merde!*" she shouts, running for the showers as if she's on fire.

It takes less than a minute for the owner to send me home for the night. I walk out the back door of the building with everything just as the sirens scream.

Perfect timing, as always.

I jump into the first cab I can hail, directing him to the *Hôtel de Crillon*. Their suites are the ritziest in Paris, and it's my go-to hideout when I'm here. I used to only stay in the Bernstein Suite, but some rich fuckwad purchased it six months ago. If I could track them down and beat the hell out of them, I would, but I booked my schedule until late 2025. Assassins with my skill set and accuracy are getting harder to find. They forced the old guard into retirement because they refuse to adapt to the digital age. Too many cameras, crime labs, and hackers running about to do everything Cold War style.

The future of murder for hire is millennial, people. We're old enough to be stable, but young enough to be agile with new technology. Plus, most of them are broke AF from crooked ass student loans.

It's not an issue I have, but I've been in the business since I hit double digits. You don't survive *l'Academie des Invisibles* if you haven't killed someone before the end of primary school. It's unheard of.

I was eight the first time I used the weapon that would become my signature.

Shivering, I tap on the window of the cab and bitch the driver out. He's taking a longer route than necessary to raise my fare, and I'll have his guts for garters if he doesn't knock it the fuck off. A string of curses in French erupt from him when I voice the accusation, and I slam my palm on the window with enough force to crack the plexiglass barrier. He almost drives into another car, but when he regains control, he makes the requested adjustments to our route.

We arrived at the front entrance after a few more arguments and a traffic jam around the *Champs*. I throw the euros at him in disgust, memorizing the medallion number for later. He's not worth my time, but I have quite a few contacts who might be interested in blackmailing a cabbie in town. Getaway cars are cliche in the crime world now. Most ne'er-do-wells like myself find greater comfort in anonymous taxis or ride-share accounts hacked through the deep web accessed on burner phones. If your ride doesn't know you're a villain, there's no one to flip if law enforcement comes looking.

I never look the same for any job—ever.

I will not use Arabella Montaigne as a cover in the future, and once I move to the location of my next job, I'll ensure that she meets with a terrible fate. It's a lot more work to slowly kill off my alters once I've used them, but it's also why I've never even come close to being caught. The dancer with long wavy red hair, freckles, and big green eyes will never grace the streets of Paris again after I hop a plane. She will, however, get a minor story in the paper and an obituary when I decide how she tragically dies.

The Guillotine will rise from her ashes and be reborn.

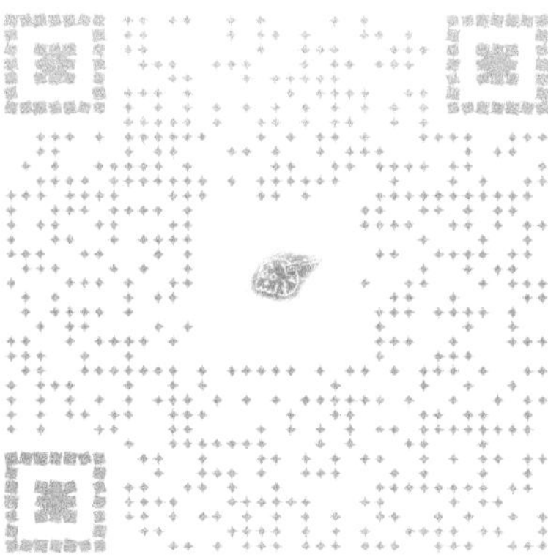

ABOUT CASSANDRA FEATHERSTONE

Cassandra Featherstone has channeled her lifelong passion for writing into a flourishing career, a journey that started when she first grasped a pencil as a gifted child with ADHD.

Her debut novel, born during the solitude of COVID lockdown in March 2020, draws on a tapestry of personal encounters and insights that resonate deeply with her readers.

An international bestseller, Cassandra has topped Amazon charts in categories such as LGBT Anthologies, LGBTQ+ Mystery, and Bisexual Romance, among others. Her works navigate the complexities of bullying, PTSD, body dysmorphia, mental health struggles, personal reinvention, and the empowerment of claiming one's own space. Importantly, Cassandra offers a thoughtful and respectful portrayal of LGBTQIA+ relationships, subtly reflecting her own connection with the community through her narratives.

Her literary repertoire spans sci-fi fantasy, urban fantasy, paranormal, and comedic genres in academy whychoose settings, with a strong commitment to portraying consensual, safe, and accurately depicted BDSM and kink lifestyles. Her books are an invitation to explore transformative stories that are both inclusive and engaging.

Often affectionately called 'The Muppet' for her wacky theater kid personality, she resides in the Midwest with her tech-savvy husband, their creatively inclined college student, a literary-minded dog, and four scheming cats.

READ MORE AT CASSANDRA'S WEBSITE OR HER FACE-BOOK PAGE. SIGN UP FOR EXCLUSIVE CONTENT AND UPDATES HERE.

Join her Master List for promo and ARC opportunities by scanning the
QR below:

ALSO BY CASSANDRA FEATHERSTONE

THE MISFIT PROTECTION PROGRAM SERIES

Road to the Hollow

Return to the Hollow

Home to the Hollow

Rejected in the Hollow

Revealed in the Hollow

Healing in the Hollow

Revenge in the Hollow

AUDIO OF THE MISFIT PROTECTION PROGRAM SERIES

Road to the Hollow

APEX ACADEMY CAPERS

Come Out and Prey

Let Us Prey

In Prey We Trust

Oh Holy Spite (3.5 novella)

Eat. Prey. Love.

Prey It Ain't So (4.5 novel)

Prey It By Ear

AUDIO OF THE APEX ACADEMY CAPERS SERIES

Come Out & Prey

Let Us Prey

Ruthless (Book Two)

Wicked (Book Three)

AUDIO OF THE VILLAINS & VIXENS SERIES

Bloodthirsty

Ruthless

TRIANGLES & TRIBULATIONS

Hoist the Flag (PQ)

Yo-Ho Holes (Book One)

CHILDREN OF THE MOON- WITH SERENITY RAYNE

New Moon Rising (Book One)

Waxing Crescent (Book Two)

Waxing Gibbous (Book Three)

Samhain Secrets (Novella 3.5)

Full Moon (Book Four)

Waning Gibbous (Book Five)

Waning Crescent (Book Six)

RISE OF THE RESISTANCE

Ream Exclusive Prequels

Hooked on a Feline (Book One)

Peacock Me Like A Hurricane

Love The Way You Lion (Book Three)

Snake It Off (Book Four)

REAM SERIALS

Secrets of State U

Discordia University

Faetal Attraction

Rise of the Resistance

F.E.A.R. Academy

ANTHOLOGIES